Praise for Dathan Auerbach's

BAD MAN

"Spellbindingly terrifying. . . . High-test, 151-proof horror."
—Nick Cutter, author of *The Troop*

"Dark and disturbing. . . . Readers will be reminded of the young Stephen King."
—*Publishers Weekly*

"[A] nasty little slice of Southern gothic. . . . Auerbach [keeps] readers on the edges of their seats for the whole ride."
—*Kirkus Reviews*

"Auerbach vividly turns an innocent small-town Florida grocery store into the place where nightmares go to replenish themselves. . . . *Bad Man* [has] a marvelously dark and horrifically satisfying conclusion."
—*Shelf Awareness*

"*Bad Man* will slowly but surely creep you out. . . . [Auerbach] wrings terror out of the every day and every night of the semi-urban Florida Panhandle and makes the world stop for the time it takes to read this work."
—Bookreporter

DATHAN AUERBACH

BAD MAN

Dathan Auerbach lives in Florida. He is the author of *Penpal*.

1000vultures.com

Also by
DATHAN AUERBACH

Penpal

BAD MAN

a novel

Dathan Auerbach

BLUMHOUSE
BOOKS

BLUMHOUSE BOOKS | ANCHOR BOOKS

A Division of Penguin Random House LLC

New York

FIRST BLUMHOUSE BOOKS/ANCHOR BOOKS EDITION, AUGUST 2019

 Published in the United States by Anchor Books, a division of Penguin Random House LLC, New York, and distributed in Canada by Penguin Random House Canada Limited, Toronto. Originally published in hardcover in the United States by Blumhouse Books/Doubleday, a division of Penguin Random House LLC, New York, in 2018.

Anchor Books and colophon are registered trademarks of Penguin Random House LLC.

Blumhouse and colophon are trademarks of Blumhouse Productions, LLC.

The Library of Congress has cataloged the Blumhouse Books/Doubleday edition as follows:
Name: Auerbach, Dathan Kahn, 1984– author.
Title: Bad man : a novel / by Dathan Auerbach.
Description: First edition. | New York : Blumhouse Books, 2018.
Identifiers: LCCN 2017048799 (print) | LCCN 2017053610 (ebook)
Subjects: LCSH: Missing persons—Investigation—Fiction. | Brothers—Fiction.
GSAFD: Psychological fiction. | Suspense fiction. | Mystery fiction.
Classification: LCC PS3601.U347 (ebook) |
LCC PS3601.U347 B33 2018 (print) | DDC 813/.6—dc23
LC record available at https://lccn.loc.gov/2017048799

Anchor Books Trade Paperback ISBN: 978-0-525-43526-6
eBook ISBN: 978-0-385-54293-7

Book design by Michael Collica

www.anchorbooks.com

Printed in the United States of America

FOR BRIAN

(1987–2017)

We salt our lives with other people's sins. Our flesh to us tastes sweet.

—Ray Bradbury, *Something Wicked This Way Comes* (1962)

Man's life is a line that Nature commands him to describe upon the surface of the earth, without his ever being able to swerve from it, even for an instant.

He is born without his own consent . . .

—Baron d'Holbach, *The System of Nature* (1770)

BAD MAN

Prologue: A Body in the Woods

At the sweltering height of a north Florida summer, a body was discovered by two boys playing in woods they'd always promised to stay out of. Thick and looming trees made a forest that could swallow anyone who didn't know the way. But they knew it, the same way all young boys who grow up near woods know it: by trampling through the trees until they give up their secrets. Even that day they emerged safely, though perhaps a little different. The story that they would tell their parents later that day was a lie. They hadn't simply seen the body.

The truth was that the older boy had been the one to find it, and he had found it not by accident but by violence. Directing his frustration with the world back on to itself, he would save his anger for the forgiving trees. The younger boy followed and watched, the sight as natural and turbulent to him as a thunderstorm; all you could do was stay back and hope not to be caught in its path. The older one would beat trees with their own limbs and toss saplings as far as his arms and gravity would allow—not in a mindless way or in a tantrum; it was somehow more methodical. Piles of dead leaves and anthills exploded on the toes of his swinging boots, while the two boys talked about calm things, happy things.

That day in July, they were debating how big they thought the neighbor girl's bra must be, when the words stopped as abruptly as the boot did. Boots pass right through anthills. The dry ones feel like they weren't even really there to begin with. There's a soft, quick *thud,* and then it's nothing but leather chasing sand. Wet hills are a little different. Those kick back a bit, up the leg and into the knee. You have to drive harder into those or else your boot's just scooping dirt. And then what's the point? The older boy had kicked hard, hard enough to pass right through, but his leg hummed like a bat against concrete.

It wasn't until the younger one started yelling and pulling at the older boy's shirt that he could begin to make sense of what had stopped his foot. He hadn't kicked an anthill. The boy stood there dumbly for a while with his boot in the side of a collapsed face before his friend finally managed to wrestle him away.

The older boy got the switch, but it was the younger boy's parents who had been the most furious. Their anger was tempered only by a kind of unclean relief tumbling over them in a muddy wave, as they learned that their son had wandered in and out of danger before they even had a chance to know it was there. The boy never really understood their reactions. He was fine. Nothing had happened. But he was just a boy. He couldn't know how scary having a child could be, knowing there's a piece of yourself out in the world that you can protect only with warnings and rules that could be ignored and broken; knowing that the connecting nerves are so long, any message of distress would take an eternity to reach its way back to you; feeling pain at the expectation of agony.

The parents of the young boy said much to keep that summer in his mind, as if he would somehow forget or even want to. He had to be more careful with himself, they'd say. Next time, something might find *you.* Their town, small as it was, was no different from any other—the well of ghost stories no less deep, and so they drew from it and served him stories about other children who had also been fine right up until the moment they weren't.

What about that kid at the old paper mill? 'Bout the same age as you, more or less. Climbed in through a broke window twenty-five feet in the air, and then snapped both his legs when he fell from that platform. Lay there for damn near two days before someone found him.

And that little girl, the one who didn't get off the school bus that one day because she didn't never make it on? Heard her momma stood at that bus stop all afternoon figuring there had to be some kind of mistake. But the world don't make *mistakes,* you hear me? What it makes are fools who think bad luck won't notice them. Don't matter who you are, or how old neither.

Just ask that one little boy, not that you could. Wasn't nothin but a *toddler.* Just up and vanished into thin air. *Poof.*

For the parents, perhaps more disconcerting than the boy's story was the fact that he wasn't bothered by theirs. But young boys are hard to bother. They're immortal by their own measure. Only as the years wear on do they seem to see that there are fewer and fewer ahead. There's no telling when this realization will hit, but given long enough, Time makes you aware of itself. Glancing backward, we can see we've done some traveling, but at some point we all learn that the horizon ahead won't keep pace with us forever. We can only hope that there's still a ways to go before the edge sneaks up under our shoes. How far is anyone's guess, but we're gaining on it all the time. The young boy's parents decided to rush that lesson in their son, and it worked, more or less. He still went out, but he looked back more often.

The two friends returned to the place a few months later, chattering the whole way through the woods about the things the young one's parents had told him, adding their speculations and embellishments with each muddy footfall. They were talking about the missing toddler as they came to the clearing, but once they were in it the air turned as empty as the earth. They stood quietly for a moment, staring at the soil. There was only a smooth divot in the ground where the corpse had been, like the wet dirt underneath a pried-out stone. They knew the police had taken it; it had been on the news, after all. But neither boy said anything about that. Neither boy said anything at all, for that matter. They should have kept talking, though. There were few places on Earth where it would have been more appropriate to talk about that missing toddler.

But really there wasn't much else for them to say. The young boy's parents had told him what they knew, and that hadn't really been all that much. What the parents recalled was that the boy had simply vanished one day, like cigarette smoke in the wind. What they didn't know was that the little boy's name was Eric.

They'd seen flyers for Eric here and there over the years. That is to say, their eyes had touched them from time to time, but that was as far as the image ever made it. They didn't know because they never really looked. No one ever does.

They also didn't know that Eric had a big brother named Ben or that they'd actually seen all 220 pounds of him twice before. The first time was at a craft store when he was walking with his baby brother. The second time was years later when he was out looking for him.

They might have known that's what Ben was doing if they had slowed down to talk to him when he approached, but they hadn't, so they didn't. It probably wouldn't have made any difference. Not because of what they didn't know, but because of what *Ben* didn't know. It wasn't his fault, though.

Ben had no way of knowing that he should have stopped looking.

All told, there were only two people in the whole world who knew that.

PART ONE

Lost and Found

1

"Ready or not, here I come!"

The front and back yards were off-limits. Eric knew this, but Ben still locked the doors when they played. Even three-year-olds know that the only true rule in hide-and-seek is: don't get caught. Eventually, the boundaries of the game would expand. Maybe in a few years. Ben could only imagine the hiding spots Eric would discover once he was officially liberated from walls and rooms.

"I know all your spots, bud!" Ben taunted as he walked into the hallway that fed their bedrooms and bathroom.

A muffled giggle floated from Eric's room. Ben doubled back in order to add a little more time to the clock. This was the fifth time they'd played this game in the last hour, which was about five more times than Ben would have preferred, but this game at least afforded Ben some time to himself. The longer he could draw out the hunt, the less frequent the screaming and laughing fits would be. It was a hard game to play for both of them. Their house was fairly small, and Ben was more than fairly large for a fifteen-year-old. There was virtually nowhere for him to conceal himself. But Ben's turns as the hider were really only ceremonial anyway. Just a formality.

Eric's giggles were the sound track of the game, growing louder and more uncontrolled the closer Ben got. Even without his brother's snickering, Ben usually knew where he was hiding. Right now, Eric was in his bedroom. But Ben *found* Eric only some of the time. Most of the time, Ben let Eric sneak loudly back to the base.

"Olly olly oxen free!" Eric would call.

"Aw, dangit!" Ben would protest.

It was a fun enough game, but Ben's enthusiasm for it wasn't quite as strong as his brother's. It seemed like Eric might just go on playing it forever if he had his way. Ben walked into his own room and slipped his shoes on. He'd have to leave for the store soon enough. Ben tapped his knuckles against the wall behind his headboard.

Knock. Knock. Knock.

No response. Eric was getting cleverer all the time. The hall perpendicular to Ben and Eric's led to their parents' room and was lined with family photos in cheap frames. "You over here?"

In the kitchen, Ben again ran his thumb down the itemized grocery list his stepmother had left for him. Deidra cooked well and often. Half the time it was tough for Ben to imagine how the ingredients could work together, but they always did. She was talented at just about everything she tried, and she tried a lot of things. The house was speckled with scraps of her hobbies, both old and new.

An ovular table connected the dining room and kitchen by virtue of the fact that it was too big for the small space. It was the nicest piece of furniture in the house, though it was surely better suited for one with more square feet. Ben jostled the drawers and cabinets of the small buffet piece in the dining room's corner. "I'm gonna find you!"

"Olly olly oxen free!" Eric called as he barreled into Ben. Small as Eric was, Ben's left leg was weak enough that he was pushed off-balance. Ben's hip struck the edge of the buffet, and a small Hummel figurine tumbled down from the mantel. Ben lurched and whipped his arms out, fumbling with the porcelain doll until it rested safely against his chest.

"Go easy," Ben said, but Eric either didn't hear or didn't care; through chestnut curls, his bright hazel eyes smiled as he squealed and giggled around the table.

"You hide now," the small boy said.

"Can't and won't." Ben sighed, placing the figurine back on the shelf. "We gotta run up to the store, bud."

"What for?"

"So you don't starve to death."

"I don't wanna go."

Ben rubbed his left thigh with the heel of his hand. "That wasn't the deal, remember? We play for a while, and then we head on up to the store. Besides, I was gonna get you somethin, but I can't remember what it is you like. Was it peas?"

"No," Eric said, and laughed.

"Nah, I didn't think it was peas. It's mustard, huh? Big jar of mustard is what you was wanting."

Eric shook his head. "Reesees Peesees."

"Wrinkled pigs' feet? You want some pig feet, bud?"

"No." Eric laughed again and shoved his brother.

"Well, go and get your shoes on then, and you can show me what you want, because I can't understand what it is you're talking about." Ben smiled as he watched his brother run to his room.

—

The air was stifling. Ben's right hand returned repeatedly to the bottom hem of his shirt to adjust it away from his large stomach, but the attraction was undefeatable; the fabric pulled toward his body like a dollar-store shower liner. His other hand was full of Eric's.

"Look both ways," Eric said as they approached the main road.

"That's right, buddy," Ben replied.

As Eric surveyed the asphalt, he turned his stuffed animal in sync with his own movements, its black dome eyes reflecting and warping the world around it. A car whizzed by and Eric tucked the small rhinoceros under his arm. "Watch out, Stampie," he said as dust enveloped the trio. Ben felt his brother's hand squeeze harder as they stepped into the street.

Ben's walk was more of a hobble as they moved along the overgrown grass shoulder between the trees and pavement. An old injury pestered for consideration with every step. The back of his right hand shimmered with a thin layer of sweat as he drew it away from his forehead. *Shoulda gone sooner,* Ben thought.

Eric took long, exaggerated steps as he kept pace with his big brother, his feet stomping on tufts of grass and dry clods of dirt that exploded in brown plumes under his small feet. A quiet song drifted through his closed lips, one no doubt inherited from his mother. Ben had once asked if she had a song for everything; she'd said that she was working on it.

Ben felt short fingers wrap around his wrist as Eric's feet left the ground. "Don't do that," Ben said. He looked at his brother, who was hanging from his arm like a swing. Ben bent sideways to lower the boy's feet back toward the earth. Eric laughed and then went limp, his hand slipping out of his brother's.

"Quit it . . ." Ben sighed, his back feeling like an old hinge as he moved his hands toward his brother. "You're gonna stain your shirt." Eric's wrist felt thin and frail in Ben's grip as he lifted his brother back to his feet. He spun Eric around and brushed the dirt and grass from his back. "C'mon," Ben said, walking ahead.

Eric whined as he held his arm out. "Hold hands," he insisted. Ben obeyed, pulling Eric along. After a few more steps, Ben felt his shoulder jerk as Eric suddenly dug his heels into the dirt, his hand slipping out from Ben's grip once again. The boy tumbled backward into the grass, where he lay laughing, long blades of sickly green tickling against his pale skin.

"Gosh dangit, Eric!" Ben snapped. But Eric kept squirming, cackling each time he managed to slide his hand out of his brother's and fall back into the boy-shaped impression in the dry grass. "That's enough now!" Ben spat. He grabbed his brother's wrist and pulled him upright. Eric sulked but accepted it after a while.

The store was pretty much in the center of town, though the town was lopsided and sprawling, so its center depended on how it was measured. The company that built the store measured the center by population density. There were a fair number of neighborhoods near Ben's, but beyond the store, the road and the town itself wound down into nothing.

Trees and fields. Fields and trees. Those things counted as nothing to Ben anyway, even if they did seem to eat up the whole horizon. Ben stared long into the distance as he and Eric walked through the store's parking lot, a flat carpet of asphalt that shimmered like it was wet on hot days like this one.

There was nothing striking about the place other than how large it was. The enormous rectangular block sat in the flat town like it had been left there by mistake, dropped on the way to a larger, more bustling place. It was the biggest grocery store in town by far.

As Ben tripped the sensor, the automatic doors rumbled and jerked awkwardly against their frame. With great effort, the bottoms of the doors ground against the metal track, and the whole opening shrieked like a sideways mouth. Ben could feel the screech in his cheekbones. And as it lingered, it seemed to crawl through the rest of his skull.

"Jesus." Ben ducked and turned his head. Even Eric seemed to notice Ben's discomfort, though the boy looked at his big brother for only a moment before darting gnat-like around Ben as they entered the store.

Eric had set his own course, which Ben worked vigilantly to correct. "We'll get your candy at the checkout, bud." Ben reflected on the absurdity of having to make deals with such a small boy, and he regretted promising Eric candy of all things, but there was no other currency with which the boy would trade. He'd give the sweets to him once they got home. Before long, his parents would be back, and it would be their responsibility to contain this tiny whirlwind. "C'mon, bud. I need to get some water in me," Ben said, gently guiding Eric by his shoulder.

Ben tugged at the bottom hem of his shirt again, trying to force some of the cool air between the fabric and his skin as they walked toward the back of the store. His headache seemed to grow worse with each step, like there was an invisible vise clamped around his skull, threatening to cave it in.

"Cookies," Eric pleaded, pointing behind himself toward the bakery.

"Then no candy."

The small boy mulled the choice for a moment, huffed, then marched back toward Ben's outstretched hand.

Ben tousled Eric's hair. "Stampie likes Reese's Pieces better, I reckon."

"Yeah." Eric smiled.

The fountain was stingy. Without enough pressure to form an arc, the water seeped slowly down the metal bubbler. Ben placed his lips on the nozzle, the curved splash guard pressing against his cheek, and pulled the tepid water into his mouth. He put his hands on Eric's waist and lifted him with a grunt so that the child could do the same. Water dripped down the little boy's chin as Ben set him down. "You gotta use the bathroom?" Ben asked, gesturing toward the off-white door. Eric shook his head.

As they walked the aisles, Ben chased his headache with the tips of his fingers. It had traveled from just above his ears to his temples, which he now rubbed while watching Eric bounce from one side of the aisle to the other. Ben lifted a can of green beans off the shelf and herded Eric to the next aisle.

Ben's arms were encumbered by the time they reached the checkout. Cans and boxes teetered and shifted in his crossed arms as they stood in the middle of a long line, the solitary cashier making polite chitchat as she swept barcodes across the scanner. Ben's head split a little more with each piercing tone from the register, which only grew louder as the customers in front of him took their receipts. Eric reached up and tipped Stampie onto the conveyor belt among an elderly woman's groceries.

"Sorry," Ben said, lifting his occupied arms a little to show the woman that he was unable to retrieve the toy.

She smiled, plucking the rhino up by the horn. "Oh, bless his heart," she said affectionately. "I reckon he better stay with you, sugar," she said, bending down to hand him back to Eric.

"Thanks, ma'am," Ben offered.

Eric pushed the toy back onto the belt as the line moved ahead. Finally, and with great relief, Ben let his cargo tumble onto the black conveyer belt. He snatched Stampie from the woman's groceries and handed him back to Eric.

"Quit it, okay?" he said softly.

As Ben corralled the runaway cans, he felt a tug on the bottom of his shirt.

"I gotta go pee," Eric whispered.

"No, you do not."

"I do too."

"I asked you not five minutes ago if you had to go," Ben whispered.

"But I gotta go now," Eric said, pinching and pulling the crotch of his pants.

The line moved forward while Ben looked from his brother to the people behind him. "You're gonna have to hold it or else we'll lose our place."

"I gotta peeeeee," Eric protested.

Ben craned his head toward the back of the store, trying to estimate the time it would take to make it to the bathroom and back.

"You gotta go that bad? No foolin?"

"No foolin." Eric squirmed.

"I can take him," a man said through a beard so thick that Ben could see only hair moving when he spoke. He had warm eyes and a soft voice.

"No. No, that's alright. Thanks, though."

"No trouble in it, really," the man replied, holding out two dollars. "Just get me this with the rest of your stuff?" He motioned to a loaf of bread in front of him on the conveyer.

"I sure do appreciate it, mister," Ben said as he returned the grocery burden to his arms, "but I better take him. C'mon, Eric." The two brothers slid past the snake of a line. Ben stopped to dump his groceries at an empty register.

"What about my Reesees?"

Ben exhaled heavily through his nose. A spike of pain surged from his knee as if it were reaching up to be with its mate in Ben's skull. With uneven steps, Ben led Eric back toward the bathroom.

By the time they got there, Eric was bawling. The door opened with a high groan, and the smell of bleach overpowered Ben's nose. A black scar of mildew outlined the chipped porcelain sink. The urinal sat too high on the wall for Eric to reach, so Ben ushered him into the lone stall. It was too cramped for both of them, so Ben left the flimsy door open while he helped Eric with the button on his pants.

"I can do it," Eric protested.

"Okay," Ben said as he retreated. "Go ahead."

He glanced at the entrance to the restroom to see if there was a way to lock the door, but there was no bolt. Ben leaned against the stall's frame. A man entered the restroom, nodded at Ben, pissed in the urinal, and then left without washing his hands.

"I got it," Eric said, as he began urinating with his pants piled against his shoes.

"Good job, buddy," Ben said. He turned the faucet on and splashed cold water against his face.

"Oops," Eric yelped.

Ben stuck his head into the stall and saw Stampie floating in the dirty water. Ben sighed.

"I can get him," Eric said as he pulled his pants up. He reached one arm toward the rippling water, but Ben seized it quickly.

"Go and stand over there," Ben rumbled, pointing toward the sink.

Eric grabbed his own fingers awkwardly and took his assigned position while Ben gingerly fished the stuffed rhino out of the toilet. He held it aloft and watched as several streams of water merged into one. Continuing to hold it at arm's length, he pivoted on his heel and dropped the toy in the sink before turning on the faucet. Ben's large fingers slid into the metal box on the wall where the paper towels should have been but found it to be only an empty shell.

"Stay here." Ben pointed at Eric firmly and then pushed open the wooden door. As it swung closed behind him, Ben pulled open the adjacent women's restroom door. "Hello?" he called. "Anyone in here?"

Hearing no response, Ben slunk in and quickly grabbed a handful of paper towels, kicking back at the door in an effort to keep it open. Paper towels in hand, he exited the room swiftly and again moved from one door to the other.

"All clean!" Eric exclaimed as Ben walked in. Clutched in Eric's small hands was Stampie, whose large eyes and slanted smile now looked sad as his fur sagged with water—water that dripped all the way down Eric's arms. There were wet spots on his pants and shirt.

"Jesus, Eric!" Ben shouted. Eric recoiled and drew Stampie in closer to his body. "No," Ben said, snatching the toy from the kid's grasp, "he isn't clean, and now you ain't neither." The throbbing in Ben's skull was pulsing audibly in his ears.

"Don't hurt 'im!" Eric shrieked.

"I'm not gonna *hurt* him. I'm fixin to *clean* him." He jammed the rhino aggressively against the soap dispenser.

"You're hurtin him!"

"No, I'm not! He's fine. See?" Ben snapped, pushing the toy in Eric's face before moving it to the small waterfall in the sink.

"Lemme do it!" Eric said, reaching up into the sink. "You're bein mean. Lemme!"

"It's just a toy, Eric!"

"No, he isn't! You said!"

Ben squeezed the water out of the creature and then wadded paper towels around it. Eric was still reaching up for the rhino when Ben struck the large silver button on the air dryer. The machine wheezed briefly before the steady whirr of hot air began.

"I can do it!" Eric nagged, pulling on Ben's forearms.

"But you ain't gonna!" Ben screamed. He could feel his headache in his teeth now. Christ, it hurt. This was taking so much longer than it was supposed to. Ben wondered if someone had put his groceries away by now. He'd have to collect them all again.

"Gimme!" Eric cried, now yanking on Ben's shirt and arm.

"You're not gettin any candy now." Ben jerked his arm away and freed his shirt from his brother's grasp. "Leave me alone!" Ben yelled.

"No," Eric whined, lingering on the vowel.

With a click, the motor disengaged. Unable to tell the difference between dry and just warm, Ben had to wait a moment so the fabric could cool. He depressed the button again, the steady and boisterous hum of the dryer washing over his mind in the same way the air itself billowed and curled around the contours of his hands. He looked peripherally at his brother, who stood with a contorted and wet face in the exact spot where Ben had directed him.

Ben placed his forehead against the cold tile on the wall, ignoring the black veins of grout. Eric couldn't be blamed. Not really, anyway. He was just a boy—old enough to have preferences and desires, but too young to be expected to control or manage them. Whatever person he would become was still very much a work in progress. Any discord between their moods or temperaments could only be Ben's fault.

Ben forgot that sometimes. Too often he thought of Eric as being older than he really was, more in control.

A chill rolled across Ben's back and neck, and he felt the pressure inside his skull ease further. Stampie's black eyes stared up at Ben, reflecting and distorting his own face. He looked older, heavier. His eyes were sunken and dark. A selfish forlornness tugged at Ben's heart. He tried to place it, but he could not.

Ben pushed the silver button again, savoring the white noise. He'd apologize, tell Eric it had all been a joke. There'd be candy after all. Isn't big brother so funny?

As the gale dwindled, Ben ran his fingers over the rhino. A faint mist launched from the ends of the fibers that he could only barely feel. "I'm sorry, bud," Ben said, his words echoing. He rolled his head toward the sink. "Stampie's just about—"

But Ben was talking to empty space.

"Bud?" he said, spinning around and pushing the door open into the stall behind him. Ben's heart pounded and a warm wave crashed over the back of his neck. "Eric?"

With trembling hands, he set Stampie on the lip of the sink and flung the door wide open. His eyes darted and stalled awkwardly as he tried to take in as much as possible while still being compelled to scan slowly so he could actually *see* what he was looking at.

Disposable music leaked from speakers hidden in the ceiling. Ben's feet moved briskly along the back aisle of the store, his head aimed unceasingly to the right, peering down each food-lined alley that whizzed past. His chest heaved.

He stifled an impulse to call out, to yell for his brother at the top of his lungs. Because it wasn't real yet. There was still hope. Screaming would make it real somehow. The door would open, the wind would carry the words, and this would all become a part of the world. He paced the aisles three times before his voice cracked.

"Eric!" Ben shouted across the puzzled faces of leering customers.

"Eric!" Ben shouted again, his pulse quickening, his mind doing its best to stave off disorienting panic. *He'll be down the next aisle,* he reassured himself. *He'll be down the* next *aisle.*

A game. This is just a game, he tried to tell himself. *He loves to play, so why not here? Why not in this place?*

"I'm gonna find you!" Ben attempted to yell, but only a whimper emerged as he shook his head.

More empty aisles. More gawking strangers.

Ben cupped his hands around his mouth and bellowed, "Olly olly oxen free!"

Nothing.

It's okay. This was okay. Kids wander off all the time. "Eric!" Ben screamed.

Wet tracks ran down Ben's cheeks, but he wasn't aware of them, or maybe he just ignored them. They weren't real anyway. This was a dream. This wasn't happening. This *couldn't* be happening. More customers turned now, their conversations ceasing.

Ben found himself running, his stomach bouncing uncomfortably.

His left knee burned and stabbed at itself, threatening mutiny. Gracelessly, Ben dodged one customer and then another. A shopping cart collided with his midsection; his hands gripped the edges and flung it out of the way. Indecipherable curses pursued him as he bounded his way toward the front of the store. Colorful packaging caught his eyes as he approached the first register. Candy. *He left for candy!* Lane by lane Ben moved his eyes over the displays, expecting to see a small boy kneeling down gorging himself, his face half hidden behind a shimmering and wrinkled wrapper.

At the end of the row, Ben found his groceries still spilled out across an unused conveyer belt. A sinking feeling took hold in his stomach. His eyes flashed from one end of the store to the other. Bakery. Frozen foods. Grocery. Pharmacy. From almost every section, eyes peered out at him, but none were the eyes that he wanted to see.

The soles of Ben's shoes squeaked against the tile as he approached the cashier from the line he had abandoned earlier. "Haveyouseenalittleboy?" Ben begged, raising his palm parallel to the ground to indicate height. The cashier shook her head as if she didn't understand the question. Frustrated, Ben repeated himself more slowly, each pause feeling like precious time spent frivolously. Again the cashier shook her head, this time with comprehension. "Call him, please," Ben said, his voice cracking as he turned away. "On the speakers!"

Ben's leg buckled briefly as he moved toward the store's entrance.

"Hey, what's his name?" the cashier called after him.

Ben turned back, his face wincing from pain and panic. "Eric!" he shouted.

Ben moved as rapidly as he could toward the doors, which slowly opened as he approached. He misjudged the gulf between them, and they rattled as his large body struck their frames. *"Would Eric please come to . . ."*

Several cars meandered around the parking lot. To his right two vehicles were leaving it altogether. He felt his body pull toward them, but his feet were planted right in front of the store. Anxious indecision filled his breast. Every place he didn't check was a place that Eric could be. And every place he did check meant he wasn't checking somewhere else. Every choice seemed wrong.

Ben jogged uncertainly toward a truck that ambled up one of the lanes and away from the store. Sweat poured down his back and sides, stung in his eyes. It sped up as Ben approached, but he couldn't run any faster.

"Hey!" he wheezed. "Hey!" Ben waved his arms, but the truck pulled away.

Ben ran back to the store. His chest quivered as violently as his legs. The doors stuttered open, the wheels derailed from the track due to Ben's collision. Everyone was looking at Ben as he entered, their faces possessed by something. Judgment? Pity perhaps. Ben couldn't see them. Ben could see only the cashier, shaking her head and standing alone.

"Eric!" he screamed.

But there was only silence.

Eric was gone.

Once upon a tuh-time, there

wuh-was a bad man.

2

Five Years Later

By the time Ben graduated high school, he was twenty years old and desperate for a job. His father, Clint, was still delivering newspapers. Now the home's only paycheck, it was practically spent before it was printed, consumed by old bills. Ben's stepmother no longer worked. Deidra hardly left the house at all, really. She wanted to be there when Eric came home.

There wasn't a place in town that Ben hadn't approached. If it was within walking distance, it had his application, and despite his leg, Ben employed a very loose definition of that measure. Hardware stores, gas stations, landscaping groups. He had two applications floating around somewhere for costumed advertising. Put on a silly outfit and wave a sign. A bad job with worse pay, but Ben put in for it all the same.

Clint said there was no rush, that eventually Ben would find an opening. Ben knew the first part wasn't true, and after waiting all summer, he stopped believing the second part too.

It might have been for the sake of exhaustion—so that when Ben said to himself that he'd tried everything, it would be the truth. Maybe it was spite. The fact was that Ben wasn't really all that sure why he'd applied at the grocery store or why he'd agreed to the interview when they called him the very next day.

Late August was hot and sticky, but Ben walked slow—slower than he had time for and slower than his leg demanded. When he got to the doors, he stopped altogether, just outside the sensor that would trip them. Stopped and watched and thought until he was late for his appointment.

In the years since Eric had gone missing, Ben had gone near the store only a couple of times. His father less often, and Deidra not once. Inside it looked exactly like he remembered it. The same sterile lighting and bad music. But it felt different, like thinking about the last meal you had before you got sick. It felt a lot like that. It felt exactly like that.

He wanted to leave so badly that it was all he could think about. But his feet kept moving. His mouth kept speaking. His body kept doing things, until Ben found himself sitting in an office about to interview for a job he didn't want but somehow knew he'd get.

Just below a long window were two tube TVs. One screen was black, so Ben watched the other one. It was a boring show: nothing but a flickering deli cooler. Ben remembered this room, though he'd seen it only once before. He remembered the store director, Bill Palmer, gesturing toward the same stuttering image and shrugging his shoulders with exasperation while Deidra sobbed in the doorway. The man hadn't apologized, hadn't done anything at all except assure customers that everything was "under control." He kept saying that: "under control." Like it meant something. Like he had any goddamn idea what was going on.

Ben glanced at his watch. How long had the girl said it'd be? How long had it already been? He felt his legs twitch again, a prompt to stand, a prompt to stand and walk out of the room, walk out of the store. Ben rubbed his left thigh with the heel of his hand and turned his head toward the sound of approaching footsteps. He almost laughed when Bill Palmer walked in.

The man was a little balder and a little fatter, but he still moved like he was king shit. He worked a key into the lock on his filing cabinet and fished some papers out, then turned back toward his desk.

He hadn't even looked at Ben yet. Grunting as he sat, he sighed heavily as he snatched a pen from his desk. He swiveled from side to side in his chair as he slipped a paper onto his clipboard and rested it against his round belly. Ben waited impatiently for the man to look up, recognize him, and end the interview.

"I don't usually do these things," he said, shuffling through the papers, pretending to scan them and doing a bad job of it too. When he finally looked up, Ben felt a rolling in his stomach. But Palmer had no reaction at all. His mud-colored eyes looked ridiculous behind his glasses, swollen and cowlike in his gelatin face. "Says here you ain't never had a job."

"Just graduated high school."

Palmer nodded. "You a dopehead?"

"Nosir." Ben flinched.

"Thief? You ever been arrested? These forms talk about felonies, but—"

"Nosir."

The man studied Ben for a moment, tapping his pen against the clipboard. Finally, he spoke. "Do I know you?"

"I'm sorry?" *Here we go.*

"Do I know you from somewhere? From here?"

"Maybe from shoppin in here sometime."

"Well, I don't think I need to ask if you can lift boxes," the man said after a while, gesturing with his clipboard at Ben. "Can you work overnights?"

That's it?

"As a cashier?"

"What?" Palmer glanced at the sheet on the clipboard and sighed with exasperation. "We don't need no more cashiers," he said, pushing up his glasses and pinching the bridge of his nose.

"I put in for bag boy too, sir."

"Stocker. We need someone on the stock crew. Shift is from ten to six, give or take."

"At night?"

"You're lucky you're strong, boy. Yes. At night. When there's no sun. Prime meridian."

"It's just that my daddy works overnights, and my stepmom . . . There ain't nothin during the day at all?"

"Not a thing. Pay is eight bucks an hour. Time and a half on holidays, of which you'll work every single one."

Ben hunched in his chair and wiped his hands with his kerchief as he adjusted to the offer. The clipboard rattled as Palmer tossed it onto the cluttered desk beside him.

"This ain't a lifetime stint on a submarine, son. It's refilling shelves, and I got a stack of names around here somewhere of people I can call when you leave. Someone'll be there to show you the ropes. You want the job or not?"

"Okay," Ben heard himself say.

Palmer handed Ben some things along with some papers to sign. Ben wasn't really paying attention, though. Still stunned from the breathtaking lack of awareness that Bill Palmer had displayed, it took a concerted effort by Ben to resist hurling the stacks of papers off the man's desk and screaming until he remembered who Ben was.

Ben had no sense of how he would tell his parents or how they would react. And he didn't have much time to figure it out, since Palmer wanted Ben to start tomorrow. But the money would spend. The bills and "Final Notices" in red ink would swallow up his checks like fire, and when offered a solution, Ben's father couldn't go on pretending there wasn't a problem. This was a good thing. Even if it didn't feel like it.

3

Mosquitoes swam frantically in the thick, humid air. Stepping out of the house was like walking into a warm, pliable gel, one that Ben had to push through the whole way to the store.

The talk with his dad and Deidra that morning had been strange. There hadn't been an argument. No real back and forth. Ben tried not to focus too much on how badly they needed the money. He wanted to be vague, say things like "helping out." But before Ben got to say much of anything, Clint just nodded and said, "Okay then."

Deidra hadn't said anything at all. She'd only laughed—just once—when Ben referred to his job as being at "just a store."

With his name tag clipped to the collar of his polo shirt and a paper bag with his lunch tucked under his arm, Ben stood outside the store for a minute, then leaned against an old metal cage full of propane tanks and stared out into the parking lot. Infrequent cars lit up the road at the far end of the lot to Ben's right, driving down one of the town's main arteries, then being swallowed up by the darkness that lay beyond the illuminating streetlights of civilization.

Ben checked his watch. It was 9:30. He brushed one mosquito off his arm, then another. Every bead of sweat and loose, tickling hair caused a reflexive twitch; before long, he swatted at bugs that might not have existed at all. He pulled the time card that Bill Palmer had given him out of his back pocket and tapped it against his palm. *Should've come at ten,* Ben thought.

Turning back toward the store, Ben ignored the large bulletin board that was affixed to the brick next to the entrance. He took one step, then another. The doors seized for just a fraction of a second and then moved apart with a screech. He could think about Eric later. He could think about Eric all damn day if he wanted.

A pretty cashier looked in Ben's direction. He met her eyeline with a smile while he adjusted his shirt away from his stomach to hide his belly. Ben leaned his back right next to the time clock, which sat on a wall just outside the borders of Customer Service, and passively watched customers weaving up and down the long aisles of the store.

When his watch read 10:00 p.m., Ben pushed his time card into the clock's slot and heard the metallic ratcheting of the printer head as it marked his slip. He slid the card into an empty space in the receptacle to his right and looked around. There was still no sign of his coworker.

With his spine flush with the wall again, the crown of his skull rolled against the paneling, which crackled noisily under the pressure. Above, he noticed an ancient camera dangling from the ceiling. Ben exhaled heavily and walked toward the register and the pretty cashier.

"Hi," Ben said with a small wave.

"Hey," the girl replied, setting down her magazine. Her hair was a pixie cut dyed with bottled colors: reds and blues, pinks and blonds. Her pierced nose was dotted with freckles.

"Chelsea?" Ben asked, reading the girl's name tag. "You have any idea if someone else is coming in tonight? It's my first night, but no one really told me anything. Mr. Palmer said someone'd be here." His lunch bag crinkled in his damp hand. "I'm on the stock crew," he added with haste.

"Well . . . *Ben,*" she said, exaggerating a squint at his name tag, "I have no idea." She smiled with teeth that were crooked in just the right way.

Ben blushed and laughed goofily. "I guess you wouldn't know what I'm supposed to do, then?"

"Just straighten up for a while. Make the shelves look nice. Marty will be here soon. It's hardly even ten o'clock."

"Alright," Ben said, backing away from the register. "Thanks a lot."

Swaying indecisively, Ben settled on an area and started straightening up. As he moved boxes and shifted packages, he hummed along to the songs forced upon him by the intercom. He tried to stay near the front of the store. Unsure of what constituted a good—much less a finished—job, Ben took his time.

At around eleven o'clock, Ben heard the familiar ruckus of the automatic doors and turned to see a thin guy of about nineteen walk through them. A name tag was clipped to the frayed bottom of his Skid Row T-shirt, and a red box cutter bobbed in its leather holster affixed to the waistband of his jeans. He scratched at the scalp beneath his dark auburn hair and then rubbed his eyes with his fists. Moving closer to intercept his coworker at the time clock, Ben recognized him immediately. From school? Ben wasn't sure, but the familiarity wasn't shared; he looked at Ben with new eyes.

"Sorry I'm late. Car troubles," the guy said, the end of each word conjoined to the next in a thick drawl. He looked at Ben briefly, then took a pen from his pocket and wrote "10:00 p.m." in Saturday's column before returning the card to the slot on the wall.

"What about the camera?" Ben gestured with his head.

"Huh?" He looked at the camera mounted to the ceiling. "Oh, that? That thing works less than me." He smirked as he extended his hand.

Ben dug his handkerchief from his pocket and wiped his hand dry before pressing his palm against his coworker's. "Ben."

"Good to know ya, Ben. I'm Marty." He waved to Chelsea, who smiled wide and waved back. "You 'bout ready to get started?"

"I already did," Ben said.

"No kidding!" Marty said in apparent disbelief. "Well, *alright then.* Let's see your handiwork."

Ben led Marty past the entrance to the collection of tables on the far side of the store lined with plastic clamshell containers full of croissants and boxes stuffed with cupcakes. Marty, hands stuffed deep into his pockets, stared at Ben's progress with cartoonishly wide eyes and puffed-out cheeks.

"Did I do it wrong?" Ben asked.

Marty deflated his cheeks and laughed. "Oh, man. She's gonna shit. This is the bakery department. We don't mess with any of this stuff; that's the bread lady's gig. She's real . . . *particular.*"

Ben smiled uneasily, wiping the back of his neck with his kerchief.

"I mean, *I* think it looks great, man."

"I can fix it," Ben assured, moving toward the table.

"No, no," Marty interrupted. "She'll never know who did it. Could've been a customer or some sort of freak accident that stacked everything like this . . . Don't sweat it." He gestured with his head back toward the middle of the store. "We're grocery. That's pretty much everything between the bakery and drug."

They walked the inside perimeter of the store while they chatted. The rectangular layout was a simple one, the geography of which Ben already knew quite well, though he didn't interrupt Marty's tour. They passed the long front end of the store that housed Customer Service, in front of which were several registers. When they reached the drug department, their discussion was already migrating away from the features of the store. And by the time they walked the deli and dairy racks on the long back aisle, the store had become nothing more than a place to house their conversation.

Ben felt a tightening in his stomach as they moved past the men's bathroom. The wood-patterned vinyl sticker on its face had begun to peel from around the door's edges and handle. He buried the feeling and followed Marty through the double doors and into the back room.

The contrast between the two spaces was stark. The main floor was for customers, open and airy so they could push their full carts wherever they liked for as long as they liked. High ceilings beamed with bright light that made the aisles feel spacious, even during crowded hours. But the back room was claustrophobic. Loud. Dim bulbs shone on the clutter of machinery and backstock from a much lower point. Here, the ceiling served as a floor for the store's second level, a spartan array of storage rooms and offices. Above, Ben could see the metal railing of the concrete catwalk that led to Bill Palmer's domain and, behind that railing, a colossal machine that filled every pocket of empty space with its noise.

"Air conditioner!" Marty yelled.

Marty yanked hard on the handle of a large industrial freezer. It opened after two or three attempts, and cold air billowed as it exited; Ben could feel it filling up his shoes as it tumbled to the floor. Marty grabbed an ice-cream sandwich from an open box on a shelf just inside, paused, and then grabbed another and handed it to Ben. Finally, the roaring machine wound down and the room felt a little less oppressive.

"Looks pretty full in there."

"Needs to be reorganized or cleaned out. Probably both."

"We stock the coolers too?"

"Yeah, about once a week or so. Might seem stupid, but you leave that door wide open when you go in there." He bent and snatched a piece of wood off the ground next to the large door. "And you use this wedge to hold it. I mean really jam it in there. That door's janky as fuck, and if it closes on you, you're gonna freeze to death."

Marty placed the tip of his index finger on the outside of the enormous door. "But here's the stupidest thing about this piece of shit. You just give it a little love . . ." Marty gently nudged the door back toward its home, and it glided smoothly into place, latching without protest. "And presto."

They turned and walked farther into what Marty called "Receiving," since it was where pallets of inventory were unloaded through the massive metal doors Ben could see at the far end of the room. As they walked, a foul smell coated Ben's nose and he exhaled sharply through it.

"What is that?" Ben asked.

"What's what?"

"That *smell*."

"Ohhhh," Marty said. "That's either the exotic scent of death or it's the damages." He pointed to a steel rack with cans and glass jars precariously towered on top of one another. Ben could see flies swarming wildly, enjoying their buffet. "There's really no way to tell anymore."

"Yeah. I think that's it." Ben laughed. "How come nobody cleans it up?"

"Inventory's not for another coupla months. But you go right ahead and get scrubbin if you want."

"Ya know, it's really not that bad once you get used to it."

Marty laughed. "And here we have the prize pony of the store," he said, gesturing with the this-could-be-yours pomp of a car salesman. "The Baler. Built in 1795, and last serviced somehow even before then, this enormous piece of shit will make all your dreams come true, as long as your dreams are only about crushing cardboard."

Small flakes of ancient paint scattered like green dandruff as Marty petted the side of the monster with mock affection. Regardless of when it had actually been built, Marty was right about one thing—it *was* enormous.

"I'll show you how it all works after Monday's truck," Marty said, tapping the control box on the side of the baler. "You'll get the hang of it 'fore long."

"Mondays are when the truck comes?"

"They didn't tell you a goddamn *thing,* did they?"

Ben shook his head.

"The trucks come Monday, Wednesday, and Friday," Marty said, as they walked deeper into the back room. "We block the other nights—line everything up on the shelves so it all looks like one solid block."

"Stocking and blocking," Ben said.

"And rocking," Marty said flatly, gesturing without enthusiasm to the dull music that dripped from the speakers above. "This here's the break room."

The space was fairly unadorned. There was a plastic folding table in the middle of the floor with chairs tucked underneath. The white walls looked a sickly yellow under the old lights, though the left and back walls were mostly covered with posters that were meant to be motivational. They made even Ben roll his eyes, and he was too new to be jaded already. A camera was perched in the top corner where those walls met. Ben pointed at it and Marty shrugged.

The far wall was covered entirely with metal lockers, each marked with a name written on masking tape. At Marty's prompting, Ben taped his name to a free locker and put his bagged lunch inside.

"You gotta bring your own lock," Marty said, slipping a piece of paper into the slot of a locker belonging to someone named Frank. "We don't really take breaks in here, but you can leave food or clothes or whatever in the locker. Don't put anything in the fridge unless you're trying to give it away."

Marty closed a drawer and turned back to Ben. A green utility knife docked snugly in a leather holster dangled from his hand.

Ben arched his back and dug discreetly under his stomach for the waist of his pants, then slid the metal clip of the holster onto it. The boys walked back into the heart of Receiving, where the air conditioner again screamed against the walls and floor.

"That it then?" Ben shouted.

"Yeah," Marty shouted back. "All 'cept them stairs." He pointed to a rusted set of steps just to the right of the freezer. "There's a few offices and a bathroom up there. Some stairs that spit out right around the pharmacy. Most of the rooms are Palmer's. It's where he looks down ladies' shirts. Sometimes he accidentally busts a shoplifter. C'mon, I'll show you what I mean."

Marty led Ben back through the double doors. After getting a little distance, they turned toward the back of the store, and Marty pointed at a series of darkly tinted windows that nested up against the ceiling.

"The crow's nest. You can see through all them windows. Captain Palmer sits up there all day and waits for someone to try to make off with something, since all them glass domes are empty and none of the real cameras work." The span of Marty's gesture encompassed the entire store. "Except for maybe that one. I heard that one works."

"It does," Ben muttered as he looked at the camera that hung over the deli racks. "*None* of the other cameras work?"

Marty looked at Ben curiously. "A hole in the earth could open up right where we're standing, and Palmer would just rope it off. They don't fix shit around here."

It was five minutes before midnight, and Chelsea's voice came over the intercom announcing the closing of the store.

"That's our cue," Marty said as he started walking toward the front of the store. "We got chair detail outside . . . But between the crow's nest and that camera," Marty continued, "Palmer is on the J-O-B."

"He ever catch anyone?"

"You'd be surprised, and *boy* does he seem to get off on catching people. They steal more than you'd think, especially meat and drugs. A while back—" Marty's own laughter interrupted him. "A while back, this lady grabbed a bunch of pills from the pharmacy, and Palmer saw it. Now, he usually waits for them to stroll toward the exit, ya know, so they can't pretend they were gonna pay for it. Anyway, he's watching her walk away, probably jerkin his dick, all excited to spring the trap.

"But then this lady just *bolts* for the exit. Like, out of nowhere, she just makes a beeline straight for the door on the other side of the store! When something like that happens, there's these intercom codes you're supposed to use. But Palmer"—Marty started chuckling—"Palmer comes on the intercom and goes, 'I need . . . I . . . There's . . .' And she's still gunning it. So finally, he just goes, 'Thief! Thief! Get her! She's getting away, damnit!' The speakers were all busting out because he was screaming into the mic, and everyone's just looking around trying to figure out what was going on."

"So what happened?"

"She just ran right out the door! Palmer came down all red and out of breath and looked around like she would still be there. Then he just looked at everyone, even the customers, and put his hands out like, 'You blew it!'"

Marty positioned himself to the right side of the front doors and reached up to flip a small switch secured to the trim of the metal frame. Ben watched as Marty turned the key and then grabbed the deadbolt at the center of the two doors and slid them apart, letting the air, which was thick and wet with humidity, leak into the store like a paste. The surrounding businesses were all long closed, and without their polluting lights, the stars above shone brightly in the clean sky.

Outside, Marty grabbed two plastic chairs that were stacked behind the propane cage and set them near the entrance. The two sat facing each other. Marty held his pack of smokes out and offered one to Ben, who declined as he forced his way into a chair that was a bit too snug.

Ben heard the bright click of a Zippo opening as Marty flicked his wrist. He lit his cigarette and the smoke curled in tendrils that danced gracefully upward despite the heaviness of the air, air that was so still the smoke collected in a gossamer curtain against the recessed lights in the awning above them. Ben watched small moths make puddles in the murky sheet as they tried to move ever closer to the light—Sisyphus reborn with wings.

Chelsea came outside. Ben offered her his chair, but she declined and left soon after. Ben watched her drive the last car out of the parking lot.

"Where's your car?" Ben asked.

"Hmm? Oh, I don't have one."

Ben smiled as he realized what Marty had meant by "car troubles."

Marty lit another cigarette while Ben wiped his face and neck with his handkerchief. The conversation dwindled, but not uncomfortably so, and the two sat in relative silence for a long while. Rhythmically, Marty swept his lighter open against his jeans, then closed it. *Slink. Clink. Slink. Clink.* Ben lowered his eyes from the lights above and fixed them straight ahead onto the board he had avoided hours earlier.

A silver frame outlined the large panel, hugging the two thin sheets of acrylic glass that protected the display beneath it. In big, bubbly blue letters that formed a faint arch, the banner read: HAVE YOU SEEN ME? Below this overly stylized header were a dozen or so black-and-white flyers for missing children. As if all the pieces of paper were blank save one, Ben's eyes fell upon Eric's face.

Eric's features were a little distorted in the image—the inevitable result of photocopying duplicates of duplicates. The worst part of it, if such things could even be measured, was how old his brother's flyer looked, worn and eroded. Exposed for so long the sun had stolen all the brightness from the sheet.

His eyes glazed over as they moved themselves across the board. Each flyer began with "My name is" followed by the child's name in capital letters and ended with a phone number that probably didn't ring as often as anyone hoped.

"You good, man?" asked Marty.

The parking lot was dark, and cicadas and toads buzzed and bellowed from the woods across the street.

"Hmm? Yeah," Ben blurted out. "Yeah, I'm good . . . So it's just us all night?"

"Yeah, until the bread lady shows up. Usually around five or so?"

"She know you just call her the bread lady?" Ben chuckled.

"Hope not. I call her Ms. Beverly when I talk to her, and I try to make sure that doesn't happen too often."

"She that bad?"

"Just takes everything so serious. Like, we work at a *grocery store,* ya know? Ain't never been a stocker she liked, 'cept for me, and even I don't know why that is. She used to give me a real hard time, but she's mellowed out some. She thinks we're all a bunch of thieves."

Ben nodded to a stolen candy bar that sat in Marty's lap.

"But she don't *know* anything. Just accuses everyone all the damn time. If I had a nickel for every time she's said I stole her bread, I'd have enough money to pay for all the bread I really stole." The two laughed. "You like the job so far?"

"I like chair detail," Ben said.

"Most important part of the job, right here!" Marty said, slapping his armrest.

"*You* like working here?" Ben asked.

"It's not so bad, really. Palmer's a real piece of work. But the job itself is alright. Creepy at night by yourself sometimes. Weird place."

"Why's that?"

"Gets too quiet, I guess. Shit falls off shelves. I dunno. Don't have to deal with customers, though, so . . ." Marty shrugged.

"Not a people person?"

"Depends on the people, I guess. Something about this town, man. Got real big after they finished that interstate a few years back. But in a hurry, ya know? Like people got off the interstate for gas and couldn't figure out how to get back on, so they just threw a rock and built a house. 'Fuck it. I'll just live here in this random-ass neighborhood forever, I guess.' But the town ain't never caught up. Still got just the one hospital. My brother's gotta share a desk at school. And the fuckin *roads,* man . . ."

"Too many tractors?" Ben grinned.

"Where the hell are they going anyways? Ain't no farms around here. Not no more. Shit, we're sitting where the last farm used to be before they paved and built over it."

"What about that field past the woods out there?" Ben gestured toward the store's sign, which stood as the last light for miles in that direction.

"What field? Oh, that baby field?" Marty waved his hand dismissively. "Idiots holding up the whole town so a tractor can farm some beans."

"I think maybe it's cotton."

"That's a kind of bean. Cotton bean." He smiled.

Ben dug a granola bar out of his pocket and peeled the wrapper back before biting into it. He took deep breaths to pull the heavy air into his lungs as he stared straight ahead. The toes of his right foot pushed his leg up and down like a jackhammer.

"You sure you're doing alright, man?" Marty asked.

"Huh?" Ben responded, before shaking his head faintly to snap his mind to attention. "Yeah, I'm good."

"Depressing shit." Marty sighed, gesturing at the board. "You might think about bringing out a magazine, since them don't make for good reading."

Ben feigned a chuckle.

"I reckon you and me are the only ones who've paid that board much mind at all. People just walk on by. Hardly even noticed it myself before I spent so much time sittin out here.

"I do wonder what happened sometimes," Marty continued after a short while. "Especially to the older ones. Shoot, one of them was almost thirteen, you know? I went to elementary school with his sister, but I ain't heard from her in a long time. Figure taking the little ones makes sense—perverts and all—but the older ones? You think they run away or something?"

"I dunno," Ben mumbled.

"Gotta wonder where they might be running to. I guess sometimes with the younger ones it's the folks. Maybe the daddy comes back and takes the kid. Wish my daddy woulda come and kidnapped me."

Ben ran his fingers through his short hair, his eyes lingering on the board. He thought that Marty would have recognized him by now. But they'd never spoken before. Maybe Marty didn't know anything about Ben, and Ben wondered whether he should try to preserve that ignorance. It wouldn't last forever, but it could last for just a little while longer, before the pity came and tarnished everything. How long would that take, though? How many nights could he sit out in front of this bulletin board and deny he was staring at it?

Marty's words were muted in Ben's ears, and Ben was only somewhat aware of his own absent participation in the exchange. He could feel a quivering in his chest as his lips began to push out words.

"My brother," Ben started, as he gestured toward the board and grunted through a dry throat, "my brother's up there."

Marty turned and looked at the board. "Jesus, dude." His eyes went wide. "I can't believe . . . Shit. I'm sorry; it just didn't . . . goddamnit . . . it just didn't click when I saw you, cuz you look different to me. Fuck."

"It's alright," Ben said. "You was a grade above me, I think."

The air was quiet for a moment. "What . . . what happened?" Marty finally asked, tentatively.

Wringing his hands together, Ben answered Marty's question. "I . . . I lost him."

Marty nodded almost imperceptibly. "Do you mean like someone took him? We don't have to talk about this."

"I dunno." Ben had a nauseated and crooked smile on his face as he lightly slapped his hands together between his knees. "That's all I can really say for sure, because that's all I really know. And the crazy thing is"—Ben's voice quivered as he gestured toward the store—"the thing that's messing me up so bad is that it happened right *here*." His voice cracked. "Right here in this store."

Marty breathed out heavily. Smoke twisted upward from the cigarette between his fingers.

Ben wiped his nose with his handkerchief and laughed. "Man, what am I *doing* here? All the stuff you showed me, all them departments. Even the back room. I've *seen* it all before. I saw it when the police came and looked for him."

When Ben told the story—when he talked about it with anyone—he tried his best to treat it like it *was* a story, like it was something that had happened to someone else. That was the only way he could get through it. Over the years, he'd developed a skill for it, but being at this place made him forget how to tell a story. All he could remember was the truth, so that's what he told Marty.

He told him about the heat and the headache. About looking for Stampie the stuffed rhino later that same day but finding that someone must have already thrown him away. He told Marty about the hand dryer and how he had to keep calling his house until someone finally picked up. Until his *stepmother* finally picked up. About how his parents had asked the police for search dogs, and how the police hadn't been able to acquire any from the neighboring town. And he told Marty about how the police had made him call for his brother as they walked the store.

Marty leaned forward in his chair, his elbows resting on his knees while he stared at Ben.

"He was supposed to fix the cameras after that. Palmer. He said he'd fix 'em." Ben pressed and scraped his handkerchief against his palm. Back and forth, over and over. "I'm sorry for pouring all that stuff on you, Marty. I'm not usually—it's just being back here . . ."

"Ain't nothing to be sorry for, Ben," Marty said. "*I* sure am sorry, though. I got a brother myself. I can't . . . Jesus Christ, man."

Neither spoke for a while.

"Hell of a first night, huh?" Marty said.

"Yeah." Ben laughed, wiping his eyes with his knuckles. "I'm good now. I'm alright." He breathed out a heavy sigh. "Your brother older or younger?"

"Younger. Aaron. A real pain in the ass too."

"Think that's a rule with younger brothers. Even Eric could fire me up sometimes."

Marty dropped his lighter and leaned down to pick it up. "That's his name? Eric?"

"Yeah."

Marty nodded and stared out into the clear black sky. The ashes from his neglected cigarette had formed a long, unstable cylinder that broke off and scattered on his jeans. He brushed it onto the concrete while Ben talked.

"I just want to know what happened to him. I want to see him again. More than anything." Ben wiped the sweat from his forehead with his kerchief. "Jeez, it's really hot out here. Can we go back in? Is that alright?"

Marty flicked his dead cigarette into the parking lot and walked back inside without saying anything.

4

"Fat dumb idiot," Ben muttered to himself. "Stupid fat dumb fuck." His bad leg screamed as he swung it, sending an empty cardboard box flying against a shelf. A few cans toppled and rolled along the aisle. "Can't never just be quiet. Not here five minutes and look."

A can bumped against his shoe as he limped down the aisle. He'd known Marty for only a few hours, and already Ben had solidified himself as the Guy Who Let His Little Brother Get Took. And that's who he would *always* be now, someone who demanded unwanted soft words and undeserved pity.

And what if Marty told Bill Palmer? Ben could feel his palms dampen at the thought, and he shook his head as if that would be enough to get rid of it. He'd tell Palmer—or he'd tell someone who would tell Palmer—and that'd be it. First and last paycheck on a single piece of paper. Ben couldn't help but chuckle as he rubbed his handkerchief on the back of his neck. He was pacing now. Was he looking for Marty? He wasn't sure. Ben wasn't sure he knew what he was looking for in any sense.

His shoes squeaked against the tile as he limped past one of the cans he had sent rolling a few seconds before. He glanced down the aisle toward his mess and kept walking, wishing he could think of something other than how he should have let Eric have a goddamned cookie. More and more those had become the things that ate at Ben—the small things. They added up so quickly. Ben rubbed his eyes, glanced down an aisle, and froze.

He turned and looked behind him, back toward Receiving, and then ahead in the direction of the pharmacy. Ben *was* looking for Marty now, but when he moved his eyes back down the aisle, all he could see were the cans he'd loosed now stacked neatly in a pillar in the middle of the aisle.

"Marty?" But only the bland music of the PA answered him. With slow steps, Ben approached the small obelisk. "Sorry, man!"

Grunting, Ben squatted and began ferrying the cans to their spots on the shelves. He headed to the back room, expecting to find Marty there, and when he didn't, he ran his fingers down the printed schedule to see if anyone else might be on for that night. But there were only two names, and they were both accounted for.

With a shudder, the air conditioner powered down, and Ben was left with only the tinny sputtering of old speakers. Ben listened to the garbled chutterings of the intercom, which now sounded less like singing and more like speaking. Ben suddenly became very uncomfortable, as if he had paddled too far out into a midnight lake. He stared straight ahead, waiting for the empty feeling to pass, waiting for his feet to touch the bottom. But the feeling did not pass.

The speaker crackled and then went silent. Ben's skin turned to goose-flesh, and for just a moment the room seemed quiet enough that Ben thought he could hear his own breathing.

Thunder tore through that silence. Inorganic and harsh, the crash made Ben flinch as if he'd been struck. Ben spun, his arms near his chest in feeble defense, and looked to the upper level. He held his breath. The air conditioner whirred, coughing and thudding out of its slumber, until finally it roared back to life. Ben exhaled as if in relief, but he didn't *feel* relieved.

—

The hours ticked by slowly until it was finally time to clock out. As Ben and Marty walked toward the exit, Ben saw a white-haired woman scurrying from table to table in the bakery department, undoing the damage that Ben's attempt to help had caused.

"You want a ride or something?" Ben asked. "My dad should be here in just a minute."

"Nah, that's alright. Thanks, though," Marty said.

Ben leaned his body against the propane cage. There was a sharp pain shooting up his left leg. He pressed the heel of his hand into his thigh and pushed down hard toward his knee. Ben groaned. The first time always hurt the worst, but eventually the pain would subside. Slowly and repeatedly, Ben overwhelmed his nerves until they were tired of talking.

"You all done then?"

Ben looked up to see Bill Palmer waddling toward the store, adjusting the waistband of his khakis; his tie was a little too short.

"Yessir," Ben said. "Marty just left. Store looks real good."

The man nodded, then seemed to glance behind Ben, his eyes lingering for a moment before he walked into the store. Ben turned and looked at the board. At Eric's flyer.

When he heard the rumbling of his father's truck, Ben stepped into the parking lot to meet him and climbed into the passenger seat.

The truck churned noisily down the street. On their right, Ben caught a glimpse of Marty on the side of the road. He wasn't walking, though. He was just standing by the tree line gazing into the woods.

He didn't ssstart out all the way

buh-bad. It stuh-started in his head.

He thought bad things.

5

The loose rocks of their driveway popped under the weight of the truck's tires. "She alright?" Ben asked, nodding toward the home. Clint only scratched his beard and shrugged.

When his father opened the front door, the powerful aroma of eggs and sausage wafted out, and Ben couldn't help but smile.

The three of them sat at the oversized table. Two dinners and a breakfast made from the same food. No one mentioned the store. In fact, no one mentioned much of anything, but it wasn't a bad silence. Wavy brown hair fell over his stepmother's eyes, which were swollen from either bad or absent sleep, but her spirits seemed high, even if the corners of her lips seemed to tremble when she tried to smile. Ben stayed up a little longer than he had intended, just sitting at the table with his father and stepmother.

He thanked Deidra for the meal, cleared his plate, and walked sluggishly toward his room. And as he paused in his doorway, he listened to the clattering of dishes in the kitchen and tried to pretend that things were like they used to be.

How old had he been? Eleven? Maybe just ten, when his father remarried. He had known that his father had been seeing a woman; Ben had met Deidra a handful of times, and he liked her. But it never registered with Ben that anything serious was developing. The proposal had seemed to come out of nowhere in Ben's mind.

Their new house had been a little too big, Ben thought. It was in worse shape than the house where Ben had grown up, and for a while the third bedroom was just a workspace for Deidra's painting and other hobbies. It wasn't until Deidra got pregnant that Ben understood why they'd really wanted a third bedroom.

Clint had moved Deidra's easel and her desk, her typewriter and her fabrics, into the garage, where they would sit untouched and forgotten. A crib and later a bed furnished the room, resting on top of carpet that was still stained with paint. Ben remembered hearing new noises coming through the wall, coming from a room that was finally serving its intended purpose. Anytime Eric cried or laughed or crashed one of his toys into the partition, and anytime Eric's mother sang him a song or read him a story, Ben could hear it. When walls are thin enough, it's almost as if they aren't really there.

Ben walked a few extra paces past his room and stood for a moment at the entrance to Eric's. As quietly as he could, he turned the knob and gazed backward in time.

Eric's room existed in a kind of stasis, frozen like a capsule that waited to be reopened. Unlike most of the other rooms in the house, there were no ceiling leaks in Eric's room. Everything was clean. Strangely, everything felt new. And there *were* some new things. There were new toys, still tightly wrapped in colorful paper, placed on the shelves and dresser after each missed Christmas and birthday by Eric's mother. From time to time, Ben thought about opening them. But he didn't. He left them untouched, because they weren't his. Whether they belonged to Eric was hard for Ben to decide. But he supposed they did in some way. The whole room was full of things Eric had loved and might have come to love. A mausoleum for a boy and who he might have been.

With quiet steps, Ben slunk back to his room and shut the door. The sound was what Ben noticed the most. There was so much less to hear now, but Ben still listened. And Ben still sometimes lay on his back in bed just staring at the ceiling before going to sleep. And sometimes when he did, he tapped the wall next to his headboard with his knuckles like he would when he was just a little younger and a little less lonely in his own home.

The mattress sank as he lowered himself onto it, a cordless phone gripped in his right hand. A few times a year, Ben called Officer James

Duchaine, and a few times a year Ben was told that the police hadn't found or heard anything.

There was a time when Ben could talk to any officer at the station, when they all knew the details of Eric's case. But that time had long passed. Now there was only Duchaine. Ben could remember when that transition had begun, when his calls started being rerouted. But what he couldn't remember was when the calls had become a kind of empty habit. He supposed it might have started around the first time he heard annoyance in Duchaine's voice, when Ben was made to feel that he was wasting the man's time with stupid questions.

It didn't matter, though. This time there was no answer at all.

The feeling that had come over him in the back room when the air conditioner rumbled to life wouldn't leave him. And that almost would have been fine if Ben had been able to make some sense of what that feeling was exactly. It wasn't fear. It might have been at the time, of course, but it couldn't *still* be fear, not all these hours later. No, it was something else, something that made him blush even in the solitude of his room.

Because as silly as Ben knew it was, he didn't trust that noise or its source. He didn't trust it at all, and despite how hard he tried to shake it, he felt in some small and slippery way that he had caught the store not only *doing something* but also trying to pretend that it wasn't.

Ben slid his hand from the receiver to a sketchbook that lay right next to it. He touched the cover as the cold pillow on the back of his neck made his eyelids feel weak. Plates and silverware clashed together under a running faucet in the kitchen as Ben's breathing slowed. He lifted his hand off the embossed leather cover and brushed it against the wall by his headboard.

Knock. Knock. Knock.

6

Ben awoke suddenly in the middle of the day, the sun screaming violently through the blinds. His mouth was dry and tasted bad, and he unconsciously pressed his tongue against his palate, curling it toward his teeth in an attempt to wet his mouth. A loud heartbeat thudded in his ears as he lay there drawing in quick and shallow breaths. Uneasily, Ben let his eyes wander around the room, his heart accelerating as he turned his head to spy on the spots where the walls met. No faces, only furniture.

His head returned to the damp pillow with a heavy sigh escaping his nose. The dream itself was bad, but that it was back was somehow worse. It had to have been at least four years since he'd had it. As he lay there with the afternoon sun fighting its way into his room, he hoped that the dream was just an aberration of his brain, that it would pass and be forgotten by all parts of him just as it had before—that it was nothing more than a kind of mental indigestion bucking at him after a testing night.

As the pulsing in his ears receded, the muffled and monotone droning of his father's snores trickled through his closed door. Under it, there was another noise. A song. Softly, almost timidly, it snuck into Ben's bedroom through the wall behind his head.

It was Deidra's voice, whispering a melody punctuated with words that Ben could not make out. Ben felt a sinking in his chest. Quietly, he stepped into the hallway, stopping just shy of Eric's door, which he was surprised to find open. The song was sweet and unfamiliar—probably one she had come up with on her own after Eric disappeared.

Ben grimaced and mouthed obscenities. He looked down the hall.

There might be a chance that his father didn't know, and maybe some fleeting chance that this wouldn't happen again, that it was a fluke.

"I love you, baby," Deidra said softly. "I miss you more than you know."

Ben could hear her breathing words into the air like a child entrusting her most closely guarded secret to a friend. Ben knew he should leave. But the longer he lingered, the more he fixated on the idea that while the secret might not be meant for him, it might indeed be *about* him. That in the wordless rustling of her quiet conversation, Deidra might be telling Eric about the bad and stupid thing that Ben had done. About how he'd gone to work at the store. About how it wasn't *just a store.*

Ben leaned closer, the old wood creaked, and then there was no more whispering to hear. Suddenly, Eric's door slammed shut so forcefully that a family photo jostled and fell from the wall. The glass cracked, and the pressed wood frame split almost completely in half.

Ben took a tentative step toward the closed door and then turned away from it. He squatted, inhaling sharply at the stabbing pain in his left leg, and began collecting the pieces of the frame. A door opened at the end of the dark hall.

"What was that? Everything alright?" Clint asked.

Ben ran his fingers over the ear that had been closest to the door, realizing only now that it was ringing. He told his father that everything was fine and silently tried to convince himself of the same.

7

Ben had been the one to choose the photograph that was used on Eric's flyer. His hands had combed through dozens of smooth pictures from boxes that were hauled out of the garage and albums ferried from the living room. There were no pictures of Eric by himself, not since the time when he was an infant.

Deidra had hated every picture that Ben chose. She would look with damp eyes at each photograph, press her lips tightly together, and then dismiss it. Ben had asked her to explain her criteria only once. She'd sobbed, shaking her head. "He didn't like that shirt . . . He said it itched him, but . . . but he looked so *handsome* in it."

In the privacy of his room, Ben had held a family photo from the previous Christmas and cut into it with a pair of scissors. His hands trembled as he moved the blades around the curly locks of dark hair that fell onto his baby brother's face. When it was done, the sight of the scraps twisted his stomach, but he couldn't bring himself to throw them out, as if keeping them might change the fact that the scraps were all that was left.

For years afterward, Ben kept that photograph in a frame next to his bed. Some time ago, even Ben couldn't recall exactly when, he had moved the photograph onto the dresser that sat across the room. The picture was roughly oval in shape, with swooping curves cut into the longer edges. Light creases arced across his brother's face from a brief time when Ben hadn't handled it with the necessary care.

Since his third night of work, Ben had carried the photograph in his back pocket inside an Ultra PRO baseball card sleeve like a secret talisman. It did nothing to ward off the uneasy feeling the store gave him. But it was nice to be able to look at Eric whenever he felt the urge, which was often.

Truth be told, almost every day since starting at the store, Ben had fantasized about showing customers too. He'd come close once or twice, approaching shoppers only to walk right past them, feeling short of breath as he pinched the picture in his back pocket.

He wasn't sure why he felt that way. Ben had been afraid of losing his job since his very first night, when he'd told Marty about his history with the place. But near as Ben could figure, that particular danger seemed to have passed. If Marty was going to tell Bill Palmer, he likely would have done so in the past two weeks.

Whatever the nature of his apprehension was, Ben let it push him out of the store and into the great wide world beyond, onto a path he had walked before but not as often as he should have. Not nearly as often.

Outside, the lazy summer sun stalled just above the horizon. Ben tucked his sketchbook under his arm and started walking. By his watch, he had a little over two hours before work.

The contrast between the houses of the new neighborhoods and the ones that had first settled the town seemed stark—at first anyway. Most of the older homes flaunted their age without embarrassment; if they couldn't be called ruins, it was only because they were still occupied. The homes that arrived with the interstate were young things, confident and sharp. Even their arrangement was well styled, lined up like rows of corn along the drive, then swaying with the winding asphalt of the cul-de-sac: guiding the road then following it, dancing.

From the street, the homes really did seem nice. Picturesque even. But distance could do that. In reality, the houses were nothing more than cheap gifts in vinyl wrapping. Some of them were already starting to show their wear in charmless cracks and creeping mold.

Opening his sketchbook from the back cover, Ben ran his fingers down rows of addresses and dates. Six months ago, there had been as many houses for sale in this neighborhood. The fact that there were now only two realtor signs meant that this trip wouldn't be a total waste. Four new doors to knock on.

Right after Eric disappeared, the whole area, if not the whole town, was whipped into a frenzy. Woods, abandoned houses, creeks—there was virtually no place that hadn't felt a human foot. Everyone—police and parents alike—conducted themselves outwardly as if the situation were only temporary, as if it had all been some mistake and Eric would turn up. He had simply wandered too far away and gotten lost. And since nothing stays lost for long in small towns, he was only ever a day or two from finding his way back home. Ben knew that wouldn't last forever, but it didn't seem to last at all. After what seemed like just a day or two, people began to act like they had done all they could even when they had done next to nothing at all. James Duchaine held out a little longer, but not long enough.

Mostly, people just talked, guessing and speculating. From what Ben could tell they all seemed to be in independent agreement: that the same new road that brought in business might just have taken something with it in return, that Eric must have slipped right off the edge of the earth. And as that feeling spread, he began to slip from their minds as well. There was nothing to be done about that, really. The same process would probably play out inside the walls of the house that Ben now stood in front of, just as it had in the one before. And just as it would in all the ones to come.

Ben knew he couldn't really blame them, even though he did. Gradually, even the buzzing flurry of voices in his own mind—*Have I checked here? Did I look there? Could he have gone there?*—was joined by just one more companion. It was quiet at first, barely a whisper, easily swept aside and overpowered. But it was tenacious, clawing and pulling itself against the muddy walls of Ben's brain until it was all he could hear anymore.

He's not coming home.

It was the only echo that seemed to get louder over time, and Ben couldn't deny that it had changed him, worn him down. The fervor and intensity that came with every sunrise all those years ago had slowly burned out in the town, at his home, and eventually in his own heart. Hell, Ben had been out of flyers for almost a year. He'd let that happen.

And now he couldn't even make more since the only copy he still knew about was at the store.

But Ben still made his rounds. Even walking up the hollow-sounding steps, preparing to insert himself into the lives and minds of these new homeowners, he could hear that taunting, defeatist mantra. But he still climbed. He still slid Eric's picture on top of his sketchbook and took a deep breath. And, most important, he still knocked.

8

Ben had to hustle to make it back to the store in time for his shift. The guy at the new home had been nice, though it was doubtful the conversation would lead to anything. He said he'd tell his wife when she got home from work. From the looks of things, they hadn't even unpacked yet. Near as Ben could tell, the couple didn't have any children of their own, but he wasn't sure that mattered either way. It used to be that Ben thought those with children would be more empathetic, more in tune with this particular kind of crisis. He didn't think that anymore.

Still, it had to be the right approach. Catching people who were new to the area was the best thing to do. Maybe they'd keep their eyes open since they now knew what to look for. Maybe they'd even talk about it with the new friends they'd come to make, remind them of something they shouldn't have forgotten in the first place.

Ben put his sketchbook in his locker and got to work. Marty was nowhere to be seen. Frank was there, though, standing by the time clock, tapping the butt of his utility knife against his open palm.

"Heya, Frank."

"Big Ben," Frank said, and nodded, "how was your weekend?"

Ben had met Frank on his third night and liked him instantly. Although he had a bit of an overbite, Frank's smile was brilliant, which was a dangerous thing, since he laughed at just about everything. He always dressed a little too nicely for the job he worked—slacks instead of jeans, pressed and stain-free collared shirts, and always light colors: the worst colors a person could wear when moving products from dirty boxes to filthy shelves. His eyeglasses were just a little too big to be fashionable; they were better suited for a much older man, though Frank did have a few years on his coworkers. Maybe ten. Still, he reset his eyewear like a kid would, middle knuckle of a bent index finger pressing against the glass, smudging it each time. Frank's name tag, which actually took two days for Ben to notice and an extra day to inquire about, said BLACK FRANK.

The story, as Marty told it anyway, was that when Frank was hired, there was already another employee named Frank who worked at the store. This proved to be only an occasional and minor source of confusion for a handful of people, but at some point the new Frank was mistakenly written up due to the rudeness of the old Frank. In response, new Frank used the label gun to alter his name tag, and it had stayed that way until long after old Frank quit.

When measured cumulatively, Frank had worked there for almost as long as Marty had. While his work ethic was strong, his dedication and resolve were not. He quit. All the time. Sometimes, in the middle of a shift, Frank would simply resign. The thing was only the rest of the crew ever knew about it. Since Palmer never found out, Frank would show up a few days later and clock in like everything was normal, and the ticking clock would be reset. Everyone always covered for him because he was a nice guy. Ben had been there only two weeks, and he had already seen Frank quit once.

Ben and Frank made their way into Receiving under the auspices of beginning their nightly project, but in reality they wanted to avoid being asked to retrieve shopping carts from the sprawling parking lot. The backroom doors swished open for Marty at around half past ten.

"Jesus. What happened to your face, man?" Ben shouted over the air conditioner, tapping Frank with the back of his hand.

The right side of Marty's lip was swollen and split, as if someone had pumped it full of air until a seam burst. A dark red line marked the chasm. Dried blood mixed with new and old skin as his body attempted to sort the mess out.

"Oh, I bet I know," Frank said, moving closer. "He finally slipped one of his pecker drawings into the wrong person's locker."

"Vat mean that yer the *right* person?" Marty flashed a crooked smile, the right side of his mouth sagging like it was full of chewing tobacco.

Frank huffed. "Well, you ain't makin it easy to feel sorry for you."

"Sowee. What I meant wus yur mmamasa veye-ter," Marty mumbled, saliva spilling out of the stubborn gap between his lips.

Frank looked at Ben, who shrugged his shoulders. "What?" Frank hollered.

Marty leaned in, speaking slowly and loudly. "Your momma's a *biter.*" His smile grew wider as Frank started yelling about how his momma didn't take to rednecks.

"You okay for real?" Ben asked.

Marty nodded, wiping the spit from his chin with his forearm. "No vig deal," he said. "We gohtta make a vale."

This would be the fifth bale that Ben had helped make—well, the fifth that he had watched Marty and Frank make. Most accurately, this would be the fifth bale that Ben had watched Marty make pretty much by himself. Frank hated the baler, hated every rusted, unreliable inch of the thing.

There were two parts to the machine: the box and the ram.

The box was simple, maybe six feet across by five feet deep. Each side was about a foot thick: solid steel that was further reinforced with welded slats about three inches wide. Graffiti covered almost every surface—names, insults, drawings—scribbled on and among the flaking green paint and deep rust spots. The front was adorned with a lock-wheel that looked like it belonged on a submarine. Its spokes and rim were more black than green from the wringing of rough hands. The whole front face of the baler was a door. Shorter than the left and right sides, the front rose only to the middle of Ben's rib cage. There, it met with a heavy slide gate, a pinecone-seed tessellation, through which Ben could see mangled cardboard that seemed to cower below a brutal rectangular plate. That was the ram.

A cylinder that was more than a foot thick rose out of the plate and ran parallel with what looked like steel girders to well above Ben's head. It seemed almost like the ceiling itself had moved to get out of the way of the beast's support beams and the small pipes and boxes and wires that completed tasks that outpaced Ben's mechanical understanding. But he knew enough. Every aspect of the machine—its density, its thickness—was built to mangle.

The power of the thing was even greater than its size, and the way in which it loomed wasn't something that seemed to diminish with time, nor was it something that was altogether tangible. Like standing near the low railing of a tall bridge, it imposed itself, extending a mad invitation that couldn't help but be heard. *Climb in,* it seemed to say. *Just sit down inside. There's room. Experience the procrustean wonder.*

When there was so much cardboard in the chamber that not even the ram could budge it, the machine would be run through a half cycle. With the heavy plate pressing down, Marty could spin the lock-wheel and open the front of the monster, and the pressure was more than enough to hold the crushed boxes in place. It was then just a matter of keeping them that way. This was where the wires came in.

Looped on one side, they were about fifteen feet long but only about an eighth of an inch in diameter—nowhere near thick enough to inspire confidence in anyone. Ben slid seven of them out of the repurposed PVC pipe next to the baler. Marty hadn't asked him to do this, but Ben didn't want to volunteer to punch tunnels. On Ben's very first bale, Frank had taken on that job. Whether it was his turn or he was just trying to make a good impression on the new guy, Ben would never know. What he saw, however, was a pretty nervous and well-dressed man stab what looked like a bent piece of rebar into the small slots between the cardboard and the bottom of the baler so that there'd be room for the wires, jamming and spearing until his knuckles inevitably cracked against the invincible machine.

Frank couldn't even watch as Marty cleared the tracks in preparation for Ben's wire, walking away, yelling that Marty's hands were going to match his face. Marty called him a chickenshit, and Ben laughed, despite the fact that he wasn't looking either.

"He break his hands yet?" Frank asked as he dragged a pallet past Ben, letting it slam in front of the baler.

Marty cursed through clenched teeth as he continued to ram the gullies clear. "I'm workin on it," he grunted. "This vuckin bitch."

"You want help tying it up?" Ben asked.

"No. And don't you vorry neither, Frank—I'd just as sthoon step into the machine than be anyvhere near it after you ran the wire."

Frank sucked his teeth in annoyance and snatched a cable out of Ben's hand. Squatting, he fed it into a channel that Marty had already cleared, then walked to the back of the machine to push it through an opening at the top. Ben watched as Frank fed the wire through its loop, then bent it around itself in a kind of metal knot. It really did seem like Marty had just chided Frank into doing a job he didn't want to do. But when Marty tugged on the wire, pulling it off the cardboard like a handcuff off a small wrist, Ben saw that Frank was just genuinely bad at it.

"Don't matter none," Frank said as Marty ran a fresh wire.

"Not to you. You hide in the other room every time."

"I still say we'd be better off letting Big Ben here squeeze the boxes. Prolly wouldn't even need no wires after."

"I guess," Ben said, chuckling. "If they wanna pay me extra to sit my fat ass on the boxes, then that's fine by me."

Frank looked at Ben with a confused expression until the sound of the baler being started made him flinch. The massive cube whined as it struggled against the wires. The whole block shifted, turned ninety degrees, and slammed onto the empty pallet Frank had placed in front of the machine. The wires held.

With the machine empty, the crew set about stocking the store, taking far more breaks than they needed, but that was fine. It gave Marty a chance to nurse his lip with a bag of frozen peas. As long as the shelves were full and the aisles were clear when the store opened, Bill Palmer couldn't give less of a shit about what went on between midnight and six in the morning. They moved faster with better music, or at least the night did. After the doors were locked, Marty jammed a paper clip into the intercom button and put the receiver in front of his boom box, and the three boys became DJs for the duration of their shift.

At just past five in the morning, a harsh clatter burst through the store's speakers and T. Rex's "Metal Guru" stopped abruptly. Ben, Marty, and Frank looked at one another curiously before walking toward the intercom they had rigged in Customer Service.

"Welp, that's it for you, Marty," Frank muttered.

"This ain't yer house!" Ms. Beverly yelled across the gulf that shrank between them as she rounded the corner of the counter. "You can't just . . . just do whatever you damn well please here." Her deeply southern voice seemed off-key, if such a thing were possible when simply speaking. There was a dull, unnatural tone to her every sound.

Frank retreated a step or two, as if he could use Marty and Ben as human shields. Ms. Beverly's feet moved as swiftly as her legs would allow, her shoes stomping against the tile. Her white hair rested in a loose but tidy bun on the crown of her skull. A single curl of sugar-string hair bobbed against the wrinkled skin of her scowling face.

Ben could see Marty attempting to prepare his uneven lips to communicate clearly. "We didn't know you was here, Ms. Beverly," Marty offered, his palms turning upward while his shoulders shrugged faintly. "We woulda turned it off."

"Well, I *am* here," she snapped. There were tremors in her hands and head. Her eyes darted among the three men before she closed them tightly and brushed a white curl behind her ear. Ben could see the large hearing aids that seemed to grow out of the sides of her head.

"I just thought that was yer favorite song is all," Marty pleaded carefully over his swollen lip.

A smile brought new wrinkles into the ancient woman's face. "Just please be mindful, wouldja?"

"Yes, ma'am," Marty said. He smiled and winced at the pain in his lip.

She narrowed her eyes. "Boy, what in the world did you do to your face?"

"You don't like it?" he asked, feigning insult. "Magazines said full lips are in this year."

Ben and Frank chuckled.

"Always got something to say." The old woman sighed, walking away from the counter and back toward her own department.

"Let's wrap it up, boys!"

Marty and Frank kicked and shoved their trash down the aisle. Ben looked again at Beverly, who paced the bakery department making small, imperceptible modifications to containers of pastries, taking her time to work against the unhelpful tremor in her hands. Every step was deliberate—a thing that Ben sometimes understood all too well. It was more than just a quirk of old age, though. They were the same shakes that Ben had seen in his grandmother. Beverly had Parkinson's disease.

"Ms. Beverly," Ben said softly.

When she didn't turn, Ben said it a bit louder. Still, she didn't react. He reached a hand out to touch her shoulder, thought better of it, and slid his feet to the side so that he might occupy Beverly's peripheral vision. Finally, she turned toward him with a jolt.

"Sorry," Ben said. "Sorry, I wasn't tryin to sneak up on you. I hope you ain't too mad about the music."

"No harm done." Ms. Beverly tugged on a latch until a large metal door swung open.

"And . . ." Ben began. "And I guess I might as well fess up for the other week. My first night, I moved a bunch of your displays. I thought . . . Well, I'm sorry is all, and you can bet that if it happens again, it wasn't cuz of me." Ben managed a laugh.

"Alright," the woman said, squinting at heat that even Ben could feel, despite the shield that the metal door should have provided. She pushed a tray cart of raw bread dough into the walk-in oven. "That everything?" she asked, turning back toward Ben. "Any more sorrys?"

"No, ma'am." Ben smiled. "But if you ever need something, just ask. Happy to do something other than stock shelves."

The woman wiped her hands on her apron. She had to raise her eyes a bit to look into Ben's, her head shaking just enough that the steadiness of her eyes seemed almost surreal. "I remember you," she finally said.

"Yes, ma'am. I been here for about a couple weeks."

Beverly shook her head. "I *remember* you, that was a terrible thing. He was your brother?"

There was a quivering in Ben's stomach. "Still is," Ben said, forcing a smile. "Yes, ma'am." He pinched the edge of the stiff sleeve in his back pocket. "His name's Eric."

Ben handed her the photograph, and her eyes lingered on it for a while, long enough that Ben eventually lowered his hand and let her take her time.

"He was so young."

"He was three. He'll be eight years old now. In a few months, anyhow."

"God." Beverly sighed. "I got two grandchildren of my own. I just can't imagine . . . It's all I can do to keep these two eyes on 'em. And there hasn't been any news in all this time?"

Ben shook his head, but had to speak it aloud since Beverly was still studying the photograph, adjusting the distance of her quivering hand like a microscope stage. "No."

"Bill Palmer ain't said nothin to you?"

"No, ma'am."

"It must be so hard for you to be here," she said in a quiet voice. "In this place."

"I've done easier things."

"I couldn't even hardly *look* at the house where my daddy died. But he's in a better place. That's what I tell myself, anyhow. That makes you brave, I think. You bein here."

"He . . ." Ben chewed the inside of his lip and considered Beverly. "Eric ain't dead, Ms. Beverly."

"I wasn't trying to say that he was . . . that the boy had passed, and I think you know that," she said sternly enough that Ben actually tensed. After a moment she continued with a softer voice. "I'm sorry. I see you wandering around here after all this time . . . I just know that must be a hard thing for you. I'll pray for you and your family. No matter what, everything will be fine, Benjamin. I really do believe that. Things happen like they're supposed to."

Ben nodded uncertainly and rubbed his hands with his kerchief. "Like God's plan and all that?"

"Makes you think, don't it?" The woman smiled.

"I think maybe sometimes things just happen. They just happen and that's it."

Beverly pressed her lips into a slight frown. "Well," Beverly said, turning back toward her department, "you're certainly entitled to believe that, son."

"Ms. Beverly? My picture?"

"Hmm?"

"Eric's picture." Ben gestured at her apron.

"Oh," she said with a confused look, her trembling hand slipping into her pocket. She handed the photo back to Ben. "I'm sorry about that . . . Listen," Beverly whispered as she placed her hand over Ben's, "you look different, enough that I almost didn't know who you was, and maybe Bill never will. But you can't let him see you with that."

"No, ma'am. I don't think he'd be too happy."

"It's more than . . ." She sighed and seemed to try to steady one trembling hand with the other. "This ain't none of my business. I don't like gossip, talkin behind people's backs and such. But . . ." She rubbed the tip of her index finger against her philtrum. "But I believe that you got some kinda right to know what kind of man you're working for.

"We had a cashier once. Sweet enough, but dumber than a box of rocks. Broke too. She started skimming off her till. Not too much, from what I understand, but enough that she got caught. Bill fired her, of course. Now dumb as she was, I doubt very much that she listed this place on her résumé, but Bill called every place he could think of and told them what happened, what she did. And when she finally did get a job and he found out, he told the owner, and she got cut loose.

"She came back here and screamed at him about it. Told just about everybody what he done, even though she couldn't prove it. But I believed her and believe her still. She was workin at a toy store. Bill's never been married. Ain't got no kids or nieces or nephews, so what in the blue hell was he doing in a place like that? Could be for any number of reasons, I guess. But I think he was lookin for her. Still. Weeks after he fired her. Because he's *mean*.

"He's always been mean. But the state he was in when your brother went missing. The things he said about your family . . ."

"What things?" He could feel a warmth creeping up the back of his neck.

"Nothin kind, son. He'll fire you. Do the same as he did with that cashier to you and your friends just for knowin you. Maybe find out where your folks work—" The woman pressed her lips together and closed her eyes. "I feel awful for yelling at you and for what I said about your brother. For you to come back here and work for that man . . ."

Ben could only nod, and he considered the old woman and her words. "Thank you," he said at last. "I'll watch my step some."

But Beverly only bobbed her trembling head and frowned.

"If it makes you feel better," Ben continued, "I might be workin for him, but I don't do a very good job."

Beverly laughed.

"And hey," Ben added with a smile, "maybe me bein here is because I'm supposed to."

"Maybe." Beverly smiled back. "Maybe."

And he thu-thought and huh-hhhe thought and he thought until thinkin wasn't enough no more. But thinkin is all a head c-c-can do. He needed some huh-help.

So he asked his feet.

9

Come the middle of October, the air was beginning to cool, but like every year, it was happening slowly. It was hard to even feel yet. But the woods could tell. The orange-and-red requiem for the hotter months played vibrantly on the leaves of the oak trees that peppered the side of the road, a beautiful and warm foreground for the choir of deep green pines beyond.

Although Ben never asked, he wondered from time to time why they always took their breaks away from the comfort of mechanically controlled air and in the treacherously thin plastic chairs. Maybe it was the camera that hung in the break room's corner. Even if it was busted like everything else, it still made like it was looking at you. Could just be a tradition inherited from some previous incarnation of the stock crew—one passed down silently as the result of a single person's preference that outlived the person who started it—but even in the worst weather they dined just outside the sliding doors with no complaint or objection.

Even when Ben worked alone, he'd walk all the way from the break room with his lunch just so he could plant himself on the concrete and listen to the quiet dark. Every now and then, a car would drive past, either going to or coming from town, and Ben would close his eyes and see how long he could hold the engine in his ears as it disappeared to nowhere in particular.

Most nights weren't that quiet, though. Most nights buzzed with loud chatting and louder laughter. Ben could never remember what they talked about. After the fact, he could never trace where they ended back to where they began. The subjects banked like starlings, the three of them just along for the ride.

"Tell him what happened!" Marty pleaded to Frank again.

"No," he snapped, his head shaking back and forth. "Fuck you."

"C'mon, man." Marty's voice quivered with suppressed laughter. "It's cool. Don't worry about it. Just tell the story."

"Yeah," said Ben, who was tracing the contours of his green utility knife with a black marker, "what's the big deal, Frank?"

Frank crossed his arms and shook his head, slower now.

"He ain't gonna judge you for it." Marty giggled.

"Just a misunderstanding is all it was," Frank said.

Marty clutched his stomach and laughed until his eyes watered. Even when he'd recovered, his voice shook and fluttered until the laughter would break through again. It took him almost ten minutes to tell a two-minute story.

On Ben's day off, Marty had finally convinced Frank to talk to a girl he'd had a crush on since long before Ben worked his first shift. Frank hadn't tried to hide it. Or if he had, he'd done a poor job: staring at her and occasionally offering to "help her with her bags," even though she only ever had one or two and Frank was a stocker, not a bag boy. Marty's comments had either worn Frank down or built him up enough that he decided to act on his feelings.

"I was sittin right here," Marty said. "I was sittin right here, and Frank was sittin where you are, and she comes out, and Frank just gets up. He walks after her, and I'm like, 'Well, goddamn,' ya know? Fresh Prince comin through. So he walks up to her. But he doesn't say nothin, and he doesn't stop walkin neither. He just kept on walkin behind her. Dude, he kept walkin until they were both out of the parking lot and around the corner.

"And then . . ." Marty leaned forward in his chair and laughed so hard he coughed. "And then I just hear, 'Help!' " Marty's voice strained through his whimpering giggles. " 'Help me!' She thought . . . She thought she was gonna *die*! What a stud!"

Ben didn't want to laugh at Frank, but he couldn't help it. Even Frank smiled as he cleaned the lens of his glasses with his shirt. Finally, Frank couldn't help it, and the three were lost to laughter.

Through his waning, tearful chuckles, Ben could hear a familiar sound echoing across the parking lot, rumbling and shrieking. "What the . . ." he mumbled to himself, as his dad's truck pulled up parallel to the curb.

"Hey, Pa. Everything alright?" Ben said, approaching the vehicle. "This ain't on your route, I don't think."

"Is now. I switched with Reggie so I could take the store. Saddles me with a few extra stops on top, but that's alright." There was a brief but not at all uncomfortable silence. "I figured you and me could have lunch."

Ben glanced back at his coworkers. "Yeah. Yeah, I guess that'd be okay." He climbed into the truck beside his father.

Clint pulled to the far side of the parking lot and set a brown sack with a rolled-over top on Ben's lap, then produced one of his own. "I wasn't sure if you'd be hungry," he said over the rustling paper bag. "Hell, I wasn't even sure how I'd get your attention when I pulled up."

"Didn't have much of a plan, did ya?" Ben joked as he opened his lunch sack.

"Well, I brought the sandwiches. That's about as far as I got." Clint killed the engine and the stridulation of cricket legs seemed to rise up in its place. "So how are those guys?"

"I like 'em," Ben said, unwrapping his sandwich. "Funny. Nice guys."

"You ain't gonna believe this," Clint said, pointing through the windshield, "but I just found out that Frank is Reggie's boy."

"No kiddin?"

"Nosir. Came up yesterday in the lot. Small world. You know, they live just a little up the way, Reggie and Frank."

"Everybody does, I reckon."

They ate in relative silence for a while. Clint brushed the crumbs off his hands and into the brown paper bag between his knees. "Deidra's having a real hard time with this . . ." He tugged on his beard lightly. "You made some friends, and what with them livin close by . . ."

"You want me to quit?" Ben asked, though it sounded more like a statement than a question. "What am I supposed to do for work?"

"You can come back and work with me again . . ."

"I don't want your money, Pa."

Clint shook his head. "We could get you your own route; Reggie's looking to shave off more stops as it is, and he ain't the only one."

"I ain't got no car, though. Did she say somethin? I never even said anything about any of my shifts. I don't even leave my name tag out where she can see it."

"She didn't have to say anything. She's been in that damn room near every night. Day too sometimes. She hasn't done that in ages. We gave this a shot. But you been here for near two months, and I think that's enough. C'mon, Ben. You know how hard this is on her."

"It ain't easy for me neither, Pa."

"Don't remember saying it was, Ben. But this was a choice that *you* made."

"Yeah it was," Ben said sharply.

"Beg your pardon? Of all the goddamn places—"

"Weren't no other places to go. We ain't got no money, Pa. The roof leaks. One of the bathrooms don't work. We got no money, and Deidra hasn't worked in five years. She only leaves the house like once a year for that stupid present thing she does—"

"Ben," Clint snapped.

"I didn't wanna work here. I didn't want to, but I gotta work somewhere. Someone has to do something."

"I *am* doing something."

"That ain't what I meant, Pa. I know you are. But now there's two of us. I make almost as much as you do. I can help out—"

"This ain't help, Ben. This is selfish, what you're doin."

"What about when I sign my checks over to you? That still selfish of me?"

"You think you can fix things by bouncin from one fuckup to another?"

Ben exhaled slowly. He wiped a few tears away with the heels of his hands. "Thanks for lunch, Pa," he said, tossing the remains of the sandwich back in the bag and opening the door.

"Yeah. Anytime."

Ben shut the door and heaved a bundle of newspapers out of the back of the pickup before walking into the darkness of the parking lot. Ben felt the truck's headlights on his back only briefly as they swept across him like spotlights. The papers' plastic binding ribbon dug into his fingers, and the limp in his leg made the heavy stack bang into his good knee. Truck tires squealed as they transitioned from parking lot to road. Marty and Frank had gone back inside.

Ben let the stack of newspapers slam on the Customer Service counter. He rubbed his eyes with the heels of his hands again, then scraped his fingernails against his scalp, back and forth, faster and faster, until he could feel it burn. He tried to curse but made only stunted sounds through his clenched teeth. Pounding his fists against the counter, Ben hurled his foot against a cardboard box that hung over the lip of a shelf below, sending it skidding and rocking along the tile. He drove the knee of his bad leg into the lower cabinet. The pain was blinding. So he shut his eyes and did it again.

He pressed his forehead against the counter's plastic laminate and tried to breathe, wincing at the throbbing in his leg. For all his objections, Clint sure had cashed Ben's checks in a hurry. Ben hadn't expected a parade in his honor—hadn't even really expected a thank-you—but for his dad to just show up like that . . .

Fuck them, Ben thought. His father hadn't said it, but he'd come close enough: *Every little bit of this is your fault, Ben. Everything that's led us here, and everywhere we might end up. It's all because of you.* Ben struggled to even out his breathing, struggled even harder to lean into the indignation he thought he should be feeling.

His leg screamed, and Ben hissed through his teeth as he turned and braced himself against the counter, sliding down until he sat with his back against the fractured cabinet door. He tapped the back of his head against the drawer behind him, then rolled it from side to side.

On the floor to his left were a pair of eyeglasses and a set of keys. The side of the box he had kicked was collapsed, but he could still read that it said LOST & FOUND.

Ben stared at the box for a long time. A strange kind of hum was collecting in his ears, low and constant like the feedback from an amplifier, a deep static inside his brain. He sat there in dumb silence as the buzzing built and built until it finally broke across his chest like a gray wave. With a hollowness that he hadn't felt since his first night in the store, Ben sat there and stared into the large black eyes of an unreal thing.

Even as his fingers touched the box to pull it closer, his mind tried to push it farther away, back where it belonged—some other place, some other world. Not here. Not with him. It didn't feel right in his hands. The last time he'd felt it, it had been soaked.

The last time he'd felt it, it had belonged to Eric.

Ben couldn't help but laugh as he cradled the small stuffed rhinoceros and tried to conceive of what slow series of steps would have been necessary to place it here in this box after all this time. They were unimaginable to Ben. The last place he knew it to be was in this store, so in some way it was right where it should be, wasn't it? It would actually be *more* confounding to find it literally anywhere else in the world. Right? No. That wasn't true, and Ben knew it. He knew it because he had seen this box before—more than three times in the weeks following Eric's disappearance—and there hadn't been any goddamn rhino in it.

"Where did you come from?" Ben muttered to the toy, like it might answer. Stampie just smiled. And just like Ben's first night, it felt almost as if the store were smiling back.

10

Ben was the first one to leave for once. The truck wasn't all the way unloaded, but he hadn't been that big of a help anyway. He couldn't even remember if he'd clocked out.

As Ben limped through the ratty grass, the plastic bag swung and the small rhinoceros thudded softly against his leg. The sky was only just beginning to tease morning. Occasionally, headlights would cut through the dark, and Ben would try to tuck himself closer to the clutching shadows of the tree line. Whatever his father's new route was, Ben didn't want to risk being spotted.

By the time Ben approached the police station, he had to squint against the sun. Had he even told Marty and Frank that he was leaving? He couldn't remember. He'd talked to Marty, though. Alone in the back room, he'd asked him about the toy, if he'd ever seen it before. But Marty had only shaken his head.

There were two chairs in the small lobby. The relief Ben's leg felt when he sat was immense. Ben swallowed against a sore throat. It stung like he'd been screaming. Ben glanced around the room for a water fountain but found none. A young deputy scribbled on what seemed like an endless cascade of papers. Those shuffling pages and the crinkling of Ben's plastic bag were the only sounds in the building, aside from the infrequent squawking of a radio somewhere.

Almost like a tic, Ben turned and leaned to look out the glass entrance doors. Sometimes he'd see a car. More than once the door rattled open, and Ben's head jerked to look at someone he didn't recognize. "Duchaine's on a call," the deputy had said. "He should be back shortly."

Ben stretched the thin bag over the face of the stuffed animal inside, making the rhinoceros's coal eyes the color of dirty milk. His hands moved back and forth over the plastic, slackening and tightening. Slackening. Tightening. Bringing the toy into existence and then sending it away. Only sometimes did he take it out, turning it over in his hands, examining it, confirming what he already knew and then doubting it right away. When he fell asleep, the bag was clutched in the crook of his elbow.

His heart was pounding when he woke up. He thought he might have yelled, but the deputy at the desk was still scribbling onto his papers, paying Ben no mind at all. Gasping, Ben patted his hands against his stomach and legs, then snatched up the bag, which had rolled onto the seat beside him. Ben stood and glanced outside, then looked into the room behind the deputy. And there he was, James Duchaine, sitting at his desk, pecking slowly at his keyboard.

"You coulda woke me up," Ben said as he walked past the counter.

"Tried," the deputy replied.

It had been a long time since Ben had seen Duchaine, and Ben had seen him so seldom back then that it was hard to tell whether time had been kind to him. His hair was perhaps a little grayer. The wrinkles seemed to cut a little more harshly into the sides of his eyes. But he still had the same resting frown on his mouth and the same twisting burns on his left forearm.

He didn't look up right away when Ben took a seat across the desk. He glanced from the papers in his lap to the monitor in front of him, stabbing his fingers awkwardly into the keys.

Ben adjusted his shirt away from his stomach and waited for the man to finish. Or at least he tried.

"Deputy Duchaine."

"Lieutenant," the man said absently as he concentrated on his typing.

When he was finally done, Duchaine took off his glasses and tossed them on his cluttered desk. His mud-colored eyes ran over Ben's face. "You lost some weight," he said, squeaking back in his chair. "Or moved some around anyway."

Ben shifted in his seat and bit his tongue. James Duchaine wasn't going to mock him out of the station. Duchaine laced his fingers over his stomach, then after a moment nodded and moved his thumbs apart, encouraging Ben to please hurry up and get to the point.

"I want to talk to you about Bill Palmer, the store director over—"

Duchaine nodded. "I know him."

"I work there now," Ben said. Duchaine raised his eyebrows but didn't interrupt. "Started about two months ago. Back when everything happened, back when . . . he wasn't no help at all to us—to me and my dad and . . . Always seemed real lazy about everything, annoyed and mean all the time. He's not no different now.

"None of the cameras work. He said he'd fix 'em, but he never did. That's what everyone says."

"Ben—"

"I catch him lookin at me sometimes," Ben continued. "He don't see that I see. Standin at the end of the aisle, just starin at me. I can see him out of the corner of my eye."

"Do you have any sense that Bill Palmer knows who you are?"

"Nosir. Never said nothin to me about it."

"Your parents know? About you workin there?"

"They do. Listen, I felt funny about the place ever since I started there. And then this morning . . ." He reached for the bag.

"Funny like how you felt about Bob Prewitt?"

Ben stared at Duchaine but did not speak.

"Son, I wanna ask you to bear with me here, okay?" Duchaine sighed, then leaned forward in his chair. "Now, about a month or so ago I get a call from someone who tells me that some big fella showed up at his door, says he wants to talk to him about a missing person. That he keeps him on his porch for about thirty minutes, talkin about his lost brother, talkin about the town, talkin about how he knows they're new to the area, talkin about all kindsa things, really. And all the while he's glancing past him into the house where his stuff is still sitting in boxes. Along with his pregnant wife, who's standing in the hallway listening, scared to death that this big guy might decide to just walk right on in.

"That's not the only call like that I've gotten. Now, that's fine. I'll keep on takin them calls, but I think you might be heading down a path here," Duchaine continued. "Why in God's name you would work at . . . Anybody in the world who'd been through what you been through would have a funny feelin about that place. We had Bill Palmer down here, okay? More than once. He's got all the grace of a pigeon, but . . . listen, how things seem to you and the way they really are can be very different things. And that store ain't doin you no favors when it comes to seein things straight."

"Ain't nothin doin me no favors in any damn thing," Ben said. "And it wasn't no thirty minutes."

"Son, I just think that you need to slow down and not work yourself up too much. It's not—"

"Not work myself up . . ." Ben muttered. "Maybe I could get myself a big desk, hmm? And I could just sit at it, just wait for everything to work itself out. Why don't you just finally say it? Just say that you're done." Ben struggled to get his voice back under his control. "You came into our house, took a bunch of his clothes and pictures and toys. And then you just gave up.

"And now, first time you had to see me in years, and all you wanna talk about is how long I keep people on their porches? You ever *think* about Eric? He ever even cross your mind when I'm not talkin to you about him?"

"He does," Duchaine said, squaring some papers on his desk and scooting them to the side. "Bob Prewitt ever cross yours? You sounded just like you're soundin now, you know that? When you told me about him peeling out of that parking lot. Refresh my memory, Ben. How'd that turn out?"

"That's not on me," Ben snapped, punching the chair's armrest. "Not the whole thing. I got it wrong, but—"

"Got it wrong?" Duchaine's voice pitched. "You *lied,* Ben. Right to my face. That's what you did." Duchaine shook his head and said almost whimsically, "All that wasted time."

Ben stood, squeezing the plastic bag in his fist. "You don't punish my brother for that. You don't do it. And you don't get to blame me for everything. Not when you lied to me too. You looked *me* right in the face,"

Ben grunted through a tight jaw, "and said that you'd find him. That no matter what you'd keep lookin. That's what you said.

"But you ain't lookin anymore. Not none of you are." Ben turned toward the deputy at the front, who was looking back toward the commotion now. "Would he even know who I was talking about? Hey!" Ben shouted to the deputy. "My little brother's missing." Ben's voice broke as he fished the photograph out of his back pocket and held it up. "His name's Eric. He'd be almost eight years old now. Have you seen him? Have you ever even fucking heard of him?"

The three men were quiet for a little while. Ben stuffed the photo back in his pocket. Duchaine wasn't looking at him anymore.

—

Ben's steps were slow and painful as he walked home. Although the sun was at his back, he still held his hand in what looked like a sloppy salute to shield his eyes from the light skipping off the dewy asphalt. The town was awake now, and each time a car shuddered by, Ben had to turn away from the dirty cloud churned up by its tires. He held the bag on his right side to guard it further.

Every few minutes, he found himself glancing inside the plastic sack again, but his thoughts were on Duchaine, not Eric. Ben had gone there to give the police the stuffed animal, to give them what might be the first piece of new evidence anyone had seen in years. Even if it was only evidence that the toy had been in the store since Ben had lost it, Ben was prepared to hand it over, and James Duchaine had managed to talk Ben out of it. Without ever seeing the rhino, he'd managed to convince Ben that Eric's favorite thing would be stuffed into the same box that held his favorite shoes and God knew what else—a whole collection of things the police had taken and kept, saying they needed them for the scent dogs that were coming from some other department or county or state. Scent dogs that they never got.

Ben wouldn't be surprised if Eric's whole file could fit on an index card. Apparently, Ben's convictions were a currency, and he'd spent everything he had on Bobby Prewitt.

"Fuck!" Ben screamed as loudly as he could.

When he approached the entrance to his neighborhood, Ben stopped and stood on the side of the road for a few minutes. Maybe more than a few. He didn't need to look at his watch to know that his father would be home by now, but he still glanced. Despite everything, Ben knew that his dad was right—his working at the store was bad for Deidra. Ben could admit that. He'd known it since before he put in his application. But what his father seemed to either overlook or ignore was the fact that nothing much at all seemed to be very *good* for Deidra. If that was just the way it was, then there was really no arguing against it, but there wasn't a whole lot Ben could do with that information.

But maybe he'd already done what he needed to do.

His front door moaned when he opened it. The television was on, as was the kitchen light, but there was no sign of Deidra. Ben didn't have to wonder where she was, though.

Her voice drifted through Eric's door, a soft song for a summer morning. Ben listened for a while. Even as he shut himself into his own room, he could still hear her through the thin wall. Melancholic. Alone.

As quietly as he could manage, Ben slid the stuffed rhinoceros out of the plastic bag. Its large, shiny eyes skewed and bent the world like black fun-house mirrors. After he'd had it long enough to stain and fray, Eric had asked Ben if his stuffed animal was real. Obviously it was *real,* just not *alive,* but neither of those things seemed to be what Eric was getting at. It was an odd kind of question, but one that Ben could tell made perfect sense to his baby brother, and that had been good enough. After a moment, Ben had grabbed a pair of scissors, and Eric watched as the tag was carefully snipped from the back of the rhinoceros's leg. "Now he is," Ben had said.

Ben could still feel the old ragged strings from the amputated tag. Eric had been too young to know what kind of beast the toy was. Stampie never crashed or rammed anything; he was too much of a friend to be an animal. Ben might have made him real, but Deidra had made him Eric's. And as much as Ben wanted to—as much as he thought he probably should—Ben couldn't bring himself to ignore that fact.

The bed squeaked as Ben stood and walked to his door with the stuffed animal. In the hall, he couldn't hear Deidra's singing anymore, but he knew that she was still in Eric's room. He would explain where he found it. There was no real way to know how Deidra might react, but Ben hoped that she'd smile. At him. And, most important, *because* of him.

Deidra didn't say anything when Ben knocked or when he opened the door. Even when she saw Stampie, she didn't speak. Which wasn't to say that she was quiet. It was just that the noises Deidra was making weren't quite words. And whatever was twitching onto her face wasn't a smile.

11

A misty yellow glow replaced the usual white sterility of the store. Ben looked at the face of a man he felt he knew but didn't recognize at all.

"He'd be older now," Ben said as he held out the photograph. He wasn't sure if he'd said anything before that, but it felt like he had. It felt like he might have said a great deal indeed.

"Are you sure?" asked the stranger, who crumpled the piece of paper and let it fall to the ground.

"I think so," Ben muttered, looking at the jagged paper ball in the spindly grass. Ben wanted to crouch down and grab the photograph, but he didn't. A light breeze tousled his hair.

"Ask *him*. He might know." The stranger pointed to a man leaning against a register, his eyes aimed so directly at the ceiling above him that his mouth hung open slightly.

"Have you seen this boy?" Ben asked, again holding out the photograph.

"Oh, sure," the man replied without lowering his gaze. "I've seen him lotsa times. Lots 'n lots 'n lots. Hey, waddya think's in there, anyway?" He gestured above him, but Ben did not look.

"When did you see him?"

"How long's it been there, I wonder. Seems like maybe a long time. A long, long time. I keep on waiting for it to move. You think it will? I reckon it will."

"When did you see him?" Ben repeated.

"You were just talkin to him."

Ben turned and saw that the store was empty. Of course, he couldn't see the whole store, behind the shelves and around the corners, but he knew, somehow he knew. He turned back to face the cashier, who had lowered his head. His lips moved as if he were speaking, but there was nothing to hear. Ben stared into the hollow black socket and felt the cool air that seemed to seep out of the fleshy cave. The lips kept bending and pursing in silent conversation, and finally there *was* a voice, but it wasn't coming from the man's mouth.

"You didn't see him, didja?"

Ben looked up and followed the ghost of the man's gaze into the mossy, overgrown forest floor that sat where the pipes and fluorescent lights should have been. Among the angled greens and straight browns stood a taut mass of curved white. It seemed to grow closer, and all at once Ben could feel brittle leaves under his feet. Pearlescent ribbons of frayed cloth stretched tightly over what Ben knew was a body, but still he touched it with the fearful curiosity of a child discovering sea-foam for the first time.

As soon as his fingertips grazed the fabric, it seemed to disappear. He could hardly see the sheet now. Something was wrong with his vision. Something had happened to his eyes, his sight. It was slipping away. No. No, his sight was fine; it was the world that had blackened. The darkness seemed to have come all at once, as if someone had shut off the sun like a gas lamp. *I don't like this part.* He couldn't move his legs. Ben shivered in the cold forest. Leaves shook in the cool wind. *Something happens here.* He wanted to leave. It was *time* to leave. But there he stood. *Something happens. What is it?* And as he lingered, he could feel something in the darkness noticing him.

There was no noise at all now. No breeze. No birds or bugs. Maybe there had never been any to begin with. Maybe none of this was real. Ben's legs wouldn't work, wouldn't move at all. He had the thought to clap his hands together, to clap noise back into the world, but his arms had quit too. In fact, Ben couldn't feel his arms at all. But he could feel his hands. And as small fingers wrapped around one of his own, Ben realized that this was as real as anything that had ever happened.

"Can I come home?"

Startled, Ben's eyes darted to the voice. Eric was so small, smaller than

Ben expected. He was older, but he didn't look it. There was something wrong with his face, like someone had made a skin mask from an old memory. Then it moved. *I know what happens.* Not like it was supposed to, though. Not his jaw or brow. It was the whole face. Cheekbones, skull. The boy's features shifted slowly as if to age before Ben's eyes, and then they clicked back into place. Ben could hear them reset. *I know what happens now.*

"Can I come home?" The fingers tugged.

Ben felt pressure inside his body; he wanted to kneel, to scoop the boy up, to hug him. But there he stood. *Yes! Oh, God. Yes, of course!* his mind roared. "No," his mouth said.

"Please? Please, can I come with you?" Eric's bulging eyes glistened in the moonlight. "I'm sorry."

Ben struggled against his own mouth, screaming at it to obey. *Don't say it. Don't say it to him.* "You gotta stay here, bud."

The boy pouted. "But I don't wanna. I don't wanna stay."

There was a loud pop, and Ben felt a tremor in his grip. Eric's wrist had broken, now bent and curved like a goose's neck. His hand trembled in Ben's, and Ben felt himself pull away from Eric's grasp. Something twisted in Ben's stomach at the pain on his brother's face. Pain that had nothing to do with the broken bone.

"Will you stay here with me?"

I'll never leave you, Ben's heart sobbed. *Tell him. Tell him that I'll stay with him forever. Even if that means neither of us can never ever leave, I'll stay. Please hear me. Please, I need you to hear me. Tell him, you piece of shit!*

"I can't," Ben's lips said.

Eric sat on the rags. They were silver now. That was new. "Will you sing me asleep?" He lay down.

"I don't know the songs."

"Please," Eric blubbered.

"Little boy blue . . ." Ben's voice cracked. ". . . come blow your horn . . ."

Eric's shoulder dislocated and jerked toward his face. He smiled sweetly and closed his eyes.

". . . The sheep's in the meadow, the cow's in . . ."

Ben could hear more bones cracking and grinding as Eric wrapped his arms around himself with new joints. His skin grew taut, rising in peaks where bends weren't supposed to be.

"... the corn. Where is the boy who looks after the sheep? He's ..."

The boy's skin seemed to be getting thinner, like peeling away layers of tissue paper. Finally, there were no layers left, and Ben could see withered muscle and old bone as his brother settled. Ben soon ran out of words, so he hummed the melody until Eric seemed to sleep. As he stroked his brother's hair, he realized somewhere in the back of his heart that the boy looked too asleep to just be sleeping.

"Good night, bud," Ben said with a hitched breath; he gritted his teeth to shut in a sob. *Don't leave. Don't leave him there. Not like this!* Ben turned to go. There was even less light in this direction, but Ben could still see, not that there was anything to look at. Behind him he heard shifting leaves under shuffling feet. *No. I don't want to see.*

Ben pivoted on the cold ground and saw Eric standing now, his body crooked and disjointed. Each step was an unnatural hobble that Ben could practically feel in his own bones. But what Ben felt the most was disgust at just how profoundly afraid he was that Eric might catch him.

"Do you see me?" the boy whined, his face a puzzle of bad bones and sagging skin. "Are you lookin?" The thing limped faster now, its eyes angry, every movement a struggle. Like an insect, it shuddered toward him, chattering, losing its balance, falling, shambling. "I'm here, brother. Don't go. It's me. It's *me. Itsmeitsmeitsmeitsme.*" Ben tried to step backward, but he couldn't. His legs wouldn't work.

Suddenly, Ben was on his back, the cold ground driving its chill into his spine. There was a pressure on his chest. Ben felt the scrambling of limbs. A small voice squeaked against the struggle. Eric's eyes were jaundiced, his teeth cracked and eroded.

"IT'S ME."

Ben's heart hammered in his ears. He sat up in bed and he struggled to catch his breath, as if the nightmare had been on another world with a different atmosphere. Leaning over the edge of his bed, Ben snatched the waist of his jeans and fished Eric's picture out of his back pocket. Moving it until it caught some stray light, Ben stared at his brother's face.

Still fogged with sleep, Ben tried to orient himself. Needles danced against his palm when he squeezed his hand into a loose fist. Numb and clumsy, Ben tried to shake the life back into his extremity, his movements no freer here in what appeared to be the waking world. He looked at the ceiling for a long while and at last decided that he was awake and resolved to act as such.

Sitting up in the gloom, Ben looked at his clock and saw that it was just past eight in the evening. Cautiously, he dragged his eyes across the darkness of his room, chasing shadows out of his peripheral vision, worrying that one might linger, that one might move and grin and speak. His legs wobbled under him as he stood. A dull throb pulsed in his left thigh; Ben gritted his teeth and pushed his palm into the muscle.

His room was in shambles. Ben had to step over and around his scattered belongings. His cheek was still sore. There was a moment when Ben thought maybe that had all been a dream too. He hadn't even moved when Deidra screamed and struck him. Even when she started using her fists, he hadn't moved. He'd just watched—watched her curled lips, her swinging arms. Watched her eyes glow with the same mad fire that had torn through his closet and dresser and bookshelves looking for other hidden things. As if she might find a whole cache of Eric's belongings that Ben had stolen away. Stupid as it was, Ben had actually wanted to help her look, help her rummage through everything he owned in search of imaginary treasures. But he'd just watched her until his father had come home.

Ben picked up and sniffed his shirts until he found one that was clean. He turned away from his mirror to put it on, and as the box cutter rattled home into its holster, the silence of the rest of the world grew conspicuous. Ben listened hard for the expected hum of the television, the voices of his parents. But there was nothing more than the whispering of his ceiling fan.

The hallway was as dark as the rest of the house. Ben checked his watch to make sure of the time. Usually, his father would be up by now, his stepmother not long for bed. At the back of the hall, his parents' door sat flush with the wall. Ben took two steps toward his bathroom before he was frozen by a shape at his vision's edge.

Deidra stood motionless in Eric's room. Her white nightgown was as still against her back as draped marble, her coffee hair made onyx by the surrounding darkness. Ben could only just make out Eric's empty bed in front of her. If she had been lying on it, Ben would have felt compelled to check for breath in her statue-still body. Hesitating, he cleared his throat softly to signal his presence, but it was a null transmission, swallowed by the black cube of his baby brother's room.

Ben began to wonder if he had made a mistake when deciding that he was awake. Bits of light from dingy streetlamps crept through the closed blinds and glistened against the foiled ribbon on some of the presents along the wall. The longer Ben stood there, the more he found himself wondering how long Deidra had been standing in that pose. Her elbows were bent, her hands hidden somewhere in front of her body. Ben didn't have to see them to know that they were clutching Eric's old friend. He wished she would move, that she would turn around so that he might see that she was alright. Just a little movement, a little noise. But there she stood. And behind her, there Ben stood, perhaps just as still. Because he was also afraid that the house might creak under the weight of his step and that she *would* turn. And that he would see that she was very much not alright.

Suddenly, the alarm on his watch sounded. The noise was cacophonous in the vacuum of the hallway. A lock of his stepmother's hair shifted against her alabaster dress, and Ben disappeared down the hallway and behind the bathroom door. The exhaust fan whirred sickly, like a baseball card clipped to the spokes of a bike tire. He splashed water on his face and let the faucet run long after. With a jerk, he slid the far drawer out of its socket, blocking the door. Inside, Eric's toothbrush and bathtub toys rolled and collided with one another.

His reflection stared at him as he stood, and at once Ben wanted to look away. But he forced himself to stare back: stare at his stomach overflowing onto the counter, at his stupid round face that drooped low enough to hide his neck, at his quivering and grimacing mouth. It seemed to tremble, but that wasn't quite right, was it? No, there was a rhythm. Ben could feel it in the tickling wisps of hateful air that spilled past his lips. Soundless words that Ben didn't need to hear to understand. *"Itsmeitsmeitsme."*

And his fuh-fffeet said, "Ok-k-kay, wuh-

we'll take you there, but we're not bad."

Buh-but when they guh-g-got there, do you

know what hhhappened? They STOMPED.

And STOMPED.

And SS-STOMPED until they

couldn't stomp no more. But there was

still muh-more that needed doin.

And so he asked his hands . . .

12

"Trick or treat!"

Ben stirred in his bed and listened to the murmuring through the wall. The next time the doorbell rang, he sat up and stretched his leg, got ready for work, then walked toward the noise.

Clint laughed as he talked to the children and their parents who stood outside. Two little boys, maybe about six or seven years old, dressed as a pirate and a mummy and standing with paper bags dangling from the ends of their outstretched hands. The mummy's costume was made of toilet paper and was already tattered to the point that it sagged in huge loops, exposing the boy's clothing underneath.

The three plastic spiders tangled in Clint's beard appeared to move on their own as he talked. One of the boys noticed and shared his disgust with his cohort. Ben leaned against the wall and watched his father laugh at the squeamish kids. "Dee, come look at this," he called. But Deidra didn't move from the couch. Stampie was on the cushion next to her.

The sun had set, and a slow breeze drifted lazily through the thinning trees. Clouds collected somewhere off in the distance, as if the round moon had repelled them like soap in a grease trap. All around were the sounds of children screaming and laughing. Phantoms and ghouls, monsters and princesses, swarmed the usually quiet neighborhoods, outnumbering the houses nearly five to one. They darted and banked like fireflies, stopping only to receive their bounty before rushing to the next house. Ben stepped into the street to allow a large family with five children to avoid the asphalt themselves as they crossed paths, their little girl inconsolable over a broken fairy wing.

The store was teeming. Ben had never seen so many people wandering the aisles. There weren't many convenient spots in the sprawling and scattered town for families to go trick-or-treating. Eric had had to be driven from neighborhood to neighborhood on his first and only Halloween. Luckily for the town, Bill Palmer never missed a chance to be a part of the community—especially when he could sell tickets.

"He's charging?" Ben asked, taking a small chocolate bar from Chelsea's bowl.

"Two bucks," Chelsea answered. It had actually taken Ben a beat to realize that it *was* Chelsea under the black wig. Her dark eyeliner swept into points near her temples.

"Cleopatra?" Ben asked, chewing.

"Stock boy?" She smiled, gesturing at Ben's clothes.

"Think I'll win the costume contest?"

"Well, it looks pretty authentic."

"Been workin on it for a few months." He took another piece of candy and put it in his pocket.

Chelsea laughed. "That'll be two bucks."

"Put it on Palmer's tab."

Despite how late it was, there were still employees stationed with bowls of candy in most departments. The sounds of "Trick or treat!" seemed to ricochet off every wall. The pharmacy and bakery were vacant, but it took an effort to even notice that much through the rolling waves of hustling children and their visibly fatigued parents. Some costumes were nothing more than masks, a sneering devil or snarling monster draping loosely over the collar of a T-shirt, some so ill fitting that little hands gripped and twisted the latex to realign the eyeholes. Other kids had simply raided their mothers' bathrooms. Bright red stitches that bore the smeared and glossy shimmer of cheap lipstick and sunken sockets dug with seldom-touched eye shadow turned children into vague ghouls or undead things.

Halloween was always tough. They'd started handing out candy at Ben's house again only last year. Deidra had been alright. Not quite comfortable, but this year . . . What had Ben been thinking? What could he have possibly thought would happen when he gave her that toy?

Ben blocked the store for almost an hour, folding into his thoughts until a quick series of prods in his side pulled him out.

He turned gracelessly to see a mask made of newspaper hovering at about the height of his stomach. Small holes had been torn for the eyes, but that was about it. There were no other adornments. The paper enveloped the child's head and was tied lightly around his neck with a length of twine, the ends curling outward like the bottom of a lollipop wrapper. The rest of the getup was less a costume and more of an outfit. Like many of the other children, this one was celebrating Halloween only from the neck up.

"Hello," Ben said, then waited for the inevitable "Trick or treat." It didn't come. The longer he waited, the more uncomfortable the absence grew, until finally Ben said it himself. The child raised his candy bag, which Ben noticed had come from one of the store's own registers. Ben also noticed that he appeared to be this child's first stop.

"That's quite a costume you got there," Ben said awkwardly.

The child responded with a movement rather than words. He held the bag aloft and jostled it with outstretched arms, the newspaper flexing delicately with his breathing. Ben slid his hand into his pocket and retrieved the treat that he had stolen from Chelsea's supply, dropping it into the kid's bag.

"Alright then," Ben said, but the kid lingered. After a while, he shook the plastic sack again. "That's all I got," Ben apologized, patting his pockets.

The child's small hand disappeared into the bag and emerged after a moment, clutching the small wrapped chocolate bar. Ben surveyed the kid briefly before speaking again.

"There are lots more people who have lots more candy," he said, gesturing back toward the registers. He bent over a bit more and pointed. "See that nice girl there? Go talk to her. You'll have that bag full in no time."

The smile on Ben's face grew uncomfortable as it became something he had to think about. But still the boy didn't move.

"Okay . . ." Ben chuckled with bewilderment, shuffling to his left to let a customer by. But the person stopped right behind the boy.

"What're you doing?" a voice stabbed.

The boy's body jerked hard to one side.

Ben straightened his back quickly. Beverly's face was tense and strained with anger as she attempted to wrestle the bag away from the child. "Ms. Beverly, what's going on? I—"

"What's going on," she interrupted, "is this little good-for-nothing snuck right out so he could come get some candy. Ain't that right?" The boy started to turn away, holding the bag out of Beverly's reach. "Give it here," she said sternly.

The child's arm darted and banked. This was a dance that must have been familiar to both of them, for rather than attempting to flank the boy's quick hand, Beverly withdrew her own, only to run it down quickly from his bucking shoulder. Her hand moved with his now, rather than at it. "Let go," she grunted.

Clenching his hand within her own, she pried his fingers apart so that the bag slipped free and floated down to the tile. Beverly's other hand moved against the boy's thrashing chest. The child's shirt shifted, exposing a gnarled necklace of twine that bunched near his throat. As Beverly moved her eyes to Ben, Ben watched the boy put the candy down the front of his pants.

"Where's it at now, boy?" Beverly snapped louder than before. Customers were gathering at both ends of the aisle now. Some children had even ceased trick-or-treating to watch. "You know your momma's rules."

The boy squirmed but hadn't twisted free of Beverly's grip. It struck Ben that the boy was surely big enough to resist the weak clutches of the old woman. Without a doubt, he could have pulled free at any point he wished. But he stayed there, ensnared by her brittle hands like an adult elephant restrained by the memory of the rope that stopped it as a calf.

"What's he sayin?" she snapped at Ben.

Speechless, he shook his head. "Ms. Beverly, it's just a piece of candy. It's Halloween."

Underneath the newspaper mask the boy was heaving audibly now. He still didn't speak. The newspaper just crinkled and crackled as the boy huffed.

Beverly's face flushed red with exertion and anger. Her thin, pale lips retreated like window blinds, exposing teeth stained by age and worn by use. As the boy writhed, Beverly's arm slipped upward, pulling the child's necklace free from under his shirt. A flat red ring bounced at the end of the grubby string, thudding lightly against his chest. When the boy moved to touch it, Beverly's arm slid against the newspaper mask and ripped it free from the yellow string that anchored it.

A dark spot had seeped through the thin paper where the child's mouth had been, obliterating the ink. The mask tore at the puddle of saliva when Beverly's arm finally slipped up and over the kid's face, resting just above his eyebrows.

For a moment, Ben thought he had been mistaken in thinking that he had been talking to a little boy. The slender, pointed nose and soft shape of the child's eyes gave his face a distinctly feminine quality. But when he parted his lips in a snarl, the masculinity was revealed in his jaw. He was about thirteen years old and beautiful, even in this state. His amber eyes flashed wildly; then his body seemed to relax.

"You about done?" Beverly's voice had quieted after she noticed the crowd. The boy nodded and stuffed the red ring back into his shirt. "Man alive. Just what in the world has gotten into you?" Beverly asked with an exasperated laugh. The white cotton of her nightdress draped over her thin frame like a sheet on a pole.

"Did he ask you for candy?" Beverly turned her attention to Ben, and in the same instant, the boy's bright golden gaze fixed on Ben's eyes, which were now oscillating rapidly between the two stares.

"I . . ." Ben's esophagus made a swallowing gesture, but nothing moved but time. The boy just looked at Ben, his eyes aflame with anticipation.

"Oh, don't let him play you," Beverly said. "He can't have none. Di'betic, this one."

The four eyes lingered impatiently on Ben's fumbling mouth until the words finally sloughed out. "He put it in his pants. Down the front. I didn't know he couldn't have it." Ben attempted to look at Beverly but could see only the angry glower that had washed into the kid's lips and eyes, eyes that still hadn't blinked or broken away.

"You can't make like a demon and think the devil won't notice, boy." She placed a hand on the boy's shoulder and tucked him behind her. "Thank you for bein forthright with me, Benjamin."

The two walked past Ben toward the end of the aisle that was closer to the store's exit. Ben's shoes squeaked against the tile as he pivoted to watch them leave. His heart was racing with guilt for the boy's ruined Halloween. Only as they turned to leave the aisle did the kid look at Ben, and when he did, he smiled like he was posing for a photograph.

"I'm sorry," Ben mouthed.

13

"Down his pants?" Frank asked in disbelief.

The baler shuddered as the ram bore down. Marty held the collar of his shirt over his nose and tapped a button on the baler's controls to bring the plate down another inch, then two, before he was finally satisfied.

"Of all the nights to be scheduled," Frank muttered.

"Jesus *Christ,*" Marty said, walking up to the damages shelves. "You probably woulda missed it anyhow, Frank. Off somewhere avoiding work." Marty squinted against the half-can of air freshener he was emptying onto the foul racks.

"That don't make it smell better," Frank choked out.

"Smells just like"—Marty studied the label—"fresh linen to me."

"Where you wash your sheets at? The toilet?"

"She said the kid was diabetic," Ben grunted, sliding a pallet in front of the machine.

"The way you tell it, that kid would've been better off eating the candy," Frank said.

"That kid doesn't have no diabetes," Marty said, tapping the bent rebar against the baler.

"How do you know?" Ben asked.

"Like Frank said. You ever see someone go apeshit on a kid for tryin to eat a piece of candy? And all that about the devil watching or whatever? I know you think she's alright, but Beverly's crazier than a shithouse rat, Ben."

"C'mon, man," Ben objected.

"She sets the table in the break room. Place mats and metal forks and everything," Marty said, pointing at Frank with the rebar. "Tell him about the time you seen her."

"Nah, man," Frank said, smiling uneasily. "C'mon, Marty."

"You're the one who seen her. Fine." Marty sighed as Frank slipped some wires out of the tube near the baler. "Few months back, Frank here says that he was blocking the store when he turns a corner and Queen Muffin is shopping for groceries like it ain't three in the goddamn morning. Didn't even know where she was. You tell me there ain't something wrong with her."

"Fuck you, Marty," Frank shouted.

"Hey, if you'da told it, maybe you coulda told it a little sweeter than I did. I didn't see you getting all butthurt when you was laughin about the break-room table."

"That's a different thing."

Marty shrugged and Frank whipped the wires to the ground and left the group. The swinging doors thudded as Frank exited the back room altogether.

"You forget his granny's sick?" Ben asked, scooping up the wires.

Marty jammed the rebar into one of the gutters at the base of the baler. "I wasn't talkin about his damn granny," he grunted. "What? I can't say anything to anyone just because it might remind them of something? Give me a fuckin break. I was just sayin that Beverly's a little off sometimes. That was it."

"Yeah. Yeah, I know. But you know how Frank gets sometimes . . ."

"Of course I do. He storms out all the time over just about everything." Marty's words jabbed in rhythm with his efforts to clear the cardboard. "It's fuckin exhausting, and I don't need someone tellin me how to avoid something that's not my fault in the first place. Frank's granny has Alzheimer's. Ain't nothin wrong with Beverly's brain. She's just a bitch."

"Alright," Ben said, feeding wires into the slots that Marty had burrowed. "I wasn't gonna tell you to do something different. You guys are friends. We're all friends. That's all. Just . . ."

Marty tied off the wires one by one while Ben watched.

"It's hard to know how people are gonna take things. That's all. Good or bad. You remember how I found Eric's toy? That rhino? I gave it to my stepmom. To be nice. I thought about taking it to the police, but I thought she needed it more. I thought it would make her happy, and I was wrong. She got upset, but whose fault that is isn't really the point. Still gotta try."

Marty held the button to run the baler through the rest of the cycle. The block of cardboard shifted and moaned against the metal strings.

"Marty," Ben called, but Marty kept holding the button, staring straight into the machine through glassy eyes. "Dude!" Ben shouted as he put his hand on the mass of cardboard, grabbing his friend by the shoulder and pushing him backward. The machine disengaged and the massive block of cardboard rested awkwardly on its corner.

"Jesus," Ben said.

Marty looked down at the pallet he was standing on and laughed with what seemed like mild wonder. As he stepped off the wooden slab, Ben held the cardboard back with both hands and moved to the side. He let go as he stepped off the wooden slab, and a thousand pounds of bundled boxes teetered and fell, slamming onto the pallet.

14

"Let's get this over with," Ben muttered as he yanked on the metal latch to the freezer. The first three attempts felt like trying to pull a car sideways by its door handle. Finally, it opened and a cloud of frigid air rolled out of it. Ben stepped back instinctively, like a child dodging a crashing wave on the shore. He looked for the wooden wedge to prop the door open, until he decided that he'd looked long enough. He wanted to move this miserable process right along. Reaching into the freezer, Ben hooked his fingers into the taut plastic that enveloped six half-gallons of ice cream and dropped it in front of the door.

Ben stepped inside and the cold hit his bones immediately. Iced wind surged audibly out of a grate in the ceiling that was thankfully nested near the far wall. Pockets of frost hung in the corners like glass spiderwebs.

It looked like Marty had sorted the room with a snowplow, and Ben treated it with the same gentle touch, heaving the arctic boxes clear of the threshold before they could sting his hands too much. Usually there was someone there to catch the stock, but not tonight. No one else was scheduled, and Palmer wouldn't believe that Ben hadn't seen the note.

His leg ached, but as long as Ben made a point to stay in motion, it was unlikely that it would seize up entirely. So that's what he did. Even when he paused to consult the inventory listings on the back of the note, his legs kept moving in a kind of pathetic cancan.

Ben wiped his running nose with the bare skin of his forearm and shot another box into the warmth. The freestanding aluminum racks clanged as Ben rooted through them. Mercifully, most of the items were at a manageable height, but as the list shrank so did Ben's luck. A geyser of steam sighed from Ben's mouth as he looked at a box that was nestled so high it might actually be touching the frostbitten ceiling.

The thin metal rails of the rack burned against Ben's palms as he hoisted himself onto the first shelf. There was a slight tremor in the frame, but it seemed to steady as Ben spread his feet apart. Tall, but not tall enough, Ben stretched his arm upward, grasped at the box, and then settled for the shelf below it. As he pulled himself up and stepped on the second shelf, the whole rack suddenly twisted and threatened to topple. There was a fluttering in Ben's stomach as he reeled backward. Quickly, he heaved his great weight forward, slamming the whole shelving unit against the wall. With a snarl on his face, he clawed and struck at the box. *Fucking frozen peas,* Ben thought as he hooked his fingers into the box's seam. *Gotta get these stocked up ASAP or else no one will ever really notice or give a shit.*

Packages surrounding the box he needed crashed to the ground. Ben cussed under his breath and realized that he was mad not only at both Palmer and the cold of the freezer, but also at peas and people who liked to eat peas. With one last pull, the keystone finally began to shift, but as it moved, so did something in Ben's peripheral.

The door was closing.

Silently, the massive slab glided on its bearings like a pivoting wall. Ben scrambled. The whole rack twisted at the center and buckled. Ben reeled for balance as boxes and bags collapsed on and around him.

His foot clipped the edge of a package, and Ben's good knee smacked against the cold concrete. Still the door swung in its lazy and carefree arc. *But here's the stupidest thing about this piece of shit.* The floor was cold against Ben's palms as he tried and failed to regain his footing, slipping once, twice. Ben hurled a frozen box at the door, but it was too light. The door kept moving, pushing the box back toward Ben indifferently. *You just give it a little love . . .*

Ben planted his left foot on the ground and yowled at the pain of burdening his weaker leg with the entirety of his weight. The box scratched against the filthy floor as the door pushed it, but it looked like that sound might not last much longer. Ben lurched forward, uncertain whether his bad leg would be good enough, but certain that no one would ever hear him over that fucking air conditioner. The latch clicked against the lock plate.

And pres—

The moving wall stopped and Ben cried out as its heft and momentum traveled squarely into his index finger. He gritted his teeth and rammed the thick door with his shoulder. It flew open and thudded loudly against the wall, and Ben found himself hoping that it hurt.

Ignoring the pain in his knee, Ben kicked the ice cream, which was sitting just outside the arc of the slowly returning door. The bundle hardly moved, skidding abrasively in the quiet back room, then stopping dead. Ben stood there for a moment blowing hot air into his hands and trying to think. Where had he put the package? Closer to the middle of the door? Maybe the edge? Ben grabbed the ice cream and rocketed it back into the freezer, ignoring the obvious sound of tumbling inventory beyond the fog.

Near as Ben could figure, the door had started moving and the ice cream had slowly spun out of its path. That was what had happened. But as he watched the door creep home, he didn't feel like that was the answer. His mind squirmed as if it could overcome the rising thought, but the fact was it wasn't a *thought.* It was something that Ben had come to laugh about in the privacy of his own heart: that silly feeling from the first night—a feeling that he thought he had outrun.

The latch clicked as the door stopped. The air conditioner roared to life. Right on cue.

Ben blew heat into his cupped hands as he kicked the Receiving door open. It yelped at the top of its arc and then swung angrily back toward Ben. He kicked it again, ignoring the cries from both of his legs, and moved quickly away from the back room.

As he stood at the urinal in the bathroom, Ben ran his eyes over the graffitied tile and placed his hand against his back pocket to feel the hard sleeve of Eric's photograph, a motion that seemed to have gone from habit to tic over the past few weeks.

Since the first night he'd brought the photo, he'd come to think that it was reassurance that he belonged in the store just as much as anybody. *More* than anybody, in fact. But the ache in his good knee and the lingering chill in his blood seemed to contradict that so strongly that as Ben left the bathroom, he did so with the timidity of a scolded child.

There was no yelling waiting for him, of course. Nothing but the toneless melodies and industrial rumblings that were saved for those who walked the aisles when no one else did. A sound track of isolation that amounted to nothing at all for those who heard it often enough. And for just a second, nothing was all there was. But as the bathroom door whined home, something else joined the chorus.

TAP, TAP, TAP.

Ben's body jerked; he tried to smile his nerves away. He moved to check his watch and tried—

TAP, TAP, TAP.

He moved cautiously toward the front of the store.

TAP-TAP-TAP-TAP-TAP-TAP-TAP.

It could be a customer. It wasn't unusual for a person to try to walk into the store after it had closed. But those pleas always came in the form of knocking knuckles or smacking palms. These taps were unique to those who knew which sounds traveled through the store and which ones didn't. This was metal on glass.

TAP-TAP-TAP-TAP-TAP-TAP-TAP.

Ben felt for the key to the front door in his pocket. Reflections of displays and registers swirled on the glass doors, making the bright store appear to extend beyond its borders and into the blackness of the world outside. But there was something wrong with the symmetry. A hazy and black shape. A figure. As Ben came into full view of the locked entrance, he could see that the apparition looked a lot like Marty.

Ben sighed as he fished the key from his pocket. The doors screeched apart.

"Jesus, dude. You scared the crap outta me." Ben mustered a smile, but it was unreturned. Smoke crawled and twisted up Marty's arm like powder vines. A cigarette burned between his fingers. Seven more lay at his feet, charred and used up. Ben stepped outside.

The music seeped through the closing doors, growing quieter with every lost inch of open air until it couldn't be heard at all, the vibrations too faint to compete against the double-paned glass. The light in the awning above them flickered softly. It would need a new bulb soon;

whether it would get one was another question entirely. A wrapper crinkled as Ben removed a candy bar from his pocket. He took a bite. Smoke whipped gently around Marty's face in the still air while mosquitoes and gnats began to swarm around Ben's neck and head. Their wings squealed in his ears like a balloon slowly running out of breath.

Marty had made no reply. Ben studied him in the fickle light. A faint bruise colored the corner of his eye. "You alright?"

"Huh? Oh." Marty touched the edge of his socket with his thumb.

"You come to lend a hand?" Ben joked. "You just missed me almost getting locked in the freezer."

Marty was scratching his arm next to the inside bend of his elbow. A dark red streak was forming in the wake of his nails. He turned his head toward Ben, who was blinking in hard squints to reroute the sweat that had begun trickling down his brow.

"I been thinking about this since your first night, man," Marty said. "Jesus, I been running it around in my head again and again, and I still don't know what to say or how to say it exactly. Less than that, I don't know what *you'll* say . . . or what you'll do, even."

And that was enough. Somehow, Ben felt he knew what Marty was about to say, and he found himself wishing that he were anywhere else at that moment, that he were about to listen to someone say something that didn't matter, something that was so trivial he could ignore it and the conversation wouldn't miss a beat. But Ben wasn't anywhere else right then. Ben was there with Marty and Marty's words.

Sound leaked through trembling lips and echoed like cannon fire in Ben's ears.

"I seen your brother."

15

For a second or two Ben felt dizzy, like his brain was on fire and it was rolling to extinguish itself. No emotions had come yet. They were lurching and colliding with one another like a slow black avalanche. But his eyes still watered, and the hairs on his neck still stood erect, as if Marty's words were some germ his immune system was trying to shut out. Ben looked at Marty stupidly for a long time.

"Say somethin!" Marty's voice shook Ben into comprehension.

"You *saw* him?" Ben's fists were balled tightly. "I don't understand. What do you mean, you saw him? When?"

" 'Bout six months ago."

"Six *months*?" Ben's heart was pounding. He squeezed his skull between his hands.

"I wanted to say somethin sooner." Marty fumbled with his lighter. "But . . ."

"But what?" Ben's words were weaker than he'd intended.

Marty stared at the cement. He took another step backward and bumped against the propane cage.

"No," Ben said. "You . . . You're telling me . . ." Ben fumbled at his back pocket. He put Eric's photograph so close to Marty's face that it would have been impossible to actually see it. Marty flinched. "You're telling me that you saw *this kid.* That you seen him before I ever started workin here? That you seen him six months ago and you never said nothin to nobody? No—"

"I did," Marty cut in, "I said somethin. I called."

"No." Ben was inches from Marty's face. "The fuck you did."

Marty pressed his back harder against the metal cage, as if he could be absorbed by it, disappear into it. "I don't know what I'm supposed to say to that. I ain't lying to you, Ben. Why would I?"

"Why would *they*? I talked to the police. I called 'em. I was at the station two weeks ago, and they didn't say nothin about anyone calling—not in the last six months. Not any goddamn time. This ain't somethin you want to mess with me about, so you quit it."

"I ain't lyin to you, Ben," Marty said flatly.

"Yeah you are!" Ben screamed violently. He shoved against Marty's chest hard enough that his body ricocheted off the cage. When Marty said nothing, Ben pounded his fist on the metal next to Marty's head once, then again, then again and again, until his hand went numb and the rattling of the frame was louder than the screams in his own mind. Marty had shrunk into himself more with each strike. The rims of his eyes were lined with water, but he said nothing. For a while neither of them did.

"This whole time," Ben muttered. "This whole time I been walking around like . . . like some kind of idiot."

A pain swept into Ben's jaw as he clenched his teeth. He looked at the bulletin board, at his brother's flyer. One face among a dozen, shining out to him like a beacon that only he could see. Ben felt a wave of heat move through his body.

"You put the toy in the box." He rolled his head back toward Marty. "I asked you about it, and you said you never seen it."

"I didn't ever see it, Ben! And you didn't *ask* me nothin. You got in my face and screamed at me about it. You put your fuckin hands on me and scared the shit outta me. I didn't have any goddamn idea what you were talking about until later."

"Fuck you!" Ben shrieked, turning away from Marty. Ben clutched the sides of his head with his fists, then clacked one near his right temple until his knuckles stung and he didn't feel like screaming anymore. Ben could feel something caustic swelling in his chest as his anger ebbed: an unclean mixture of despair and something poisonous that sat in Ben's heart like oily water. "Where? Tell me where you saw him."

"Up the street a little ways. Maybe half a mile or so."

Ben turned his head toward the dark and empty parking lot. "Show me," he said.

"What?"

"Take me to where you saw my brother."

"It's the middle of the night."

"I don't care," Ben snapped, sliding his aching and bruising hands from his head. "You wasted enough time already."

It wasn't a long walk, but it was a dark one. There were no streetlights to guide their path, and the moonless sky loomed indifferently above. Small creatures rustled and cried in the blackness, invisible to all but one another. Although Marty knew the location, he walked a pace or two behind Ben, whose feet trampled the tall grass with long, uneven strides. Ben could barely hear Marty's gentle movements over his own. Every dozen or so steps he'd turn to make sure he was still there, and Marty would look up, wide eyes shining out in the smothering darkness, as if something were about to happen. While they walked, Marty played with his lighter. *Slink. Clink. Slink. Clink.*

Ben's gaze crept crablike to his left. It must have occurred to Ben when he and Marty first set out where their path would lead. He must have known what lay on that black horizon, and of course he *did* know. But it wasn't until his neighborhood crept out of the darkness that his stomach began to knot. Irresistibly, his thoughts turned to Deidra, alone in the house, a festering hermit who would hate her stepson even more now. Ben winced and tried to bury the thought, but the ground wasn't deep enough for that. Ben had already buried too much.

The asphalt horizon shimmered with a sliver of light that exploded as a car's headlights crested the hill. Ben squinted into them until he was forced to look away. Power lines that hung over the street like loose stitching were wrestled briefly from the dark sky. The air grew quiet as the engine churned down the road, and the darkness returned, more consuming than before—a punishment for looking at the light.

"Here," Marty said. Ben stopped and turned toward Marty, who was gesturing toward the woods to their right. "It was right around here."

"*Here* or *right around* here?"

"Here," Marty said forcefully.

The trees that made up the forest blurred together into a dense visual singularity. Ben could see nothing in the dark contours of the impenetrable wall before him. But it felt familiar, like he'd seen it before, though not with his eyes. This black woodland void.

"Tell me what happened." Ben's voice quivered. "Don't leave nothin out."

Marty held Ben's stare for a moment. There was a kind of faint pain on Marty's face. He breathed out heavily through his nose.

"I was . . ." He cleared his throat and then put fire to another cigarette. "It was like eight in the morning, and I had stayed late to pick up my check. Something was busted, the printer or the computer or something." Marty waved his hands in front of him like he was fanning away the unimportant detail. "Whatever it was, it was taking forever.

"I get my check, and I start walking home. It was sunny as hell, and I had this *splittin* headache from this bad tooth I got. All the birds were chirping and making it worse, but then all at once they all piped down. I could hear this crunching in the leaves, so I turned and looked." Marty swallowed hard. "And I see this kid. Real young. Dirty and whatnot. And he's just staring at me from behind this bush, standing still as a statue; he's just looking at me."

"How did he look?" Ben interjected. "Did he look alright?"

"Yeah, man. I guess. Yeah, he looked alright."

"Tell me what he looked like. Was he scared?"

"No. No, it didn't seem like he was scared. That was the weird thing," Marty said nervously. "His face was . . . was like a painting or something. It was just all froze up."

"What do you mean?"

Marty cleared his throat, trying to pick his words discriminately. "I don't know how to put it exactly. His face was just *blank*—like he was wearing a mask or something, but it wasn't no mask. It was like he was staring at something really far away, like he wasn't even looking at me. It was like a doll's face . . ."

The pit in Ben's stomach deepened.

"It all felt real weird, him just standing and staring like that. I didn't know what to do really, so I just kinda waved at him." Marty raised his hand and Ben watched his palm rock slowly back and forth. "He stuck his hand up a little and waved back, and I said, 'What're you doing out here?' But he didn't answer. I asked him if he was alright, if he needed help, but he didn't answer me still. Then I asked where his momma and daddy were. I took one step toward him, and he just ran off into the woods yelling for his momma."

"You didn't go after him?"

"No . . . No, I didn't want to chase a little kid through the woods, ya know? He was calling for his mom, and I figured it wouldn't look too good for me if she seen me running after. So I just shrugged it off and kept walking home."

Ben exhaled with exasperation, his fingers interlaced and crowning his head.

"But I kept picturing the kid's face. It looked real familiar to me, but I couldn't pin it down. Got weirder and weirder the more I thought about it. Why would he be out there? Why would a mom have her little kid out in the woods? He was so filthy. My momma would beat my ass when I came home that filthy as a young'n . . .

"I thought he maybe was homeless. You know that shelter up the road?" Marty gestured and Ben nodded. "I thought he might be from there or something, but homeless people still look after their kids and all, so that didn't seem right. Still, he looked so familiar. I kept thinking that maybe I'd seen him bumming with his parents somewheres. It was the only thing I could figure."

Marty chained the old cigarette to a new one and held the smoke in his lungs before continuing.

"But right before I got home, it just hit me like a goddamn sledgehammer." He pounded his fist against his upturned palm. "'That's the kid from one of them flyers at the store!' So I turned around and ran my ass back here . . ."

"And?"

"And he was gone. Shoot, he was long gone almost as soon as he started running back when I left him. I thought about going after him, about going into the woods, but I figured if I couldn't see him from here, I wouldn't see him at all."

"So you went back home?"

"No." Marty shook his head rapidly. "No, I went back to the *store.* It took me just a second to pick out his poster, and I snatched it off the board and went inside to call the number. I told them that I seen the kid, and they were like, 'Are you sure?' and I was like, 'Yes, I'm fucking sure!' ya know? They took all the information and told me to hold tight."

"Why?"

"In case the police needed to talk to me? Shit, I don't know. I didn't really ask."

"You didn't keep looking for him?"

"The fuck you want from me, man? They told me to stay put, so I stayed put. Weren't no one in the store hardly, but I damn near tackled a kid that was leavin just for movin too fast. I had that place locked down . . . Anyways, the cops never did come. I figured they'd gotten all they needed from me and were off doing whatever cops do."

Ben ran his fingers over his head, his hair flinging droplets of sweat like thousands of miniature catapults.

"They didn't have a record of any of this," Ben said painfully. "If all this really happened, then why don't they have any record of it?"

Marty ran his index finger over the faint scar on his lip. "I don't know. I mean, I really don't have any goddamn idea. Maybe you talked to the new guy and he was looking in the wrong drawer. Or . . . or maybe they do got a record and they can't tell you because you're not the dad?

"I never heard anything more about it. I started thinking that maybe I was wrong. The picture on the flyer is all fucked up, and what are the odds, anyway? I started figuring that it *wasn't* the kid from the flyer. I spent months making myself think that. Then you told me what you told me, and what the hell was I supposed to say then? Tell you somethin I didn't even believe was true?"

"But you think it's true now?"

Marty nodded. "I . . . I wanted to say something when you found the toy. I knew I needed to, but you scared the hell out of me that morning. I'm really sorry, Ben."

Ben exhaled a trembling breath. The last vestiges of his counterfeit peace slipped through his fingers like silt from a dead river. As false and fleeting as that peace had been, as Ben stood there in the darkness, he was somehow sure that it would also be as close as he'd ever come. It was a state now lost to him forever, as alien to Ben as a brand-new emotion would be to the whole of humanity. Warm wind rattled through the trees, and Ben turned back toward them.

"C'mon," Ben said as he walked toward the tree line.

"No way." Marty took a step back toward the road. "I ain't going in there."

"I need you to show me where he ran to."

"I got *no idea* where that might be."

Ben grabbed Marty's arm, and Marty snatched it away angrily. "I'm not fucking going in there, Ben. It's pitch black, and we can't see shit."

"I have to look."

"He's not out *there.* Not now."

Ben turned back toward the trees and moved. He felt Marty's hand on his shoulder.

"Have you lost your goddamn mind? You're not gonna find anything out there. Not tonight. Not like this," he said, gesturing to the darkness that enveloped them.

Ben jerked his shoulder away from Marty's grasp. "You don't know that. How could you? You saw him, and you didn't do anything. *No one* has done nothin at all. Not the cops. Not my parents. Not anyone in this whole damn town! Nobody looks at them flyers. You said it yourself, man. No one *ever* looks. They may as well put that board *behind* the fucking wall! I'm his *big brother.* I was supposed to protect him, man. But I didn't do that. I didn't protect him, and now I can't do nothin at all for him. No one can! I can't do this by myself anymore!" Ben's voice echoed in the darkness for a moment before being swallowed up by it.

"Your momma and daddy can help. It ain't all on you; doesn't have to be."

"No," Ben said, shaking his head, thinking about his stepmother. "This is just a story. You understand? This is just a story, and a story won't do nothin good for them."

"I . . . I'll help you, Ben. I promise I will." Nervousness tugged at Marty's vocal cords. "But you goin out there now? That's not gonna help anything at all."

"I have to find him, Marty." Ben's jaw tightened as he failed to stop himself from crying.

"We will, Ben." Marty's eyes glistened briefly in the dim light before he wiped them against his forearm.

"I'll kill 'im," Ben said, his eyes lost in the gloom of the forest. "I swear to God I'll kill whoever took 'im."

And his hhhands said, "Okay, wuh-we'll help you here, but we're not bad." But they SSSQUEEZED. And SQUEEZED.

And SQUEEZED until they cuh-couldn't squeeze no more. But was he done?

Of course he wasn't done.

16

"Yeah, thanks a lot," Ben snapped. He slammed the phone back on the hook and tried to steady himself. He tapped his palm against his brother's flyer and looked at his face, tried to use it for balance in the bland lighting of Customer Service. But his eyes kept creeping back toward the phone number.

For the first time in years, Ben had called the North Florida Missing Persons hotline, and the woman who answered was about as unhelpful as fucking possible. She wouldn't even say whether Marty had called, because "they couldn't give out that kind of information." The only information Ben *had* managed to coax out of her was that the hotline kept a record of each call and that everything was forwarded to the police. Everything.

Police? Well, that meant Duchaine. How nice. It would be hours before he'd be at his desk, and Ben wasn't even sure it would be worth the time and aggravation to call the man. Six months and not a word.

Eric's face was an inky ruin of poor contrast passed down one too many times. The boy's smile seemed more like a sneer now, and the longer Ben looked, the more he saw the thing from his dreams staring back at him, rattling its jaws as it shambled through the mist, chattering, *IT'S ME.* Ben blinked the image away and slid the photograph out of his back pocket to compare the two faces.

The photograph was larger than its deformed twin on the sheet. Ben thought for a moment, then used his shaking hands to slip it from its case and crease folds into the rounded edges of the picture until it would fit the same space. Then he thought for a long while as he looked at the photocopier.

Faceup on the glass, Ben laid the flyer down and placed Eric's photograph on top. Then he wrote his own phone number on a slip of paper and added it to the collage of Eric's flyer. The new numbers fit squarely in the frame, as if they belonged there, positioned over the digits that had done fuck all. Flipping the stack carefully, Ben lowered the lid, set the machine for 250 copies, and punched the button. A column of white light fused the scraps together.

Ben grimaced while he put the original flyer back on the board, but he wasn't going to let Duchaine string him up on some kind of technicality. It was fine. The police could keep this one. Ben jerked the transparent screen closed and walked back into the store.

Come morning, Ben carried his stack of flyers back to the spot Marty had shown him. There was nothing in the woods—nothing but trees and dirt, anyway. At night, with the space between the trees clogged with darkness, the plot of land had seemed immense, unending. But as he stood among the trees, with the singular and all-consuming shadow from the night before reduced to splotches under the power of the morning sun, he saw that it was nothing but a patch. The trees on the opposite side of the road, past Ben's neighborhood, the store, and everything else for that matter, looked as if they might actually stretch on endlessly, but the woods he was standing in now, the woods where Marty had seen Eric, did not. Almost as soon as Ben entered the woods, he could see his way out. That was fine. He would just keep walking, day after day, until he'd handed out and hung every last goddamn flyer. Fuck Duchaine.

Ben could see other shapes beyond the trees: houses and sheds. Yellowed vinyl siding and horizontal planks of dead wood moved from background to foreground as trees whispered in the wind behind Ben's back.

The houses in the neighborhood were old: slouched and rotten, the buildings sat defeated in the same orange dirt that seemed to be a part of the atmosphere here. Nothing stirred behind their hazy glass windows. A collapsed porch awning was held aloft by a vertical piece of lumber. A few houses down, chickens squabbled in their pen.

Ben had been here before. He couldn't remember when, but it would have been at the very beginning, before there were any addresses in Ben's sketchbook, before Ben could have even imagined that things would go on for so long he'd have to make a distinction between old and new neighborhoods and neighbors. He hadn't been wrong to focus on the new residents. That wasn't quite it. But he had been wrong to ignore the old ones. There were dozens of doors to knock on. Ben wrote addresses down on the back of one of the flyers.

By the time Ben saw the large man hunched over the engine of his truck, he'd been walking the neighborhood for a few hours. Another, much younger man sat in the driver's seat with his foot resting on the gas pedal. Ben could see the orange fenders shaking as the vibrations from the engine shook the chassis. When the truck began to lurch, the older man raised his hand and the mechanical bellow subsided, taking the seizures with it.

Placing his fingers as close as possible to the base of his spine, the large man bent backward, cracking his back like a plastic water bottle, then pausing when he saw Ben approaching. Ben raised his hand near his stomach and waved. The truck's engine idled, and the man at the wheel put one foot on the dirt and leaned back in the seat.

"Afternoon," Ben called over the thudding of the truck. With hands stained by dirt and grease, the large man made a gesture and the vehicle was silent. "Problem with your truck?"

Coarse gray hair spilled out of the top of a shirt that might have been white at one point, intertwining with the man's long beard. "Problem? Just put a new engine in 'er."

"Is that right? Sounds real nice."

The two men laughed. The older man pulled a dirty rag out of his back pocket and wiped the beads of sweat off his hairless head.

"Where you come from, boy?"

"Up the road a ways. Ben." He extended his arm to shake the older man's hand, whose thick fingers squeezed like a vise.

"Jacob," he said. "This's my boy Eddie."

"Good to meet you both." The air hung still, without noise from man or machine, while Ben wondered if he should try to make more small talk.

"You just come to shoot the shit, biggun?" Jacob asked.

"Nosir," Ben said, smiling, appreciating the man's candor. "Nosir. I'm out asking about my brother." Ben pinched a flyer off the top of his stack and handed it to Jacob. "He went missing years back. I got reason to believe that somebody might have seen him sometime recent."

"This paper says it was five years back?" Jacob said.

"Yessir. I came through here once or twice before around that time. We might have spoken then?"

Jacob shrugged and ran his dirty fingers through his brown-and-gray beard and tugged on it lightly, an action so perfunctory the man probably didn't even know he was doing it. "I can't say I seen him." Jacob handed the flyer to Eddie, who pushed his tobacco deeper between his lip and gum. He looked at it for a moment before shaking his head and stretching to hand the flyer back to Ben.

"You can keep it, if you don't mind. Someone said they seen him around here a few months ago."

"That right?" Jacob said, casting a look back at Eddie. "Only kids I seen around here are the Cotter girls and Darlene's boys. You might could check with them." As Jacob said each name, he pointed to two different houses that hugged a thick, untamed copse.

"I will. You live here a long time? The neighborhood, I mean."

"All my life," Jacob said.

"Any cops come 'round here in the last few months? Asking after a missing kid?"

Jacob ran his dirty rag over his head again, soaking up the sweat that had reappeared. The two men looked at each other before Jacob turned back to Ben. "The only time the po-lice come out this way is because of Ty Cotter," he said. "And that's just to make sure he don't do nothin too stupid, which is just about the only thing he knows how to do. His lady's okay, but you don't talk to him, you understand me? You knock and he answers, you just walk back into the yard."

Ben glanced at the Cotter house and nodded. "You'll call that number if you see anything? Or hear anything?"

"We will," Jacob said, folding the photocopy and sliding it into his back pocket. "Check with the Cotters and Darlene. Might be a bigger help than we been."

"I'm fixin to do just that," Ben said. "Thanks for your time, the both of you."

The Cotter home looked like a prison from head-on, unchecked hedges obscuring where the windows might have been. Dirt and mildew bent the light reflecting off the yellow paint, making it appear a dull greenish brown. Children's toys lay like hidden relics, forgotten by everything but the overgrown grass.

The screen door whined as Ben pulled it open. His knuckles struck the splitting wooden door three times, then twice more, before he could hear movement in the house. The door cracked just enough that Ben could see a tired eye behind it.

"Yeah?" the woman asked softly.

"Mrs. Cotter?" Ben was relieved that the right person had answered the door, but that relief was short.

"Who is that?" called a nasally voice from behind the woman.

"Mrs. Cotter, I'm sorry to bother you," Ben said quickly. "My brother was seen around here a few months back. I was just wondering if maybe you'd seen him."

"Who *is* that?" yelled the voice again.

"I'm sorry," she said, "you gotta go."

"Here, just—"

With a gasp the woman was jerked to the side and the door opened wider. A man with heavy, burning eyes gripped the doorway and snatched the flyer out of Ben's hand. His lips moved and chattered as he read broken pieces of the text aloud.

"Mr. Cotter? I—"

"I don't know you," the man snapped with ugly teeth. "Why are you on my porch? *I don't know you.*" He rattled the paper. "Is this a trick? You can't come in here. You *can't come in here*! You fuck! You big fuck! Go away!"

Suddenly, the man lunged at Ben, reaching for his stack of flyers. When Ben turned to the side, the man struck Ben's shoulder and lost his footing, tumbling onto the old wood of the porch.

"You motherfucker!" the man screamed, and squeezed the paper in his hand. He squinted into the sun, his teeth like pebbles as he snarled. "Oh. Oh, I *do*. I know you. You big fuck. I remember what you did. I'm glad he's gone. You motherfucker! Me and Bobby Prewitt are both glad." The man laughed and crushed the paper into a ball, flinging it into the grass. "Get the fuck on outta here!"

"Get back in the house, Ty," Jacob said from the yard behind Ben.

"It's alright," Ben said.

"Eat shit," Ty growled as his wife hooked her arms under his and helped him to his feet. "I'm glad he's gone!" the man screamed emphatically. "I'm glad!"

"Take him in, Kell," Jacob snapped.

Kell Cotter dragged Ty back in the house, closing the door with her foot. But it wasn't thick enough to completely muffle the yelling. Almost lost to Ben's ears was the sound of what must have been the Cotters' daughters, crying as their parents fought.

"Don't let Ty bother you none. Blames everyone in the whole damn world for what happened to his cousin, 'cept the man himself, of course. That's family, I guess." Jacob shrugged and turned back toward his own home across the dirt road.

Ben stood there for a moment, trying to take stock of what had just happened. Trying to decide if he was mad or just confused. The blinds rustled to his right and then were pulled away and replaced with the face of a little girl. A deep scar disfigured her right cheek. She looked at Ben until the yelling returned, then she ducked back into the room.

Ben plucked the wadded flyer out of the weeds and stuffed it into his pocket. He walked past a small and intruding tangle of trees and into what Jacob had said was Darlene's yard. The sun was growing tired, but its powerful glow still caught on the aluminum foil that covered the window at the left corner of the house. Gaps large enough for thick fingers had formed between the warping wooden boards, the barrier between this family and the world slowly rotting. Ben's shoe knocked against bricks from an old landing buried in the dirt at the base of the porch. The first step leading up to the door was completely broken.

The screen door leaned against the side of the house, attached to the frame by a solitary and bent hinge. Ben knocked and then stepped back so that he could be seen through the window. A rogue breeze tumbled across Ben's back and then disappeared entirely, as if to show him the air didn't have to be so thick; it simply *wanted* to be.

A thin woman with dark hair appeared between the door and its jamb. She looked at Ben with weary, reddened eyes. A cigarette hung from chapped lips. When she pulled it out of her mouth, smoke rolled over and across her nicotine-dyed teeth.

"Yeah?"

"Are you Darlene?"

"Who are you?"

"Sorry, ma'am. My name's Ben. I was in the neighborhood—"

A child cried in the background. The woman turned her head back inside the house and yelled for the noise to stop, but the cries grew louder, almost savage.

"And?" She turned back to Ben.

"And . . ." Ben collected himself. "I was just wonderin if you'd seen this boy anywhere." Ben held up the flyer of Eric.

Her eyes barely even took the time to look at the picture before she responded. "No, I haven't."

"Could you please look at it for just a second?"

"Me lookin for longer ain't gonna make it so I seen him." She took a drag off her cigarette. Ben saw a blond boy pass behind her, moving from one room to another.

Ben held out one of the photocopies, the paper slightly warped by the sweat from his hand. "Yes, ma'am. If you could just—"

"I don't have time for this shit," she muttered before turning back into the house. "Hey! Come take care of this."

The blond-headed boy peered from the hallway and then disappeared into the house.

"What is it?" a voice called.

Ben wiped his hands on his kerchief and tucked it back into his pocket. He turned and surveyed the rest of the neighborhood, trying to figure if he could reach them all before it got too dark to knock on people's doors anymore. As a boy, he learned that it was rude to call someone's home after nine in the evening; he wondered if that rule still held if he was calling on them in person.

Behind him, the door creaked back open.

"Ben? What're you doing here?" Marty stepped out onto the porch, pulling the door closed in the same motion. Ben held up the flyers, and

Marty lowered his eyes and lit a cigarette. The door opened again, and the blond boy stepped outside.

"What do you want?" Marty asked the boy, the cigarette seesawing in his half-closed lips. He shoved at the boy's bare chest, his thin frame retreating before lunging back toward Marty as if they were connected by a spring. Marty wrapped his arm around the boy's head and rubbed his knuckles against it. The kid's arms flailed; Marty's chest muffled what might have been shouts.

"This is Aaron," Marty mumbled, his right eye squinting at the smoke. He turned his brother loose and deflected an insincere barrage of fists and open slaps. "Go wash up for dinner. Chef Marty's on top of it."

Aaron huffed in disgust.

"No good? Eat summore of them boogers then," Marty said, reaching for his brother's nose.

The kid smacked Marty's hands away with a bashful smile before disappearing again. Voices rumbled quietly behind the thin walls. The cry returned and became a scream.

"Everything okay?" Ben asked.

Marty looked at him quizzically until the crying returned. "Huh? Oh, yeah, everything's fine. That's a neighborhood kid. Nags to come in and then cries because he wants his momma. Bounces around like a Ping-Pong ball."

"Sounds bad."

"Always is. What was my momma goin on about?"

Ben waggled the stack of papers in his hands.

"She take one?"

Ben shook his head.

"You talkin to everybody 'round here?"

Ben nodded and gestured to his left. "Just came from the Cotters' place."

"Oh, Jesus," Marty said. "He try to score off you?"

Ben shook his head and squared his stack of papers against his stomach.

"Did . . . did you tell my momma what I told you?" Marty asked weakly.

A Jeep pulled up onto the lawn and stopped over a large, circular patch of dead grass.

"Shit . . ." Marty whispered.

Ben turned to see a man of about forty-five climb out, his boots stepping heavily on the brittle grass. His thinning hair hung down in untamed wisps that bobbed as he bounded past the missing step, lightly shaking the entire porch.

"Heya, Marty," he said. Marty flinched as his cigarette was plucked from his mouth. "Relax, kid," the man huffed, placing the cigarette between his own lips as he walked into the house.

"That your dad?" Ben asked.

Marty pushed air out of his mouth. "Shit no. That's my momma's boyfriend, Tim."

Ben decided not to press the issue. The murmuring that Ben could hear crescendoed until the voices were shouting. With a half-smile likely born of mild embarrassment, Marty grabbed the doorknob and pulled until the sounds were quieter.

Ben told Marty that he had looked through the woods, and Marty nodded solemnly at Ben's mentioning that he'd found nothing. A scream followed by a crash sounded from inside the house.

"I gotta go, man," Marty said abruptly. "See you at the store?"

"Yeah, I'll see you up there." Ben turned toward the broken step.

"Hey," he heard over his shoulder. Marty was holding out his hand. "Gimme a few of them flyers."

Ben thumbed through the papers and handed Marty a stack.

"Sorry, my momma . . . just sorry is all. For everything."

Ben watched as Marty disappeared into the riot of his home. The steps creaked under Ben's weight as he walked away. His left leg throbbed with pain, hobbling him; he'd need to ice it before his shift if he was going to be any use at all. He made his way to the next house and then the next one after that, trying to remember which ones he'd need to return to and trying to ignore the whispering voice that said it wouldn't matter.

A few hours later, he walked back to his house with a thinner stack of paper. He had a long way to go, a lot of doors to knock on. But he was off to a good start. There wasn't a home in either neighborhood surrounding those woods that Ben didn't visit.

And there wasn't a home in either neighborhood that remembered a recent visit from the police that had anything at all to do with a missing boy.

17

Ben hurled the cordless phone across his room. It smacked against the wall, sending the battery tumbling across the carpet. James Duchaine had actually laughed. It wasn't a big belly laugh, but Ben heard it in his voice all the same. "I think someone's playin games with you, son" was all Duchaine could offer. Duchaine was lying. Or Marty was.

Sitting on his bed, Ben found it hard to orient himself, to make out what he felt. Or maybe it was just hard to admit. Ben never thought that Eric was dead, not once in the last five years. But as strange as it was, it had been a long time since he considered that Eric might actually be alive, that something good might happen instead of nothing bad. But what stirred inside Ben sure felt a lot like despair.

Ben had found peace. He hadn't known it until now, but as sure as he had lost it five years before, he'd found it again and in the same goddamn place. It didn't look like what he might have expected, but it was something. But now, Ben could feel it slipping from his grasp, and he clung to it with the feverish grip of a thief—because that's what he was. He hadn't earned a thing. He wasn't vigilant, dedicated. He hadn't handed out a flyer in almost a *year.* And now there was a sickness in his gut; not because Marty's news had come late, but because it had come at all.

Ben didn't want to think, and he didn't want to sleep. He started transferring addresses from the back of the new flyer to the back of his sketchbook, got frustrated, then turned some pages. With the pen cradled loosely against his fingers, he tried to figure out what was wrong with his drawing, what was wrong with the eyes staring back at him. A trench of gutted pages attested to Ben's failed attempts. He wanted to make some progress, but almost ten minutes had passed since he'd last marked the page. Ben closed the cover and his eyes, but he tried not to sleep. He fought it like he was behind the wheel of a car that couldn't stop.

Ben couldn't remember how many times he'd had the nightmare; it had been dozens at least, probably hundreds. And as bad as that first time was, the second appearance had been worse, because that's when he knew it wouldn't stop, that his mind had built something special for him. Before long, nights, which offered the only real respite in his life, had been taken from him completely, destroyed by the promise of the dream's return.

But the dream stole more than sleep. It stole his memories. Less than a year after Eric disappeared, it started to become difficult to remember what he looked like. More and more, Eric's features seemed to sit just out of focus, like a melody floating just out of reach. The dream had confused Ben. It had replaced Eric's face with a rotten puzzle, shifting and writhing, as slippery in Ben's mind as the skin had been on Eric's bones.

Out of desperation, Ben started carrying Eric's picture with him and that helped to clear the fog. He'd bear down and force himself to see his brother's face, giving up only when the effort became too painful. But Eric's face always came back, peeking out of the corridors of Ben's brain like a nervous animal. It always came back. Until the day that it didn't.

Ben had sat at his desk, clutching his head in his hands, trying to will himself to remember. But he couldn't. The picture wasn't helping. Just as soon as Ben would set it down, it was like he hadn't even looked at it. Each time he tried to conjure Eric back, he seemed to slip further away, until Ben was picturing faces he wasn't sure he'd even seen before, wasn't sure even existed. His teacher's words suddenly didn't make any sense to him. Nothing about that room or any rooms in the whole damn building made sense. Maybe they hadn't for a long time. So Ben left. He just walked out.

By the time Clint found out that Ben had stopped going to school, he was already destined to repeat a grade for the second time in his life. In the grand scheme of things, Ben found it impossible to care.

And it seemed like Clint didn't care either. The man never asked where

Ben had been spending his time, never saw the catalog of addresses in the back of Ben's sketchbook. New residents. Suspicious neighbors. Vague stories. He wrote them all down. Dozens of names and addresses. Walking five miles a day, then ten, then too many to figure—hundreds of miles. Kept walking. Kept writing. Long after he figured out that he'd be scratching them out later, having learned nothing. Found nothing. Done nothing.

But Ben had done something with the front of his book. For every wasted walk and fruitless conversation, there was a drawing. Ben drew Eric's face so many times, he didn't even have to look at the picture anymore. Drew it until a piece of his mind hardened and turned so inflexible that all it could do was remember. Ben carved his brother's face into his brain.

And it worked. Ben never forgot again.

As he lay in his bed, dragging his thumb against the soft edges of filled pages, he could see Eric's face, dancing beneath his eyelids like sunspots. He tried not to think of the new drawing he had started. The one he just couldn't get right. The one with the bad eyes.

Ben dragged his knuckles against the wall above his head. She was in there now. Ben could hear her moving. And he could feel himself slipping. Over and over he stopped himself from stumbling over the edge of consciousness, his heart thudding in his chest each time he'd snap back. But he couldn't hold out forever. Maybe this time he could stay in the forest. Maybe just this once.

—

"Be My Baby" was the ninth track on the Bay City Rollers CD in Ben's stereo alarm clock. The fact that he was hearing it meant that he had overslept. The fact that it was the fourth CD on the carousel meant that he had overslept by quite a bit. Ben lay in bed feeling the slow creep of stiffness climb back into his body. He fought with his eyelids, commanding them to stay open and attempting to rub out their insubordination with his knuckles.

Scraps of the nightmare pulled at his mind, and he did what he could to resist. Wearily, he let his eyes observe his room, and only then did he realize that no sunlight burned through the drawn blinds; the darkness was nearly absolute, contested only by the faint wisps of light meandering from a neighbor's porch light. The clock on his stereo read 1:26. He was late.

Ben groaned and rolled away from the bright clock and dark window. He was reaching for his box cutter when he saw a small boy standing in his doorway.

Ben steeled himself. No matter how many times it happened, Ben was never ready for it. He never really expected to see Eric's ghastly face peering at him from the black, snickering like it was a game, like he had snuck into the waking world through the door Ben had left open when he climbed out of the dream. All Ben could do was hold his breath and watch the mirage fizzle like vapor under the heat of his stare. But this shape was more than just a face. And it didn't fizzle.

Warm tears built in the corners of Ben's eyes and blurred his vision. He shut his lids hard and tried once more to reset the world, as if the figure were a stain on his cornea that could be wiped away. It was only an outline, a silhouette, a looming shadow with no features or expression, but it was enough to glue Ben to his mattress. There was a trembling in Ben's throat, and he felt like he might scream or cry hysterically, but he did neither. Ben lay there stewing in sweat and the sour feeling that was spreading from the center of his stomach.

"Eric?" Ben whispered.

The shape tore from the threshold, slamming the door as it moved. Small footsteps thudded in the hallway. Ben felt faint as he struggled to get out of bed, his legs tangling in the sheets. He rolled onto his carpet, striking a table with the side of his head. Ben rose and flung his door open. The hallway was empty. He moved deeper into the house and tried to listen, but he could hear only his stereo.

Eric's door was open, but his room was empty. So was the bathroom. Carefully, he pressed his ear against his parents' door. No noise. His father would be at work now. Gritting his teeth, Ben squeezed the doorknob and turned it slowly. With a creak, the door swept into the room. The small amount of light that spilled past Ben was enough to make Stampie's eyes glint in the dark. They seemed to dance as Deidra stirred in bed.

"What?" she snapped.

"Sorry," Ben said as calmly as he could.

"What is it?"

He felt a throb in his palm. If he were any stronger, he might have crushed the knob. "Nothing," Ben said. "It's nothing."

The latch clicked back into the frame, and Ben rolled his feet against the carpet to keep his steps quiet. Weak moonlight speared through the living-room blinds and cast the furniture in gray. The more time that wedged itself between what had stood in Ben's doorway and what stood before him now, the less sure Ben was about what he'd seen.

Reaching for his back pocket, Ben found his handkerchief missing. After a few moments of patting, he realized he was wearing only boxers and a shirt. He slunk back into his room and got dressed.

The still, dark air of the open world felt uncomfortable as he hustled along the overgrown shoulder toward the store. The only sound accompanying his grass-muffled footsteps was the blended screech of countless crickets.

In the distance, beyond the trees to Ben's left, a confused rooster called out, and for a few seconds afterward there were no real sounds at all. Except for one. And it was very, very close.

Ben stopped and turned toward the rustling woods, though there was nothing he could see; the trees at the edge of the copse sparkled in the pale light but shielded everything beyond themselves. That there had been a ruckus in the undergrowth meant nothing to Ben, but that it had stopped when he did made Ben feel noticed, and he didn't like that.

Stooping, Ben squinted into the trees, and when he saw more of the same nothingness, he took a step forward, and this time the darkness *acknowledged* him.

Leaves and sticks cracked and snapped. A shadow moved within itself, and then the black was still. The noise plunged deeper into the trees, and Ben bounded toward it, his heart pounding, but his feet stopped sharp at the tree line. He could see his brother's face, crooked and wide-eyed, sneering and begging. There was nothing but blackness before him, but Eric's face danced in his mind and arrested his legs.

Ben extended his hand toward the trees and then slowly withdrew his grasp. Nothing moved. But nothing felt still.

PART TWO

The Boy in the Moonlight

18

Ben was ten years old the first time he had to repeat a grade. None of his friends had been held back, so as far as Ben was concerned, he may as well have been at a new school in another state. He didn't know any of the other kids, and now he was a year older, a foot taller, and thirty pounds heavier than everyone but the teacher. No one made fun of him. He wasn't a pariah. It's just hard to make friends when you can't do what friends do. Ben couldn't play. He couldn't run or skip or jump. Thanks to the car accident, he could hardly even walk.

His class had recess every day, and twice a week was "free play," where the kids could do whatever they wanted. These were Ben's favorite days, because he would stay inside and play checkers with his teacher or read from a children's book that told softened versions of Greek myths. The other three days, Ben walked the track and watched Daniel.

Daniel didn't seem to know or care what free play was. He ran every day and went faster and farther than anyone Ben had ever seen. He and his two friends blew past Ben like bullets, racing one another, lapping Ben as he hobbled on the inside ring of the dirt circle. The other boys were quick, but Daniel was a force of nature.

Physically, Ben was incapable of running. He'd been heavy before his accident, but now he was obese. Even walking took a lot of concentration, and it hurt. It hurt a lot. He wasn't even able to stand without his leg brace, and it sometimes took two people to steady him without it because of his size. Once a year, he was evaluated and measured for a new brace, though he would get a new one only when the knee joint no longer lined up right; his father's insurance paid for the doctor's appointments but not the equipment. The brace rattled and squeaked when he walked, a sound that became so habituated by Ben's mind, he noticed it only when it wasn't there.

Ben wasn't jealous of Daniel. Not really. He watched him with the kind of awe that someone might have for a bird banking and diving, soaring and arcing—enamored of abilities you not only lacked but couldn't even comprehend. Ben wasn't racing Daniel. Ben wasn't competing with anyone other than himself. And while it might not have actually been true, the whip-strike pain through the muscle of his left thigh made it feel an awful lot like he was losing. He tried for a long time to ignore the pain, but that was impossible. What he *could* do, however, was pay attention to something else.

As Daniel and his friends made their rounds, Ben concentrated on the whining of his brace. A mild and rhythmic screech, like a swing whose bracket needed oil, sounded with each careful and uneven step. The slower the gait, the more pregnant the pause before each protracted cry from the metal hinge against his knee. He didn't try to walk faster, not consciously. That was hard. So Ben focused on the noise and tried to make *it* move faster. It worked so well that for weeks Ben tuned everything out except for the sound of his progress. Then Daniel sprained his ankle.

He'd tripped playing in "the Ditch," he'd said. Just slid right down the side of the dirt valley and landed wrong. The sprain wasn't too bad. At least not until Monday, when he tried to run on it. When he did, he twisted up his leg bad enough that Ben was actually walking faster than him come Wednesday, though Ben hadn't noticed right away.

Ben was so fixated on the cries of his brace that he barely heard Daniel speak as he passed him and his friends. Daniel asked if Ben wanted to walk with them. Ben had to slow his pace, but he did so gladly and circled the track step for step with a group for the very first time.

It was nice—nicer than walking alone in a lot of ways. And it was helpful. Carrying on a conversation was even more effective than listening to the squeaks and screeches of his brace. It was a little difficult to think of things to talk about sometimes, but he managed. After a few days, Ben started walking the track during free play. His leg hurt like hell, but it was worth it.

After about two weeks it started growing more and more difficult for Ben to keep pace with the boys. They were moving faster—fast enough that Ben had to swing his arms to propel himself forward, wincing against the pain in his leg. He matched them step for step for as long as he could. But then, one day, Daniel was all better.

Ben tried once to slow Daniel down with a question as he ran past, but the boy didn't stop, didn't slow, didn't answer. They never really talked again after that. It was like the whole thing had never happened, and maybe that would have been fine, but Ben couldn't remember how to do his trick anymore, how to focus on the squeals of his brace and make *them* move faster. Or maybe he just missed the talking.

It wasn't that hard to see what had happened, to see that while he'd never been competing against Daniel, Daniel had been competing against him. And he didn't want to be slower than Ben. Not for three weeks. Not for one day.

When Ben thinks of that year, he remembers the time he and Daniel were equal. How he was as fast as the fastest kid. He doesn't think about Daniel's trick, even though it's part of who he is now. Every person has a day that transforms trust into a choice, when he learns that people lie for reasons all their own. That day on the track was Ben's.

And Ben had made his choice about Marty, though he tried to steel himself against it. Marty was a liar. There was really no way around it. Ben had told Marty about Eric, and then over two months later it just so happened that Marty had seen him? Before Ben even started working at the store? The *only* person in the last five years, and it was a person who wasn't even looking. A person who said he'd called the hotline, despite the fact that there was no record of it with the police. Marty lied and Marty played games. He'd found Stampie, put him in the lost and found box, waited for it to be funny, and then when it wasn't, he made up a story.

Marty was a liar, and it didn't matter. Because Ben wanted to believe him.

There had been a fire in Ben. A long time ago, the same breath that had first carried the words "Have you seen my brother?" had blown ember to flame, and that flame had endured for a while. Kept alive by dreams and wishes, it lived longer perhaps than Ben was capable of bearing, so when its flicker finally started to dull, Ben didn't fight it. He couldn't; he had nothing left to fight with. Starved of life by every stranger's indifferent shrug, every disinterested response from James Duchaine, Ben could only let the fire die in the vacuum of his heart.

That fire, Ben now knew, had been hope. He'd felt it the very instant Marty had told his liar's confession. More than anger, more than confusion, Ben could feel hope swelling in him with every breath, even if he didn't like it.

Hope had exchanged Ben's delusion of peace for the mocking whisper that told him he would never have any. Good. Keep whispering then. Go on and yell if you've got a mind to. *Eric is alive.* Ben could feel the urgency of that fact each time he handed out a flyer, and he'd handed out hundreds.

For a whole month, it was practically his second job. Every day after work, Ben would pull his stash of flyers and his sketchbook out of his work locker and walk somewhere either very old or very new, updating his list until he absolutely had to rest, sometimes ignoring even that. He stapled papers to telephone poles and put them in and on newspaper vendor boxes. Day in and day out, until he was well into his second batch.

When Ben worked alone, he'd sometimes walk the aisles not touching anything, but trying to feel something all the same. And sometimes he would just close his eyes and listen to the store, in case it had something to say. Almost every other night Ben checked the lost and found. He didn't tell Marty about those things. They didn't talk about what had happened.

All that mattered was that Eric was somewhere to be seen, and the more eyes that knew to look for him, the better. Every "no" that Ben heard was one "yes" that he might hear in a week, or even a day. And Ben heard a lot of "noes."

He didn't mind, though. He hardly noticed at all. Because that's the thing about hope—when it seems that there's no point in moving, it pushes us so forcefully that we come to feel like we *need* it to keep going. It was out of that very need that Ben decided to believe Marty. Even if what he said seemed implausible, even if it was the cruel tale of a liar, it had given Ben hope and he embraced it like an old friend. Because it felt good.

And that's what hope really is, after all. An anesthetic. Something that takes the sharp edges of reality out of focus just enough that we can keep looking at it, keep moving forward with steps that are guided by the assurance that every inch of ground can't possibly be covered in broken glass. And then when it *is*—when your feet are left as coiled ribbons of wet skin—you forget what guided you there in the first place.

It's a kind of sneaky narcotic, one produced by thoughts and words and refined by time. It doesn't fix anything. It just numbs and reassures, until it can consume the desperate for the sake of its own brilliant incandescence. And as hope comforts us, it becomes easier and easier to forget that it too was in the jar that Pandora carried. It's the one horror of the world that wasn't loosed when she opened the lid.

It's the one horror that lives in us.

But wuh-with his hands and feet quittin ah-out on him, well, there weren't muh-much he could do. So huh-he thought, *Muh-maybe I'll be good.*

And he tried.

But there weren't nuh-nothin good in him. He had to find somethin good.

So he crawled to it.

19

"It's called pride," Frank said, yanking a box open. "Everything you throw looks like garbage. Look at that. Sloppy as hell. Now look at this. *Magazine.*"

"Yeah, okay," Ben said, unloading a heap of marshmallow bags onto the bottom rack.

"What fuckin magazines are you readin that got pictures of grocery shelves, Frank?" Marty grunted as he flung an armful of pie crusts onto the shelf.

"I'm sayin it *could* be in one. Because it looks good." Frank spun the evaporated milk cans he'd just shelved so the labels faced outward.

"And I'm sayin that it *couldn't* be in one, because no one gives a shit so hard that the magazine it was in would go out of print and everyone at the printing place would kill themselves."

"You care more than me," Frank said as he slid some cans around on the shelf. "You're throwin twice as much because you keep givin me the shitty tags. Keep hustlin. I'm gonna take my time on these cans."

Marty looked around at the division of labor and cursed.

"I just wanna know who scheduled the holidays. Bustin ass to fix the store after Thanksgiving when Christmas is right around the corner don't make no sense," Frank moaned.

"You think we oughta just wait until next year?" Ben asked, ripping open another box.

"No," Marty cut in, "Frank thinks everything should all just be in one big bin. Just a big-ass cage with everything all piled up."

"Lower people in on ropes. They get whatever's on top," Frank said.

"Goddamn idiot."

"You can have your own bin, white boy," Frank snapped playfully. "Full of cigarettes and clam chowder and fuckin sherbert."

Marty laughed hard. "That what white folks eat? Clam chowder and sherbert?" He laughed again, and then Frank and Ben followed.

"Oh, Christ." Marty sighed. "Well, boys, I can't really take any more of this goddamned aisle. Feels like lunch to me."

The three of them each dropped his box.

"I got leftovers." Frank smiled, dusting his hands together.

"So do I," Marty said, slipping a cigarette between his lips and gesturing to the miles of food that surrounded them. "See you out front."

"You have a good Thanksgiving?" Ben asked, pushing open the doors to the back room.

"Yeah," Frank replied, patting his stomach with his hand. "Too good. Turkey, mac 'n cheese, sweet potatoes. My pops can cook, boy."

"You know our folks work together? My dad and yours?"

"That's what he said! They known each other for a long time, huh?"

"Seems that way. That where they met, you reckon?"

"Oh, I dunno. He's worked there . . ." Frank tapped his hand on the fridge handle. "Eight years?"

"My pop's been there for longer, I think."

"Before the papers, he was at the mall, doin cleanup-type stuff."

"Like a janitor?"

"Yeah. That's what he done for a long time at different places, way back when he was still young. Schools like Blackwater and then Bradley Park."

"That's where I went to elementary," Ben said. "Bradley Park."

"Long as you never pissed on the floor, then we good." Frank laughed.

"Blackwater like a private school or somethin?"

"I dunno exactly. It ain't around here. That was back when my daddy lived up in Alabama, and he don't reminisce too much about when he was younger. Don't know why he stayed doin stuff like that for so long. You can bet my next job ain't gonna be in a place like this.

"Y'all should come over sometime," Frank said, reaching into the refrigerator. "We live just over on Chemstrand, behind the theater."

"The old busted one?" Ben spun the combination dial on his locker.

"Busted?" Frank huffed. "You can move the tables and chairs, man. Ain't nothin busted about that."

"True enough," Ben said, reaching for his chips and pulling them out with a folded note. "Motherfucker. Marty still leaving you them pecker drawings?"

"Near every night. One day it's gonna be a real picture and then I'm gone for good. I mean that's gotta be it, right? A man putting a goddamn picture of his dick in my locker. I can get unemployment for that."

Ben laughed and slipped the note into his pocket. He and Frank carried their food out of the break room.

Outside, Marty chewed an enormous sub sandwich he'd constructed out of a whole loaf of French bread and deli meats. Crumbs covered his cheeks and shirt. There was a chill in the air, but nothing too biting.

"Frank said he's jealous, thought he was your dick buddy," Ben said, tossing the folded paper into Marty's lap. Marty pinched it between his index and middle fingers, the only two not covered in condiments and ham water.

"Butt buddy," Marty mumbled through his food. "What's this?"

He wiped his hands on his pants and unfolded the piece of paper. Marty's brow furrowed and he looked at the paper for a long time, running his fingers over the frayed corners, glancing at Ben once and then again with intense uncertainty in his eyes.

"You disappointed in your work?" Frank asked, prying the lid off his container of leftovers.

Marty refolded the paper and tapped its corner against his knee. Then he handed it back to Ben. "This ain't anything I did," he said to Ben intently. "You understand me?"

A car shambled up the road as Ben opened the note.

"That ain't anything I did," Marty repeated.

Ben flattened the page and felt his stomach turn. It was Eric's flyer.

"C'mon, man," Ben moaned. "C'mon. What're you doing? What the fuck are you doing?" he screamed.

"Fuck this," Marty snapped, standing and lighting a cigarette.

"Oh, Jesus," Ben yelped as he stood, still clutching the paper. "His face. What'd you draw? Why'd you draw on his fucking *face* like that?"

"I coulda kept it, you fuckin idiot! You didn't even know what it was. I coulda just thrown it away, but I gave it back to you, because *I didn't do it.* You can't just keep accusing me of every goddamn thing that happens."

"Yes!" Ben shouted. "I can!"

"I spent the last month passing out those fucking things. Why would I put one in your locker when I been handing them out?"

"The same reason you'd put his stuffed animal in the box and then lie about seeing him! What the fuck is wrong with you?"

"What stuffed animal?" Frank asked.

"What exactly do you think my plan would be here?" Marty yelled. "To taunt you until you decided to just beat me to death? Think about all this for one goddamn second! Why would I even have that fucking toy? How would I know that you'd find it? I'm not the fucking bad guy here!"

"Are you guys talking about the little rhino?" Frank asked uneasily. Ben and Marty stopped shouting and stared at Frank.

"You *told* him?" Ben asked, but Marty only shook his head.

"That was me," Frank said. "I put it in the box." He shifted in his chair, picking through his sweet potatoes with a plastic fork, then pressed the outside knuckle of his index finger on his glasses to push them up his nose.

"Where did you get it?" Ben asked.

"I found it," Frank replied.

Ben's whole body tensed, flinching against what he knew Frank would say next.

"In the bathroom."

—

The crew walked inside and toward the back of the store.

"I don't know what I can show you," Frank said. "Like I said, I just found it is all."

The smell of bleach and urine choked the air inside the bathroom.

"There," Frank said, "in the sink."

Ben's cheeks flushed, and the vandalized flyer burned in his hand.

"I came in to take a piss, saw it sitting there. So I took it to the lost and found like you're supposed to."

"When?"

"Shit." Frank shrugged. "I don't remember. It was a little while ago."

"Before I started working here?"

"I think so . . . Maybe it was after, though."

"Jesus Christ, Frank," Marty said.

"It coulda been before! Ben, if I woulda known . . ."

Ben stared at the sink until his eyes lost focus. "Was it wet?" he asked listlessly. "When you found it, was it all wet?"

"Yeah," Frank said.

Ben blinked hard and held his eyes shut. His breath wavered as he exhaled and looked at Eric's flyer. Ratty and worn, it seemed almost ancient. But it was new enough to have Ben's phone number at the bottom. The markings, however, bothered Ben the most.

They covered Eric's whole face, stretching down into the text of the flyer. He tried to place where he'd seen the shape, turning the paper to the left, then right. Turning it until it looked like something. From one angle, he saw letters eating one another: *Cco.*

The first *C* was a crescent outline, and it gorged itself on its thinner twin—a single curve that was itself consuming a smaller *o.* A line moved through the middle arc of both *C*s, bisecting everything but the *o.* If he turned the image so the line pointed up, it became a tower of smoke rising out of the small *o*—a train light hurtling through the dark tunnel of the larger *C.*

Frustrated, Ben cursed under his breath. It meant something to someone. Whoever had scribbled it on his brother's face knew exactly what it was and wanted to show Ben. But that wasn't really necessary, was it? Because the longer he looked at it, the more he felt like he'd seen it before.

"Do you know what this is?"

Marty took the paper and looked at the drawing. "No," he finally answered.

"Frank?"

Marty handed Frank the paper and he turned and tilted it a few times like Ben had, then shook his head.

"Really look at it. You never seen that before? Not either of you?"

Frank looked again but kept glancing up. "I never seen it. What does this have to do with the rhino?"

"Look at the name, Columbo," Marty said.

"The name?" Frank studied the page. "Oh, jeez, Ben. I had no idea. Oh, *Jesus,* man. And someone tore this down?" Frank held the paper up.

"What? Oh, fuck," Marty said, turning away in exasperation.

Ben looked at the rips in the flyer: uniform and evenly spaced, just like how he'd tried to fix the flyers to telephone poles and trees. There was a trembling in Ben's legs and a fluttering in his chest.

"Who would do that?" Frank asked.

Ben whipped the door open. He could barely hear Marty and Frank as he walked into the back room, despite them being very close behind him. The metal steps rang like untuned bells under the stomping of their feet.

"This is a real shit idea, dude," Marty said as they passed the sleeping air conditioner.

"He might have cameras and stuff," Frank added.

"Then go back downstairs!"

"Well, we still wanna see you hulk out."

"Marty, c'mon. Ben, we don't even know if that camera works."

"He's got two monitors up here and two VCRs. One's for the deli. Marty, you steal so much time here, there's no way the other one's for the time clock."

"Yeah, but then what?" Marty asked. "If the camera don't work, Palmer fires all three of us for breaking into his office. If the camera does work, then maybe you see what you see, and then that's it?"

"No," Ben said, yanking on the doorknob to Palmer's office. "No, that ain't it."

"He will fire you, Ben. Press charges. Probably sue you and whatever else he can do."

"Let him then. Fuck him and this whole damn place."

"Ben—"

"Someone tore down Eric's flyer and drew on his face! Someone had his toy and put it *right* where I left it that day. Someone's fucking with me, and I'm gonna know who it is."

"Wait," Marty said, grabbing Ben's arm.

Ben tore free. "You ain't gonna stop me from seeing this tape!"

"I ain't trying to!" Marty shouted. "Just listen to me for one goddamn second and you can get in there without getting canned!"

Ben's fists were squeezed tight enough to hurt, so he jammed his hands in his pants pockets. "Okay," he said. "Okay, let's hear it then."

"Alright," Marty said calmly. "Lemme see that flyer."

20

After they finished stocking the shelves, Marty and Frank stuck around for a while, waiting to see what would happen. But as the morning dragged on, Frank said he had to leave. Marty stayed. He said it was because what was about to happen was his idea; Ben suspected that Marty just wanted to prove that he wasn't afraid of what would be on that tape, or at least wanted Ben to think that was the case. Marty had sworn up and down that the graffitied flyer wasn't his doing. If Ben was being honest with himself, the fact that Marty insisted on staying left little doubt in his mind that there wouldn't be any tape to see at all.

Everything relied on a functional camera in the break room that was actually connected to something and Bill Palmer somehow agreeing to show them what it had seen. A perfect storm of unlikelihood. Ben knew, however, that if the first two conditions were met, then the third wouldn't really matter in the end. He'd get into Palmer's office with or without the man's consent.

"You boys been standing there for a while now," Beverly said as she approached.

"Yes, ma'am," Ben said.

" 'Bout two hours, I think," Marty added, tapping the back of his head against the wall by the time clock.

"You waitin for somebody?"

"No. Just can't get enough of this place. Thinkin about just movin on in."

For whatever reason, Marty could always make Beverly laugh, even when he was giving her a hard time. "Least the pantry's always full," she replied.

"See? She gets it. Can I ask you somethin, Ms. Beverly?" Marty said, and the woman nodded. "Have you ever seen this before?" Marty patted Ben's side with the back of his hand and then held it out. Ben handed him a folded piece of paper. "For the life of me I just can't remember what it is."

She looked at it for a long while, her hands and head trembling with disease. "What is it?"

"Just something I saw somewhere. Been tryin to remember what it is and where I seen it. Just one of them things, I guess."

"But Benjamin's got it in his pocket?"

"Hmm? Oh, yes, ma'am. Said he'd try to help me remember what it was."

Beverly nodded. "Well, I wish you both luck. It don't get no easier the older you get."

"No, ma'am," the boys said almost in unison.

The woman walked away, slow as ever, the strings of her apron swinging as she shuffled along the tile. Ben slipped the sheet of paper with the copied symbol back into his pocket, right next to the defaced flyer.

"I couldn't do it," Ben said.

"Hmm?" Marty grunted.

"Be that old and work in a place like this with assholes like us . . ."

Marty smiled briefly. "Shit." He moved a little away from the wall. "Here we go."

The doors screeched closed behind Bill Palmer as he walked by the registers. When he saw Ben and Marty, he slowed and frowned at his watch.

"Hope you two are off the clock," the man said, stroking his palm over hair that was too thin to conceal the scalp beneath.

"Yessir," Marty said. He opened his mouth to speak again, but closed it and looked at Ben.

"I need to talk to you, Mr. Palmer. About a theft."

Marty and Ben followed Palmer through the store. It wasn't at all clear that Palmer was actually listening, but Ben stuck to the script while

Palmer interrupted here and there to call attention to some flaw in the work the crew had done the night before. This went on until Marty interrupted.

"Should we clock back in? Since we're talking about work and all."

"Okay, so your CD player was stolen." Palmer shrugged. "If the lock or locker wasn't broken, then that means you didn't lock it."

"I was just wonderin if that camera works. The one in the break room. Maybe I could see who went into my locker."

"Sorry, but no," Palmer said. "No. Those lockers are provided as a courtesy. Securing what you put in them is your responsibility. We're not gonna spend all day playing detective because you left yours open."

"I didn't leave—"

"Just put in a police report like I said, man," Marty muttered to Ben. "Don't cost nothin, and they can watch the tapes and whatever."

Palmer sighed, and Ben realized that the man still hadn't said anything about the camera not working or there not being a tape. Of course, he wouldn't want to admit that unless he had to.

"I just figured this would be simpler," Ben mumbled to Marty, who smiled just a little bit.

Palmer squinted and rubbed his forehead. "Fine."

The portly man practically stomped the whole way to his office. Ben thought that at any moment Palmer might change his mind and send them away, but on they marched, right up to the door that Ben had almost kicked in.

Inside, Palmer threw his keys on the desk and then jabbed at buttons on the VCR and its monitor until the black screen turned blue. A whirring rose out of the machine as the tape zipped backward. Ben glanced at Marty, who looked very tired now.

The office was as messy as it had been the day Ben was interviewed. Paperwork lay strewn on Palmer's desk. In the corners, boxes were stacked so high they almost reached the ceiling. From the looks of it, Palmer had lost the key to his filing cabinet; the lock was drilled out, and the handles of the top two drawers were fastened together with a chain. Looking at the clutter while Palmer fussed with the machine, Ben found himself wondering what the man did with all the old tapes.

Palmer touched the VCR again, and when Ben turned he could see a grainy image of the break room.

"Well, I'll be goddamned," Marty said under his breath.

Each boy dragged a chair away from Palmer's desk and sat it in front of the screen. Palmer grunted as he practically fell into his own chair.

Based on the time stamp on the screen, the footage was from the previous morning, which was as far back as the tape went, according to Palmer. Capturing only a handful of frames a second turned a six-hour tape into one that could record a whole day, but it made the tape worse than a flipbook a kid might produce on his first attempt. Still, it was coherent enough, and it had a view of the lockers.

Ben asked if he could fast-forward.

Again, the tape whirred, and the screen became almost incomprehensible. Finally, there appeared to be some kind of new shape in the frame, but it was garbled and distorted. Ben mashed the play button and watched the jerky movements of a bag boy putting something in the microwave.

Each time the room emptied, Ben leaned toward the monitor to press fast-forward. When there was movement, he played the tape and watched each frame. The first few hours of tape went by relatively quickly, but when the lunch rush started, Ben finally had to sit all the way back in his chair.

Marty rested his cheek in his hand and stared ahead like a boy stuck in a lecture about the importance of proper shoelace maintenance.

"Was your CD player one of the nice ones?" Palmer asked.

"Hmm?" Ben glanced away from the screen. He'd been staring at the jittery recording for so long that looking at the smooth motions of the real world was almost dizzying. "Yeah," he finally continued, "it was pretty good. Anti-skip and everything."

"How many seconds?"

"Um, ten I think?"

"I sprung for the thirty." Palmer leaned over and tapped on a boxed CD player. "Figured why not? Reckon it's gonna be a big hit."

"Maybe I'll go for that one if I don't get my old one back."

"You say they left a note? In your locker?"

"Yessir," Ben said quickly, leaning forward to pause the tape. Marty sat up as Ben reached into his back pocket and handed his boss the piece of paper. Ben studied Palmer intently as he unfolded the note. Palmer squinted as he looked at it, then turned it just as Frank had.

"Just this on a blank sheet of paper?" Palmer asked, rattling the page. "What's it supposed to mean?"

Marty slumped in his chair, then leaned forward and unpaused the tape.

"I dunno," Ben said. "None of us did."

"Looks like a kid," Palmer muttered. "Right here," he added after Ben turned in his chair. "Raisin his arms up."

"What about the other shape?" Ben asked.

"Might be a light. The moon maybe. Little stick-figure kid raising his hands in front of the moon? A crescent one. Do you see it?"

"I think I might," Ben tried to say calmly as he pictured that shape scrawled over his brother's face. "Yeah, I think I can see it." And he could. It was all he could see now.

"Ben, look at this," Marty said. He was leaning forward in his chair, his eyes fixed to the screen.

"Beverly?" Ben said. "Did she go near the lockers?"

"No, but just wait a second. I bet she'll do it again."

Ben watched the jerky images of the old woman eating her lunch as two other employees prepared their own. One of them sat at the table opposite Beverly and quickly scarfed down a sandwich. Neither of them seemed to say anything other than "bye" when the man stood to leave.

"Okay, watch," Marty said.

And Ben did. The tape jerked forward. Beverly took another bite of her food. And then she started talking.

"There," Marty said. "What the fuck is that?"

Ben watched the old woman. She moved her mouth and then her hands. And then she seemed to laugh. She was having a conversation. And she was alone.

"What in the world?" Marty whispered.

"People talk to themselves," Ben said.

"Like that?" Marty pointed.

On and on she went. And then, seemingly in the middle of a sentence, she stopped. Frames later, another employee walked in.

"I mean, what the hell, dude?"

Ben shrugged. "Who cares?"

It was clear that Marty wanted to say more, but he didn't.

"She does that sometimes," Palmer said. "Talks about her day and her customers. No one's ever complained about it, so . . ." The man tilted his hands, then looked back down at his paperwork.

Marty and Ben scanned through the footage, fast-forwarding and rewinding, going frame by frame anytime someone went near the lockers. Each time Palmer wanted to leave the office, the boys paused the tape and stood outside his locked door until he returned. Sometimes Marty would leave too. And when he was late coming back, Ben would just resume the tape without him. It took almost three hours until the tape showed Ben and Frank walking into the break room the night before.

Ben didn't recognize himself at first, but as soon as he did, he stopped the tape and slowly stood.

"Nothing?"

"Nosir." Ben strained as he stretched. "Must've happened sometime before yesterday."

"Let's watch the rest of the tape."

"Pardon?"

"Just to make sure," he encouraged as he slid his paperwork to the side.

Ben resumed the tape and sat back down, glancing at Marty. On the screen, Ben and Frank moved around the room chatting. Ben pulled his chips and the note out of the locker. The two boys laughed and then left the room.

"You don't look too upset there, son. About finding that your CD player was missing."

"I didn't realize until later," Ben replied.

"Oh," Palmer said. "I only mention it because this wouldn't be the first time that someone lied about their property getting took in my store. Usually it's so they can ask for some kinda compensation, but it doesn't seem like that's what you want.

"I'm not exactly sure what you boys' game is here, but I am certain that it *is* a game. From where I'm sittin, here in the big chair, it looks an awful lot like you just made up a story so that you could come in here and watch this tape."

"Like I said, I didn't realize—"

"I don't know what for. To see who took lunch when. Or see who's using the unmarked lockers. Don't matter. It's weird to me that Frank's not here, since it was you two and not *you two* on that tape.

"What's even weirder is that I've never seen any of you with headphones on. Not one time. From what I understand, you usually play your music over the intercom with that little boom box of yours, right? So I don't know what you would even be using a CD player for.

"I don't like my time bein wasted, and I'm not gonna waste more tryin to figure out just what in the hell the two of you are up to. Marty, this'll be your second warning. But Ben, I think maybe it's time we moved you to a new position. Bag boy or cashier, wasn't it?"

"Mr. Palmer," Marty said, pointing at the screen.

The man adjusted his thick glasses and followed Marty's gesture. On the monitor, Ben walked into the break room, opened his locker, and peered inside. After a few seconds, he slammed the door shut and stormed out of the room. The seconds sped by on the time-lapse tape, and before long, Ben returned with Marty and Frank. Ben gestured at his locker and waved the paper at them. The paper was blank, of course. They hadn't copied the graffiti onto it yet.

Marty had told Ben to look angry about things, and as Ben watched the tape, he thought he'd done a pretty good job, even if all he was screaming was "My locker!" over and over again. The frames ratcheted by, and the three boys walked out of the break room.

Marty stood and stretched. "Sorry to eat up your day, Mr. P."

"I wouldn't do nothin to disrespect you on purpose, Mr. Palmer. Like I said, I didn't realize that it was missin until later. I hope—"

"Yeah, okay," Palmer said with exasperation. "Just get out."

"I ain't tryin to be a pain," Ben said calmly, "but do you have tapes from other days? So I can see who done it?"

"No, I don't have any other tapes," Palmer replied harshly.

In the corridor, Ben walked with heavy steps, while Marty rubbed the back of his neck with his hands. "Did you move my flyers?" Ben asked.

"Yeah, the first time I went to smoke. I put 'em under a pallet out back."

"Sorry for wastin your whole morning, man," Ben said.

"That's nothin," Marty replied, smiling. "You're about to waste my whole day."

21

Most stores and shops had been helpful when Ben had come to them with his new batch of flyers. They didn't want him patrolling the aisles and talking to customers, but they had no problem with him using their bulletin boards or light posts to hang Eric's flyer. It had taken a while, but when he'd finally exhausted all the prominent places to tape, tack, or staple the paper, he started putting them on almost anything a person might see, including spots that were out of the way, like the telephone pole just past the store where the town intersected with the great wide nothing beyond.

The idea was that the flyer might catch the attention of people coming in town on foot or by bicycle. Ben couldn't really take credit for the thought; the pole was littered with yard sale and lost dog posters. Still, a good idea was a good idea. But as Ben approached, he could see that he'd been wrong. Eric's flyer couldn't have caught anybody's eye. Because it wasn't there.

"No. Oh, c'mon, dude," Ben said.

He circled the pole a few times, then checked the ratty grass, sweeping it back and forth with his feet, finding only cans and bits of plastic among the dirt and rocks. If the flyer had fallen, it wouldn't be down there anyway. It would have blown away. Ben knew that the flyer hadn't fallen, though. He could see the staples he'd used. All five of them.

Marty lit another cigarette and took a drag. He didn't say anything while Ben circled the pole again. Cursing, Ben slid a flyer from the top of the stack that Marty had hidden. Holding it taut, he pushed the top edge against a nailhead until it broke through. After a moment, he pinched another nail between his fingers and gritted his teeth as he pulled it free of the wood. He used one of the rocks at his feet to pound the rough spike into the bottom of Eric's page.

"You okay?" Marty asked.

Ben hurled the rock and didn't answer.

Marty walked a little ahead of Ben, whose leg hurt enough to slow him down noticeably. For a while he tried to conceal his limp, but eventually he just gave up. He couldn't concentrate on imaginary sounds or grit his teeth to save face. All he could think about were the flyers in his arm and the one in his pocket. By the time Ben pointed them to where they had been heading, he was sweating from the pain.

"It ain't here," Ben muttered. "I put it right here." He stabbed the pole with his finger. "Look, you can see. You can see the staples I used."

Ben tried to find a way to secure a new flyer, pulling at the staples with his fingers and then scraping at them with his nails. When he could get no purchase, Ben pressed the paper against the sharp and prickly surface until it was too torn to even use, then pushed and dragged it out of spite until it was in ribbons. He didn't think he had screamed, but his throat hurt like he had. Marty didn't say a word. He stood there and smoked until Ben was ready to walk on.

"I can't fucking *believe* this," Ben said. "I can't believe it."

A few times, Ben had to rest. Leaning his back against whatever he could, he drove the palm of his hand into the muscle of his left thigh, while Marty held the stack of flyers.

"We can call it quits for today," Marty said once. "Might not be a bad idea."

Ben laughed in frustration and pushed away from his tree. He walked ahead of Marty.

"This one's still up!" Ben shouted back at Marty when they got to the next spot. "Still right here. If they got the other two, I figured they woulda got this one."

The one after that, right in front of a gas station, was still there as well. They kept walking, and Marty kept smoking.

Ben had almost managed to convince himself that the first two were flukes and somehow unrelated to what crinkled in his back pocket. One more happy stop might have done it. Just one. But it wasn't a day for happy stops. And after five more missing flyers, it ceased being a day for stopping of any kind.

Ben didn't try to replace them anymore. His hand was still bleeding from the second attempt, which he'd botched when he'd lost his temper. He had to practically lunge with each step to keep going, pushed by anger and pulled by what felt like hope. Ben moved from empty spot to empty spot until his leg finally gave up, spilling him to the ground.

After a few seconds, Marty's footsteps crackled in the drying grass. He sat down crisscross next to Ben.

"Let's call it quits. Maybe call the cops and tell 'em about these flyers and the one that was in your locker."

"I can't. Sit on my leg."

"Pardon?"

Ben stretched out his left leg with a whimper, then tapped the spot with his hand. He lay flat and brought the inside of his elbow over his eyes to shield them from the winter sun. "Sit on my leg."

"Alrighty," Marty grunted, rising from the grass and then lowering himself onto Ben's thigh. Resting his arms on his knees, Marty lit a cigarette and smoked. "It ever been this bad before?"

"Not in a long time. I think it was goin up and down them steps at work."

"That and you been practically sprinting for an hour now. How'd it get fucked up?"

"Accident when I was a kid."

"You ask someone who was too big to sit on your leg? You had this fetish since you was a kid?"

Ben laughed and then moaned at the pain. "Car wreck."

"That'll do it," Marty said through his smoke. "You get around pretty good, though. Considering."

"It's how come I got so heavy. I was always a little big, I guess. But after the wreck . . . I don't eat that much. Not really anymore. I try to exercise, but it don't do nothin . . . Don't matter, I guess. Just hard on my leg." Ben rubbed his face with his palms. "You think Frank's upset? That I never told him about Eric or anything?"

"Maybe," Marty answered. "He gets upset real easy—dunno if you can tell. But he shouldn't be upset with you. He'll be okay."

"He's a good dude."

"Yeah. Ya know"—Marty paused to take a drag—"I used to drive Tim's Jeep to work sometimes. My momma's boyfriend? He don't live with us, but he stays over so much it's like he does. When it'd storm, I'd drive his Jeep.

"Well, Frank lives kinda far from here. The days where his daddy don't come get him, he walks up the road to catch the bus, but that bus only comes every couple of hours. Like if he misses the bus around seven, he's waiting until ten—"

"That why he just bails sometimes?" Ben strained to say against the pain.

Marty nodded. "So one morning it's like the end of the goddamn world outside and I offer Frank a ride. Have to insist. Then he points me to the bus stop, and I'm like, 'Motherfucker, just tell me where your house is at.' Well, we get there. To the street anyhow. We get there, and Frank tries to give me twenty goddamn dollars. It's like four miles away. Wouldn't get out until I threatened to drive his ass back to the bus stop."

Ben smiled. "How come you ain't never driven me home when it storms?"

"Cuz Tim don't let me take his Jeep no more."

"What for?"

"How'd he put it? Oh, yeah. 'For drivin around a nigger.'" Still sitting on Ben's leg, Marty drew on his cigarette.

"Christ."

"Yeah, he's a real prize."

Ben rubbed his face with his palms. The grass beneath his head tickled his ears. "I called Missing Persons," Ben said after a while. "The day you told me you seen him . . . I need to know . . . I need to know if you're lyin to me, man, if this is some kinda joke or somethin . . . Because even though you been helping me, it makes sense. It makes sense to me that you did this."

Marty pulled on his cigarette. "I don't understand this, Ben. Any of it. This"—he gestured around himself—"ain't fun to me *at all.* You're about the last fuckin person in the world that I'd mess with. You're big as fuck. Plus we're friends. I don't got a lot of friends. But this accusin me of shit?" Marty shook his head and pointed at the flyers with his burning cigarette. "I don't know what this is. Maybe someone's got Eric and they're tryin to tell you something, but . . ."

"But what?"

"This don't look like help to me, man. This looks like *hate.* And I don't hate you."

Ben looked at the stack of flyers on Marty's lap and felt a warmth in his gut. "That mother*fucker,*" Ben said. "That toothless shithead."

"Who?"

"That tweaker *fuck*! Help me up. We're gonna go ask him how he's been spending his time lately."

"Who?"

"Ty Cotter."

22

By the time they reached Marty's neighborhood, Ben was practically dragging his leg. Clutching his stack of flyers, Ben winced and cursed.

"What're you gonna say to him?" Marty asked.

Ben huffed. "That I know what he's been doin. That I know what he done."

"I just don't see Ty goin around doin that. I don't see him goin around doin much of anything."

"You didn't hear him that day," Ben said. "You'll see. Watch how he is."

"I ain't goin to Ty's house with you," Marty said, stopping just before his own yard. "I don't fuck with Ty or any of the Cotters."

Ben dismissed Marty with a gesture and kept walking.

"And, dude," Marty said, catching up, "you don't tell him about me, you understand?"

"Tell him what?"

"Anything. Don't say nothin about me. Don't even say my name. *Listen.*" Marty grabbed Ben by the arm but failed to stop him. "We live here. Right next door. Police is over there all the time. I don't want any fucking attention from that man or Kell or even his goddamn little ones."

Again, Ben waved Marty away and kept walking.

"Ben!"

"Alright!" Ben replied without turning. He could hear the hollow thuds of Marty walking across his weathered porch.

"I'm glad he's gone," Ty Cotter had said. Ben could hear the nasally voice in his head. "I'm glad he's gone, you big fuck!" Ben clenched his jaw in anger. Why was Marty so desperate to avoid the man? Why was it suddenly so important that Ty Cotter not know they were friends?

A man waved from his seat on an upturned milk crate next to his truck. The engine sounded the same to Ben, but that didn't mean much of anything. Ben waved back, searching his mind for the man's name before giving up. He fished the graffitied flyer from his back pocket, wincing at the sight of the moonchild on his brother's face.

He pulled himself up the Cotters' rotted steps and slammed his fist against the door. Swallowing, he tried to control his breathing. The little scar-faced girl peered through the blinds. Each time he tried to collect his thoughts, they danced away. That was fine. Ty Cotter didn't deserve and likely wouldn't understand coherence anyway. Ben pounded on the door again and finally it opened.

"I need to talk to Ty," Ben said.

"What for?" replied Kell Cotter.

"He'll know what for." Ben held up the piece of paper so Kell could see it, but she only looked confused.

"No," Kell said uneasily. "I think you ought to leave."

"Let me talk to Ty and I will."

"I want you off my porch. You ain't got no business bein here."

"I got business. This how you handle things, Ty?" he shouted. "Hidin in the house?"

"Get the fuck on outta here," Kell snapped, pushing the door closed.

"You get that piece of shit out here right now, or I'm gonna come in there and get him!"

Ben felt something knock against his side. He looked toward the dull clattering sound near his feet and saw a plastic doll rocking against the old wood. In the yard, the small Cotter girl with the mangled face stuck her tongue out at Ben.

The door slammed shut in his face. Ben smacked it with his palm, then reluctantly hobbled back onto the grass.

Ben made his way across the orange road toward the rumbling truck. *Jacob.* That was his name. He didn't say anything, just gestured at the Cotter house with a puzzled expression.

"You know where he's at? He in there?"

"What do you want with Ty?"

"He did this." Ben held up the stack of flyers and tapped on the marred one on top. "He's been playing games with me and rippin my brother's flyers down. It took me a *month* to hang all them flyers."

Jacob nodded and seemed to consider Ben for a moment. "You mean this past month, I reckon?"

"Yeah."

The man pulled his dirty fingers through his beard, then spit on the ground beside his foot. "Sorry to say, but I think you got the wrong guy there, Ben." Jacob fixed Ben with a long look. "Ty's in jail, son."

The man seemed to wait for Ben to calm down and listen.

"You really riled him up when you came by. Heard him hollerin for two days until I guess Kell finally called the police. Came real late, around two a.m. He's been gone since. Safe bet is Ty failed his piss test, so he's gonna be there for a bit."

Ben looked at the flyer, then at the Cotter home. A breeze curled through the mangy trees.

"Shoot, have a seat and wait if you want, but he ain't in there."

"You heard what he said." Ben's voice cracked out of his trembling mouth. "You heard him. That he was glad."

"I did," Jacob said. "I heard. But whoever did *this*"—the man pointed at the paper—"it wasn't Ty Cotter."

Ben wanted to argue but had nothing to offer. Frustrated, Ben walked back onto the dirt road. When he turned to say something else to Jacob, he saw that the man had gone back into his home. Maybe Ty Cotter had friends. Maybe Kell—

"Psst."

Ben turned toward the sound. Peering into the copse next to the Cotter home, he watched and listened. When he couldn't find anything, Ben took a few more steps toward the neighborhood's exit.

"Pssssst."

Tucked behind the wild branches of a shrub was the small Cotter girl. Tentatively, Ben raised his hand just above his waist and waved, and the girl waved back. Then she flicked her wrist excitedly, signaling Ben over.

Ben glanced at the Cotter home, thought for a moment, then walked into the grass.

Her dirty-blond hair was draped down the sides of her face, almost completely obscuring the scar on her right cheek. She smiled at Ben and waved again.

"Hi," Ben said.

"Hi," she replied.

"My name's Ben."

"I'm Ellen."

Ben waited for a short while, and when it seemed like the girl had no more to say, he smiled and said, "Okay then," and turned to leave.

"My daddy said that you was the one who sent him to jail."

Ben stopped and looked at the little girl. "If that's true, I really didn't mean to."

"He said it when we seen him up there. You're that big fuck from before, right?"

Ben couldn't help but laugh. "I guess that's right. I didn't mean to send your daddy anywhere."

"It's okay." Ellen smiled. "He's always nicer when he gets back."

"Ellie!" another girl barked as she stepped out of the backyard.

This girl looked a lot like Ellen, even though she seemed a good deal older. Ben guessed that this was the other Cotter girl.

"Hi," Ben said, but the girl ignored him completely. She grabbed Ellen's arm and pulled, just like a big sister would.

"I ain't doin nothin!" Ellen protested.

"Shh!" the older girl hissed, pulling her back.

"Quit shushing me," Ellen snapped.

As she worked her arm out of her sister's grasp, her hair was brushed to the side, exposing the disfiguring scar: a swooping ridge that puckered her right cheek.

"Jessica!" Ellen wailed. She wrenched her arm free and brushed her hair to cover her cheek. She held it there like a bandage. Her eyes were wet. Jessica took a step back and looked mortified.

"It's okay," Ben said softly. Ellen glanced at her sister with uncertainty. "No, it's okay. I promise. Lots of people have scars. See?" Wincing, Ben lowered himself to his right knee and pulled up the left leg of his jeans. A red river of hardened skin carved a jagged line through his leg hair.

Ellen's hand fell from her face as she gawked. "Did it hurt?"

"Still does. It's even worse up here." Ben tapped his thigh. "Does yours hurt?"

"No. It feels okay."

"Alright, Ellie," Jessica said.

"How'd you get it?" Ellen asked, expertly ignoring her sibling.

"I had an accident when I was a little kid. Littler than you, even."

"Oh," Ellen said, considering Ben. "I got mine from a boy."

"Oh, no," Ben said. "Was it an accident too?"

"We gotta go, Ellie," the sister said.

"Everyone says so, but I don't think so." Ellen put her face close to Ben's and whispered, "Aaron's brother is a mean boy."

Ben leaned back and followed the line of Ellen's outstretched arm. She was pointing at the aluminum foil window. "Who, *Marty*?"

"No," Ellen said, walking backward as her sister pulled her toward the house. "The other one!"

Ellen waved and shouted a farewell to Ben, who replied so faintly the girl couldn't possibly have heard. Ben's eyes were fixed on the bright shine of the taut foil. There was a tightness in his stomach that he didn't understand.

And wuh-when he found it, he tried to be like it. But he couldn't. Nuh-now his knees were bad. His ssstomach. His chest. There weren't no muh-m-more room at all for nothin but bad.

So you know what he did to the guh-good thing he found?

He did bad things.

23

After a few days, Ben had made it to almost half the spots where he remembered posting flyers. More than forty were missing.

At home, each time he tried to draw in his sketchbook, he wound up doodling the symbol. Five strokes. Four curves and a line and there it was: a child dancing before a smiling moon. Jacob didn't recognize it. Clint didn't know what it was. No one seemed to. In middle school Ben had learned about hieroglyphs. He'd always wondered how people figured out that the symbols meant what the books said they did.

His shifts at work were mostly spent walking around the store, hoping it would show him something. When he arranged boxes and cans on the shelves, he'd sometimes push them aside to scrutinize a spot of rust that might have been something more.

When he was alone, he wandered the back room. Taking his time to ascend the metal steps, Ben walked the upper corridors and checked the few rooms that were unlocked. It felt like crawling into the attic of an enormous house and realizing that the world below hasn't stopped. Something might have happened while you were tucked away. Something might be waiting for you.

Of course, nothing ever was. If there had been, Ben would have shown it the symbol and asked it questions. He'd seen it before. Somewhere in or on the store, he'd seen it. He glanced at the copy he carried in his pocket so often it bordered on compulsion.

He walked the outside perimeter a few times. Both sides of the building were graffitied, but only with girlfriends' names and tags for imaginary gangs. When he was back inside, Ben would look at the symbol, doubt his eyes, and go back outside to check.

It didn't take long for Frank and Marty to notice. They helped, or at least they said they were. Ben couldn't tell whether they were looking for or just at things. It was tiring work. Even Ben sometimes zoned out as his eyes searched for something that might not even exist.

There was someone out there who knew more about what had happened than he did. Ben had always known that. But now that person had touched Ben. If all this was real, that person had grabbed Ben by his throat and screamed, *Look at all the things you don't know!* And Ben's imagination was not kind to him when he wondered what those things might be.

He knew that he wasn't on any kind of trail. Not really. If he'd first seen the symbol on a wall, then his journey would end at that wall. Marty seemed sure they'd find something, and Ben stayed close by while they looked. He glanced at Marty's face a lot. He wanted to be watching if Marty found the symbol, to see just how surprised his friend really was.

"The other one!" Ellen Cotter had said.

But Ellen was young, and children get confused about simple things. Marty was the one who suggested he and Frank help. And Marty seemed to search more doggedly than anyone. They were always mindful of the clock, though, stopping before they could hear the chimes and clattering of register tills, stopping even before they could smell fresh bread in the air. It was far too early for either of those things as they stocked the cereal aisle. And that's probably why none of the boys moved when they heard the scream.

Ben looked at Marty and Frank, who looked back with distressed uncertainty, until a loud crash shook them from their stupor.

Ben peered out from the end of the aisle. Nothing. He took a few cautious steps behind Marty, who was moving with the confidence of a much bigger man. Frank was in the party only in the sense that he followed in its general direction.

The sound had come from the front of the store. Ben could see that the doors were closed, that there was no sign of anyone at all. Marty stopped at Customer Service and stood on his toes as he leaned over the counter.

Ben kept walking until he reached the main doors. He tugged on the lock cylinder and they slid apart.

"It's *unlocked*?" Frank asked.

"It's always unlocked."

"Go on out there, Frank," Marty said. "See what you can find."

"Eat my ass."

Ben limped just a little behind Marty, who moved away from the doors and toward the bakery department. The area looked empty. Marty made his way behind the glass display in front of the counter.

"Oh, Jesus," Marty said.

"Don't say that," a weary voice replied.

Ben stepped behind Marty. Beverly lay slumped against the back of the counter, clutching her forearm. A dozen or so rolls were scattered on the floor.

"Ms. Beverly? You alright?" Marty asked.

"What happened?" Frank called, stretching his body as if he might see from his faraway vantage.

"Oh, I'm fine," the woman said with an embarrassed smile, a moderate tremor in her head. "After thirty some odd years, you'd think I wouldn't be so stupid. It's these damn shakes."

She moved her hand slightly to look at her arm. Ben knelt slowly so that he could pick up the steaming rolls and toss them onto the baking sheet by his knees. He glanced sidelong at Beverly and saw the red scalds on her arm mingling with bruises that never seemed to heal.

"Does it hurt?" Marty asked.

"No. Not yet, anyhow." She let out a timid laugh.

Marty supported the back of her forearm with his palm and examined the red streaks. She looked at Marty with soft, tender eyes.

"I'm alright," she said. She clasped his fingers in her trembling hand. "You really are an angel, boy. Thank you. I wish my oldest grandson was more like you." Her voice was calm and sincere.

"Can I get you anything?" Ben asked with a grunt as he struggled to his feet, his dark shirt covered with flakes of brown and white bread.

Beverly's eyes lingered on Marty's. A warm smile spread over her thin lips.

Ben adjusted his shirt away from his stomach. "Ms. Beverly?"

"Hmm?" she said. "No. No, I think I'll be alright."

Marty squeezed Beverly's hand a little tighter and stood, helping her up.

"I'll be just fine." She looked at Ben and then back at Marty.

"Go get some bandages, Frank," Marty said loudly. Frank nodded and hurried off into the store.

Ben grabbed a rag off the counter and picked up the now cool baking sheet. He slid the bread into the garbage can before setting the metal tray on the counter behind him. The three of them stood there for a moment.

"What're you doin here so early?" Marty asked.

"I haven't been getting my things done on time. Figured if I can't work faster, then I can just work earlier."

"You need any help?" Ben offered, looking around her department.

"No. Thank you, though. And I owe you an apology, Benjamin."

"What for?"

"My grandson. That night in the store. I *told* that boy he couldn't go out, but the way that one acts, you'd think no one ever let him do nothin at all." Her spotted hand shook along her forehead as she closed her eyes. "Got shook awake sometime after he left. Didn't even realize I wasn't dressed for leaving until after you did, I reckon. I just wish that I could open that boy's head up and shovel some sense in there sometimes. But he's my boy, so that makes it my fault.

"I'm sure you already went and told everybody about it," she added, and laughed. "But I never did say anything to you, and I should have."

"No, ma'am," Ben said. "You ain't got nothin to say sorry for."

"You should see the kinda hell my brother gives me," Marty said. "Sometimes you just gotta put the hurt on 'em, Bev." He smacked his palm with the back of his other hand.

" 'Bev,' " the woman echoed, and rolled her eyes.

"You sure you don't need anything?" Ben offered again.

"I am," she replied, shooing them away with a rag. "Go on and get back to work."

Just then, Frank emerged from the end of an aisle, jogging back toward the group with a box tucked under his elbow like a football. He handed the package to Marty, who studied it briefly before shoving it back into Frank's arms.

"These are fucking tiny-ass bunion bandages."

Frank shrugged.

"She sure seems to like you," Ben murmured to Marty. Frank trailed behind, reading the box.

"I guess so."

"You *guess*? She called you an angel."

"Yeah, but that's *true,* man."

For the rest of the night, Ben made sure to glance Beverly's way every so often to make sure she was okay. The woman moved slowly, humming as she worked. Ben asked Marty if he'd ever heard the tune before, but he shook his head.

It was still dark outside when the doors rattled and screeched open—too early for a cashier and way too early for Bill Palmer. But there he was. He didn't seem to notice Marty's sarcastic salute or how silly he looked bounding forward like a cartoon general. But the man was far from disengaged. Ben could see a sparkle somewhere in the bogs of Palmer's eyes. They almost seemed to dance when he told Frank and Marty to take a hike.

Marty glanced at Ben and then gestured toward the back. "Find me when you're done. I'm gonna go real slow, so I don't do all the work."

"Sorry," Ben said after Marty and Frank took their leave. "We was rotating some stuff to put the old dates in the back of the shelf."

Palmer wasn't listening. He seemed excited for his turn to speak. "When I hired you, I asked you if I knew you from somewhere. You remember me asking you that?"

Ben felt a rolling in his stomach, but that reaction wasn't all that uncommon whenever Palmer spoke. There was nothing objectively wrong with Bill Palmer's voice; it wasn't unpleasant in itself, but every word it intoned seemed to be.

He nodded.

"You said that I might have known you from around the store, from just shoppin. But I tell ya, it bugged the hell outta me every time I had to put your name on the schedule. *Where do I know him from?* Where *do I know him from?*

"Had you pegged as a shoplifter, but you weren't in my files—and believe me when I say that I looked through them files about fifty times. I didn't find nothin.

"But then," Palmer continued as he reached behind his back, "I found this."

He produced a piece of paper and unfolded it, studying it with his muddy eyes for a moment before abruptly jabbing it into Ben's chest. Ben pulled the piece of paper away from his body and looked at his brother's face.

"You're fired." Palmer said.

The creases were thoughtless and uneven, the paper dirty and wrinkled and torn.

"Where'd you get this?"

"You listenin to me? I don't know what you came back here for, but it's over. Clock out and get out."

"Okay," Ben replied. "But did you hear *me*? Where did you find this?" He turned the flyer so the man could see it.

Palmer reached for Ben's name tag, and Ben swatted his hand away.

"Get the fuck out of my store!"

"You can't fire me for *this,*" Ben shrieked, rattling the paper.

"Well, I'll be. A lawyer on the stock crew!"

There was a flash of heat at the base of Ben's skull, and he did everything he could to dowse it. He was fired. That was done. But there was still more of the store to check. Not much, but some. And if Ben couldn't restrain himself now, then whatever fleeting chance there was that Palmer would say where he got the flyer would be blown away on the wind of Ben's anger.

Ben could see Beverly looking out from the bakery. She held his gaze until he unclipped his name tag, ready to place it in Palmer's hand.

"Lemme—" His words clogged his throat; he cleared it with a grunt. "Lemme work through Christmas."

Palmer let out a loud laugh that died after one syllable.

"The trucks are real big until the end of the month. It's all Christmas stuff."

Palmer sighed. "You shouldn't have lied to get this job. You slow everyone down. Trucks ain't never finished anymore and I think that's because of you."

"You been watching me since I started," Ben muttered. "You know I been workin."

"You know I drove past the store one night. Saw you sittin outside, and I *did* watch you. I watched you sit out in that chair for two and a half hours. Not smoking or eatin. Just sitting and staring into the parking lot. I was watchin just to see how much time you was stealin, and then I was just watchin. That ain't just *slow.* That's . . . what *was* that?

"This place ain't no good for you, but more important to me, you ain't no good at all for it. You can finish out the *week,* and then that's it. I don't want to see you in here no more, even as a customer."

Bill Palmer turned, looking satisfied with himself, the fluorescent light shining on his poorly concealed bald spot.

"Mr. Palmer," Ben started, "can you just tell me where you got this?" He held up the flyer.

"I found it. It was just lyin on the floor."

Ben nodded and clipped his name tag back on to his shirt. He watched Palmer walk away and wondered if the man knew what a bad liar he was.

24

Ben woke up and stared at the red numbers on his clock. He didn't have to move to know that it would hurt. It was a lucky break that he was off tonight, though soon he'd be off every night. Strange as it was, Ben was relieved. Almost from his very first shift, it had felt like he would stay at the store forever, like almost every night for the rest of his life would be spent in a place that loomed so heavily over him he could barely breathe. It was hard not to embrace what had happened with Palmer. He hadn't left. He'd been kicked out. It was out of his control.

And his parents would be happy. After his last shift, he would tell them that he'd quit. For them.

He could hear their voices floating through the house. Clint did most of the talking. Ben listened for hours, until everything was quiet. Only then did he force himself out of bed.

Frank would be alone at the store tonight. Ben stood in his room holding his pants in his fists, still undecided.

Opening his door slowly, Ben stepped out into the black hall. Eric's room was empty. The bed was neatly made: sheets nicely tucked, the pillow round and uniform. It smelled cleaner in this room than it did in the rest of the house. Maybe it was. Or maybe it was just his imagination. Ben set his pants on the comforter and sat on the bed. Light flirted with the ribbons on the presents that encircled the room.

Tomorrow was his last night at the store. His last night working with Frank and Marty. His last night parsing lies and truth.

And that was the core of it all, wasn't it? If Ben just assumed that Marty was a liar—that he was not just a bad friend but a bad person—then everything fell right into place. If Ben could summon the energy, he could walk to the store and have a chat with Frank alone. Not about everything. Just about Marty. A nauseous tingle danced in Ben's stomach. Maybe Marty knew Bob Prewitt too. Hell, maybe they were related.

Ben ran his eyes over the green stars on Eric's ceiling as he pressed his head against the boy's pillow. Marty didn't have any love for Ty Cotter, never mentioned being related to him. Only love he seemed to have was for his brother. Ben tried not to think about Ellen Cotter.

Lightly, Ben tapped his knuckles on the wall behind his head.

Knock. Knock. Knock.

Ben could feel the pressure in the air change. Or maybe he'd heard something. The crack of a door down the hall. Naked feet sweeping against old carpet. Whatever it was, Ben moved as quickly and quietly as he could. Because someone was coming.

He hardly thought he'd fit, but he did, right between the wall and the bedframe. Gravity did most of the work. Ben sank as far down as he could, breathing lightly and peering through the narrow space between the bed and the floor.

The longer he waited, the stupider he felt. And there was the pain. He'd lain on his right side, but that didn't spare his bad leg entirely. The angle was wrong. Getting up was going to be rough. If he could just move his leg out a little, straighten it. But he couldn't. Not anymore. Because he could see Deidra's feet in the doorway.

She stepped into the room and then didn't move for a while. She was whispering something. Ben strained to make it out, but he couldn't. The hushed words continued as she moved toward the bed.

Ben's heart thundered in his ears. His pants. He'd left them on the bed. Deidra's feet turned away from him and the mattress squeaked under her weight. Biting his lip, Ben slipped his hand onto the comforter and felt for his clothes. He reached until his arm hurt. He had to be careful; he couldn't pull on the bedspread. There. Ben squeezed the jeans in his fist and inched them into his hiding place.

Deidra didn't notice. She seemed to be facing the hallway, still whispering. The bed creaked again as she stood up. She'd started humming. Ben watched her feet as they moved around the room, moved to Eric's shelves. It was only then that Ben noticed that his feet were extended past the edge of the bed. Gritting his teeth, Ben tried to tuck his legs in, but he couldn't. He placed his hand on the back of his bad leg and forced it to bend, rolling his face into the carpet, hoping that it might muffle any whimper that escaped his lips. The floor smelled dirty.

He moved his head and watched Deidra sit on the ground. Through the narrow opening, he could see only her legs and hands, and what she held.

The ribbon danced as Deidra gently shook the box. She placed it on the floor, unknotted the ribbon, then unwrapped the box without ripping the paper. From the box, she withdrew a toy robot and set it on the carpet, catching it when it nearly toppled. Still humming, she stood, walked to the shelf, and then sat down again with a new package.

Ben knew that he had lost the opportunity to leave the room. So he watched. He watched his stepmother first shake, then unwrap another gift, and then another, always setting the paper to the side before arranging the present in a very particular way: like it had a place it was supposed to go. Like this all had a *way* it was supposed to go.

A small box rattled as she shook it. Again, Deidra hummed her song and freed another gift, this time into the palm of her hand. She poked at whatever it was and then dumped it onto the carpet. Deidra sat there for a moment, then stood. As she turned back toward the shelf, she kicked the pile she had made, sending something skipping against the carpet until it landed right in front of Ben's face.

It was a tooth.

The next box Deidra brought down was bigger, heavy enough that she grunted as she lowered it to the ground. With the same gentle motions, the woman removed the ribbons and paper. Grunting again, Deidra reached into the large box and heaved the gift out.

Ben tried to scream but he couldn't, tried to get up but couldn't do that either. Even when he shut his eyes he could still see the limbless torso. Ashen and thin, it lay on the carpet just below the pile of teeth.

The metal bedframe rang out as Ben smacked his head against it.

Clang. Clang. Clang.

But Deidra didn't hear or didn't care. There were dozens of packages in the room. The night was still very young.

The next gift didn't have a box, and the wrapping was poor—poor enough that Ben could see the fingers sticking out of one end. Despite that, Deidra still took her time unwrapping it. She placed it next to the torso, paused, adjusted it slightly, and then stood.

On and on she hummed and sat and stood and retrieved and unwrapped and arranged. On and on Ben watched her perfect her project, still screaming, still shouting, still silent. He watched her build a boy.

The smell was overwhelming. Ben thought he could taste it, the sloughing skin, the wet bones. The rot of all things.

Eric's head wobbled as Deidra set it down. It didn't look like Eric, but of course it had to be. Its mouth was a pit. Blank eyes that now saw nothing. With her fingers on its chin, Deidra turned the head and dropped the small teeth into the endless black mouth.

"Smile big for me, sweetie," she said.

What if it moved? What if it *spoke*?

Ben could hardly even adjust his head now. He could hardly move at all.

"What's wrong with your smile, baby?" Deidra asked. "What happened to my beautiful boy? Something's missing," she snarled.

Deidra's hand thudded on the floor at the edge of the bed, then shot underneath it. Her fingers scraped and clawed at the carpet, raking for the tooth. Her breath became heavier and heavier as her hand moved closer to Ben's face. Her fingers shimmered even in this dark place, damp with what used to be her son.

"Something's missing," she hissed again. "Something's *gone*!"

Ben's ears rang. His mouth was dry. He panted and tried to swallow as he stared at the glowing neon stars above. He was still in Eric's bed. *I'm awake.* Over and over he repeated the thought until he believed it. Because although he was free from the dream, its feeling wouldn't leave him. Uneasily, he turned his head toward the door, knowing that Deidra would be standing there, staring with rage and disbelief. But there was no one, only the empty doorway.

Sitting up, Ben ran his hands over his face, then dried them on his shirt. He looked around the room at the colorful gifts tucked into the shadows against the wall. Standing, he limped toward the darkest corner. There really were dozens of them. Maybe it wasn't so strange. There was no grave to go visit.

Ben picked up a small box wrapped in newspaper. It was light. The ends of the ribbons that crossed it were curled like a pig's tail. He wanted to shake it. It felt like he actually might. What would he hear? he wondered. His hand began to tremble. Ben put the box back on the shelf.

25

"Talk about a sendoff," Marty said, cutting into the plastic that enveloped one of the pallets.

"This is like double," Ben moaned.

"Wish Palmer would fire *me,*" Frank muttered.

"We gotta make a bale," Marty said.

"It ain't that full," Frank objected.

"It's gonna be by the end of all this shit." Marty gestured to the roomful of towering pallets. "And you haven't vanished like goddamn black Batman yet—"

"I ain't gonna leave. It's Ben's last night."

"Oh, well, gee whiz. In that case . . ."

They set about downstacking the pallets. Ordinarily, they might have hauled them out of Receiving, but given their size and the fact that customers were still milling around the store, they thought better of it. Along with the usual stock, there were dozens of boxes of mashed potatoes, gravy, cornbread, and green beans.

"Got any Christmas dinner plans, Frank? Your daddy cookin again?" Ben asked.

"Yeah, boy," Frank answered, smiling. "Gonna bring this girl I been talking to."

"Yeah, boy," Marty mocked. "You mean that girl you chased through the parking lot? How long is your table that it can fit you two and that restraining order?"

"Don't be butthurt at me just because you're having Campbell's soup."

Marty huffed.

"You doin anything for real, Marty?" Ben asked.

"Supper of some kind, I reckon."

"You got any family comin in?"

"I hope not. They're liable to be mighty disappointed."

"So just Tim and Aaron and your momma?"

"Yup, the whole stupid gang."

Ben lifted some boxes from the towering pallet. "And that's everyone?"

"Yup," Marty said after a beat. "What're you, my fuckin biographer?"

Marty looked at Ben in annoyance. It was hard to tell if Ben had really seen it, but for just an instant he thought there'd been something else.

They didn't take any breaks. There just wasn't time. Despite his limp, Ben moved almost as quickly as Marty, or at least he tried. Even Frank was hustling, his glasses streaked and spotted from constant adjustment. It was never stated, but it seemed like each one of them was determined to finish the truck before the store opened, before Bill Palmer waddled inside, before Ben clocked out for the last time.

And they were going to. Stacking the cardboard next to the baler, they'd focused on throwing the truck. They were almost done with still a couple hours left before dawn.

When Ben walked into the back room with Marty, he saw Frank forcefully sliding his last piece of cardboard box into the overfilled baler. Frank saw them but tried to pretend that he hadn't, and he moved away from the machine.

"Nope!" Marty shouted. "Nope, nope, nope. You're livin the dream tonight, pal. You wanted to wait until the most fucked-up truck of all time—"

"I didn't know it was gonna be this bad!"

"And yet, it is! You can take a picture of *both* the bales we're gonna have to make, buddy. Show 'em to that girl."

Frank lowered the gate, forcing it past the cardboard that jutted out of the mouth of the baler. He squatted and lifted his legs, hanging from the handle like he was on a jungle gym, until the frame locked into place.

While Ben slid over an empty wooden pallet, Marty grabbed six of the eighth-inch metal wires and the long iron rod.

Ben pushed the green button on the panel that controlled the press, and the high-frequency groans of the slow piston disturbed the air. The thick metal slab descended, and the dry cardboard creaked and popped as its shape changed under the enormous pressure. When it stopped, Marty spun the lock-wheel to open the steel door, exposing the crushed cardboard and clogged tracks.

Marty went to work with the iron rod immediately, slamming it through the tracks like a small battering ram to clear a tunnel between the cardboard and the frame of the baler.

"Great fucking idea, Frank," Marty grunted. "Fucking A-plus planning."

Ben and Frank winced almost imperceptibly each time he'd clear the end of one of the metal gullies, but Marty had done this enough times that he knew the rhythm, and there was little risk of him splitting his knuckles on the metal frame.

When the tracks were cleared, Marty and Frank ran the wires, and then Marty tied them.

"Look at this shit," Marty said, gesturing to the metal knot and its limited slack. "This thing's gonna be a monster."

Ben wouldn't miss this place. Not one bit. But he'd miss Frank and Marty. In spite of everything, he knew he would.

"Alright, let 'er rip," Marty said.

Ben pushed and held the faded green button to restart the pneumatic press. As it raised, the small platform below moved with it, and the reformed cardboard monolith groaned as it flexed against the metal wires and began its slow ninety-degree pivot.

This machine Ben would also not miss. Old and stubborn, it seemed to have that effect on everyone who met it. Decades' worth of frustration and resentment were tattooed on the giant's chipping skin, undoubtedly directed squarely at the beast itself. SHITBOX, one read. FUCK YOU! said another. Well, maybe that one was for Bill Palmer.

And that wasn't all that strange, really. Because there was one for Ben too.

As the enormous brick was slowly heaved out of the baler, it began pushing the pallet away from the machine. Ben couldn't hear it sliding.

"Goddamnit!" Marty ran to anchor the pallet with his foot, as if he were trying to stop a soccer ball.

"Stop, Ben!" Frank yelled.

"If it rocks back, we'll never get it out of there!" Marty said. "Just stop when I say."

"Fuck that. Ben, shut it off!"

But Ben just stared—stared at the special message just for him: four curves and a line, a child dancing before a grinning moon. There it was, right there on the machine.

The protests from the bale rose an octave, and the cardboard bubbled past and engulfed the wire like clay through a chain-link fence. But the cardboard block wasn't moving.

"C'mon, you bitch," Marty grunted.

Ben thought the graffiti must be new. It had to be. But it wasn't. This hadn't been drawn onto the machine. The way it felt under Ben's fingertips, the lines had been carved all the way down to the metal, back and forth, like a broken Spirograph. There was rust. It was old.

Marty stepped onto the pallet and began shoving the block like it was a stingy vending machine. He fought against and rocked with the whining cardboard bale until their movements were longer and smoother.

"Okay, stop," Marty shouted.

The platform continued to rise slowly as Ben held the button, the bottom of the bale pivoting up the back of the machine.

"Stop!" Marty repeated. "Ben!"

Even as Marty shouted, Ben thought he saw the beginnings of a smile on his face. "Guys . . ." Ben said.

The heavy brick teetered on its edge, and Marty jumped off the pallet to get out of its way. But he didn't move fast enough. A sound like a gunshot echoed loudly off the walls. One of the six wires wagged in the air like an upside-down pendulum, the end jagged and twisted.

"Fuck!" Frank screamed as he rushed out from the side of the baler. "Oh shit!"

Ben stood frozen with his hand still faintly pressed against the control button, his eyes fixed on the image carved into the baler. He should have been looking up. When his mind finally returned, he saw the swaying cable. It didn't look like he expected it to.

"Ben!" yelled Frank.

It was the wrong color.

"Jesus, Ben! Help me goddamnit!"

It was too red.

26

Ben closed his eyes tightly, and when he opened them again, he was already moving toward Frank, who was crouched on the floor.

Crouched down over Marty.

Marty's chest heaved erratically. His eyes were wide and rolled wildly in his skull like two ball compasses. He had his hands pressed against his neck like he was trying to choke himself, and Ben could see blood seeping out between his fingers like a breaking dam. Frank floated his hands above Marty's throat frantically and indecisively while blood pooled next to Marty's head and soaked into the knees of Frank's pants.

"Help him!" Frank cried. "Fucking help him, man!"

A low gurgling noise rode the river of blood out of Marty's mouth, and he kicked and scraped his feet against the concrete floor as if he were trying to get away from what was happening, from what had already happened.

Ben took off his overshirt and shoved it into Frank's hands.

"We need to call an ambulance," Frank said, his voice unsteady.

"I know. Where's the first aid kit?"

"Huh?"

"The first aid kit! Where's it at?" Ben bellowed.

"I . . . I think it's somewhere upstairs. I don't know."

Ben took Frank's hands and guided them to press the shirt against Marty's throat. Marty's face was white, like all its color was collecting on the floor beneath him.

Ben ran for the double doors, turning around midstep but not stopping. "Talk to him, man! Don't let him fall asleep!"

Just before barreling through the double doors, Ben noticed a fire alarm affixed to the wall. His heart sped up, and he ran to it, plunging his fingers into the recess and violently ripping down the metal tab.

Nothing.

No! No! No! his mind roared.

Heaving the doors open, he screamed for help. Then he remembered they were all alone.

Ben burst back into Receiving. Marty was still moving, though less and less. Frank's face was twisted in fear. "Did you call someone? He needs help!"

The metal steps thundered under Ben's uneven steps. He tried to skip a stair and almost lost his footing. He ran along the narrow walkway. He knew which doors would be locked, but he still tried. One by one he tried them all.

And one by one he found them locked or cluttered with seemingly everything but what he needed. Crates of paper. Displays.

C'mon!

Ben ran farther down the curving hallway. Sweat poured down his face and back, and his breath stuck in his dry throat. There was a stabbing pain in his side. Ben pressed his palms against his knees and stole more time than he knew he should. If he could just get his breathing to slow, maybe his heart would too. He concentrated on that as he glared at the end of the hallway. There was only one door in this area. No one had called for help yet. Frank needed bandages. Gauze. What a waste of time.

Slowly, Ben groped his way along the wall. There was no keyhole in the handle, and Ben's stomach tingled when he twisted the doorknob and felt it move. But it wouldn't open. He hurled his large body against the door again and again, but it wouldn't budge.

Frank was calling for him, though his voice was muffled and weak by the time it traveled from downstairs to Ben's ears.

Ben's eyes and nose were wet. He kicked the door hard—hard enough that it seemed to give just a hair, but that might have been his leg buckling. Ben moved back down the corridor.

Back among the other rooms, he picked a door at what felt like random and kicked it, striking the doorknob, which punched right through the cheap wood. Ben tumbled inside.

There was a phone on the desk. Ben lunged for it and pounded in 911. He spoke quickly. Too quickly. He repeated himself and then did it again, despite not being prompted. He rifled frantically through all the drawers of Palmer's desk, throwing papers onto the floor. The phone said that an ambulance was en route and to stay on the line. He hung up. Turning toward the filing cabinet in the corner, he shot a quick glance over the old TV monitors and out the window of the crow's nest, hoping he might see red lights flashing through the glass, but it was way too soon for that.

It's okay, his mind pleaded. *He'll be okay.*

The top two drawers of the filing cabinet were locked together and would hardly move at all, despite how hard Ben pulled. But the bottom drawer would.

Ben wrenched it open and plunged his hands into the clutter. "Fuck," he spat as his hands scrambled over things he didn't need. Paperwork. Videotapes. A half-empty bag of chips. Ben cursed again. Tears pricked at his eyes. "C'mon, goddamnit!" He almost couldn't believe his eyes when he saw the plastic box.

"Yes!" Ben screamed, snatching the first aid kit. He hurled the wrecked door free from his path and ran—ran faster than he had ever run—ignoring everything his leg was telling him. The sound of his footsteps clattered with an uneven rhythm, echoing off the narrow walls of the corridor. Free from the chambered hallway, he looked over the railing.

Marty wasn't moving anymore. His feet weren't kicking. His arms lay limp and useless on his still chest. Frank still knelt behind his head, leaning over Marty.

"Here!" Ben shouted, and flung the first aid kit from the second story. It smashed against the ground, sending its contents skidding across the concrete. "Help is coming!"

Ben limped down the stairs.

"Marty?" Ben's voice cracked. But Marty didn't answer. His face was white and lifeless.

Frank held a roll of gauze in his shaking hands. The shirt he'd wrapped around Marty's throat had soaked up a lot of blood.

"I don't know how to do this," Frank whimpered. The fabric sagged impotently. It was a sponge and nothing more, nothing that would help.

Ben tried to tighten the slack and Marty's head slumped. Frank made a noise like a nest of cockroaches had just scurried over his hands. Leaning, Ben lowered his ear to Marty's chest, but he couldn't hear Marty's heartbeat over his own. Ben left his head there so he could pretend he was doing something. After about a minute he sat up.

Frank and Ben sat silently. Ben tried to find a pulse in Marty's wrist but wasn't sure if he was feeling in the right spot. Frank held Marty's head in his lap. Marty's chin was red with blood and slouched against his chest. The rest of the boy's face had no color at all. The baler hissed, its pneumatics resetting.

They waited for what felt like much too long before the Receiving doors burst inward.

Two men rushed into the room. Before Ben could say anything, the EMTs were shooing Frank and Ben away. They issued commands to each other that Ben didn't understand.

Frank had scooted backward. Now he sat awkwardly on the floor, wiping the blood from his hands onto his pants with a lightless look in his eyes.

"Is he alive?" Ben asked the paramedics. The men continued talking between themselves, frantically swarming around and over Marty. Finally, they lifted his body and placed it on a gurney. They hurried back through the swinging doors. Once again Ben and Frank were alone.

"He's gonna be alright," Ben said. Frank didn't reply.

Ben felt his vision blur as he stared at the baler. The red-tipped wire was still. Whatever menace Ben thought he might have felt was gone, like it had been discharged.

Legs shaking, he walked toward the machine. He moved his fingers over the symbol that had been carved into the metal, relieved and nauseated that he hadn't imagined it. Then he let his feet carry him out of the back room.

There were no flashing lights. The ambulance was long gone. That was a good thing. It had all happened so quickly that Ben couldn't quite shake the feeling that the paramedics had never come at all. That Marty was still back there on the floor. Had Ben even called for help? What were they supposed to do now? Finish the truck? Ben looked at his feet, looked at the blood he'd tracked onto the tile. He followed the trail back through the double doors.

Frank hadn't moved. Still sitting on his feet, he rested the backs of his hands on his thighs. He seemed to be staring at the blood that shimmered on the concrete. At the edge of the dark pool was a Zippo. It must have fallen out of Marty's pocket while he kicked. Ben slid it away from the mess with his foot, then picked it up. He wiped it against his pants, then tucked it into his pocket.

"Are you okay?" Ben asked. Frank nodded.

It took just a few more minutes for the police to arrive. A deputy by the name of Green confirmed that Marty had been taken to the hospital, but he couldn't or wouldn't comment on his condition. Green didn't do much of anything. He seemed to be waiting for someone, and it wasn't long before Ben saw who.

One of the doors swept inward, and Lieutenant James Duchaine walked into the room. He shot Ben a passing glance, then turned to his deputy. They exchanged quiet words.

Duchaine's black boots clunked against the hard floor as he walked. "You okay, son?" he asked Frank. He repeated himself when Frank didn't answer, then asked Frank his name, asked him if he knew Bill Palmer's phone number.

"Nosir . . . but it's wrote down on a sheet somewhere in Customer Service."

"Okay, that's good. Can you stand? Why don't you go with Deputy Green here and get it? Someone's gonna have to give him a call."

"I don't want to."

Duchaine squatted in order to move closer to Frank. He tried to coax him away from the blood. Out of the room. Back to coherence. Turning his head to meet Ben's gaze, Duchaine asked for help in getting Frank to his feet. He began asking about the accident, directing most of his questions to Frank but accepting answers from Ben when they weren't forthcoming.

Even though Ben could see the value in what the man was doing, watching Duchaine deviate from the usual script of their short conversations made his jaw clench. Duchaine seemed engaged now. It seemed like he cared, like Ben wasn't wasting his time. He kept asking about the accident, about how the wire snapped. Had it ever snapped before? Where was Marty standing? Where was everyone else? He seemed so *interested.* Ben looked to Frank, but Frank could only shrug his shoulders while tears welled in his eyes.

Ben tried to respond intelligently to Duchaine's inquiries, but all he managed to mutter was that a wire broke, which the officer already knew. What more was there to say? Why was Duchaine so engrossed in an industrial accident, of all things? The officer rephrased his question, and the sides of his lips turned up. For all Ben knew, the smile was meant to be comforting, but suddenly Ben was picturing Duchaine's office, picturing that same stupid and handsome grin on the other end of the phone. Ben could hear him chuckling. *Call from* who? *About* Eric? He felt words filling up his own mouth like vomit.

"Son," Duchaine huffed in annoyance, "I just need you to answer my questions so we can figure out exactly what happened here."

"Wouldn't *that* be somethin," Ben snapped.

Duchaine flashed another, now vaguely frustrated smile and tapped pen to pad. He was silent for a moment before continuing. "We can talk about Eric. I got no problem with that at all. But first we need to talk about *that.*" He pointed to the blood that still glistened on the concrete floor. Ben turned but quickly looked away.

Duchaine waited another moment, then added quietly, "Everyone's gonna say this lands on you boys. That this wasn't on them or their equipment. Bill Palmer's gonna blame you three. If he blames the machine, then whoever made that thing is gonna blame the three of you. The company that owns this store is gonna blame you. The maker of them wires is gonna be pointing at whoever tied it. Do you see what I'm sayin? No matter what, this is gonna bounce back. It always does.

"I need this all wrote down in its full account. You understand? So that when it *does* bounce back there's a piece of paper sayin, 'Nosir, this ain't on them boys.'" Duchaine lowered his voice and asked, "You wanna tell me off, or you wanna help your friend?"

Ben answered Duchaine's questions. Some of them seemed the same as earlier questions, just phrased a bit differently. But Ben still answered. Deputy Green walked Frank out of the room, presumably down to Customer Service to locate Palmer's phone number.

"Now, you were sayin something about some markings?" Duchaine asked.

Ben walked the man over to the machine and gestured at the symbol scraped into its side. "That mean anything to you?" he asked.

Duchaine leaned forward and seemed to study the shape intently. "It mean anything to *you*?"

Ben shook his head.

"Was you lookin at this when the accident happened? Distracted?"

"No. Nosir," Ben said, butterflies in his gut. "No, I seen it sometime before."

"So it's got nothin to do with what happened here then." Duchaine grunted. "Ben, whatever you might think of me or the kind of job I do," he said, turning back toward the markings, "I can't do it very well if people don't talk to me."

Ben didn't respond.

"Anyway," Duchaine said, standing straight, "from what you've told me here, everything with this machine and that bale went normal and then the wire just popped. That sound accurate to you?"

Frank reentered the room, and the officer escorting him nodded to Duchaine. Frank looked lost. Blood was caked on his hands like a dry riverbed, and some had smeared on his face and glasses.

"Green, make sure to get pictures of that wire, wouldja?" Duchaine said. "The wire and the sides of the machine. Close so you can see all the drawings and such."

"It didn't have nothin to do with . . . The wire just popped," Ben said to Duchaine. The camera flash burst as Green took his pictures.

Ten minutes later, Bill Palmer stormed through the double doors. Ben watched as he made what appeared to be casual conversation with Duchaine. How nice. Maybe they could become friends. Palmer shook his head when Duchaine pointed toward the camera nestled in the far corner of the room. The metal steps sang as Palmer ascended them as rapidly as his portly body could manage. He hardly even looked at Ben, and when he did, it was with annoyance, not worry or remorse.

Duchaine and Green talked quietly off to the side. Ben tried to speak to Frank, but it was no use. So they just stood there until Palmer lumbered back down the stairs, his eyes trained on Ben.

"We'll fax you a copy of the police report," Green said to Palmer as he approached.

"The fax machine hasn't worked for two years. You can bring it to me yourself." Palmer grabbed Ben's elbow as he tried to move away. "There are bandages in front of the pharmacy."

Ben tore his arm out of Palmer's grasp, annoyed and embarrassed.

"Hey," Palmer spat. Then the thought seemed to leave his mind as he grimaced. "Jesus, what the fuck is that *smell.*"

The man followed Ben's eyeline to the damages shelves.

"What happened?" a voice cried. Beverly shuffled toward the group. "What happened here?"

Ben shifted past her and pushed his way through the swinging doors. The time clock rattled as Ben slid his card crooked into the slot, printing the time illegibly along a line. So Ben pushed it in again. Then again. Over and over, until the card was mangled and unreadable, Ben's knuckles red. He let the gnarled card fall to the ground.

A frail hand gripped Ben's arm. "Is he okay?" Beverly asked.

"I don't know," Ben said a little too forcefully. "No. Probably not."

"Well, did you see him?"

"Yeah," Ben said harshly, exposing the red-stained palms of his hands to the woman, "I seen him. And he didn't look okay to me. I dunno. I guess it depends on what the big grand plan is."

A pained smile moved across her mouth, and as her cheeks contracted, they seemed to squeeze tears out of the corners of her milky eyes. "I reckon it does." Beverly turned and walked deeper into the store.

Outside, the black sky had only just begun to give way to daylight. To Ben's right, Frank sat quietly in one of the plastic chairs.

"If we'd have made a bale before, when Marty said. Even the other day . . ."

"This ain't cuz of you," Ben said. "I . . . it was my fault. I wasn't payin attention. I saw . . . I should've . . . I kept holdin the button down."

"He wasn't breathin. He wasn't movin at all, man. What took you so long up there?" Frank tried to scratch some of the blood off his glasses with his fingernail and then gave up. "I'm gonna catch the six fifteen up to the hospital."

Ben checked his watch. "My pop will be driving by 'fore long. He won't know what to make of all this. You can ride with us."

"That's okay," Frank said, standing. "I ain't in no kinda hurry now."

"I'm sorry that it took me so long. I moved as fast as I could, faster when I heard you hollerin."

"Hollerin?" Frank turned his head, his eyes squinting with uncertainty.

"When I was upstairs."

Frank shook his head softly as he pushed his glasses up his nose. "I don't think I did."

Ben was going to argue the point, but instead he watched Frank walk away. Flashes from the previous hours kept looping in Ben's brain. He couldn't stop seeing Marty's face. But Ben had seen other things, hadn't he? Things seen in a blur as he tore through Palmer's office. Things that hadn't truly registered until he could spare the attention.

When Ben asked if he could watch the other security tapes, Bill Palmer said there weren't any.

So why were there tapes in his filing cabinet?

And what was on them?

PART THREE

The Rot of All Things

27

Ben hung up the phone and turned toward his closet. Tucked back on the top shelf was a suitcase. It had been given to him by his grandfather when Ben was just a boy. The maroon leather was dark and smooth, bound to the stiff shell by a line of brass rivets that were only visible if the case was open and elevated. When it was new, the matching interior hinges were so polished and shiny they seemed to emit their own light.

Ben's grandfather had purchased the three-piece set from Montgomery Ward for eighty dollars in 1949. It was a gift to Ben's grandmother, meant to symbolize that they were finished moving on the military's itinerary. These were their bags; where and when they went was wholly up to them now.

The pieces fit inside one another like nesting dolls, and when the couple came to visit Ben and his mother and father, for whatever reason children take to things, Ben took to the matching suitcases. At least once a day, they'd find Ben in their room playing with the brass draw bolts, amazed at how, with just one tease of the latch, the loop would become free and the trunk would spring open.

When they returned the next year, Ben's grandfather brought the third part of the set. Identical in design to the other two pieces, this one was much smaller, only a little bit bigger than a shoe box. Ben's eyes lit up when he saw it, and he immediately set to finding things of his to pack in it. For a while, he brought the suitcase with him on any outings the family took, full of all the necessary toys and crayons to get him through the day.

As the years wore on, Ben's grandparents visited less and less, until they hardly came at all anymore. Each year was *the* year, each holiday *the* holiday, but they never came. Finally, and to Ben's astonishment, he and his baby brother were getting in the car and going to see *them,* even though it wasn't a holiday. It was supposed to be a surprise.

Ben tried to get Eric excited about meeting his grandparents, but the boy had no reference for what grandparents were. They played slaps in the backseat while their parents murmured to each other in the front. The rest of the long drive was passed with quiet dreams.

When they arrived, the fighting began almost immediately. Ben's father exchanged shouts with his own father, while Deidra tended to the horrible state of disrepair the home had fallen into. Ben saw his grandmother only once that trip. She lay supine in bed, frail and broken, already half a ghost. Ben didn't understand. She'd been sick for so long, it was just a part of who she was. Before Ben left, he told her that he hoped she felt better soon.

The next time Ben saw his grandmother was just a few weeks later. She looked more peaceful then, sleeping on white sheets, surrounded by the flowers arranged around her casket. There were no more tremors, no more moans. Ben was sad but didn't cry. Before they left the funeral home, Ben's grandfather led him to his car. It was a quiet walk. His grandfather eased open the trunk.

"I want you to have this," he said.

The leather on the suitcase was still as smooth and rich as that on the miniature version Ben had at home. The brass closures were untarnished by use. Ben tried to refuse, but his grandfather simply said, "A suitcase can help you get to where you're going, but only you can decide where that is, no one else."

The two hugged, and Ben realized that he'd get the third piece of the set one day. He could only think of how much he didn't want it now. It felt so heavy in his hand, too heavy for him to carry.

A month later, his grandfather died.

Eric had bounced around the room as Ben arranged his funeral clothes on the bed. With a heavy sigh, he pulled the dark leather case from his closet and set it beside his folded shirt and suit jacket. He released the latches for the first time since they'd become his. When the lid glided open, Ben could see why the suitcase had been so heavy: there was another one inside it. Sitting on his floor with his back against the mattress, he cried for the first time in years. Not so much for the deaths of his grandparents, but at the thought of a man who knew he wouldn't need a suitcase anymore.

Ben put the two larger suitcases back in the closet unused and never touched them again. The small one, however—the one that Ben truly felt was his—sat tucked away on the top shelf.

Even as Ben got older, the most prized possession of his childhood remained the home for everything he held dear. There were two smooth stones that he had taken from the creek when he and his father went fishing, only to spend most of the time skipping rocks atop the barren water. There was a note that his first and only girlfriend had written him, full of salacious flirtations in the awkward phrasing of inexperience. Some Garbage Pail Kids cards. A silver dollar. The family photo scraps from Eric's flyer photograph. There were even some trinkets in the suitcase that Ben kept even though he was no longer sure why they were in there. He figured he had nothing to lose by holding on to them in case he remembered one day.

For a week Ben carried Marty's lighter in his pocket, as if his friend might just show up to reclaim it. With the suitcase sitting on the edge of his bed, Ben held the lighter in his hand for a moment, before tossing it inside his maroon treasure box. Then, without any thought at all, he plucked up Eric's defaced flyer and slipped it into his pocket.

A shadow swept across the wall and Ben closed the lid to his secret box. His father stood in the doorway holding two boxes of candles, weighing them as if his hands were scale platters. Somehow, Ben had forgotten that Eric's birthday was in two days. He smiled like he was happy.

He k-kept crawlin and tryin, cuh-

crawlin and tryin, until there weren't

hardly no more good things left at all.

But there was still one more

guh-good thing, and he knew it.

Suh-somehow, he knew it.

28

The weather was turning. Never snowing but sometimes freezing, the cold was coming more quickly than normal for a Florida December. The chill felt nice in Ben's lungs as he walked to the store.

Frank had finally quit. For the first time, he'd resigned officially, citing higher wages up the road. Ben had just stood there and watched it happen. He wanted to talk him out of it. Hell, he wanted to leave in his place, but he'd done neither. Regardless of what Frank said, he wasn't leaving for better pay. Ben was sure of that.

Every time Ben saw Bill Palmer, his eyes looked more swollen and tired, but they had a lot more looking to do if they were going to find someone to replace the kid who'd had his throat torn out doing the very job they'd be putting in for. Palmer had granted Ben a reprieve, if it could be called that. It was an act of desperation. Ben was all Palmer had, and neither man seemed to relish that fact.

Palmer wouldn't stop threatening to take the cost of his office door out of Ben's paycheck. And each time they talked about anything at all, Palmer found a way to mention the mountain of applications he had for prospective hires, but it had been a week since the accident, and Ben's name was still alone on the schedule. It wasn't all a bluff, though. Ben knew that as soon as Palmer could, he'd cut Ben loose.

So Ben didn't have much time to waste if he wanted to see what was on those tapes.

The doors slid open with their expected graceless rumblings. Chelsea stood solemnly behind her register, her face still beautiful but now fixed with an expression of restless confinement, like an animal standing at cage doors she hoped might open at any moment. That same atmosphere loomed like low clouds over anyone who punched a clock there, their eyes searching for a way out of the fog caused by what happened to Marty.

After pulling the pallets onto the main floor, Ben worked the damages while he waited for the store to close. After enduring the smell the morning of the accident, Palmer would just not shut the fuck up about it. So every couple days, Ben would haul soggy boxes and dented cans into the bathroom to wash them off, so they could be scanned against inventory.

On his fourth trip to the sink, the bottom of the cardboard box gave way just in front of the exit into the store. Ben jumped backward as glass shattered and rancid mayonnaise splattered near his shoes. Holding air in his lungs, Ben squatted and picked the larger shards of glass out of the sludge. The air conditioner banged and roared to life. Sliding the box aside with his foot, Ben stepped away from the curdled puddle and leaned against the wall. He pulled his kerchief down under his chin and checked his watch. *Close enough,* he thought.

Ben climbed the iron steps. For a few months, the store had been transformed in Ben's mind from a permanent reminder of the pain he had caused to a place where he might find . . . what? Peace? Redemption? Had that been what he was looking for? How stupid.

Well, he was free to look for whatever he wanted to now, not that he knew what that was. He'd found the symbol right where he should have expected to find it. Right on the side of that cruel machine. A beacon shining sickly in dull rust amid ancient green, calling out to bad people and bad things, calling them home to a store that wasn't a store at all. A cruel, laughing void. An echo chamber where the devil once spoke.

More than any part of the store, Ben hated the upstairs. More than the freezer or the air conditioner. More even than the baler. It might have just been the narrow, dark hall lined with all those locked doors, but it didn't feel like that's all it was. The whole area reeked of Palmer, reeked of the man who never fixed his cameras, who fired Ben for being the brother of a stolen boy. Who lied about tapes.

Gently, Ben pushed aside Palmer's crumpled and sagging door. The office was dark, but Ben could still see enough to navigate, thanks to the light pouring in through Palmer's voyeur windows and the deli cam TV.

Chelsea's voice sounded over the intercom. Ben watched her through the window. Occasionally, she'd look around as she counted down her till. He waited for her to leave the store.

The filing cabinet rattled as Ben pulled on the bottom drawer. Ben squinted and tried to move his body out of the light, only to see what he had expected to see: that Palmer had moved the tapes. Ben sighed through his nose and almost shut the drawer, then he slipped his hand inside. He twisted and bent his wrist like he was digging in a raffle bucket. Papers. Magazines. The same bag of old chips. A pair of Pop-Tarts. An action figure.

A tape.

Ben's heart fluttered. The plastic spools clattered as he pulled the tape free from the drawer. "Fuck," he whispered. He put his hand back inside and dug until he was sure he'd touched everything.

There were three tapes.

He held them up to the light. He wasn't sure what he expected to find on them. There wouldn't be a label that said I'M A LYING FUCK #1, but there weren't any labels at all. How long would it have taken to slip the flyer into Ben's locker? How long would it take Ben to find that sequence within days of footage crammed into three six-hour tapes?

"Fuck," he whispered again. He should have brought a VCR. He couldn't take the tapes home, could he? No, that would be a mistake. Could he wait? Bring a VCR in tomorrow? He could see the tapes weren't rewound—the spools were all encumbered differently. Maybe Ben wouldn't need to do much looking.

Ben punched the eject button on the VCR for the break-room camera, forcing himself to commit. He powered on the monitor and slipped in the first tape.

The time stamp on the grainy video said that Ben was watching footage of the break room from three years before. There was only one person in the frame. An employee standing in the corner of the room with her hands over her face. Doing what? Laughing? No. When she moved her hands, Ben could see that she was crying, and suddenly he forgot why he'd started watching the tape in the first place.

The tape whirred backward and choppy blobs poured into the room. Ben waited a few more seconds and then pushed play.

Seven people were in the room now. They moved around unsteadily on the tape, talking, preparing food or eating it, some just avoiding work. Ben could see the girl who'd be crying soon standing near the microwave. He watched the seconds tick by on the counter.

This tape had nothing to do with anything that concerned Ben, but he couldn't help himself. He didn't want to know what distressed the woman, but he did want to know why Palmer cared.

Another employee entered the room, and before Ben could comprehend what he was seeing, the newcomer struck one of his coworkers in the back of the head. There was no reaction from the victim. He slumped over onto the floor and out of frame. Two people left the room; the others stayed while the beating continued. The quality of the tape and the recording speed made the assailant's arms look like wings as he swung his fists repeatedly into the person beneath him. Finally, the guy grabbed a chair and brought it down with tremendous force. The attacker left and so did his audience, all except for the crying woman and the beaten man, who must have been lying out of frame when Ben first started the tape.

Ben jabbed the eject button. He'd forgotten to note the time the tape started. His heart was thundering. He turned quickly to face the door. There had been a noise. Or maybe not. He stood and looked out into the store.

Ben picked up another tape and let it rest halfway in the mouth of the VCR for a while before he slid it in completely. His throat was dry. He pressed play and noted the time.

A dark-haired woman in a floral dress stood in front of the deli cooler six years ago. Ben was just about to rewind the tape when a man in a checkered shirt appeared at the far end of the frame. He moved slowly, parallel to the cooler, and as the frames flickered by, it was clear that the man wasn't just walking in the woman's direction. He was walking toward her. Ben's palms began sweating. He wanted to stop the tape, but instead he watched the man. He was very close now. The woman still had time, if she started moving. But she didn't move. Where the fuck was everyone else? *Anyone* else?

The man approached the customer from behind and slid his hands over her stomach. Ben winced at his own expectations, but the woman didn't fight. Instead, she leaned back into him. They seemed to know each other.

She looked around as the guy slipped his hand down from her stomach and up the front of her dress. Though the image was distorted, Ben could see the woman smile for a few frames before she craned her head back and kissed him, could see that she was grinding her hips against him.

Suddenly, the couple parted and scurried away from the camera's gaze. A few frames later, an employee was standing where they had been.

Ben rewound the tape. He understood why Palmer would have it. He supposed he understood why he had the other. But Palmer had them both. And there was something about that, something about the presence of them together—unmarked and uncataloged here in this place—that made Ben want to leave.

The VCR hummed as it swallowed the third tape. Ben noted the time and—

"Oh my God," Ben said. "Oh my God."

Two customers stood in front of the poultry section five years ago. Twenty minutes before the last time Ben saw Eric.

"Oh, Jesus," Ben said through his hand. He turned to look at the door, then faced the screen. A family at the cooler walked down an aisle and was replaced by other meandering customers.

Ben cupped his elbows and slouched forward, as if he could somehow make himself so small he'd disappear. Minutes ticked by on the counter. A man with a beard picked up a steak, put it back, then picked up a different one. It was Bobby Prewitt.

Another customer came to shop the same section, and the two talked for a while. The man left, and Prewitt turned back toward the cooler, swapping his steak again. Then he walked out of frame.

The aisle was dead now. Ben watched the clock. He knew what he was seeing before the tape did, when the image was still mangled and unclean. Ben watched himself materialize on the tape, holding Eric's hand. They were on their way to the bathroom.

"Oh, fuck," Ben sobbed. "Oh, jeez." Eric looked so small next to Ben. Even as they got closer, Ben couldn't see his brother's face, couldn't see his own for that matter. They walked side by side, Eric trailing just a little behind. The boy stopped at the cooler to scrape ice from its rim. Stampie was tucked under his arm.

Eric lurched forward. Ben flinched as he watched the tape, watched himself pull Eric so hard the boy almost fell over. There was a sick feeling in Ben's throat. And then Ben did it again for no reason at all. Eric pulled back. Not toward the cooler. Maybe not even to defy Ben. He turned in such a way that it was almost like he was hiding Stampie. Protecting him.

"What the fuck?" Ben whimpered. He watched his past self drag Eric out of frame. Ben stood in front of the monitor. His legs were shaking. His whole body was shaking. Gripping his head in his hands, he stared at the screen, stared until he could see himself again. Panicked. Frantic. Alone. "What the fuck?!" he whimpered. "That's not what happened! What the fuck did you *do*?"

He jammed his finger hard enough into the VCR that the monitor rocked backward. His hands trembled as he snatched the tape from the machine. He collected the others and threw them back in the filing cabinet, slamming the door.

29

Ben stocked what he could, but most of the truck would still be sitting on pallets by the time the store opened. The bag boys would throw the rest, or Ben would finish when he came back in half a day. It didn't matter.

No matter how he tried, Ben couldn't get the grainy image of Eric's tape out of his head. He could still see the choppy movements of his baby brother, the fuzzy frown on the blown-out picture as Ben jerked and yanked on Eric's small arm. It hadn't happened like that. Again and again, Ben returned to that day in his mind. He tried to imagine it even as a hypothetical, and he failed. Because that tape wasn't real.

As impossible as that was, it was the only explanation that made any sense. Standing there in the baking aisle, Ben could remember all sorts of things. See Clint, he brought home a chocolate cake every year for Eric's birthday, but that was wrong. Eric liked *yellow* cake. Everyone else had forgotten that, but not Ben. And if he could remember *that,* then he sure as shit could remember the worst day of his life.

Staring at the boxes of chocolate cake and containers of fudge frosting, Ben knew he wasn't going to be able to choose. Every option was wrong. Someone else could decide, then. Someone else could think about cakes and birthday parties. When Ben left the aisle his legs were stiff, as if he'd been standing there for ages.

Ben walked back into Receiving, again stepping over the mayonnaise. The jar had exploded like a rotten bomb, and Ben had left most of the cleaning supplies in the bathroom on the other side of this moat. He could use a mop, but then he'd have to clean the bucket and the mop itself. Maybe the dustpan or the broom. He could scrape up the mayonnaise like spackling paste—

Ben stopped thinking about cleaning the mess when he saw the pattern stamped into its outer edge. Ben's face puckered as he moved around the sour puddle. It was only a sliver, but it was there, right on the rim. Geometric and alien: the zigzagging hills and accompanying valleys of a shoe print.

Puzzled, Ben stared blankly at the lines, pressing his lips together in befuddlement before walking away. He took only a few steps before returning. Bracing himself against the wall with his hand, Ben winced as he tried to bend his weak leg across his locked knee, stopping when the pain became too much to bear.

With a groan, the heater wound down, and Ben stepped toward the puddle. He tapped his fingers against his leg and looked around as if someone might confirm just how foolish he was. Taking great care, he pressed his foot into the mayonnaise, which rolled like mud from under his shoe. Withdrawing it slowly, Ben felt a fluttering in his stomach. He backed up and leaned against the wall, trying to rub the prickling sensation off the back of his neck. But he could feel it spreading to his whole body. The treads didn't match.

He looked for a long time—longer than he needed to—trying to make them the same print in his mind. The doors swung inward, and Ben's body jolted. Bill Palmer cursed as he nearly barreled into Ben.

"Godfuckingdamnit!" Ben shouted.

Palmer looked at Ben in disbelief, then yelled for Ben to clean up the mess. He tried to shake the mayonnaise off his shoe, then cursed again and climbed the iron stairs, disappearing down the catwalk.

There were no more patterns to look at, only streaks and smears. The heater whirred back to life, and Ben walked back into the store.

Ben kept stocking the shelves until he finally caught sight of Beverly in her department. A little late today, she hurriedly ran a serrated knife through a warm loaf of rye. Ben watched how easily the blade moved through the steaming bread.

"Chocolate, hmm?"

"Yes, ma'am."

"This for a birthday?" Her eyes moved up to Ben's as she continued sawing the bread.

"Yes, ma'am," he said again, nervous that his eyes were now the only ones watching the blade.

She squeezed her lips together in a thin line as she put down the knife, wiping her hands on her apron. Ben followed her over to the display case. "This'd be the one for you, I reckon," she said, hooking her fingers under the edge of a large plastic container. Browns and blacks swirled and crested atop chocolate icing flowers that marked the treat's circumference.

"That looks great," said Ben.

"You want it to say somethin? A message?"

"Huh? Just 'Happy Birthday' would be good."

"Bill decided to keep you on, hmm?" the woman asked, prying the plastic lid off the cake.

Ben nodded. "Hey, Ms. Beverly, I was wonderin—was I rude to you? The morning Marty—"

"You were," Beverly said, working an icing bag over the cake.

"I didn't mean to be. I want to say sorry. I just . . . Well, I'm sorry is all."

"It's alright. It was an awful thing what happened. Awful. I'm sure Martin's laughin about it now. Real shame."

Ben winced but smiled through it. He stood without saying anything more until she was finished.

"Hope this is alright," she said, spinning the cake on its platter so he could see it: HAPPY BIRTHDAY, ERIC!

A floating feeling moved into Ben's stomach. "M-Ms. Beverly? I . . ." Ben tried to remember if that's what he had asked for.

"Did I get it wrong? I just assumed. Is it alright?"

"Yeah, Ms. Beverly. It's real pretty." Ben paused, weighing the cake in his hands. "You got a sticker or something? For the price?"

"No price."

"Ms. Beverly, I can't—"

"Why not? Cuz the sun's up?" She smiled knowingly at him. "You get on out of here," she said cheerfully. " 'Fore I change my mind."

Ben thanked her again and hurried out of the store, avoiding returning Palmer's gaze as he passed by the registers. The third letter in his brother's name was dotted with a star.

"Hey there, Ben," a voice called from behind him.

Ben turned to see James Duchaine leaning out of his Crown Victoria.

30

Duchaine's radio crackled as they drove. The exchanges were curt and in a language that Ben didn't speak. But that was fine; it was something to listen to. Duchaine didn't say anything. That would come soon enough, Ben supposed. He'd put everything in Palmer's office back where it was supposed to be. It was possible that Ben should have pushed the tapes deeper into the drawer, but Palmer wasn't likely to notice that. Maybe he would, though. They were special tapes, after all. Magic tapes from other worlds.

There were only a few cars at the Finer Diner, but the parking lot was small enough that it almost always looked full. Even before Ben had come close to the front door, his stomach was rumbling at the smell of bacon and waffles.

The place was old but clean, and the food was dynamite. All of it. Everything was cooked in lard, butter if you wanted to go light. By the looks of it, the branding hadn't been updated in fifty years, but there wasn't really a need. It was called the Finer Diner only when the owners were in earshot. Everywhere else, it was called Grits and Shits.

Both the waitress and cook knew Duchaine by name, and he greeted them in return as he led Ben to the loneliest booth. Both men ordered without picking up a menu.

"So what did you want to talk to me about?"

Duchaine's brow furrowed. He took a cautious sip from his cup, then lowered the steaming mug of coffee back to the table. "That a birthday cake for Eric?" he asked, gesturing to the dome on the bench next to Ben. "That something your family does every year?"

"Yessir."

"It bother them any? You workin at that place?"

"No. It's just a store, and we need the money."

"How is it for you? Bein there. You like it?"

"Lieutenant, I'm real sorry. I just really don't feel like talkin this mornin."

"This ain't no big talk. Just a chat. Just askin if you like your job is all."

Ben sighed. "What's there to like? It's stockin shelves."

"Job's a job." Duchaine nodded. He ran his fingers over the ragged burn on his left forearm. "What about your coworkers? You get along with them?"

"Yeah."

"You guys friends and everything?"

"Yeah."

"What about you and Marty? Y'all ever fight about anything?"

"Nosir," Ben replied, then added, "Maybe work stuff."

Duchaine nodded, then took another sip of his coffee. Ben did the same.

"Ya know, I talked to Frank. He's worked there longer than you, right? Him and Marty have worked together for a long time."

"They was on the crew before me, yeah."

"Before that, even." Duchaine's voice pitched. "They was bag boys at the same time. 'Best friends' is the way Frank put it."

"Okay," Ben said, shrugging.

"Real broken up about everything. Nice guy. Anyway, he told me that you and Marty did fight sometimes. More than sometimes. Nothing physical. No, nothin like that. Just yellin. And see, Frank said it *wasn't* about work."

Ben shrugged again.

"What'd you guys fight about?"

The waitress arrived at the table and divvied up the plates. Ben had ordered more food than he now knew he'd be able to eat. He picked at it with his fork, then took a small bite of his grits.

"What's it matter what we fought about?"

Duchaine chewed on his eggs, then swallowed. "It's just a question. Just tryin to get a sense of things. You know that place has been open for almost as long as where we're sittin, and there's never been an accident like that? See, you tell me that you and Marty didn't fight. Frank says you did. You say that the wire just popped. But when I talked to Frank, he said that *you* said you were distracted. That it was your fault . . .

"I'm wonderin if Marty was the one who said he seen your brother."

"Wait." Ben put down his fork and ran the heel of his hand against his bad thigh. "You think I did this on *purpose*?"

Duchaine pushed the runny yolk of his eggs around with a piece of toast, then ferried it to his mouth. "No. But I'm glad you can see why I might be inclined to think something like that. You couldn't've made that wire snap on purpose. That I think was an accident in the most technical sense.

"But you didn't stop holdin that button. Marty said to stop. Frank said to stop. But you didn't. Why was that?"

"That's not how it happened." Ben reached into his pocket.

"Don't get me wrong. Shoot, if someone was playin games with me like what it seems like Marty was with you— "

The plates rattled as Ben slammed his hand down on the table. "Marty wasn't the one playin with me." Ben lifted his hand so Duchaine could see what was underneath it, could see the flyer and its markings.

"Someone put this in my locker. I been hangin these up all over town and someone tore a whole mess of 'em down. Drew . . . whatever the fuck that is right on Eric's face and put it in my locker. I don't believe for one second that Marty did that. I wouldn't never hurt him.

"You know Palmer tried to fire me because he found out who I was? That he's got tapes in his office? Got one from the day it all happened—the day Eric went missing."

"I know," Duchaine said. He lifted his coffee cup and took a sip. "I've seen it. So did the judge who wrote the search warrant for the Prewitt place."

"This tape is different. And *he* has it. Why would he keep something like that?"

"A record of somethin major that happened? I dunno, Ben. I think maybe a better question is why would he get rid of it? Look, I believe you.

In spite of it all, I do. I think that you really do think you wouldn't hurt your friend, that you believe that so much it feels true . . .

"Now," Duchaine continued, tapping the flyer with his index and middle fingers, "I know that some bad things have happened to you. But you put anyone through what you been through, and you'd have to *look* for someone to come to a different conclusion. Marty says that he seen your brother after five years. And then all this." He tapped the flyer again. "Am I leavin anything out? You're a smart guy, and you tell me you don't think for *one second* that Marty did this?

"You know anything about him? About that family of his?" Duchaine opened his eyes wide and huffed with exaggeration. "Listen to me. I'm not putting any of this into any kind of report. I don't work for that store, and I don't particularly like Bill. You can buy as many Christmas toys for poor kids as you please, but that don't mean you ain't a sumbitch for the rest of the year.

"I ain't tryin to trap you, alright? We're just talkin. I'm not gonna ask you how you know about what's in Bill Palmer's office. I don't care. But this is Bob Prewitt all over again."

"I didn't do nothin wrong by Bob Prewitt."

Duchaine leaned back in the booth, slumping in frustrated defeat. "In what honest interpretation of what you did to that man could you say that you did right by him? By that boy of his? In what possible world do you come out of what happened smelling like a rose?"

"He asked to take Eric to the bathroom *two times.* That ain't polite. That's something else, and you know it. You didn't see. You didn't see the way he looked at my brother."

"And what else did you see that day, Ben?" Duchaine let the question go unanswered. "Now look, I don't think that you were tryin to kill Marty—"

"Jesus *Christ.* If I'd've known that you asked me to come here—"

"Okay, now hold on. That's the second time you've said that. *You* asked me to meet with you. You called me and said you wanted to talk."

"I wouldn't've picked this place. I got no way of getting here."

"I picked the place, but *you* asked to talk to *me.* Now listen, if there's any chance at all that some part of you hurt Marty on purpose . . ."

Ben rubbed his head with both palms. "Someone did *this* on purpose,"

Ben snapped, jabbing the symbol with his fingers. "Why don't you look into this?"

"I don't need to," Duchaine said, finishing his toast. "I already know exactly what this is."

Heat flared in Ben's face. He waited with an expectant look, then spoke when Duchaine refused. "You gonna tell me then?"

"Supposing I did. Supposing that this really did mean something. What possible good would it do to tell you, Ben?"

Ben scoffed in annoyance. "Sounds to me like you don't know shit about any of this."

"I know that this ain't no mystery to no one but you. It's a *game,* Ben." Duchaine's tone was casual. "A joke. You keep doing these things, keep workin at that store, keep stompin around town with your ire up like this, and I worry that things are gonna get a whole lot worse than what happened to that friend of yours. In fact, I know it. Because I know you.

"But what I'm mostly interested in right this very second," the man added, "is how your phone number managed to find its way onto this flyer."

Ben snatched the piece of paper back, folded it, and jammed it into his pocket. "Ya know," he said, "the first time I met you, my daddy asked you about cases like Eric's, about if you always found the kid, and you said yes. Then you said, '*Nearly* every time.'" Ben dug some cash out of his pocket and tossed it on the table. "I remember that because you slipped that word in there like it didn't make much difference. But there's fifteen kids up on that board. Fifteen of 'em. How's that for 'nearly'? I hope that this ain't how you treat all those families. That you're different with them."

"I reckon it's you who's different, son." Duchaine leaned in with a low voice. "Because you killed somebody."

31

It was a long walk home. Ben's uneven steps made it difficult to carry the cake. He tried to focus on his walking, to not get too frustrated or emotional. One tilt too far in either direction and the icing would smack against the side of the container.

"Supposing I did . . ." He did. He knew what the markings meant, and the asshole wouldn't say. Every word out of the man's mouth was an effort to torment Ben. That's what the whole chat had been about. To get under Ben's skin. To shrug off responsibility for anything at all. No, not just that. To place it all squarely on Ben. That had been an interrogation, Ben realized. Duchaine had accused him of things. "We're just talkin," the man had said. *Goddamnit.*

Ben hadn't said anything, had he? Admitted that he'd been distracted? Or that there was a very persuasive part of him that had already pictured Marty doing the very things Duchaine had suggested? As he walked, Ben tried to recall everything that had been said. The conversation seemed to unfold differently each time he played it back, but Ben knew that he hadn't tried to kill Marty. He hadn't tried to kill *anyone.*

Strange as it was, what gnawed at Ben the most was Duchaine's claim that it had been Ben who'd asked for the meeting. Ben remembered making the call; he remembered that very clearly now. But he couldn't recall who'd asked to see whom.

"What a fucking *asshole*!" Ben shouted to himself as he limped along the road. "How'd you get that scar? Pushing someone back into a burning building, you lazy f—"

Ben's leg buckled, and he lurched sideways. It was everything he could do to keep from falling, but he managed to catch himself. Not that it mattered. He'd felt the dull thud in his hands. The once smooth chocolate icing was smeared all along the inside of the plastic dome. Ben's jaw clenched, and before he had any sense of what he was doing, he smashed the container on the asphalt, sending the cake bursting over the road.

Ben placed his hands on top of his head and took deep, heavy breaths. He made fists in his cropped hair and tried to calm himself by pulling.

Good. Fine. This would be the year he would finally say something to his parents. That he'd bought a cake and smashed it—smashed it because it was grotesque. No. Maybe just that he hadn't bought a cake because there was nothing to celebrate. That might still be too much. But something. He would say something, and then they would respond. And it would go back and forth until it became a conversation.

By the time he reached his porch, Ben could practically feel the words on his tongue. But when his father asked where the cake was, what came out of his mouth was that he'd forgotten and he'd get it tomorrow.

Ben slept for a few hours, then left for work.

Every night Ben had to pass by Marty's neighborhood on his way to the store, and he fought with himself over whether he should knock on Darlene's door. Ben had worked sixty hours the past week. With overtime pay, that was quite a chunk of change. Whether it made sense or not, Ben couldn't help but feel that some of that money belonged to Marty. *Go right on up there then,* Ben thought. *Hand Darlene some cash. She'll forgive you for sure!*

It was too late in the evening to even consider now, though. It pained Ben to admit he felt relieved.

Ben walked into the store and waved at Chelsea.

"Didn't think you was gonna make it," she said, glancing at the wall clock.

"Yeah," Ben replied, looking at his watch, "timed it wrong. Gotta walk slower if I want a night off, I guess."

She smiled and pushed her magazine to the side. "Listen, I wanted to say that I was sorry to hear about your brother."

Ben nodded.

"That's an awful thing, and I wanted to say that I think it's real brave of you to be workin here like you are."

"I dunno about brave. I—"

"Don't argue a compliment, Ben."

He smiled and rubbed the side of his face like it might hide the fact that it was a little red. "Thank you," he said, pulling his shirt away from his stomach.

"And if you ever wanted to . . . talk about it. Or just talk . . ." She let the words hang.

"I'm okay," Ben said. "But thank you. That's real nice."

"Okay," Chelsea said.

Ben wished Chelsea a good night. He wasn't sure how it had happened—who had said what to whom—but sometime after Ben emerged as the only stocker left, the reason Palmer had tried to fire him became common knowledge. It was hard not to see the irony in it. People were apparently whispering about Ben and Eric thanks to the mighty efforts of Bill Palmer to prevent that very thing.

He didn't like the pity in people's eyes when they looked at him—but at least, for Eric's sake, they *were* looking.

Ben had asked everyone he knew if they recognized the moonchild. Someone had told him to go to the library, as if there were a book called *Symbols* with every glyph known to man. The library did have internet, but it wasn't all that clear how that was supposed to help.

For all Ben knew, the shape could be the logo for an old brand of fabric softener. But then why the hell was it on the baler?

Chelsea's voice crackled over the intercom and Ben met her up front. She handed him the key to the doors, and he locked them behind her. He stood at the glass, watching her get into her car, watching her until she was safely out of the parking lot. *It really was nice of her to offer to listen,* Ben thought. *She didn't have to do that.*

Turning back toward the aisles, Ben tried to remember where he had been in his thoughts and in his job. Not that it mattered; he'd find his way back to both places inevitably. The phone in Customer Service rang. "Sorry, we're closed," Ben said to himself, walking toward the aisles.

It was only recently that Ben had come to enjoy block nights. Of course, they were preferable to throwing an entire truck by himself, but it was more than that. Now Ben appreciated their quiet monotony. It was as close as he could get to sleeping without having to worry about where he might end up or what his mind might show him.

From the time the store closed, Ben had six hours to himself. He could think if he wanted to, but he was so tired all the time, it was easier to let his mind drift. There were a few times when he practically blacked out, when he remembered clocking in and nothing more—until suddenly the sun was up and he was surprised to see that the store was finished.

But tonight, for whatever reason, the relief was not forthcoming.

He still had to get Eric a cake. He'd have to buy the ingredients this time so Beverly wouldn't ask what had happened to the one she'd given him. He'd have to sit at the table with his parents and light the candles and—

Across the store, the phone in the pharmacy chimed.

"Fuck this," Ben muttered, and left the aisle.

The baler sat in a cold slumber, like an unconscious Titan. Ben wrapped his hand around the dozens of bale wires and pulled them from their PVC quiver. He laid them on the floor, spreading them out with his foot, and grunted as he sat down crisscross in front of the new metal rug.

With his right hand, Ben grabbed one wire by its loop. He pinched the shaft with his other hand and then pulled the loop end away from his body. It took four pulls to feel the entire length of the wire, four pulls to make sure there were no cuts.

What would the plan have been? Ben considered the question as he fed another wire through his fingers. Sabotage one of the wires so that it would snap? It was hard to say if Palmer would do something like that, hard to imagine him hatching such a scheme. If the idea had been to hurt Ben, why? He'd already been fired at that point. And obviously, there was no guarantee of who would be in the wire's path. The only people who could have guessed that were Ben, Frank, and Marty.

Still, the wire could have popped at any point. It could have popped on the truck, long after it had been hauled away from the store. And that was the other thing: the wire had *popped.* If it had been cut, then it probably would have failed much more quickly and without incident, like a paper clip that had been bent too many times.

So what? A single wire had been sabotaged somehow so that it failed at just the right time and in just the right way?

Ben fed wire after wire through his fingers, checking some more than once, and growing increasingly irritated with Duchaine's smug dismissal of everything Ben had said. The fact that Duchaine had suggested things about Marty that Ben had already suspected made him feel queasy. He didn't want to think like Duchaine. Had Marty known that Frank had found Stampie?

All the wires were smooth. Ben stood and kicked the center of the pile, scattering the metal strings across the floor. He looked at the baler, at the wretched colossus, scaled in sour green. A tribal king scarified with the symbol of his god. He looked at it for a long time. Then he stooped and pinched a wire from the ground; it skidded faintly across the concrete as Ben walked toward the machine.

Ben could feel the eyeless stare of the moonchild watching him and watching the dull end of the wire as it bobbled in the air. *Good,* it seemed to say. *Finally.*

This wasn't stupid. Not any stupider than Eric's tape. And that was real. This was the point. Something would happen, like a key in a lock. Something would *happen.*

The wire scraped against the glyph and the world seemed unaware.

Ben sighed and gathered the rest of the cables, then fed them back into the tube.

In the body of the store, the phone in Customer Service was ringing again. Ben breathed with annoyance and began walking toward the sound. It wasn't all that unusual to get calls after the store was closed, but never three in one night. When Ben was almost halfway to the counter, the ringing stopped and so did Ben.

"Idiot," he said.

Then a phone behind him rang, and Ben felt a kind of hum at the base of his skull. The ringing sounded like it was coming from the deli. As quickly as he could manage, Ben hustled back toward that department, pushing his way through the swinging doors and into a room he'd never been in. Not knowing where the phone was, Ben followed the sound.

On the wall, just before the entrance to the area behind the deli case, the phone blared. Ben let it ring two more times before he answered.

"We're closed," Ben said. No one replied, but Ben lingered. He could hear the faint hiss of an open line. "Call back at six." After a second or two of silence, Ben hung up.

The phone rang again.

Ben yanked the handset from the hook and pressed it against his ear. He pressed hard, as if it might help him hear better.

"Hello?" a young voice said.

"Hi," Ben replied. "We're closed for the night."

"Um. Is there . . ."

"Is there what?"

"Who is this?" the voice whispered.

"Who is *this*?" Ben replied, whispering without meaning to. "I work here." He checked his watch. A little past three. "We closed at midnight."

"I'm not supposed to use this." In the background there were hushed mutterings that weren't meant for Ben. He tried but failed to pull them from the hiss of the phone.

"A little late for you to be up, huh? Who're you tryin to call?"

"I think he tricked me," the voice said. "I'm gonna get in trouble."

"You—" Ben started, but the line died. He waited awhile before placing the handset back on the dock.

32

Ben hadn't seen Bill Palmer enter the store, so when Bill's voice droned out a summons through the overhead speakers, Ben sighed and looked to the wide windows of the man's office. He knew that Palmer could see him, was probably watching him right at that moment. That there was no way to get out of going upstairs.

Palmer's eyes stayed fixed on the papers in front of him as he waved Ben inside. The bottom of the door scraped against the floor. Ben had really done a number on it. In the small amount of time since Marty's accident, a dull, ragged arc had been etched into the tile by the corner of the broken door.

Ben took a chair and sat silently. He checked his watch and let his eyes lose focus on Palmer's mad pen, scribbling away on pieces of paper. The man seemed to be in no hurry. A few more minutes passed before Palmer leaned back and took off his glasses.

"So, the wire," Palmer said. "The one that got Marty. You said that it just up and popped. Just like that?"

"Yessir," Ben said.

Palmer pinched a spot between his eyes, wobbling his glasses. "I know one of you screwed up. You or Frank or Marty. Hell, maybe even all of you together in some massive collaborative fuckup. But there ain't no way in hell that wire just snapped like that. Okay? That's what I know."

Ben didn't respond.

"I already talked to Frank. He told me that it was *you*. Now, I don't think I need to explain just how serious something like this is. So I wanted to give you the chance to get something wrote down. I need you to write down exactly what happened and who messed up so that we can get this all taken care of."

"I already told the police what happened. That it was an accident."

"And that's fine. They won't ever see this. This is strictly internal."

"You want me to write down that it was Frank?"

"No. I want you to write down whoever it was," Palmer said, placing a piece of paper and a pen in front of Ben atop a seemingly mindless arrangement of other papers. "I know Marty was a reckless kid, that he was standin in front of that bale just like you're not supposed to." After a moment, Palmer added, "This won't affect anything having to do with Marty or his family or anything like that."

"Can I see what Frank wrote?"

"No."

"You show me what Frank wrote," Ben said, shifting in his chair, "and I'll write you somethin."

"I never said Frank wrote anything. I said I talked to him."

"So you just want something written from *me*?"

Palmer pushed the paper closer to Ben, who for no reason at all remembered that he needed to pick up cake mix for that night.

"Here," Palmer said, placing another sheet of paper in front of Ben. "This might help you get started."

This page had writing on it. Scratchy to the point of near illegibility, it looked like Palmer's hand. Ben struggled through the first few sentences, but it wasn't long before he'd read all he needed to. Ben chuckled with disgust. "You want me to say it was *Marty*?" Ben shoved the papers back toward his boss. "I ain't gonna do that. This ain't on anybody but you and that machine."

"I ain't askin you to lie," Palmer said. "But I know what happened wasn't just some fluke."

"What? You think we was playin around? Seein how crazy we could get with that old piece of shit?"

"We made *thousands* of bales here, and the machine worked fine all the way up to and including now. Them wires is all the same. You boys are the only things in this equation that ain't reliable."

Ben offered nothing but an exaggerated shrug. It seemed like Palmer was trying to wait him out, which was fine with Ben, since he was on the clock. They stared at each other across the desk in silence. Then Palmer reached for his phone.

"Beverly to the office, please. Beverly to the office."

Ben's brow furrowed. Tapping his knuckles against his knee, Ben considered Palmer. Beverly hadn't even been in the room for the accident. She'd shown up after it was all over and done with, after the police had talked to everyone. But maybe none of that mattered. What was one more lie on the "strictly internal" report? And what was one more oversight for James Duchaine? *Fuck.*

From the corridor, Ben could hear Beverly humming. The notes sounded a bit sour, but it was the same tune she carried with her wherever she was. She stopped in the doorway, flour dusting her hands and forearms like ash.

"C'mon in," Palmer said. He slipped his glasses off, exposing the bright, painful craters the pads had left on the bridge of his nose. "You got anything in the oven, Beverly? Anything gonna catch fire?"

"No. I had just pulled the racks out when you called for me."

"That's good." Palmer gestured that the woman should take the seat next to Ben. "The other stuff's already baked?"

"It is," she said after a moment.

"It comes that way, right?"

Beverly stared at Palmer, her eyes fixed despite the tremors in her head.

"You two are friends, right?" Palmer asked.

Ben and Beverly looked at each other but didn't respond.

"C'mon now. You two talk in the mornings, sometimes even after Ben here clocks out. So let's *all* be friends and talk. What have you two been doing?" When there was no response, Palmer sighed. "Let's try it this way." He turned toward Ben. "You never had a CD player. I don't know what you was really in here for when you said it got stolen, but I know you been back in here since, and I ain't talkin about when you broke my damn door." Palmer skipped his fingers along the scattered paperwork. "I know where every single piece of paper goes."

"That ain't true," Ben said, clearing his throat. "I ain't been up here." Even as he made the claim, Ben knew it didn't sound convincing.

"Beverly, what do you guys talk about? All those chitchats in the morning."

The woman shrugged her narrow shoulders. "Just things. Whatever comes up."

Palmer sifted through some papers and retrieved one, placing it in front of Beverly. "This ever come up?"

Ben's heart fluttered.

"That's his brother's flyer," Beverly said.

"Yes, I know," Palmer said patronizingly. He swept his hands out to invite more words that never came. "You ever see Ben hand these out in the store?"

The woman shook her head. "Not that I recall."

"I never did that," Ben snapped. "I never handed not one flyer out here."

"That's real interesting, cuz I been finding them. All over." Palmer exhaled through his nose. "Well, someone's gonna have to say something here. C'mon now. You two are friends. You get along. Chat with each other. Help each other. Bev, you even made Ben a birthday cake the other day, ain't that right?"

"I don't know what you mean," Beverly said. "I don't know what any of this is," she added, gesturing to the room itself and all its confounding accusations.

"Alright, let me ask a simpler question." Palmer set the papers down and looked at them with his swollen, muddy eyes. "Who paid for the cake?"

Ben felt his stomach fall into his bowels.

"Who paid for the cake?" he repeated. "I know it wasn't you, Ben. I watched you walk right out with it."

"It was a gift," Beverly said. "For a birthday."

Palmer didn't reply.

"I can pay for it," Beverly added after some delay. "I shoulda done that anyhow. I can go do that right now."

Palmer's chair squeaked as he leaned back. "I'm sorry, but that's just not going to work."

"I'll write the fucking letter," Ben said.

Palmer plucked up another sheet of paper and pushed it across his cluttered desk toward the old woman. He laid a pen on top of it. "We'll hold the paycheck you got coming. Come and get it anytime."

Frail and shrinking smaller still, Beverly leaned forward, trembling. "I can pay for the cake." When Palmer made no reply, Beverly placed her hand on the desk to steady herself. "I've worked . . ." The woman cleared her throat and swallowed. "I've worked here for thirty-five years." She paused and waited for a reply that didn't come. "I don't understand. What is this? The customers like me. I know they do. And I like them. I need this job, Bill."

"No, they don't!" Palmer spit.

A shade of red had crept into her wet eyes. She blinked a tear free, and Ben saw it spread through the wrinkles on her cheeks like splitting glass. Her mouth hung agape and trembled as it seemed to search for more to say, but all it could find was "I like baking the bread."

Ben's own eyes stung. Whether he wrote the letter, this was going to happen. It was always going to happen. Palmer had made the decision before Ben even stepped into the room.

"This is horseshit," Ben said.

"You know it occurred to me," Palmer said with that same peat fire in his eyes that Ben had seen at his own termination, "that apart from using my paper to make these, you would have had to open up that bulletin board outside. Now I know for a *fact* that that's a no-no. Waddya say we call and see what they say about all this?"

"You cruel, small man." Beverly stood and leaned with hunched shoulders over Palmer's desk. "I've known people like you my whole life. You're a bully, and if you think I'm gonna let you terrorize this boy"—she gestured toward Ben and then jerked Eric's flyer off the table, scattering much of the surrounding paperwork—"then you're dumber than everyone says you is."

"We'll mail you your check, then. I don't wanna see you back in here, Beverly. You understand?" Palmer asked. "I'll call the police. I'll call them and have you arrested for trespassing."

"You can't do that," Ben said.

"Only one way to know for sure," Palmer replied.

Beverly stood as straight as her crooked back would allow and stared at

Palmer as if she might pour the rest of her hate into him. Her lips seemed to tremble separately from the tremor in her head. In the lingering silence, she unfolded the flyer and finally moved her eyes from Palmer to look at it. She seemed to consider it for a very long time before she smiled unhappily and placed the paper back on Palmer's desk.

Palmer held out his hand and asked for Beverly's key. The woman dug it from her pocket and tossed it onto the floor.

"Ms. Beverly, I'm sorry," Ben said meekly. Perhaps it fell from his mouth too softly for her hearing aids to pick up, because she said nothing more to either of them as she turned and left.

Ben's handkerchief was in tatters; he'd fussed and picked at it with mindless, brutish fingers for too long. Palmer busied himself with straightening the papers that Beverly had disorganized. The satisfaction that Ben had spotted in the sewers of Palmer's eyes was gone. Something else had replaced it, though Ben couldn't tell what.

"You didn't have to do that," Ben said, pointlessly. "Fire her over a cake just because you're pissed at me. You can't do things like that—"

"So quit then," Palmer said flatly. "You got no idea what's goin on here. I don't expect you to, and I don't find myself carin too much either way. I done all I can do, and it ain't no business of yours anyhow. She'll get her check. She'll be alright."

"I'm gonna tell her what you done and why you done it."

Palmer shrugged and Ben rose and moved toward the crippled door. His desire to tell Palmer just what he thought of him was strong, but not as strong as his desire to leave the room and the company it housed.

"I wouldn't get too worked up over her, if I was you." Palmer rubbed at his eyes with the heels of his hands. Ben might have thought that Palmer looked remorseful if he believed the man was capable of such a thing. "I kept her around as long as I could. You don't know anything about that woman. Besides," he continued, tapping his fat finger on Eric's flyer, right next to Ben's phone number, "she's the one who told me who you were."

33

After Ben left Palmer's office, he'd looked for Beverly. He'd walked with purpose, hoping that he might outpace her slow steps, but there'd been no sign of her at all. It wasn't surprising that she'd decided not to linger.

In the back room, Ben checked the baler again, looked at the markings. Then he stepped over the deep brown stain on the concrete as if it were a hole in the earth that might swallow him up. He stepped naturally, like it was just something that happened to be there, like he hadn't put it there himself.

Everything outside was cold and wet. Morning dew glinted off the asphalt and turned to mist under the spinning tires of passing cars. The temperature would likely drop only a little more, but by the way some of the folks in town were dressed, you'd think thermometers had bottomed out. People moved more quickly, as if they might outrun the world itself, but the rest of nature seemed to be winding down like an old clock. The mosquitoes had all died or gone back to hell, or whatever they do when the air itself starts to bite and sting. Tree frogs moved less energetically after the sun sank below the earth, and there seemed to be fewer squirrels around all the time.

Ben had never bothered a customer—never even talked to one about Eric. He'd left everyone alone and done his job. So what the fuck had just happened? Ben was sure that he had never met a worse man than Bill Palmer. Whatever doubt there had been had shuffled out of the room with Beverly. There was something wrong with Palmer.

More cars cast up more mist as they moved in the direction of the store, and Ben fantasized that this was a different day—one with an enormous truck that he hadn't shown up to throw, leaving Palmer no choice but to fucking do it himself. Ben really could do that to Palmer, but he knew he wasn't going to. Ben knew he wasn't going anywhere.

Eric was *somewhere,* and the path to finding him started at the store. Ben felt it in the marrow of his bones, and in a way that was the most torturous part. Ben knew that there was some door he could open, some window he could peer through, that would end everything, that would be enough to bring his brother home. Just one brief look and life would reset.

Ben stood at the entrance to Marty's neighborhood. For what felt like the hundredth time, he stared down the dirt road and wondered what might be going on in Marty's weathered home. Did they hate him? Did they even know that they should? He could find out. Just walk a little farther and knock. Just tap on the door and it would all be over.

So then do it. Do it, you fat fuck. Tell Darlene what you did to her son.

Ben rubbed his left leg with the heel of his hand and walked home.

Huh-he moved so ssslow-like, crawlin
luh-like a snake, that no one thought he
was real no more. Nuh-no one believed.

And the guh-good thing sssaid,
"Well, he wuh-won't get muh-me."

And the bad man whispered
back, "Yes, I will."

But all the guh-good thing
heard was the wind.

34

By the time Ben got home, his father was asleep.

Eric's birthday cake sat as the centerpiece of the dining table. Evidently Ben's father had picked it up. A melody drifted through the air, calling to Ben like a siren's song.

Deidra's coffee-colored hair shone vibrantly in the sunlight that poured through Eric's open window blinds. Her nightgown draped loosely over her delicate frame and billowed gently as she ruffled and whipped the sheets on Eric's bed. Ben watched as she smoothed the sheets, her hands running over the fabric like irons, tugging and stretching until there were no wrinkles left. The doorframe made a cracking noise as Ben leaned against it, and his stepmother turned with a gasp.

"I didn't mean to scare you," Ben said, gently pushing himself away from the threshold.

"Not scared," she replied, smiling, "just startled."

"I heard you singing when I came in. It sounded nice."

"Was I? Oh. I guess I was." She smiled again. "I'd sing that song to Eric in the mornings sometimes."

"You sang to him a lot, I remember."

"Different songs for different occasions. I guess we'll all be singing later today. Still have to run out to the toy store. Got one last thing picked out I think he'd really like."

"Oh, that's great." Ben patted his palm against the molding as he took a step back. "I should probably get some sleep then."

"I'll try to keep the singing down."

"No, that's okay. It's okay."

"Thank you, Ben," she said as he turned back toward his own room.

Ben's lips pressed together in a thin and confused line, but he decided not to prod. The woman smiled so seldom that Ben had almost forgotten what it looked like. It was a nice smile. Pretty. But it came always at the wrong time, always at this time of year. Ben didn't like the way it looked anymore.

With his door shut, Ben put Eric's defaced flyer back into his treasure box. He stripped off his pants and lay back on his bed, his sketchbook resting on his stomach. Leaning, Ben snatched up his discarded jeans and fished Eric's picture out of his back pocket. The soft sounds of Deidra's morning song drifted through the wall behind his head.

Opening his sketchbook, Ben flipped past the volume of repeated portraits of little Eric, the ones that he'd drawn to fight the nightmare. Flipped past all the newer ones that were failures, the ones with the bad eyes. He'd get it right this time. And then it would finally feel like it fit the title scrawled at the top of the paper: "Eric, Age 8."

Maybe they could even use it on a new flyer. The ink flowed in long and smooth lines here and short and curt ticks there. Gradually, the gentle throb in his leg retreated as he lost himself in ink and paper. Now and then he could swear that he heard a sob interrupt his stepmother's song. The sound of slicing paper and tearing tape had joined the choir. Regardless of whether she really was happier when winter fell, Ben knew that she *wasn't* better. If she was better, *really* better, Clint wouldn't have had to buy a cake. Ben wouldn't be hunched in his bed listening to her wrap presents in his brother's room.

In truth, she was worse this year. Maybe worse than ever. For the second time, Ben had caught her making Eric's bed. That was something new.

Ben set his sketchbook down on his table. He closed his eyes and tried to dream of a world where sometimes new and good were the same things.

And the dreams did come, combative and noisy, but there was something else. Something new and warm. Already he could feel it disintegrating into dust in the atmosphere of the waking world. Breathing deeply, he lay there for a while trying to call the images back, grasping and groping at them, trying to hold on for a little while longer. What was it? He had been running. They both had. He and Eric—older now—in front of Ben, then alongside him. They were running so fast—fast enough that his leg didn't hurt. Nothing hurt. It was sunny, but Ben could remember feeling like it wasn't as sunny as it should be, or at least not as bright.

Ben's eyelids quivered as he awoke and fought against the numbing drag of sleep. Eric had said something in that other world, but Ben couldn't hear it. Nor could he hear his own responses. Ben put the back of his hand against the cold wall and sniffed mucus back into his nose. With dwindling awareness, Ben's knuckles rapped three times on the drywall.

Knock. Knock. Knock.

Drifting slowly in the silence, Ben's dream called him back, only to be scattered like dandelion seeds by something bleeding through from the waking world, something that Ben hadn't heard in five years.

Knock. Knock. Knock, the wall replied.

The rhythm was slow, the sounds themselves faint, but they wrenched Ben's mind back into his body. He sat up too quickly, the dull thudding of his heart playing in his ears. For a moment he felt dizzy. His eyes swept toward his clock: 3:12 p.m.

The house was quiet and still. The door at the end of the hallway was closed, his father snoring somewhere behind it. In the kitchen, Ben filled a glass from the sink and chugged it. He filled it a second time, and as he brought it to his lips, he saw, from the corner of his eye, that his father's truck was gone.

And then he remembered that it was Eric's birthday, the one day a year Deidra could be counted on to leave the house, out buying one last emergency present that she remembered to forget. Just like every year.

Quietly, Ben set the glass in the sink and walked back into the hall. He stood at Eric's closed door. He'd heard knocking. He'd heard it. But Deidra was gone. Ben raised his hand like he might touch the door. But he didn't. Something felt very wrong, like the air was buzzing with noise he couldn't hear. There was a kind of charge in his skin, one that made his eyes water.

Clint was snoring in the bedroom. Deidra was gone. Ben tapped on Eric's door, but no voice called out to him. Delicately, he turned the knob and paused. He squeezed the knob hard, then pushed the door into the room. "Deidra?" Ben whispered. But the room was empty.

White sheets with a rainbow of dinosaurs lay messed and twisted on the mattress. Ben glanced back into the dim hallway, then stepped into the room.

He lay on his brother's bed and gazed at the plastic stars above and let his mind play tricks, his fingers teasing at something in the sheets. A leaf. Sleep took Ben before he thought to wonder. Ben could almost see Eric's face. They had been running, yes. Through the trees. God, how they ran.

35

"Wake *up*." Ben felt a hand pressing firmly against his shoulder, firm enough to rock his whole body. Opening his eyes, Ben could see Deidra's long, spiraling curls swaying around her snarling face as she again leaned into Ben's shoulder and chest. "What in the hell's the matter with you?"

Beyond Deidra's burning eyes, Ben could see a collage of white stars on the ceiling, and only then did he feel his feet dangling off the edge of the bed. His heart hammered in his chest at the full and engulfing realization of exactly where he was. And on today of all days.

As soon as Ben lurched out of the small bed, Deidra set to making it. "It's filthy. You got leaves in it. Look at what you *done*!" Her shouts became mutters, and after a moment it seemed like she wasn't talking to Ben anymore. As she fussed with the sheets with Stampie tucked under her arm, she didn't even seem to notice that Ben was still there. So he left.

In the kitchen, Clint was splitting a head of lettuce in his hands, setting the leaves next to a toppled stack of tomato slices. Ben craned his head under the faucet and took a long drink of water. Deidra walked past Ben without a word and began assembling Clint's work.

A few minutes later, they were eating. After only a few bites, Ben set his turkey sandwich down. Deidra always used too much mayonnaise. The cake sat at the center of the table, green candles impaling the chocolate skin. Ben stared across the table at the empty plate that accented the empty chair.

"Not hungry?" Deidra asked.

"Just saving room for cake," Ben said with half a smile.

"Uh-huh" was all she said.

One by one Clint lit the candles until there were eight glowing columns of fire. Their flickering cast erratic, disfiguring shadows on the faces of Ben's parents.

"Made it to the toy store today," Deidra said to her husband. "Think I found a winner."

"Good." Clint smiled.

"And I put Stampie on Eric's pillow, right where we used to put him. And we'd pretend the pillows was hills, and he'd gallop up and down 'em."

The fire danced defiantly in the family's silence. Liquefied wax oozed down the paraffin pillars, making green craters in the deep brown frosting. One wax puddle overran and bled into its neighbor, reaching over like a squid's tentacle. Ben thought about how fast he and Eric had run under that dark sun, keeping perfect pace, neither pulling ahead, neither falling behind.

"I remember," Deidra began, as the wax continued to drip. "I remember when we took him to the mall to meet the Easter Bunny. He had on that little button-up shirt. The one with the stripes. He was so excited. But when we finally got to the front of the line he just hugged my leg and wouldn't even look at the Easter Bunny. We finally got him to sit on his lap and Eric just cried and cried." She laughed. "But when I asked him later, after we got home, if he liked the Easter Bunny, Eric said yes. Big ol' smile on his face."

Clint chuckled. "I remember the time he put on your high heels."

"Oh—" Deidra interrupted her own exclamation with delight and clapping hands.

"He stood at the top of those porch steps when we were out cutting the grass. 'Mama, look!' and then *whack*. That boy took a *tumble* down them steps. By the time I got over to him, I was already figuring how long it would take to get to the hospital. I even had the color of his cast picked out. But when I picked him up, he was laughin that laugh of his."

Steadily, the candles disappeared. Ben could feel his parents' eyes on him as he stared at the dancing flames.

"Son?" Clint nudged him verbally. "What do you remember?"

"I . . ." Ben shook his head. He didn't want to talk, didn't want to share any memories. For the first time in years Ben had hope that his brother was alive, that he was really out there somewhere. But this . . . this *ritual* didn't help anything. It didn't help *anyone.* It was like they were sitting around telling ghost stories, and Ben was being forced to acknowledge again and again that he had been the one to write the first tale.

"I remember . . ." The words tasted like bile. "I remember when we played tag and he kept chasing me even when I was the one supposed to be chasing him."

Silence hung in the air for a moment. "Go on . . ." Deidra encouraged.

"That's it."

"Okay then," she said tersely.

"Maybe we just skip my turn? I ain't feelin too good."

"No," Deidra said.

"Honey . . ." Clint started.

"I ain't gonna let him just sit there and not say nothin."

"I don't wanna do this anymore," Ben muttered. "Any of this. It's not . . ."

A silence passed. The flames crackled and flickered on the ends of their wicks. Finally Deidra said, "I wish we had more stories to tell too. Say . . . you know what *I* remember? *I* remember *you* had a birthday party once."

"Don't," Clint said.

"I remember that you had a birthday party once, and we made—how many invitations did we make?" she asked Clint. "Must have been twenty or twenty-five at least. Handmade too. Each one was different. Animals in birthday hats. I used glitter glue. You helped with the googly eyes. Remember? And you came home from school with almost all of them. Do you remember that? I remember that. I remember that we had all that cake and all that food and no one to eat it. Well, no one except for *you.*"

An uncomfortable silence descended over the table, and Ben could feel his eyes clouding. He'd brought the invitations back home, even though he'd wanted to throw them away, to leave them in garbage cans and say he'd left them in hands. But Ben had brought them home because he thought his stepmother might want them back since her art was on them.

With red cheeks, Ben leaned forward, filled his lungs with the quiet air, and blew out the candles.

Deidra gasped as thin tendrils of smoke curled at the ends of black wicks. "Why . . . why did you do that?" she whimpered. "Why did you do that?" she shrieked.

"What the *hell,* Ben?" Clint growled, reaching for the lighter on the table.

"No, don't bother," Deidra said, resting her hand on the fist that clutched the lighter. "We wouldn't want to waste Ben's time. Gotta get back to the store! Keep stocking those shelves, that'll fix *everything*!"

"At least I'm tryin."

"Why didn't you try back then, hmm? Why didn't you try when you let my little boy just wander away?" Her eyes were dark in the new absence of candlelight.

"At least I looked for him."

"What?" she snapped.

"Ben—"

"No, I want to know what the fuck that means."

"I went out every *day*"—Ben's voice fluttered—"to look for him. I'm *still* looking for him, and I'm gonna find him. You didn't look for him once. Not one time. You leaving presents in his room? Rushin out for that one last gift you made sure to forget? Throwing cakes away every year? Like he's going to just show up one day? Now we're fighting because I blew out some *candles.* You think he's going to want *this* if he comes back?" Ben grabbed at the present that sat next to the cake.

"That's enough, Ben," his father snapped.

Deidra latched her hands onto the box. "Let it go!" she screamed. She drew her hand back and smacked Ben's face. He dropped the box.

"Jesus Christ." Ben rose fast enough to send the wooden chair sprawling into the kitchen. "I gotta go to work."

"Big hero. Thank *God* for you," she sobbed. "It's good you have so much time to help now that you finally graduated high school."

Tears welled up in Ben's eyes. "We can't all stay home messing up sheets at night just so we can make them in the morning!"

Confused pain twisted the woman's face.

"Honey . . ." Clint said gently.

She moved her arms to dodge his grasp. "You think I do all this because I think he's coming *back*? You know, I used to wish that it had been you that disappeared, and I felt so bad. What kind of thought is that to have? But really," she snarled at Ben, "sometimes when I look at you I wish that your accident had done more than hurt your leg."

"If only," Ben said. He hooked his fingers under the cake's platter and lifted it off the table.

"Put that down!" Deidra hollered.

"Both of you sit down!" Ben's father roared.

"I gotta go to work."

"Ben!" Clint yelled as the door slammed behind his son.

36

Ribbons of deep blue hung over the horizon as the sun lost its grip on the world. It was only six o'clock; Ben's shift didn't start for another few hours.

Goddamnit, Ben thought. He shouldn't have done that. Said those things. Blew out the candles. But what was he supposed to do, sit there for an hour? *You could have said something before, when you smashed the first cake.* Yeah, that would have gone great. Just like with the rhino. *You could have said* something *about* anything *at anytime.* Fuck you.

He'd let things fester in his own mind. That was true. But anything he might say—anything at all—would only make things worse. If Ben told his folks about what Marty said, about the symbol, about anything, they'd talk to Duchaine. Now suddenly it's a different conversation about how Ben—what had Duchaine said?—caused Marty's accident on purpose without knowing it. What did that even mean? Jesus Christ.

Even as he walked farther and farther away, he knew that it was only temporary, that he'd be back. It's not as if his storming out had paused the event. He wondered what his parents might be talking about now, how much worse things might get before he came home from work. Ben kept looking down at the cake, at the wells of cooled wax at the base of each candle. "Crappy birthday, bud." His shoes swept against the dry grass.

Ben could see the hint of the store's sign in the distance, peeking above the horizon like a gopher worried that it's too late in the day to come out and see the world. As he approached the woods, his pace slowed. Even the sight of the sign made Ben's stomach turn. Kicking up dry dirt, he put the woods and the sign to his right.

"I've been finding them. All over," Palmer had said about Eric's flyers. Walking down the orange road, Ben looked from house to house, wondering. Ty Cotter was still in jail. Someone had ripped the flyers down, and they'd shown up back at the *store.* None of it made any sense to Ben. None of it.

And what if it was all just some gag? Some stranger messing with Ben. Or, worse, someone he knew. What if Eric had been dead since the day he went missing, and this was all just a joke? None of this would have happened if it weren't for the store. Try as he might, there wasn't much of a way around that fact.

The Cotter girls were nowhere to be seen. Nor was Jacob, his orange truck sitting like a hungry metal bird in the front yard, its hood open like a mouth.

Beyond the trees that bordered the small backyard of the house, Ben could see the sky had lost its color. He heaved himself past the broken bottom step and onto the rotting porch. Setting the cake down on the rough railing, Ben rapped his knuckles against the chipped wooden door. He held his breath, listening to the voices and movement inside, and hoping that whoever answered the door might not look at him with hate in their eyes. Locks rattled. Hinges squealed.

A raspy voice spoke. "Heya, Ben."

A shaking one responded. "Hiya, Marty."

In a single, fluid motion, Marty stepped across the threshold and pulled the door closed behind him. Ben couldn't help but stare. Red, puckered flesh seemed to undulate around the sutures each time Marty moved his head. Deep black and maroon flecks lay in the creases of his reoriented skin. The gash on his neck had been closed hastily and with no apparent regard for aesthetics.

"You wanna kiss it better?" Marty said with a smirk.

Ben laughed at the joke, but his eyes watered at the fact that Marty still liked him enough to make one. "It doesn't look that bad," Ben offered.

"Fuck you. That why you're cryin? Because you couldn't never look this good?"

With a step, Ben closed the distance between them and wrapped his arms around his friend. Marty's body felt so small, so frail, in his embrace. Marty patted Ben's back, but Ben didn't reciprocate. "I'm so glad you're alright, man," said Ben.

"Thanks," Marty said, moving his arms from around Ben's back. "In a few more seconds, this'll count as cuddling."

Marty spoke with a kind of precision and care that Ben had never heard from him. Anytime his words tried to move too fast, they would evaporate into airy sounds.

"You bring me a cake as a get well present?"

Ben pulled away. "Something like that," he said through a chuckle. He wiped his salty eyes with his forearm. "We thought you was dead, man."

Marty burned the end of a cigarette and winced as he pulled the smoke into his lungs. "Figure I nearly was." The smoke sputtered out from between his lips, playing stowaway on his words. "Gonna take more than a fucking catastrophic industrial accident to take me out, though."

"I came to visit. Me and Frank both did."

"I know. The doc told me."

"When I came back a few days later, you was gone already. I came by here a hundred times, but I didn't figure—"

"Don't sweat it, man." Marty gestured to his wound with the fingers that held the cigarette. "This shit got all infected. I was running a fever for days." His voice lowered. "My mom finally took me to the fucking doctor to get some pills. It's like high school all over again: if you ain't pukin, you ain't sick. I been laid up for a bit."

A piercing scream tore through the house. Marty glanced toward the closed door before turning back to Ben nonchalantly.

"Everything okay?" Ben asked.

"Yeah."

Ben pulled his shirt away from his stomach. Not wanting to seem insensitive, he hesitated before he spoke. He brought his fist up to his mouth and held it there for a moment before trying to swallow hard enough that the queasy feeling might leave. "Any idea when you'll be coming back to the store?"

"Been wonderin the same thing. While I was dealing with all this"—he gestured to his neck again—"my momma's boyfriend tried to get all the workers' comp bullshit straightened out, but Tim ain't too good at that kinda shit. They act like I want them to buy me a goddamn boat. I just want them to pay for my medical bills. The whole thing's a mess. The case is under 'review,'" Marty said, pinching the air.

"Review? For what?"

"That it was their fault and not mine. Some cop come by askin after things."

"Who?"

"D-somethin."

"Duchaine?"

"Yeah. Told him what I remembered, which is exactly fuck all. Nice guy. Said that everything looked like it was an accident. Said he was gonna talk to you. Meanwhile I got like eight hundred pages of shit to fill out from the store."

"Palmer tried to get me and Frank to write something sayin it was you," Ben said.

"*What?* What the fuck?"

"I didn't write nothin."

"Did Frank?"

"I dunno. I know he talked to that cop. Palmer said he talked to Frank, but I doubt he'd say something against you. I haven't talked to him since he quit."

"You're shittin me. Like *quit* quit?"

"He was real freaked out, man. Can't say I blame him."

"What a total pussy."

"You didn't see what he saw. I went off to call for help, and he stayed with you. You just laid down and slept through the whole goddamn thing."

Marty's laugh quickly became a cough.

"I kicked in Palmer's door to try to find a first aid kit."

Marty laughed harder, wincing and holding his neck. It took a few seconds for him to compose himself. "So it's just you? Palmer hasn't gotten no one else?"

"Not yet. I'm not even sure if there's anyone to get."

"Horseshit," Marty said incredulously. "We used to move through stockers so fast some of 'em didn't even have time to get name tags. I'll bet that cheap son of a bitch just wants to see how strong your back is. You working every day, then?"

"Yup. Don't care about overtime anymore neither."

"Hey." Marty tousled his own hair. "If you want me to come by and help out a little—just for a few hours here and there—"

"No. No, that's nuts." Ben swallowed and tried not to think about his dinner. "So, listen. I wanna tell you what happened."

Marty flicked his cigarette into the dead grass, then ran his finger against the cake, scraping off some icing. "I know what happened," Marty mumbled around his finger. "That bale was way too big."

Ben drew his handkerchief against the back of his neck and breathed out heavily. The air was chilled, but Ben was still sweating. He felt queasy. "You yelled for me to stop, and I didn't."

Marty shrugged.

"That symbol, the one from Eric's flyer, it's on the baler. Carved right into the side of it. I saw it that night." Cold needles pricked at Ben's hot neck from the memory.

"Fuck off."

"It's just I can't get my head around any of this, man. And I been trying." The quaver in Ben's voice had shaken away any control he still had. "Palmer knows we lied about my CD player to get into his office. This morning, he calls me into his office and tells me to write something about the accident. Then when I won't do it, he fires Beverly. He called her in and fucking fired her just so I could see it. I don't . . . I don't understand what's happening anymore, man. She's so old, older than my granny was even, and she was on all kindsa pills for her Parkinson's. I don't know if unemployment covers those kindsa things. Jesus, man. Can you even still get things like that if you got fired?"

Marty drew on his cigarette and shook his lowered head.

"Oh, good. Good goin, Ben!" he shouted at himself through clenched teeth as he squeezed his stomach with his hands so hard that he couldn't hear the mania in his own sobbing voice. "Jesus Christ, man. I gotta talk to her. To say sorry. To figure this all out. I don't understand, dude." There was pleading in Ben's voice.

"Ben." Marty glanced over his shoulder toward his door. He spoke quietly and deliberately. "She's gonna be fine. Look at me, dude. I'm sure she's on Medicare or Medicaid or Social Security or all three even. Okay? Maybe even some extra ones that only grouchy old ladies know about." A small laugh escaped from Ben's mouth and Marty leaned into it. "She's old enough that she probably knows the guy who invented money. That's a good friend to have if you ask me. She's gonna be fine.

"But *you*? You gotta get a handle on yourself, man. You can't be savin all this shit up for my porch once a month. You talk to anyone other than the goddamn bread lady? Anybody? Your folks? The police?"

"I talked to my dad some, yeah. Not about much, I guess, but I've talked to him. The cops, that one that came by here, he knows pretty much everything."

"And?"

"And what? He don't care. I mean, what in the world, man?" Ben put his hand on his stomach. There was a wet feeling in the back of his mouth. "I need to use your bathroom."

"My yard is your toilet," Marty said, bowing and sweeping his free arm across the breadth of his domain.

"Dude, please," Ben urged. He felt cold.

Inside, the air was still. Sour. The smell of air freshener was draped like a piece of tissue paper over the overwhelming stench of nicotine and kitty litter. There wasn't any cat, though, not that Ben could see.

Darlene and Aaron sat at a small white table in the kitchen. Their chairs looked like the ones the crew took their lunches on back when there was a crew. The longer Ben looked, the more certain he became that they more than just resembled those chairs. Cigarette smoke hung calmly in the air above the family, pooling around the yellow ceiling lights like a foul lake.

"Ben's gotta take a piss," Marty said matter-of-factly as he walked past the kitchen and down the hallway.

Sweating, Ben waved but didn't look in their direction long enough to see if the gesture was returned. He moved around an old, stained couch. More holes than fabric, the upholstery both clung to and sloughed off the frame like skin on a starving body. Black stains peppered the white popcorn ceiling. Marty stood in the corridor and gestured to a doorway.

"Flusher don't work, so you gotta jiggle the chain when you're done. I swear to God," Marty said as he left the room, "if I wind up with a face full of your turds . . ."

Marty shut the door. The chill was worse in here. Shards of broken tile teetered under Ben's feet near the toilet. Two roaches scurried across the mantel into the wall. From what sounded like the kitchen, Darlene shouted Marty's name.

As Ben knelt in front of the toilet, Iron Maiden's "Purgatory" suddenly pounded through the wall so loudly that Ben couldn't even hear himself vomit in the stained bowl. He heaved twice, then lowered his head onto his forearm and breathed heavily. Ben pulled the chain and his dinner was washed away.

The pipes rumbled when Ben turned the faucet handle, and after a second or two, water sputtered out and into his hands. He wet his face twice and rinsed his mouth. As he watched the water twist down the drain, he could see it shimmer in the light, and he lost himself for a moment. Or maybe longer than a moment. Long enough that Ben's whole body jerked when someone began slamming their fist into the bathroom door.

Ben had to slide sideways into the hallway, his path guided by Aaron's body. The boy's Thin Lizzy shirt was full of holes and billowed over his small frame—an obvious hand-me-down from his big brother. Aaron moved to the side, clearing a path back to the front door, which Ben stepped slowly toward.

The music was so loud that it made Ben's ears ache. That was the only reason he turned back toward Aaron, to ask him to turn it down a little, and that was when he saw the padlock. It dangled lazily behind Aaron, nestled against the cracked molding and peeking over the boy's shoulder like a chrome eye. "The other one," little Ellen Cotter had said. "A mean boy."

Ben raised his arm with his index finger extended limply, like his bones had turned to taffy. "What's in there?" Ben found himself muttering. Of course, Aaron couldn't hear him. But then he didn't seem to need to.

Aaron shifted his weight and glanced behind himself, toward the end of the hall. When he faced Ben again, he sighed and then hollered, "Marty!" Ben took a step deeper into the hall and felt Aaron's hands on his chest, but what actually stopped him was the hand on his shoulder.

"You clog it up? I ain't plunging your shit, buddy," Marty shouted into Ben's ear.

Ben turned. Marty's shirt was missing. Scars pocked his friend's stomach. There might have been a dozen or more, pea-sized and scattered like an ugly constellation. When Ben didn't respond, Marty stepped next to his brother. He shut the door to his bedroom, which muffled the music enough that Ben could hear himself talk.

"I was just asking what's in there is all." Ben shrugged, pointing past Aaron at the padlock.

Marty's face looked briefly as if he'd smelled something slightly off. "Can't see what business that is of yours."

Marty studied Ben in much the same way that Aaron was, though not quite as intensely.

"That's Tim's room," Aaron said finally. "Where he keeps his things."

"I thought that was your room," Ben said to Marty. "On account of the foil on the windows. For keepin the light out while you sleep? I just ain't never seen a lock like that on an inside door is all."

"You ain't never lived in this neighborhood neither," Marty replied, shaking his head. He was smiling now, and Ben felt less like a scolded child. But he also felt, somewhere deep in a place that was older than him, that if he tried to take even a single step forward Marty's smile would die on his lips and something very bad would happen.

When Ben turned, it seemed as if the whole hallway decompressed. He let the current take him. Aaron was smiling now too.

On the porch, Marty dug a cigarette out of his pack and tapped the butt against the bottom knuckle of his thumb. "I was thinking—if you really wanted to, I think I know how you could talk to Beverly."

"You got her phone number or somethin?"

"Nope," Marty said, pinching the cold cigarette between his smirking lips, "but I bet Palmer's got that and a lot more."

37

Ben clocked in early and started throwing the truck. By the time Chelsea began telling customers to get out, Ben had already finished almost a quarter of the stock. If he wasn't about to stop—wasn't just biding his time—there was a chance that he might actually finish before the store opened.

"Do you want a walk out to your car?" Ben asked Chelsea.

"No thanks, I'm good."

"Fine by me," Ben lied. "I've got some pretty big responsibilities around here anyway." He tapped the handle of the cart in front of him.

"Well, don't let me slow you down." Chelsea smiled. Ben locked the doors behind her and dropped the key into his pocket.

Ben made one stop by the photo center before walking into the back room. Surrounded by the thrumming of machines upstairs, Ben pushed the cart of go-backs so deep into the room that he could reasonably claim that he'd never even seen them. Then he hustled up the metal stairs as quickly as his leg would let him.

Palmer's door still sagged on its hinges. White light—the only thing of its kind in the long darkness of the upstairs corridor—flickered through the opening. Ben's steps were quiet. He spied the television monitor through the jagged gap in the door, stuttering silently in the black box of Palmer's office.

Taking care to move the door as little as possible, Ben squeezed into the room. His box cutter snagged on the frame and rattled loudly as Ben jerked it free. He paused and collected himself, his eyes stinging a bit as he looked into the room's only light source. The deli cooler sat motionless on the screen. Ben brushed his hand against the wall until it found the switch.

The overhead lights beat back the weak glow of the television, and all at once the room became exactly what it was—just a box where a sad little man sat hatching schemes that would serve him and him alone. Yesterday, Palmer had called Ben into his office just so he could set one of those schemes in motion, and Ben had felt in a very real way that he would have liked to beat the man to death—something he had never felt in all his life.

James Duchaine said he'd talked to Bill Palmer a number of times. Ben had no reason to doubt that. Nor did he doubt the nature of those talks—that Duchaine may have actually leaned on Palmer some and found that he was empty. Of course, it didn't matter if either of those things was true. Ben didn't need to speculate. Because there were a few things that Ben *knew.* Palmer had fired Ben just as soon as he'd learned who Ben was. When that didn't take, he tried blackmail, and when *that* didn't take, he'd fired an old woman.

Near as Ben could tell, Palmer had fired Beverly either out of spite or self-preservation. Whatever the case, Ben needed to talk to her.

On the desk was a wire container for pens and a nearly full coffee cup, on the corner closest to the door. Everything else was paper: hundreds of sheets, some in folders, some loose. And Ben believed that Palmer did in fact know where every single sheet belonged. He walked around the desk twice, just looking. Ben tried to take mental pictures of everything so he'd know where it all went. But for other things, Ben had a much better camera.

It was disposable, but it had a flash and twenty-seven exposures. Ben needed to find Beverly's address; he reckoned that should be on her termination form, which might have other information worth seeing. The other pictures were for quite literally anything else that seemed important. A little bit of time and just over ten bucks to fuck up Palmer's world? What a bargain.

Ben moved next to Palmer's chair and looked over the stacks of paper. He tried to get acquainted with the forest enough that he could tend to the trees. Most of the papers were meaningless to Ben, but he ran his eyes slowly over each one of them. Then he lifted each page, one at a time, and read the one below it. He stopped after every piece of paper, stepped back from the desk, and surveyed. He took his time.

After about an hour, Ben found Beverly's termination letter. There was no address on it. It wasn't even signed yet. He squared it in the eyepiece anyway. *Click.*

Slowly and methodically, Ben combed through every piece of paper on the desk, reading each one. And when he was done, he still had twenty-five pictures left. The papers—the whole lot of them—were all receipts and order forms, applications and inventory reports. The copy of the letter blaming Marty was gone.

He tugged on the drawers of Palmer's desk until he found one that was open. Nothing but a sweater in the top drawer.

Ben sat in Palmer's chair, careful not to move it by much, while he played with the drawer. It would still be worth going out to Beverly's, even without the note, even if just to tell her what had really happened. And maybe in exchange, she could tell Ben a little more about Bill Palmer. Ben listened to the rattling of the drawer as he pulled it out and pushed it back in. Leaning forward, Ben extended the drawer out as far as it would go and peered into the shadowed box. He slid his hand inside and felt near the top until he found something other than wood. A latch. He slid it to the side and pulled harder until the drawer was free from its socket. But this desk wasn't as cheap as Bill Palmer. With his fingers, Ben pried at the panel that protected the bottom drawer. And when it wouldn't budge, he slid the drawer back in its slot.

Sighing, Ben leaned back in the chair and stared at the flickering screen of the deli cam. Then he stood. The filing cabinet rumbled as Ben pulled open the bottom drawer, and he cursed under his breath as he dug through its contents: books, magazines, old food. But no tapes. Not a one. He hadn't found Beverly's address, hadn't found anything of value. Frustrated, Ben yanked on the middle drawer, but just as when he'd tried after Marty's accident, the top and middle drawers wouldn't budge more than an inch. Ben pulled on the chain that connected their handles.

He stepped back for a second, an angry heat burning on the back of his neck. Then he lunged at the metal box, working his hand under the handle of the middle cabinet and pressing his shoulder into the face. He squeezed and pulled and twisted. He clenched his jaw and used the bones in his hand as a fulcrum, grunting and hissing swears, wobbling the whole cabinet. Until something snapped.

Gasping, Ben pulled his hand free and flexed it. Deep red tracks marked his skin. "Fuck," Ben whispered. He pulled at the handle. It hadn't snapped. The screw that fixed it to the drawer had. Ben thought for a moment. Fine. It could be replaced. Ben slipped the chain underneath the handle, freeing the drawers from each other.

Ben pulled the middle drawer out and ran his fingers over the employee files. There were dozens of tabs and many names Ben didn't recognize. He was just about to open the top drawer when he saw Beverly's name. It was a tome compared with its peers, unwieldy enough that it was held together with what might have been the world's largest rubber band. Thirty-five years of employment recorded in a stack of papers that Ben could still lift with one hand.

All Ben needed was an address. Delicately, he pried the band off the file. It was so old and dry it didn't make any noise when it broke.

Ben cursed under his breath as he looked at the limp band. Fine. It could be replaced too. Slowing his breathing, Ben opened the folder, and there it was, right on top: Beverly's home address, printed in the spry hand of a woman not yet beset with the tremors that would steal her dexterity in the years to come. Ben jotted the address down, checking it more than three times for accuracy. The paper was her job application. *Click.*

There was a noise, a kind of clatter that made Ben's lungs seize. He stood and listened, straining to hear something and afraid that he just might. Rubbing his palms with his fingers, Ben first looked into the hall, then filled it. He walked the corridor slowly, quietly, hearing nothing but the sound of his own footsteps. The room below came into view and Ben looked over the railing. There, near the baler: the tube of wires had fallen. Metal threads lay scattered on the floor. Ben stared for a second, then walked back to Palmer's office.

His fingers picked at the corner of the folder while his other hand riffled through the pages. They seemed to be ordered by date. Ben kept the edge of the cover pinched between his fingers, as if he might close the folder at any moment, but he didn't.

Ben knew he had a number of files to go through. Marty's, for one. His own if there was time. But there he sat. There was something captivating about the pages, like drawing life out of a barren well.

Palmer had meticulously collated customer endorsements. "Beautiful cake!" "Always says hello!" "We love Beverly!" and on and on. Things that Beverly would have loved to see but likely never had. *Click.*

Ben didn't read every sheet. Not at first. He skipped around, skating through Beverly's life capriciously, thumbing away huge chunks of time, until he saw that the tone shifted somewhere in the pages. "Messed order up." "Snapped at customer." The folder read like it contained the histories of two different employees.

At first, Ben assumed he was seeing the grasping paranoia of an unkind man. But partway through the list of grievances, Ben began to doubt. There was a rhythm to things, a structure, a line. Any page toward the beginning glowed with the happy words that had set Ben to reading in the first place. It was only later in the file that things soured. Somewhere along the way, there was a split, and Ben wanted to find it.

So Ben stopped skipping and just read.

It became hard to track, since many of the papers were benign or otherwise hard to categorize, but eventually Ben found the schism. It wasn't clean or sharp, but it was there. A gray period when the file spoiled. Over the course of several months almost a decade ago.

There was nothing in the pages themselves that explained it, but the change was there. Ben could touch it, pinch it between his fingers. The file told a story. So Ben kept reading.

With no music overhead, the only sounds in the room were the squeaking joints of the chair and the soft shuffling of old paper, like the chittering of insects in the dead leaves of winter. As Ben read, he found himself humming. The song seemed to creep into his mind rather than emerge from it: a tune he could not place, one that he'd learned from the mother of these pages.

It was hard to say how long he'd pored over the file. His eyes were dry and tired. He stood with his legs still bent and craned his neck so that he might see the sleeping store below. A feeling of restlessness had crawled into his bones. He sat, shuffled more papers, and tried to ignore the fact that that restlessness was really something else entirely.

It had been coming since he'd opened the folder. Of course it had. He had been gaining on it with every page he'd turned, as sure as the sum of his entire life had been gaining on it all those years before. And just like the first time, he hadn't seen it barreling toward him until it was too late, until it was staring him straight in the face with the unblinking and unfeeling eyes of Time that said only, "What took you so long? I've been waiting."

Perhaps he hadn't expected to see the date. Not every day had made it into the file, so why should this one? But it had. And there it was. The date Eric had gone missing, scribbled at the top of the page like it was just any other day. There was a fuzzy feeling at the back of Ben's skull, and the small room was beginning to feel smaller still, like it might actually crush him with his hand still caught in this paper snare.

The text itself was without substance. Beverly had been late that day. A customer filed a complaint about the fact that his cake wasn't ready on time, when he'd needed to pick it up before work. It went on at some length, droning trivialities that Ben slogged through only because of the date in the header. His mind kept trying to help him skim through the inanity with such insistence that he almost missed it, almost breezed right past that final line, those final words stuck to the end of the paragraph like they belonged there. Like there was nothing wrong with them at all.

HI BEN

38

It felt unreal in the most literal sense, like a thing that was not happening because it could not happen. Like he'd found the world playing games with itself. A mistake in the very tissue of life.

And there it was, waiting patiently for him. All in capital letters. A different-colored pen stroke maybe? A darker shade? Or was that just an artifact of Ben's eyes? Or even his brain?

It wouldn't go away. No matter how long he looked, or how many times he turned the page as if it were a Magic Slate that might simply erase itself, it was there. It was a part of the world.

HI BEN

He was going to cry. Not for any reason he had access to. He hadn't even considered the meaning yet, the *why* of it all. That it *was* was more than he could weather, more than he knew what to do with. It was there, and it *had been* there, sitting in a file, one page out of hundreds, locked away inside a cabinet. A secret waiting to be told.

And Ben could feel it. He was being watched. Ben could feel a gaze scraping across his skin, burning welts into his flesh. The room had no cameras. Ben had checked before, just as he was checking now, searching for an unblinking eye that shined from a corner, its electric veins spiraling somewhere deep within the moldy walls.

Ben sat paralyzed in Palmer's chair, afraid to move so much as an inch for fear of tugging on the invisible strings that surrounded him: tripwires woven from the air itself. Connecting everything. Reporting everything.

Someone knew that Ben would look in this file—would look at this piece of paper—before Ben himself did. He was exposed, so profoundly and so completely exposed, that even his thoughts might not be free from the grasping gray hand that now waved to him.

It had to be Palmer. It could only *be* Palmer.

And yet that didn't feel quite right. Because Palmer was just a man. And this felt like something else, like this paper had arrived with Eric's tape, seeping through a membrane between worlds.

The sound of Palmer's phone tore through the quiet room.

Ring-ring-ring. Ring-ring-ring.

Ben flung himself away from the desk as if it were on fire. "Fuck!"

The panic had washed out his vision; everything was as bright and featureless as if he were waking in a hospital. His heart tripped over itself, and his breathing came and went at its own volition.

Ring-ring-ring. Ring-ring-ring.

Ben stood and looked out the window, certain that he would see Palmer standing behind the Customer Service counter, smiling and waving. Who else would call? Nobody called this late.

Leaning over the table, Ben reached toward the phone as if it were a coiled snake. "Fuck!" he snapped again.

Ring-ring-ring. Ring-ring-ring.

Someone *had* called before, though. That late-night conversation while Ben stood in the deli, talking to a caller who said that he'd been tricked. What the fuck was going on? Ben rubbed his unsteady fingers against his soaked palm, then placed them against the cold plastic of the receiver. It rattled against the base in Ben's shaking hand. Very quickly, Ben raised the phone to his ear and spoke into it.

"Hello?"

Static swirled in Ben's ear as a voice crawled through it. ". . . et . . . n."

"Hello?" Ben repeated.

"Let me in," said the faraway voice.

Ben nearly dropped the phone. He leaned his elbows against the desk and pressed the receiver hard against his ear to keep it in place.

"Ben?" The voice was lost in static. Then, "Ben?" it said again, clearer this time.

"Marty?"

"Can you hear me?" Marty asked.

Ben sighed and nearly collapsed back in Palmer's chair. "Yeah, I can hear you. Jesus, dude. You almost killed me just now. What're you callin me for?"

"I'll take near death by phone over near death by baler any day, man. I been knocking on the front door for like half an hour. Where the hell've you been? You get her address?"

"Yeah. Yeah, I got it. I been up in Palmer's office."

"Come let me in; it's fuckin cold out here, and I ain't even got my money to keep me warm because I spent it all callin you from this goddamn phone."

Fishing the key out of his pocket, Ben hustled toward the door. He could see Marty hugging himself and shivering with enough exaggeration that he looked like a cartoon character. Ben slid the key into the lock and started to turn it. When Marty grabbed the bolt on the other side and found that the door wouldn't budge, he cussed Ben and slapped his palm against the glass.

Ben hesitated, his fingers still pinching the key. This wasn't the plan. This wasn't even close to the plan.

HI BEN

"Dude, c'mon!" Marty slapped the glass again. Ben turned his wrist and freed the doors.

"What're you lockin the doors for?" Marty snapped.

"I always lock 'em."

"You got it then? You know the street?"

"Huh?" Ben muttered. "Yeah. Yeah, I got it."

"Let me see it then." Marty glanced at the scrap of paper for a while and chewed his lip. "Think this is way out in the sticks. What about the note? The fake confession note or whatever."

Ben shook his head.

"You get into the filing cabinet? He probably locked it up."

Ben felt his heart tremble. "What . . . what're you doing here?"

"I got excited, man. This is like some KGB shit. You want help? I can help you look. Read through stuff double-time."

Ben glanced at the wide windows of Palmer's office. "Listen, I got a lot to do up there. Lemme go finish, and I'll meet you where we said."

"You alright, man? I spook you or something?"

"No. Yeah. I'm okay. Just gotta wrap it up and finish the store."

"I know you're the last man standing here and all, but you ain't *that* good, dude. Store opens in like an hour and a half."

Ben checked his watch. "Fuck." He still had to fix Palmer's filing cabinet and had half the truck to throw. Before Ben could say anything else, Marty was walking toward the aisles. Ben sighed and locked the door, then hustled to the store's modest hardware section.

Back in Palmer's office, he set the superglue on top of the filing cabinet, then got to work. Wedging his hand between the folders and the inside face of the door, Ben fished the screw fragment out of its hole. Then he dug a handful of screws out of his pocket. With the broken bit resting in the trench between his middle and ring fingers, Ben pushed and flicked the other screws around in his palm until he found one that was the same size.

He bent the filing cabinet handle just enough to test the screw against the hole. Four screws later and he'd found the one he needed. After he put Beverly's file back, Ben would have to feed a screw that was just a little smaller than it should be through the hole in the cabinet's face. Then he could close the drawer, reset the chain, and glue the handle back onto the screw. Ben glanced out the window to check on Marty's progress but couldn't see him.

Closing Beverly's file, Ben couldn't help but wonder about the pages he hadn't read, about the possibility of other special things waiting for him. But there wasn't any more time. The papers hadn't been stacked or arranged nicely. As he worked to re-create their jagged appearance, Ben saw the torn rubber band.

He sighed in frustration. With hurried steps, he left the office and descended the metal stairs, making his way across the store toward the school supplies.

"Where you at, dude?" Ben called for Marty. But there was no answer. Glancing down each aisle, there was no sign of him at all. "Dude!" Ben shouted again.

Ben lifted a multipack of rubber bands from its hook.

"Who're you talking to, *dude*?" Palmer asked.

39

Ben felt his body jolt. He turned. "I was talkin to you," Ben said. *Oh, fuck.* "I . . . seen you come in, but then you just weren't there." *Oh, fuck fuck fuck.*

"Store looks bad."

"Yessir."

"C'mon," Palmer said.

As Ben stepped toward the man, he pointed to the bag of rubber bands in Ben's hand. Ben put them back on the hook.

As they walked the store, Ben again glanced nervously down each aisle. Palmer was saying something about the Christmas trucks. Where the hell was Marty?

The superglue wouldn't take long to dry. Ben had left everything in order, right? He just had to put the folder back. He should have made some kind of excuse to keep the rubber bands. Fuck. Put the folder back, fix the lock. Put the door back where it was. The camera. Ben had to grab the camera. What was Palmer doing here so early? God*damnit.*

"Okay," Palmer said. "Get to it then."

Ben felt like he was going to faint. He had to stall, but he couldn't think of anything—not a goddamn thing. Ben tried to rub the tingling in his hands off onto his jeans as he watched Palmer walk away. For a split second, he could only think to throw something at the man, to hit him with a can. They'd yell, maybe fight. That would stall him. Was there any chance that Marty had gone upstairs and fixed things? And if he did, would it even matter? He didn't know where everything went. *Just do it. Hit him with something.* Ben wished that the ceiling would collapse.

Faintly, in the air somewhere behind him, there was a sound, a nasally repetition.

"Mr. Palmer?" Ben said the words before he thought of what he'd say next, before he even understood what he was hearing. But then Ben turned and saw the blinking lights through the wide glass of the storefront. He almost cheered when he asked, "Is that your car?"

The man craned his head as if to better hear the noise. Then he hustled past Ben, back toward the front of the store.

Ben followed, unsure of what was happening and desperately hoping that whatever it was would buy him enough time to do what he needed to do. Palmer grabbed the lock cylinder and slid the doors apart. There, in the middle of the parking lot, was a solitary BMW. Its headlights pulsed in time with the horn. And between the blinding blinks, Ben saw something he never knew he wanted to see.

"Shit!" Palmer shouted, walking briskly toward his car. The driver's side mirror dangled impotently from its base. Even in the poor light, Ben could see the dent in the hood—like someone had used it as a trampoline.

Palmer kicked the plastic chair that lay toppled beside his car. "Call the fuckin cops!" he shouted to Ben. "I got you on camera, you little shit! Come back and . . ." Palmer's voice faded as Ben moved into the store, leaving the doors slightly apart.

His leg protested as he jogged back upstairs. Hurrying into Palmer's office, Ben paused to take stock of his project. File. Lock. Handle. Glancing out the window, Ben could see that the front doors were still separated. A shadow swept through the headlights, likely Palmer pacing, still yelling. Ben set the phone's headset next to the dock, pushed speaker, and dialed 911.

"Hi, um . . ." Ben said when dispatch picked up. "I want to report a car that got beat to shit." Ben gently lifted Beverly's folder and slipped it back into the filing cabinet.

"Is anyone injured?"

"No. Just the car."

There was a sigh. Ben glanced through the glass at the space between the doors, then stretched the broken rubber band down either side of the thick file.

"Sir, this line is for emergencies only. You'll have to call the non-emergency number."

"Yeah, that's fine," Ben said, lifting Beverly's tome enough to slip the ends of the band underneath. The weight would hold the band in place. If it didn't, Ben supposed that Palmer would let him know. Aloud, Ben repeated the number the woman had given him as he hung up the phone, then he dialed it. Again, Ben glanced through the window, then he cupped a small screw and slid his hand between the first folder and the inside face of the drawer.

While the phone rang, Ben pinched the screw and closed the drawer. "C'mon," he said at the outgoing ring. The sooner the police arrived, the sooner Palmer would be indefinitely preoccupied. Finally, the call connected, just as Ben was forcing the chain underneath the handle.

"I want to report a car that got beat on." Swiping the glue off the top of the filing cabinet, Ben explained the situation as he squeezed a few beads of superglue onto the metal threads and then onto the back of the handle's base. Speaking through his clenched teeth, Ben pressed the handle against the cabinet. "Shit," he grunted. A shallow puddle of adhesive crept from under the meeting point of the two pieces of metal. The call ended, and Ben hung up.

Ben scraped the glue up with his fingers, then cleaned them on his dirty jeans. He glanced through the window again. The doors were closed. There were no dancing shadows. There were no headlights at all. Palmer had either gone or he was coming.

"Fuck," Ben whispered. He craned his head, looking through the glass for any sight of Palmer, but there was none. Ben had to leave. He shouldn't even be on the second floor, much less—

Ben's hip bumped the side of Palmer's desk, and coffee from the old cup sloshed over the rim, splashing on the pages underneath it. Ben's mind reeled. He stood uncertain, shaking his hands near his chest as if he had just pulled them from a fire.

As quickly as he could, Ben lifted the cup and collected the soiled pages. He twisted the bottom of the mug against the papers, then returned it to the desk. That was it. That was all he could do. Ben shut off the light and squeezed his wide body between the broken door and the broken frame.

Ben hadn't made it halfway down the corridor before he could hear Palmer's footsteps. Ben could go to the other end, around the corner. And then what? There were no open doors down there. As quietly and as rapidly as he could, Ben walked back toward Palmer's office and opened the door across the hall.

The room was musty. Stacks of milk crates filled with old papers, which Ben could barely see in the dim light of the hallway, stretched all the way to the far wall. There was barely any room for Ben at all.

Through the sliver between the door and the jamb, Ben watched Palmer stop in front of his office door. He seemed to consider it for a moment before pushing it inward and flipping on the lights. Ben breathed through his mouth. The room stank like old cardboard thanks to all the ancient displays Palmer refused to throw away.

The man stood at his windows with his hands behind his back, posing in his solitude like a lonely king. After a minute, he fell into his chair and scooped up the phone.

"Lotta stock still on the floor, Ben," he said over the intercom.

Palmer plucked up a few pages and read them, scribbling once or twice. After what must have been twenty minutes, the man stood again, looked out the window, and picked up the phone. "Ben to my office."

Palmer wasn't going to leave the room and Ben couldn't leave his. He watched Palmer watch for him through the windows. Then all at once his throat went dry. Ben realized how stupid he'd been, saw how poorly he'd played at being a spy. Because real spies don't leave their cameras behind.

It was right next to Palmer, right next to his shoulder. Was that where Ben had left it? Hadn't he set it somewhere else? Ben's eyes watered. Palmer swayed from side to side as he looked out over his kingdom for its sole subject. It was only a matter of time before he saw it. Ben had taken only ten, maybe twelve pictures. And they were all Palmer's now.

Resting his head against the jamb, Ben watched Palmer pick up the phone again only to set it down. Ben squeezed his hands into fists as he watched his boss move toward the camera.

And then he just kept moving.

Ben's whole body tingled as Palmer walked past his broken door, then out of view. After a few seconds, Ben eased his own door open and peeked out into the empty hallway. Cautiously, he crossed the space and chanced a glimpse through the window. Blue lights strobed outside. Ben snatched the camera from atop the filing cabinet and left the room.

Then the sky wuh-was wet.

"Luh-look out! Look out!" said someone.

And the guh-good thing said back, "I ain't afraid of rain!"

Buh-but it weren't rain. The ssssky wuh-was a mouth.

40

As Ben hurried across the damp road, he gave his partner a thumbs-up. Marty shot his hands into the air and shouted like Ben was running the final yard of a game-winning touchdown. He started coughing immediately, but he smiled through it, his hands still raised.

Ben laughed. "Are you fucking *kidding me*?" He hugged his friend and lifted him off the ground without any effort at all. "Dude, what in the world!"

"I saw him come in," Marty said frantically. "He was this close to seeing me, dude."

"I was shouting for you."

"I heard you! Holy shit. I fucked his car up!"

"Did you see him when he saw it?" Ben snarled and spat, aping Palmer's frenzied reaction. Marty and Ben laughed together, laughed until Marty had to hold his throat and Ben's stomach hurt.

Ben told Marty about what had happened upstairs as they walked to the drugstore. Marty didn't interrupt, not even with exclamations. He just listened, eyes fixed on Ben, a forgotten cigarette smoldering between his fingers. Ben didn't mention what he'd found in Beverly's file. He wanted more time to think about it: what he'd seen and what he'd say. Plus, the picture would prove it was real, and then it wouldn't matter how it sounded. Of course, that was only if he'd taken a photo of Eric's day, and now he couldn't remember if he had.

Outside the drugstore, Ben puzzled over that uncertainty while he filled out the photo lab envelope. He knew he hadn't taken as many pictures as he could have, which was going to gnaw at him. He looked at the small digits near the viewfinder. If he could account for each number—

"What the fuck . . . ?" Ben muttered.

"Hmm?" Marty grunted through smoke.

"I only got one picture left. I should have like ten."

Marty slipped the camera out of Ben's hands and looked at it. Then he shrugged and stood next to Ben. "Cheeeeeese," Marty said, snapping their picture. "You was probably in the zone, man."

Ben took the camera back, sealed it in the envelope, and dropped it into the metal chute. The tag he'd torn from the form said the pictures would be ready in a few days.

"I guess," Ben replied.

The sky was a gray curtain of clouds backlit by the rising sun. Old cars ambled up and down the street, their wheels grinding loose rocks against the wet asphalt. The air was cold and full of mist.

Marty blew hot air into his hands. "Where the hell did this weather come from?"

At the crest of a hill, Ben could see a seemingly endless sea of trees with gold flakes and bright saffron leaves clinging to the end of their lives amid the emerald of the evergreens. A sharp trench of bare earth carved the forest in half like parted hair before seeming to converge at the edge of the world. Ben wondered where in that ocean of leaves Beverly's house might be as they walked down the escarpment. The store, their own neighborhoods, and the whole town disappeared quietly behind them.

"You think you'll come back?" Ben finally said.

"I dunno," Marty strained as he drew fire into his lungs. "This might surprise you, but I actually don't like Bill Palmer or his goddamn store. The way he's tryin to fuck me with this workman's comp stuff . . . Figure if he wins, I know I won't want to be there. And if I win, he ain't gonna want me around. Hate to say it, but I think that place might have seen the end of my magic touch."

"Don't sound much like you hate to say it," Ben said with a smile. "What're you gonna do instead?"

"If I knew that, I'd be doin it already." Marty smiled and shook his head. "Whatever I can get, most likely."

"What do you wanna do, though?"

"What, you mean like *dreams* and shit?" Marty seemed to ponder this for a moment, absently rubbing the wound on his neck. "Funny as it is, I always wanted to be a singer, like in a band or something. I could sing real good, if you can believe it. The doctor said my voice might heal up when all's said and done. That said, I tried singing in the shower the other day and started coughing so bad I damn near puked, so I dunno about all that, really."

"You mean like *sing* singing?"

"As opposed to what?"

Ben pointed at Marty's Guns N' Roses shirt.

"Oh, I'm sorry. Axl not good enough for you? You Bonnie Tyler–listening fuck."

"She ain't like my favorite singer or whatever," Ben replied incredulously.

"You don't gotta pretend, man. Not with me."

"I ain't."

"Alright . . ." Marty lit up a cigarette. "That cuz you're still holding out for a hero?"

"Get bent." Ben laughed. "Least she knows what a note *is*. 'You're in the jungle baby!'" Ben shouted in his most strained falsetto. "You're gonna have to move to a city if you wanna do all that."

Marty laughed as he ran his fingers over the sutures across his throat. "We was talkin dreams, man. Closest I'll get to bein in a band is stocking shelves at the CD store in the mall."

After a moment, Ben prodded a little. "Think you ever will? Leave, I mean."

"I sure would like to."

"So how come you don't?"

"Family shit."

"Aaron?"

"What? No. Just other shit. Responsibilities and all that. Aaron's gonna be just fine. He's smarter than me. Hell, he's smarter than my whole family. Problem is that he knows it. Don't never have to tell him to do his homework or study or nothin like that. That boy's already lining up colleges and he's barely got hair on his nuts."

"Sounds like he wants to get out too."

"Big time. And he fuckin better too. Go somewhere and be something. Have more'n goddamn TV dinners for Thanksgiving. When I'm an old geezer, I'll probably still be able to see the track marks from where he tore outta here, and they'll be the best-lookin part of this whole wet asshole of a town."

"Tell me what you *really* think, man," Ben said, grinning. "I reckon your brother's got the right idea, though."

"I guess. He ain't got no friends, though. If he wants to see a movie or go somewhere, he's always coming to me. And that's alright, but I tell him that he needs to slow down. Life moves at its own pace."

"What's he say?"

"That I'm a fuckin idiot. That he'll make friends later. That boy's got a lot of lip on him."

"Wonder where he gets that from . . ." Ben smirked.

"Fuck if I know," Marty said, smiling back. "Tim can't stand him. Getting backtalked by a kid like that. Now Tim, there's a real prize."

"Can I ask you somethin, man?" Ben paused rhetorically. "How many brothers do you got?"

Marty didn't respond. The two walked quietly while Marty smoked. Weak wind teased the trees high enough that Ben couldn't feel the breeze.

"I was talking to . . ." Ben hesitated for a moment. "I was talking to one of the Cotter girls. Ellen. The real small one. She's got this nasty scar on her cheek . . ."

The tall grass whipping against Ben's shoes sounded like drops of rain hitting glass. It was the only sound.

"Them girls . . ." Marty let the bitter words hang in the air. "Ty and Kell Cotter are about two of the most fucked-up people I ever met. Kell used to be alright. Good-lookin. Yeah, believe it. But Ty—I don't know where he came from or how in the hell he got his hooks into her, but when he showed up, that was it for Kell. I mean . . . you ever seen tapes of locusts on crops?" Marty gestured to the field to their left. "That's Ty. He ate her *up.* Junkie fuck put two babies in her and dragged that whole fuckin house into whatever's below hell.

"Jessica—the older one—and Aaron was friends forever. Then they got sweet on each other, or Aaron was sweet on her anyway, and she was comin over all the time. Aaron wasn't allowed to go over there on account of who in their right fuckin mind would let a kid step foot into the Cotter house?

"Then *Ellen* started comin over. And she's fine. She . . ." Marty lit another cigarette and pulled on it. "I *do* got another brother. Okay? We ain't fixin to talk about him, but Ellen would not leave him alone. She kept messin with him, and he finally messed back, just like we'd always warned those girls about. And now, because my momma ain't worth a shit, we gotta keep a lock on his door in case that little shithead comes back over. Or in case my brother tries to get out to get at her.

"I don't blame Ellen," Marty said reluctantly. "But Jessica's older. She's supposed to look out for her little sister."

"That's the job," Ben muttered.

"Dude, I didn't mean . . . Goddamnit."

Ben waved his hands. "You didn't say nothin wrong . . . How come you lied about him?"

"No offense, and I mean it, but he ain't really none of your business, Ben."

Ben considered Marty for a long while. "He real young?"

Marty looked toward the sky as if the answer were in the inky clouds. "Seven. No, eight."

"Eric just turned eight." Ben swallowed. "You eat any of that cake?"

Marty nodded.

"I been workin on this drawing of him," Ben said after a moment. "Of what he might look like now. It's been the hardest thing I ever done. I always used to think that it was the eyes that I couldn't get right. But I been thinkin that it's maybe that I don't know what to put *in* the eyes, if that makes sense. I carry his picture around, but I . . ." Ben swallowed. "I don't know him no more. As hard as I try, I can't even think of what he'd be like now."

"Still your brother. Whatever he'd be like, he'd still be that."

"I know," Ben said, mustering a fake smile that struggled to convey his real gratitude. "He had this laugh, man. I'm not kiddin, it would get in your ear and change your whole day. It was the best laugh I ever heard. I think I would still think that even if he weren't my brother." Ben wiped his nose. "I don't know where he got it. Seemed like it just showed up one day. We'd play hide-and-seek, and every time—*every time*—he'd start giggling when I got too close. And right when I'd be about to find him he'd say, 'Olly olly oxen free,' like me finding him couldn't count no more. And then he'd laugh. Sounded like some eighty-year-old frog-man.

"It's stupid, but I can't stop thinkin that he might not even laugh like that no more."

Marty left the silence alone, only scattering it after it had lingered for a long while. "You can't think about shit that way, or at least you shouldn't. If you're just gonna guess at things, I think that maybe you should guess at something good. I don't know what that might be, but maybe it's somethin to try for.

"I also think," Marty added with the pomp of a debater's final remark, "that you should just quit the fucking store once and forever. Might not solve a single problem at all, but it at least won't make things *worse.* And I hope you don't mind me sayin that it seems to me that that's all that place has ever done for you."

To their left, a flat field of withering plants was stamped into the earth. Spots of white flashed boldly against the brown, late cotton that had missed the harvest. Marty put his arms inside his shirt.

"Do you . . ." Ben blushed at just the thought of the question, but there was something about being this far away from town and everything in it that made the question easier to ask somehow. "Do you really think there's something wrong with the store?" Marty looked at Ben quizzically, so Ben tried to supply some clarity. "My first night at the store, you said that it was a weird place. Do you really think that?"

Marty shrugged. "It's a shithole that feels like a creepy shithole sometimes."

"What I mean is . . ." Ben knew what he wanted to ask but wished there was a different way to ask it. "Do you think that a place can be bad?" The last few words tumbled weakly from Ben's lips as his voice shriveled against its own foolish sounds.

"What? You mean like haunted? Like ghosts and shit?"

"No. Bad like a person. Mean."

"You seeing spooky ghosts shopping for haunted bargains?"

"No. I was just askin, man. Dumb question."

Flicking his cigarette into the street, Marty shoved his hands into his pockets. "I don't think it's a dumb question. Not really.

"Aaron asked me once—this was a long time ago, I guess—if God gets bored just watchin everything. Ya know, just sittin up there forever. So I say that I ain't got no fuckin clue, because what kind of question is that? But then later, after thinkin for a bit, I say that however old the Earth is, God's older, right? Older than the galaxy, the whole goddamn universe. Older than everything. The big swingin dick of all that is, sittin around for kajillions of years. Time's gotta move fast for someone like that, right? Like if you take a dayfly and a person, ya know? So He watches everything all the time, keeping everything running smooth. And it's never boring because it's all zipping by so fast. I think it's a pretty good answer. Good enough.

"And then Aaron, that little shithead"—Marty grunted as he pulled on some branches, considered them, then let them go—"Aaron says, 'What about when He blinks?' Like a great joke, Aaron. I don't know if he even realized how much that messed with me.

"I mean, how long would that last for dumb fucks like us down here? Minutes? Whole goddamn lifetimes? Everything everywhere is cruising along and then *wham.* God's not looking anymore.

"Let's take this cut-through."

The smell of dirt was powerful. The opening to the woods didn't look like a proper trail. Dew tattled on spiderwebs hiding high in the trees. As they plunged deeper into the infinite trees, unease coiled in Ben's stomach. Even though the sky was bright, the surrounding branches seemed to tease at Ben's dream. In each clearing he half expected to see a bundle of white twitching in the brush. It would shamble toward him, the sheet falling away. *I'm here,* it would say, and it would sound like his brother. But it wouldn't *be* his brother.

The feeling lingered like a stench, and when Ben looked at his companion, he wondered if his nerves had anything at all to do with the dream. As they walked through the leaves and dirt, Ben glanced at the ground behind them, looking for the jagged shoeprint he'd seen once before but could no longer remember.

"You sure this way is gonna be quicker?" Ben asked.

"I reckon it will. The road is back over that way. To get to where we're goin, we'd have to walk up and then cut across. This whole part of the woods is easy to figure. It's a big square. Markers on some of the trees, since this patch belonged to the paper mill."

"The one that shut down a while back?"

"Yeah. My daddy said that these was special kinds of trees. Supposed to grow real fast. He used to work there, at the mill."

"That place stank so bad." Ben ran his hands gently against the thin needles of the saplings to his right. Standing at knee height, they reached ambitiously toward the giants above them. As he leaned, he wobbled and nearly fell.

"So did he." Marty laughed. "Come home stinkin like sulfur."

"You ever see him still?"

"No. And I lost his fuckin lighter too."

"That Zippo? Dude, I have it," Ben said excitedly. "Yeah, I got it. It flew outta your pocket when the baler tried to kill you."

Marty smiled like a little boy and smacked Ben on the shoulder. "Un-fuckin-believable."

"I'll give it t—" Something caught Ben's shoe. He lurched forward gracelessly, planting his left foot against the ground with such violence that the pain blurred his vision.

"You alright?" Marty asked as he tried to steady Ben. Ben nodded and righted himself. "I ain't giving you no piggyback ride."

Ben turned angrily, as if he might punish the earth itself, but what had snagged him hadn't come from the earth. Not directly. Ben ran his fingers across the rough surface of the rebar. Swearing under his breath, he gripped it like a golf club and strained as he tried to rob it from the dirt.

"Hey, King Arthur," Marty called from up ahead, "get a load of this shit!"

41

About twenty feet from where they stood, wedged so tightly into the trees that it looked as if it had grown with them, sat what could only technically be called a car. Brown paint and red rust seemed to pull it even deeper into the foliage; the woods bent and stretched around it in slow, imperceptible acceptance. The entire front end of the car had curled and warped to accommodate the tree to which it was now forever wed. The driver's door was fully ajar. The hood was crumpled, pushed up toward the windshield like a sheet of tissue paper.

"You think it still works?" Marty asked, sliding into the driver's seat.

"Are you serious?"

"Looks like it's been here for a while . . . Man, what do you think happened?"

"I think it hit that tree."

"How much you reckon it'd cost to tow?" Marty asked, tugging on the glove compartment latch.

"To the junkyard?"

"What? No. To get it fixed up." Marty's face was red from straining. "Motherfucker," he panted, then slid out of the vehicle. "See if you can open that."

"What?"

"For the registration. So we can see if it belongs to somebody."

"It won't open," Ben replied, gesturing to the car.

"Right. So get in there and, you know, flex on it. C'mon, man. Be my streetwise Hercules."

"You sure know a lot of lyrics to that song. I don't remember the part where she wants the fat dude who works at the grocery store."

Marty looked at Ben with bewilderment. "Dude, what? You're like the buffest goddamn guy I've ever met."

"Fuck you."

"Fuck *you,* buddy. I'm not gonna stand around talkin about how your lats could use some definition or whatever. Just . . ." Marty motioned to the car.

"No."

"Dude, you—"

"I'm not gonna fit, and I'm not gonna help you make a joke here."

Marty lit a cigarette. "If you don't fit, I'll eat this."

Ben huffed as he looked at the car. Finally, he put his hand on the roof and squeezed himself into the cramped area between the steering wheel and the seat, keeping his left foot on the ground as he did.

"Ta-da," Marty said.

Ben strained to lean over and pull the handle of the glove compartment.

"Anything?"

"It's jammed," Ben said, pulling on the plastic handle. "It won't—" The handle snapped off in Ben's fingers. He handed it to Marty.

"My glove compartment!" Marty cried. "Is there anything in the console?"

Ben lifted the lid and shuffled through the contents, but he didn't see anything that looked like paperwork for the car.

"Sorry, man. I guess you'll have to keep looking," Ben said, as he struggled to maneuver his body out of the car. He put his hand on the top corner of the door and was about to shut it when he realized how silly that would be.

"Nothing?"

"Just some pieces of paper—grocery lists, directions to somewhere."

"Alright, well, dibs," Marty said, leaving the car behind.

"You can have it."

"I know I can . . . I got dibs."

"How much farther is it, you think?"

"Beats me. This'll spit us out on the right road, I know that much. But as for where the house is at, I have no idea."

The trees began to thin. Ben's leg spiked with pain with nearly every step. Soon they were met with a long strip of unpaved road. They took a guess and walked toward the sun. The addresses on the sparsely set houses indicated that they were headed in the right direction, and when those houses eventually ran out, the two friends were left with only the orange-scarred earth to guide them. But that was enough, because as he and Marty looked down from a small hill, Ben knew they had found Beverly's home. He seemed to know this innately—in the same heart that pounded as they drew closer to it.

The tall grass of the vast yard mingled with the dirt of the road and dissolved into the surrounding trees. The home itself was small and unadorned, save for a low porch whose posts were as rectangular as the house itself. The backyard was as overgrown as the front; several large pine trees peppered the landscape.

As they walked into the backyard, long grass whipped at their pant legs; some stalks were forked and peppered black seeds onto their clothing. Hard and resilient like crab or torpedo grass, it crunched like potato chips under their feet. A tattered rope lay limp in the yard, coiled in parts like a dead snake as it made its way into a knot around one of the tree trunks. A small, dilapidated shed nestled up against the tree line, its siding eroded away like an ancient ruin, exposing the skeletal wooden frame behind it. The scene looked funny to Ben, like the forest had frozen, caught in the beginnings of a slow theft.

"You think she'll pay us to mow her lawn?" Marty said.

"Maybe you should let me do the talking," Ben muttered.

Narrow and long, the front porch sat engulfed by weeds and filth. A wind chime hung motionless from the awning. Marty glanced at the slip of paper that Ben had handed him earlier, then pointed to the numbers on the mailbox fixed to the exterior.

They ascended the steps, which moaned at their weight. Each window had a layer of grime so thick that attempting to peer inside was like trying to see through a mud puddle. The mailbox was full of catalogs and envelopes that had spilled out onto the deck, some partially caught between the warping boards, all of them old and faded. Ben knocked lightly on a plastic sheet tacked to the door, his knuckles striking on the bold-typed CONDEMNED printed at the top, which made his heart sink a little. They waited for an answer, but none seemed imminent.

"Ms. Beverly?" Ben called, knocking a little louder. "I don't think she's here."

"That notice don't mean squat. Piece of paper can't stop a person from stayin in a place. What's the date on it?" Marty pressed his hands against the screen over the window and attempted to peer inside.

"About three years ago."

"I can't see shit," Marty hissed. "This window's made of dirt."

"Ms. Beverly?" Ben pounded. "It's Ben and Marty from the store. You in there?"

"Gimme your cutter." Marty said, extending this hand toward Ben.

"What for?"

"I think I see her. Gimme yer cutter."

"So you can cut the screen? No way."

"You said wasn't no one in there anyhow. Okay, I'll buy her a new one, then. How much is a screen? Like a buck?"

"I think it's probably more than a buck. Besides, I came out here to say I was sorry. I don't wanna have to apologize for the screen too."

"Just gimme it, would ya?"

Ben sighed and reached for his waist but felt only his empty holster. "Crap, I don't got it. I must've dropped it."

"Wait!" Marty hissed. "That's gotta be her. Goddamn this window." Marty dug his fingers into the frame, attempting to pry the screen off. Ben grabbed his arm.

"I don't think she's in there. I don't think anyone lives here, man."

"Then no one will care if I—" The window frame cracked loudly as the screen came loose; it settled on the porch with a clatter. As the wind made toddler music on the chimes, Marty used the side of his hand to polish the window. He peered in.

"Anything?" Ben asked.

"Just a bunch of junk. And a chair that I could have sworn looked like an old lady." Marty chuckled.

Leaning against the splintering wood of the house, Ben massaged the tissues of his leg and sighed audibly. "What now?"

"Well," Marty said as his fingertips brushed against the slowly opening door, "now I reckon that we see what's inside."

42

"It was open?" Ben murmured as he followed Marty across the threshold, holding his elbow like a leash.

"You see how much trouble I had with that screen?" Marty gently jerked his arm out of Ben's grasp. "I ain't no lock picker."

"We shouldn't be in here. This is breaking and entering."

"I didn't break the door."

"Entering then. Trespassing!" Ben whispered loudly.

The sun struggled through the dirt-tinted windows. What light did survive ricocheted against ancient dust that seemed frantic to entertain the two very unexpected guests. With the light still at their backs, two doorways down a narrow hall and a back exit were plainly visible.

"Hello?" Ben shouted tentatively.

"I thought it'd be warmer in here," Marty muttered, stepping deeper into what appeared to be the living room.

A weathered armoire decorated the otherwise barren wall opposite the entrance, its doors slightly ajar. To their right were several wooden chairs and a stubby coffee table, above which hung a framed family photograph with no glass. Ben's feet shuffled against the grit on the wooden floor and then around the pine chairs. He gazed intently at the enormous bald man in the center of the photo.

"Jesus," Marty said.

Ben turned and saw him standing in front of the armoire, its doors now fully open. He shook a stained and unattractive cloth doll in Ben's direction.

"Give me the power, I beg of you!"

Ben looked at him blankly.

"Chucky?" Marty said. "Killer doll and all that?"

"We shouldn't be looking through her stuff," Ben said, leaving the photograph.

Marty seemed to consider this for a moment before placing an unopened varnished box back on the upper shelf. He closed the doors and dusted his hands against each other. "Ain't nothin here anyway. But look at the fuckin walls, man."

It was hard to see in the poor light, but the walls were a sloppy mosaic of paints: huge patches of muted red on green, flanked by black and blue. There was no pattern. It looked as if someone had set out to paint the room, then started switching colors between each stroke.

The next room was even darker. With the blinds shut, Ben had to squint his eyes to make out the bed against the wall; it played footsie with a smaller cot where the walls joined. Dry wood creaked underfoot. The air tickled at Ben's nose, which he rubbed with his handkerchief.

Marty shuffled into the hall and through the doorway of the opposite room. "This one's about the same," he called.

Ben delicately prodded a small wooden train car with his foot, scraping it dully against the floor before tipping it over. The wardrobe on the wall to his left was empty, just like the rest of the house. It all felt so hollow and as stale as the air that filled it up.

"I think we ought to go," Ben said. "I don't think we should be in here."

But it was more than that. Ben didn't *want* to be there. He very much wanted to leave. In spite of the kaleidoscope of paint on the walls, everything there felt gray. Forgotten. Forsaken.

"How long you think it's been since someone lived here?"

"Couldn't tell ya." Marty cleared his throat. "My granddaddy lived in a house like this. Little bigger, I guess. Hard to remember, it's been so long since I been there. Hardest part about the house was keeping it clean. A lot of these kindsa houses weren't sealed. The wood, I mean." He stomped his foot on the floor. "So it warps and dirt and bugs get in. There was a great big crack in my granddaddy's floor. I remember when I'd have to sweep, I'd just push everything back through there. This the only address you saw in that folder?"

"Yeah." Ben leaned against the wall and shut his eyes. This was the second time in a day that he'd intruded on Beverly's life.

Ben tugged at the cord of the window blinds, hoping to let in some light. Dust and dirt scattered across his arm, but no light came. He yanked just a bit harder. There was a snap and the blinds tumbled down onto the piled sheets of the lumpy bed.

"Blinds cost way more than a buck, ya know?"

Ben ignored his friend and walked back into the hallway, which fed into the kitchen. There, drawers sat half open, full of utensils and rags, illuminated by the pale light of a window without dust-choked blinds. Furnished so fully, the room felt somehow heavier in Ben's mind. Metal clanged behind him as Marty curiously kicked at a wood-burning stove. Ben watched as he tapped on the tall cylinder that connected the stove with the ceiling like an iron tentacle.

"Why would she just leave all her stuff?"

"I know, right? So much great shit here. She coulda taken just half this dust and built herself a whole new home." Marty ran his hand along the dirty counter, then brushed his palms together.

Ben flicked at the handle of an old lantern that sat on the windowsill and sighed. He looked out at the scraggly lawn. In spite of everything inside his own heart, Ben had managed to convince himself that Beverly was fine, that she didn't really *need* the job like she said she did: she just wanted it very badly. A woman who had worked as long as she had must have something to catch her when she fell. But nothing in this place could catch her. It was all too brittle.

"I hate this place," Marty muttered.

They walked back into the living room, and Ben groaned as he sat in one of the chairs. Marty sat crisscross on the floor, then leaned forward and slapped his hand on a book, dragging it off the coffee table. He thumbed through the pages.

"There any chance they made that book at your daddy's mill?" Ben said, smiling through a wince as he rubbed his leg.

"This is scritta. They didn't make this kinda paper there. Need a whole other machine." Marty tossed the book back onto the table. "I think you gotta go to the cops now, Ben. I don't know what else I can do far as helpin you."

Ben shook his head.

"Whatever it is, dude, whatever you have against that one cop with the fucked-up arm . . . Go talk to someone else then. I dunno. I thought we'd find something here."

"I can't. I said that already. He ain't gonna listen to me."

"It's his fuckin job to listen to you. What, did you burn down his granny's house or something? Shit, even if you *did,* he's still on the goddamn payroll."

"He says I killed someone." Ben let the words hang in the sour air for a while before he spoke. "We was in the checkout." Ben cleared his throat. "Me and Eric was at the checkout, and I had a lot of stuff on the conveyer. I wanted to go home. Then Eric says he needs to use the bathroom.

"I . . . I don't know why I didn't just take him. He's little. He has to go to the bathroom. It don't matter if I asked him five minutes ago. It don't matter if it was five seconds. I don't remember what I said to him exactly, but I just wanted to get outta there.

"Then this guy behind us, *he* offers to take him. I say no and turn back away from him, and then he offers *again.* Two times this guy offers to take my three-year-old brother to the bathroom. He don't ask to take my money and buy my stuff with it. He don't just ignore us or leave us alone. He offers something that don't make no sense to offer. And he does it twice.

"After everything happened and the police came, I tell them about that guy. And the cashier, she goes, 'Oh, that was Bob Prewitt.'

"Do you know that name?" Ben's voice quavered.

Marty nodded. "That's Ty Cotter's cousin."

"Imagine my surprise when I learned that very thing. I didn't know Prewitt or Cotter. Not at the time. Not then. Anyway, the police are talkin to me and they're askin about him, and I know, I mean I *know,* that they don't care. Not about what I'm sayin. I can feel this while I'm telling them.

"So I told James Duchaine—that one that came and saw you—I told him that I seen Prewitt in the parking lot tearing ass outta there in his truck. I don't know why I said it, but they cared. Took 'em till the next day, but they cared. They never got no dogs for Eric, never made no statements about him. Talkin to Bobby Prewitt is the first and last thing that they ever did. And they needed to talk to him. They weren't gonna and they needed to.

"They get a warrant to search his property, but they don't find nothin 'cept for two things: that he was growin pot inside his house, and that Bobby Prewitt didn't own a truck."

Ben exhaled heavily and wiped his dusty hands on his jeans. "The end of this story is that Bobby Prewitt went and killed himself. He done it because he lost a custody battle he was havin with his old lady over their kid. He'd been fightin this woman for a long time, from what I was told. Had to make a real big case for himself.

"He lost that custody battle because of the pot. Then a few months later, that kid had some kind of accident at the lake near the mom's house.

"I told Duchaine about everything, man. About Palmer, the flyers, the symbol. He don't care. He just does not *care.* He says that I lied to him about what I seen. Figure he might have even thought that while I was telling it. I did see someone driving off. I did see that . . .

"And what's fucked up"—Ben laughed incredulously—"is that I know it ain't true. It can't be. But sometimes I can see him, man. I can *see* Bob Prewitt in that truck. Even though Duchaine says I'm a liar and even though he didn't own no truck, I can see him peelin out in my head. Clear as day.

"So I can't talk to him, okay? Him, Missing Persons . . . don't matter."

Ben leaned forward and lifted the book from the table. It felt leathery in his hands, soft and well worn. His fingers caressed the embossing on the cover. HOLY BIBLE. He thumbed through the pages, which felt as brittle and thin as rice paper in his hands.

"I didn't know this was a special kind of paper," Ben mumbled.

"You see how thin it is, though."

"Yeah, I guess I just thought they made regular paper and then split it in half, like two-ply toilet paper or something. Made sense in my head all the way up until I just said it."

On the very first page was a name written in an unsteady hand. "Beverly." It was hard to tell what trembled the writing, whether it was before she'd refined her motor skills or after she'd lost them. Ben rubbed the soft page between his thumb and index finger. Faded ink stamped in the shape of BLACKWATER SCHOOL marred the page just above the scribbled name.

There was a tremble in Ben's leg. He shifted the book to try to catch more of the lazy light, but there wasn't enough. Ben stood and moved toward the window, and as the sun touched the wispy paper, Ben felt like his skin might just slither right off his bones.

In stamped ink, faded and pocked by time, there it was: mother moon smiling at her dancing son. Four curves and a line that reached all the way to a place Ben had never even heard of. A beacon that called to Ben.

Ben wasn't sure if he had said anything. He didn't remember calling to Marty, but his friend rose from the floor to Ben's side by the window.

"L-look," Ben stammered. "You see it, right?"

"Fuck."

"That's it, right? That's the same thing."

"Yeah."

"That's the same fucking thing, right?"

"Yes."

"What is this? What the fuck is Blackwater School?"

"I don't know. You gotta go to the police. They gotta talk to Beverly."

"Frank's dad!" Ben shouted. "Frank's dad used to work there. He told me. He said that his daddy used to work there. What the *fuck,* man! Why . . . He said he never saw this before!"

"Ben," Marty snapped, "you hearin me? You need to take this book and show 'em, because someone needs to talk to that loopy bitch."

"He told me . . . he told me right before I found that flyer in my locker."

"So what?"

"So *what*? He told Duchaine your accident was my fault. Said he never seen this before!"

"You can't see it. I don't know why, but you can't see that something's wrong with Beverly. She ain't your grandma, Ben! She ratted you out to Palmer."

"Then why would Palmer fire her?"

"I don't have any goddamn idea! But I know that the symbol is in her fuckin book! You're holding it, dude. Look at it!"

There was a throbbing in Ben's skull, a kind of pain right behind his eyes that radiated outward like ripples in a still lake. With the book under his arm, Ben walked into the kitchen and turned on the faucet, hoping to wet his face and his throat, but the spout was nothing but an ornament now.

"What'd you come out here for?" Ben snapped.

"Why did *you*? You wanna say sorry to Beverly? You wanna see if she knows something about *Palmer*? Palmer ain't the one you need to be thinkin about. There's something wrong with Beverly, you dumb fuck. Open your fuckin eyes already!"

Ben inhaled to speak, but his throat tightened, freezing his breath in his lungs. There was a prickling against his scalp, like cold rain the size of small needles. Using his kerchief, he tried to clean the glass, but the grime was on the other side. "C'mere," Ben said, and motioned to Marty. "There. Do you see that?"

"The window? Yeah, I see it," Marty said, approaching. "What am I lookin for?"

"Right there." Ben pressed the tip of his finger against the glass and stepped back so Marty could use it as a sight. "Standin in them trees some. Look."

"Huh?" Marty cupped his hands on the window and leaned against it. "No, I don't see noth— Oh, Christ," Marty whispered, his breath fogging the glass. "Ben, there's a boy out there."

43

"What're we gonna do?" Ben hissed.

"We're gonna talk to him," Marty replied, never turning away from the glass.

The boy still hadn't moved, though as Ben shifted on his feet, the stained window sometimes made it seem to Ben that the child had vanished right before his eyes.

"We're gonna see if blondie here knows where Beverly's gone to."

"Look, he's movin."

"I see him."

"He might not have anything to do with this place."

"Ain't no one out here 'cept for us and him. What are the odds of somethin like that? What are the odds he ain't seen her? Don't know where she's at? How'd he even find this place?"

"*You* found it."

"I don't think he can see us." Marty moved so quickly that Ben almost missed the chance to grab his arm.

"What're you doin?"

"I'm gonna talk to him."

"He might come this way. You go out there now and maybe he bolts. Let him keep comin."

"He's just walkin the tree line. He ain't stepped foot in the yard. Fuck off my arm. I'm goin."

"He'll get away. We go out the kitchen, and we can get to him quiet."

"You ain't getting to no one quiet. Let go of my fuckin arm."

Ben squeezed tighter when Marty pulled. Sneering, Marty rammed his knee into Ben's bad leg. Lightning cracked in Ben's skull. He stumbled, and Marty hurried through the front door. He moved fast. Ben saw a blur zip by the cloudy window. Marty's voice sounded from the backyard. Ben had only reached the sink when he heard Marty shout again. And by the time Ben stepped out the door, Marty had already been swallowed up by the thick trees.

The kid had run, just like Ben had said. Why wouldn't he? The ragged steps moaned under Ben's weight as he descended them before stepping into the yard. Somewhere in the distance, Marty hollered, and Ben could only think how unwelcoming that would sound to young ears.

Ben had never seen Marty so angry or so filled with purpose. As he walked through the yard, Ben wondered where that righteous indignation might have been when Marty was keeping his own little secret.

Keeping pace with them would be impossible. There was never anytime during the whole walk to this place that Ben had any sense of where he was, and now his leg was on fire. He'd lose his way, and then he'd be the one calling out in the maze of trees.

Ben leaned his shoulder against the shed, then slammed his fist against it. Absently, Ben glanced at the side of the structure; most of the frame had bowed and split like easily peeked-through window blinds. He could see right inside. Some old tools sat on an older workbench. That was all.

Sucking through his teeth against the pain, Ben slid his back down along the warped boards of the shed and sat on its dirt foundation. Gently, he pressed his knuckles into the muscle of his leg. "Motherfucker," he muttered.

Ben opened the Bible again and ran his fingers over the symbol, then set it on the dirt beside him. Blackwater School was up in Alabama, Frank had said. The Blackwater River didn't stretch far into that state. Maybe it was close. What the fuck did it have to do with Eric? Ben didn't ask himself that question, but his mind furnished him with answers anyway: images of his baby brother alone in a classroom with whoever took him, crying for help. Learning things that no little boy should know.

Ben tried to listen to the quiet air. He plucked seeded grass stalks from the earth and picked them apart. Snapping a thick blade of grass off in the middle, Ben pinched it longways between the sides of his thumbs, just like his father had taught him when he was a boy still small enough to believe in magic. The taste of grass was bitter against his lips as he pulled air into his lungs. Ben blew, but there was no whistle, only the hollow sound of wind wisping through clutching hands.

Ben tossed the blade back to its family. Marty hadn't just wanted to talk to Beverly. He said that he'd hoped they'd find something out here. And then what do you know? They had. How lucky.

It had been a long while since Marty ran into the woods. Ben listened, but there were no more shouts at all now. Marty was still out there somewhere, chasing a blond boy through the wild trees.

Chasing a boy who looked an awful lot like Aaron.

So the guh-good thing said, "Well,

whu-what should I duh-do?"

But there weren't nothin he could do.

Because he could fuh-feel the teeth now.

It was too late.

44

Pushing air forcefully through his nostrils, Ben sat up and rubbed his face, concentrating on his tired eyes. As his knuckles pressed firmly into his sockets, Ben beat back the memory of the fight. Storming out. Sneaking in. He hadn't heard his alarm, but it must have gone off, because he woke up to the faint sound of dishes in the kitchen. Right on time.

He found his way into a shirt and pants and eased his door open. Warm light from the television flickered against the walls of the living room, but it had no audience.

"Mornin, Pa," Ben whispered.

"Oh," Clint said, then reached for another plate from the cabinet. "You off tonight?"

"Store'll be locked up by now anyhow. She sleepin already?"

Clint nodded his head, then dipped his chin toward Eric's room. "You want pepper in your eggs?"

Ben nodded and drank three glasses of water to make up for the day before. He'd sat there for an hour before Marty finally came back, cursing, saying that the boy had just disappeared. He collapsed in a chair as Clint brought their plates to the table.

"Leg seems bad."

"Ain't never been that good."

"Got a line on a job maybe."

"Yeah?" Ben replied.

Clint nodded, then brushed some egg out of his beard. "Know someone at the courthouse. Says they need a file clerk."

"What's that?"

"Somethin with files, I reckon. Getting files. Filin files." The man took another bite, then pushed his eggs around with his fork. "You want it?"

Ben rubbed his thigh with the heel of his hand. "What's it pay?"

"Does it matter?" Clint took another bite, leaving space for Ben to respond. "You let me know," Clint added curtly.

They sat in silence for a few minutes before Ben spoke again. He asked if his father wanted some company at work.

At the distribution center, all manner of vehicles idled in a line just in front of an elevated concrete platform. Carbon monoxide steamed from tailpipes as drivers waited—some fast asleep with mouths agape—for the large, paneled door to retreat so they could fetch their freight.

Yellow light poured down from a cracked aluminum cone, illuminating a man's dramatic gesticulations as he moved his mouth at a pear-shaped woman with blond hair as thin as kite strings. Following his father, Ben stepped out of the truck and into air that was swirling with wind and bickering. Even from a distance, Ben could hear the voice of the man he'd come to see.

"No way," the man said. "Uh-uh." He shook his head. Had his eyes been open, he could have seen from east to west.

"You need to make it right," the woman snarled, crushing a cigarette under her heel.

"*You* need to climb down out of my *ass,*" he said, pointing from one to the other. "Oh, hey, look here. Here we go." He frantically waved Clint over, despite the fact that he and Ben were practically at spitting distance from them.

"Reggie." Clint nodded. "Brandy. You both know Ben."

Reggie had dark skin and perfect teeth. A little heavy around the midsection, but he carried it in such a way that people would say he was a big guy, not a fat one. Little tracks of gray cut through the black hair on the sides of his head. His glasses were thick, with large frames.

"Hey! How you doin, young Ben?" Ben almost had a chance to answer before Reggie continued. "Now listen to this," he said, tapping Clint on the chest with the back of his hand. He brushed some of Brandy's ashes off his forearm. "A man can get dirty just standing *next* to you, Bran. Go on then, girl. Let him hear it."

"*Next* to me is as close as you're ever gonna get. And who is he? King Solomon?"

"King *who*? Just tell the man."

"Don't make no difference. I don't give a damn what he says—"

"I don't wanna get in the middle of this," Clint interjected.

"Oh, you right *smack* in the middle now. Spit it out, girl. You want me to tell it?"

"Then he'd have to hear two stories. The one you tell him and the truth." She smirked at Reggie, who scoffed incredulously. Frank really did look a lot like his father. "The other day Reggie asks me if I'll switch routes with him—"

"Just for the night," Reggie cut in.

"Just for the night. Says he's got to pick his son up from work—"

"He had a doctor's appointment, and her route finishes right by his work—"

"Goddamn, Reggie. Would you let me say what happened?" she spat, adjusting the collar on her denim shirt.

"I'm just saying that my route finishes way over there"—he gestured—"by the—waddya call it—the raceway."

"What the hell does that matter?"

"I'm just sayin is all."

"Go ahead," Clint encouraged Brandy, who leered with striking disbelief at a puzzled Reggie.

"*Anyway,* I say alright, *even though* I had already counted out my stacks and *even though* I ain't never driven that route since they added what stops they added."

"You said you was happy to do it!" Reggie moaned.

"It's an expression. Why would I be happy to do anything for your old, ashy ass? The point is that when I was driving through Scotty's Hardware on *your route*"—she scowled at Reggie—"I got a damn nail in my tire."

"And she wants me to pay for it! You believe that? I didn't put that nail there!"

"Weren't never've happened if I didn't take your route."

"You said you was happy to do it!"

Brandy sighed in exasperation. "So that's it. That's what happened." She lit another cigarette. "And yeah, I *do* think he should pay for it. Pitch in at least. I mean, damn. Ain't never got no flat tires on my route, and I been driving it, what? Five, six years?"

"Yeah, but neither have I," Reggie said wryly. "It was a freak accident. An act of God. I can't be held responsible for *that*."

"If you say 'act of God' one more time, I'm gonna put a nail in your damn *head,*" Brandy growled.

"So waddya think there, chief?" Reggie gestured toward Clint. Brandy's eyes were averted as she drew on her cigarette.

"I think that this is really none of my business," he replied evasively. A metallic clamoring rose up behind the small group, and the door slowly receded into the building. Truck and car doors whined open and thudded shut as several dozen feet shuffled up the concrete steps, onto the platform, and into the building, hurrying out of the cold. Ben could see the relief in his father's face as he retreated glacially, hoping Reggie and Brandy wouldn't notice until he was already gone.

"Ah, don't be like that," Reggie pestered.

Clint sighed with resignation through smiling lips. "Well, if you wanna know what I think," he teased as Reggie nodded intently, "I think that Bran was doing you a favor, so you might do her one in return."

"Ha!" Brandy shouted.

"I *had* to pick Frank up," Reggie pleaded. "She didn't have to run over no nail!"

"How's he doin?" Ben asked.

Reggie pressed his lips together. "He's doin good." He nodded, pushing his glasses up his nose the same way Frank had always done, with the bend of his index finger against the glass. "He's okay. Makin good money at that new superstore. How's Marty doin? He doin alright?"

"He seems to be getting better. Out of the woods anyhow."

"Good. That's good. I know Frankie really liked him a lot. Still rips him up, what happened."

Reggie wasn't going to offer, so Ben had to push. "You think it'd be alright if I came by to see Frank sometime?"

"You'd have to check with him. I know he's beat. More than even when he worked at your store."

"We gotta get goin," Ben's father said, scratching at his beard.

"Good seeing you, Ben," Reggie said.

Ben thanked the man and said good-bye to Brandy.

"Alright then," the woman said. "Pay up."

"What? Oh, because *Clint* said I should? I don't give a damn what he says."

Ben's father heaved thick bundles of newspaper down to Ben, who ferried them to the bed of the truck. The whole time, Ben watched Reggie haul bundles by himself, smiling and muttering to himself, pushing his glasses up each time he had to bend down for a new stack. Every now and then he glanced skyward at the black clouds that everyone seemed to think were nothing more than a bluff. If the rain did come, Clint would have to cover their cargo with the tarp from the toolbox in the back of the truck.

Ben's movements were more graceful than in previous summers. His lungs seemed more resilient as well. It was his father who finally asked for a quick break, and when he did, Ben suggested that Reggie might need some help.

"Heya, Reggie," Ben called as the man dropped a bundle into the trunk of his car. The whole body of the vehicle sagged at the new weight. "You need a hand?"

"Oh, hey there, Ben. No, I think I got it." Reggie smiled and craned his neck. "Where's your daddy at? He tell you that I needed your help more than he did?"

"Nosir." Ben grinned. "He's takin a break himself."

Reggie pushed his glasses up and huffed. "Hey! Get back to work, old man!"

Ben could hear his father's laughter in the air. This wasn't the right time—not for the whole thing—but Ben could start something here, open a door.

"I meant to ask you," Ben said. "You know if Blackwater is still around?"

"Blackwater?" Reggie replied, passing Ben with a bundle of papers. He didn't speak again until he'd set it in his car. "Don't think I've ever heard of it."

"Frank told me that you used to work there. Blackwater School? Before you was at Bradley Park, he said."

Reggie smiled and furrowed his brow. "I think either you or Frankie got mixed up about somethin there, Ben. I worked at a lot of places, but not no place called Blackwater."

Ben stood there for a moment under the low sky while Reggie ferried his stacks.

"Before Bradley Park, I was at a place called Mikey's Auto. Then . . . what was it. Shoot, I can't remember the name. Some crew that did lawns. Lawngrow. Something like that. Lawnpro Incorporated. That was it. Just some guy with a mower. Stuck 'Incorporated' on the end just for the sound."

"Ben!" Clint shouted from behind the truck. "Let's hit it."

"Guess I must've heard it wrong," Ben said. "Tell Frank I said hey, would ya?"

"I sure will." Reggie smiled.

"He let you help?" Clint asked. The door to his truck squeaked as he pulled it open.

"Nope," Ben replied.

Ben couldn't remember exactly what Frank had said. He had been certain back at Beverly's house, certain enough to let the memory carry him right up to Reggie. But now he couldn't keep hold of Frank's words.

As Clint pulled the truck out of the lot, Ben looked over at Reggie. There were still a few bundles left, but he wasn't carrying them. He wasn't moving at all now. Leaning against his silver car, Reggie stood staring into the glossy windows of a delivery van. He wasn't smiling anymore.

45

There were times, especially when driving on long dirt roads, that Ben had to remind himself that he and his father weren't the last two members of a long-dead race. The isolation at the store was less severe and certainly less quiet—even now that Ben worked alone—but there was something about *moving* through the stillness that felt odd to Ben. Sometimes the feeling lasted for miles, stopping only when papers had to be slung or someone spoke. But their stops were few and far between, and for the most part the only noise was the wind streaking in through the partially lowered windows.

Beverly's home sat in Ben's mind unsteadily, its details fuzzed and fleeting to the point that it almost felt like a dream. Of course, it hadn't been a dream. It couldn't have been, because Ben could still *feel* that yellow-haired boy standing at the edge of the tree line. Ben could still feel him in his sinking gut every time he thought that maybe that boy looked just a little familiar, even out there, even without features that Ben could make out. Staring at a house that had been condemned for years, a house with windows so muddy, he would have been invisible were it not for the strung gold that hung from his head. Staring until Marty chased him even deeper into the trees. He must have been very fast, that boy—so fast that Marty had just given up. "I couldn't find him anywhere," Marty had said.

They rode for a long time slinging papers on a route that Ben had never seen before. Many of the locations were buried on remote roads. They didn't say much, and that was fine, for a while anyway.

"I'm sorry." Ben let the words hang. "For what happened last night."

"Yeah, that was somethin."

The brakes squealed as Clint rolled the truck to a stop at a deserted intersection. He glanced down the black roads, then coasted forward.

Two songs played on the radio before Clint spoke again. "I see how she is. I see it. How she's changed. And I know *I've* changed . . ." He tapped his palm lightly against the steering wheel. "I don't think she can move on. And I don't think that makes her weak. Everyone's got that line. What do you do? Just what in the holy mother of fuck is a person supposed to do when life says to you, 'Hey, I see what you've built there. And *I don't like it.*' Everyone's got that line."

"Like Momma."

"I talked to her, you know?" Clint said. "Ran into her a few years ago. She said she was sorry. For the drinking. For a lot of things. She always tried to be a mother to you. I don't know if you remember it none. She seems to be a much better one now, for whatever that's worth. Happy. She couldn't believe that any of us were holding it together with all that was going on. Wanted me to say that she was sorry to you too."

"How come you didn't tell me?"

"I dunno. Maybe I should've. But she could have tried just a little harder. Instead of leaving when it got too tough, she could have tried. I'm not gonna deliver her sorries to you just so she can feel like she really done something."

"You just did, though. You just told me."

"Shit," Clint said with a bit of a smile. "I'll tell you this, though. As hard as this has all been, we've handled it. Right way or not, I don't know, but we've handled it. And we still are. You at that store. I don't get it, but you do, and that's enough.

"We're still together," Clint added after a while. "Even when you leave home and go start you a life, we'll all still be *together* in the ways that matter. Your momma . . ."

"What?"

The man shook his head. "I don't want to badmouth your mother."

"I ain't seen her since I was little, Pa." Ben shrugged.

"She had this look of *relief* in her eyes when I told her," Clint said with disgust. "For just a second. Like she was glad she got out before it could happen to her—like that makes any damn sense at all. I dunno, maybe I read too much into it, saw something that wasn't there." Clint exhaled heavily. "We got dealt a hell of a hand, Ben. The lot of us." His father cleared his throat. "And if you . . . if you ever needed to talk to someone . . ."

"Someone who?"

"Anybody. Like a doctor."

"About Eric?"

"About anything. Anything at all." Clint opened his mouth as if to speak, then closed it. Then he opened it again. "We saw one. Me and Deidra."

"I didn't know that."

"Never thought I'd pay someone to just sit and listen. Seems like that's all she did, anyhow, but I reckon she must've done somethin or other when I wasn't lookin, because it worked."

"Worked how?"

"I came to terms with some things, let go of some other ones. Like this dream I'd been havin."

Cold wind moved like a banshee through the cracked windows. Needles danced on Ben's skin. "What dream?"

"I had all kinds. Dreams and dreams. Good ones, bad ones, and everything in between and on either side. But there was this one . . ." Clint trailed off, shaking his head as he turned the truck. "He just came back one day. Just walked through the door like it weren't nothin at all. We was all sittin there, in the house I mean, and I look up and there he is. Older and different, but still him. Still Eric. You'd think that everyone woulda been flippin their shit, but no one made much of a fuss at all, including him. He just says, 'I win,' and sits down at the supper table and puts his head down.

"And we all just kinda go about our business like either he never even left or we didn't understand that he come back. But then he starts countin. Up. Not down like you always did with him when you played your games. Shrink made a big fuss about that one. I can't remember if she said it or if she made me say it—cuz that's what she always did: made me say the thing she figured out like it was my own damn idea—but I spent damn near three weeks talkin to this lady just to find out that Eric countin *up* was supposed to mean that I was scared of losing you too."

"Why?"

Clint tugged and scratched at his beard. "Because it was your turn."

The truck rocked back and forth over the uneven road. Its yellow headlights washed over a thin man ambling along the shoulder. He stuck his thumb out and glared into the glass as the truck rumbled by. Ben wondered where he could possibly be heading that he needed to go *deeper* into nowhere.

"I miss it sometimes. The dream. Strange thing . . ."

"How come you're telling me all this?"

His father stared out the windshield and shrugged. "Because you're my boy. You're a good son. And a good brother."

Ben thought about the tape in Palmer's filing cabinet. "Thanks, Pa" was all he said.

The old truck turned onto a road that Ben's eyes met with vague recollection.

"Hey, Pa. You ever heard of a place called Blackwater?" Ben asked.

"The river? Yeah, sure. Runs from up somewheres in Alabama down to the Gulf, I think. We used to take rafts out and coolers of beer."

"No, I meant the school. Blackwater School."

"Blackwater School. Black. Water. School," Clint repeated slowly, as if trying to coax the information from the words themselves. "Oh!" he exclaimed. "I think that was a school for live-ins up in Alabama. Or was it . . . Where's Blackwater Park? The state park, I mean."

"I got no idea, Pa. What do you mean 'live-ins'?"

"Orphan kids. Some of 'em. Or maybe abandoned kids."

"Was it a religious school?"

Clint shrugged his shoulders. "Probably. Back then a lot of places like that were, I reckon."

"It still open?"

"No. No, I don't think so. Been a long time since that place shut down as I recall. For the life of me, I can't remember what for, though. You ask me, we still need places like that."

Stop after stop, the men delivered their stacks of newspapers, and before long, the arrangement of the trees and nuanced curves of the asphalt began to look familiar to Ben. Unending woodland gradually disintegrated into flat fields. A light glowed with an exaggerated halo through the faint fog, and Ben knew what it was before it pierced the mist.

"Check your watch, boy. We made pretty good time tonight," Clint said with a great deal of pride.

Ben wasn't sure if he had ever seen the store so dark. The parking lot loomed like a black lake in front of a store vacant of life and light. Overlapping shifts ensured that the windows shined perpetually fluorescent, but now the only remaining employee who worked overnights was riding through the gloomy parking lot in wonder.

The truck idled as Ben reached into the bed for two large bundles of newspapers. The plastic ties gouged angrily at his hooked fingers, pinching and pulling more with each waddle of a step he took toward the front door.

"Lemme give you a hand," his father called from the driver's seat. Slow applause echoed off the side of the store.

"Good one, Pa," Ben grunted over his shoulder. He walked over to the spot where Marty used to sit. Pocked with scorches from his cigarettes, the concrete looked like a cratered moon.

"Classics are classics," Clint shouted as Ben unloaded his cargo in front of the entrance. The imperfect glass of the doors bent the truck's headlights at odd angles. Cupping his hands, Ben pressed them against the glass and peered inside, though he wasn't sure what he expected to see in the abyss. Ben's stomach tightened at the thought of Beverly's file and the idea that whoever knew that Ben would see it might know by now that he had.

Aisles and aisles of murky darkness stared back at Ben. Dull banners and signs hung frozen in the black air. And something else. Something curious. A light.

Not fluorescent, or even anchored to the ceiling, it flickered near the back of the store, peeking out like a flashlight's bulb through splayed fingers. Though that wasn't the image that moved through Ben's mind. He thought only of the boy's golden hair shining through the twisted bones of old trees. Wrapping his hand around the protruding lock, Ben tugged against the doors until the bolt rattled. But the light remained, staring.

Ben shouted for his father to turn the headlights off, and when they clicked off, Ben turned his attention back to the window and stared into the store for what might have been a full two minutes. There was nothing to see now; like the golden boy, the light had fled. But Ben knew he'd seen it: a light blinking closed like a glaring eye.

Ben rubbed his dirty handkerchief against the back of his neck. "Turn 'em back on!" he shouted to his father over the idling engine.

"What's the problem?"

"Just hit the lights real quick, Pop."

The bright lamps flooded Ben's thirsty pupils, stinging like cold water hitting a parched throat. Squinting, Ben peered back through the glass and moved his body, trying to force the reflection to resemble what he had just seen, but it never did. He checked his watch. Just after four in the morning.

"What is it?" his father called.

Ben walked briskly toward the truck and slid back into his seat. "Nothing," he said, brushing off the chill. "Thought I saw a light on inside."

"They got someone else workin this shift now?"

Ben could only shake his head and stare out his window, still searching for that golden light.

46

Ben slept for a few hours, dragging himself out of bed just before one in the afternoon. He lay there for a while, listening to the sounds of the house. The soft murmurs of the television through the door. The hum of a lawnmower somewhere farther away. He moved in stages, first sitting on the edge of his bed, then standing in his boxers and shirt, staring at the clutter of his room.

Quietly, Ben pulled the Bible free from the shelf, then spaced its neighbors to make it look like they weren't down by one. He pulled on his jeans, then purposefully turned away from his mirror as he took off his shirt. He paused. Then, still holding the balled-up shirt in front of his chest, Ben turned back toward the mirror.

Soft and revolting, his stomach drooped over the waist of his jeans, making his belly button a mouth that frowned at its own face. He couldn't see his pectorals; they were hidden somewhere beneath his deflating breasts. Because that's what they were. Breasts. Fat-boy tits. With his free hand, Ben squeezed. He squeezed his drooping gut, his sagging tits. He squeezed and pulled at his fat. And while he could hardly grab it at all, his hands still felt full, overflowing. Ben grimaced. He rubbed at the stretch marks on his sides, first just to feel them, then harder as if he might erase them. He stared at himself: taut and coiled, distended and porcine. He stared at a gross, fleshy body that he could see without even opening his eyes. Burying his head in his shirt, Ben pulled the fabric down. "Yeah, okay, Marty," Ben muttered.

In the living room, Deidra sat watching TV. Her feet were propped up on the coffee table. Stampie wasn't near her. Maybe he was still in Eric's room, maybe on her pillow in the room down the hall. Ben wasn't interested enough to ask, not that she would have answered him. Ben plucked his father's keys off the counter and walked out into the sun.

The truck rumbled awake on the second crank, and Ben pulled out of the neighborhood. He didn't drive very often. Most of the things he needed to get to were close, and he didn't need to get to that many things.

The movie theater was about twenty minutes away. Frank had said he lived somewhere on Chemstrand, just behind that old dump. Ben hoped that Frank was being literal, because that road was a long one. If it was farther down the street or on a side road, Ben would be looking all afternoon. Fried clams. They served fried clams at that theater.

Ben let the radio play and hung his elbow out the window. The wind felt nice, even as the truck slowed into thicker traffic. Frank's side of town was more densely populated. More stores and restaurants, more things to do. At least it seemed like it. But a lot of businesses were closed, shuttered forever in the gutted strip malls that guided the road.

Moving slower than the speed limit, Ben ambled down Chemstrand, looking for Reggie's car. He didn't know the make or model, just that it was silver with some kind of . . . thing on his dashboard. A statue or figurine or something. He drove for about a mile, moving slow enough that no car stayed behind him for long. Then he made a U-turn and doubled back before he turned down a side street.

Ben let the truck coast. There were so many garages. If Reggie's car was in one of those things, then that was that. There were miles of neighborhood here. Ben couldn't walk up to each garage and peek through the square windows. More than a dozen times, Ben slowed or even stopped at the sight of a similar vehicle before pressing on the gas and rumbling deeper into the neighborhood. Twice Ben stopped the truck completely, getting out to lift car covers. The streets weren't laid out in any sort of pattern. There were no grids, and Ben didn't have a map, so he could only do his best to drive the roads systematically.

And all the time, there were cars coming and going. Checking a driveway only really counted for as long as Ben could see it.

It had been about an hour and a half of driving the neighborhood streets, retracing his route, finding new veins, reversing out of unmarked dead ends. An hour and a half of stumbling upon paths he'd surely driven before. But finally, there it was. A silver Mercury Tracer with an orange cat statuette on the dash.

Parking in the street, Ben grabbed the Bible off the passenger seat. The house was nice. Small but brick with a manicured lawn. Screen door with no tears. Ben knocked on the wood door three times, then stepped to his right, out of the way of the peephole.

There was a murmuring behind the door, and then it swung open. The smile on Reggie's face faded, then struggled to return after a few beats.

"Hi there, Ben," Reggie said. "Everything okay?"

"Hi, Reggie. Yeah, everything's alright."

"Your dad okay?"

"Yessir. He's fine."

"Okay." Reggie's smile wavered as his eyes became uncertain. "Frank's out with some work friends. I was just about to hit the sack."

"I didn't mean to bother you," Ben said. "Do you got a second?"

Reggie stepped to the side. Heated air washed over Ben's skin. He breathed in the clean smell of the house as Reggie shut the door behind them. Dark and warm, the home felt nice but impersonal. The decorations all looked to be store-bought trinkets, vases and paintings made in factories somewhere.

"Hadn't seen you at the lot in a long time." Reggie lowered himself into a chair and motioned for Ben to sit on the couch. "You look good." The man mimed a biceps flex.

"You too, Reggie. Still givin Brandy hell."

"She gets what she's got comin." Reggie smiled. "You come to talk shop?" He gestured toward the book in Ben's lap.

"No." Ben mustered a chuckle. "Wouldn't really know where to start."

"Well, first there was the Word. And then some other things happen." Reggie laughed loudly.

"Frank doin alright?"

"Yeah," Reggie said casually. "I mean, it was hard on him, what happened with that accident . . . Frankie ain't good with stuff like that. Someone hurt. Blood. That kinda stuff. It was hard. He thought that boy *died*. You know? That he couldn't save him. They's best friends, him and Marty. I just think he feels a little bad."

"He shouldn't," Ben said. "Frank saved his life. I ain't just sayin that."

"He'll be okay. You don't tell him I said anything," Reggie snapped with mock seriousness. "I know you and Marty like to give my boy a hard time. Clint know you're here?"

Ben shook his head. Reggie crossed his legs and nodded.

"Alright then . . ." The man swept his hands toward Ben. "Shoot."

"I been thinkin about it since last night," Ben started. "Me and Frank was talkin a little while back about how long you and my dad knew each other. Frank said that you used to be a janitor before you worked at the lot, said you worked at my elementary school, Bradley Park. He said before that, though, you worked at a school called Blackwater. Now I remember that because I ain't never heard of a school called Blackwater, and there ain't too many schools around here. And it come up again at least one more time after that."

Reggie smiled and lightly smacked his hand on his knee. "You know," he said eventually, "just as soon as I was pullin out of the lot last night, I realized I'd misled you. I did work at that place for a real short time. That was back when I lived up in Alabama. Long time ago. Forgot all about it. There ain't much I could really tell you."

"You know if it's still around?"

"I mean it's been a lifetime since I heard anything about that place. If I had to guess, I'd say it wasn't."

"How come?"

"Just because most things don't stick around for very long, I guess. That's all. New zones for new parts of the town, stuff like that."

"What kinda school was it?"

"Oh, just a regular school," Reggie replied, still grinning. "Elementary."

"It wasn't a religious school?"

Reggie's eyes crept toward the Bible in Ben's lap, then darted away. "Yeah, I guess it was. Yeah. It was." Reggie laughed.

"You was the janitor?"

"Yeah, one of 'em. There was a couple."

"You still know any of 'em?"

"It ain't exactly a club there, Ben. Janitors' club." He chuckled to himself again. "I don't even remember any of those guys' names, to tell you the truth."

"Weren't nothin special about it or anything?"

"No," Reggie replied thoughtfully. "Not that I recall. I'm sorry there, young Ben. I just don't remember too much about that place. I hope you didn't drive all the way out here just for that heap of nothing."

With a warm smile still on his lips, Reggie seemed to be waiting for Ben's next question. But what it felt like, sitting quietly in the tidy living room, was that Reggie was hoping Ben would leave. Just get up and get the fuck out of his spotless home. Just get out and go away and shut up about old jobs.

Instead, Ben stood and walked to Reggie's chair. He thumbed open the cover and handed the book to the man.

"Someone's been usin this symbol to mess with me," Ben said in a quiet voice. "Does it mean somethin?"

Reggie nodded, and soon he was more rocking than nodding. "No. Not far as I know. I think that's just a logo." He tried to hand the book back to Ben, but Ben didn't take it. Instead he sat back down. Reggie rested the Bible on his lap.

"How come you didn't work there for long?"

"Just one of them things, I guess. Might've been better pay somewhere else. Yeah, I remember the pay being low. Not like what you're makin over there at the store!"

"Did you . . ." Ben paused as he tried to think of what to ask. "Did you have uniforms?" There was irritation on his tongue. He spat the sentence more than he said it.

What a dumb fucking question.

"Yeah," Reggie answered. "Jumpsuit kinda deal."

Ben nodded and looked long at Reggie. He wasn't holding the book. He sat with his arms resting beside his legs like the Bible was an animal he wasn't quite afraid of but didn't want to touch. He was still smiling, even when he spoke. But there was something. Ben could swear it. A shadow in his pauses. The ghosts of thoughts that danced across his face.

Ask another one then.

"You, uh . . . You have one of them buckets with the wheels on it? Or did you have to carry the bucket all over the place?"

"Oh, it had the wheels I think." Reggie nodded.

There was a warmth on the back of Ben's neck. Reggie wasn't telling stories. No embellishments. No real laughter. He didn't care why Ben was asking these questions; he just wanted them to end. He already *knew* what was prompting them, or he desperately didn't want to.

There was a question Ben could ask that would open Reggie up. Ben was sure of it. Everything Ben wanted was just below the surface of Reggie's strained smile. But Ben didn't know enough about the school to know what that question might be, didn't know what Reggie didn't want to talk about, and now he was out of time, because Reggie was standing.

"If I covered the gas money," Ben started, "any chance you'd take me up there?"

Reggie laughed. "That's a long drive there, Ben. Besides, I doubt it's even still around."

Ben nodded. He rubbed his palm against his leg.

"I really do gotta be hittin the hay," Reggie said, handing the book back. "I'm sorry for not rememberin what you was talkin about last night, makin you drive here for nothin. I'll tell Frankie you said hello."

There it is.

"Nothin to be sorry about, Reggie. Hey, you mind if I wait in the truck there? I'm parked on the street."

"Wait? For what?"

"For Frank. Figure he might be interested. In ridin out there with me, I mean."

The man smiled and pushed his glasses up with a bent index finger. "What you wanna go all the way out there for? Ain't gonna be nothin to see."

Ben shrugged. "That's okay. At least it'd be a new kind of nothin, I reckon. I appreciate you letting me take up part of your day, Reg."

"Well, gas money or not, I can't let you use my car. Can't risk not havin it for work. And I don't think Frankie's gonna appreciate you wastin his time along with yours," Reggie said.

"I ain't tryin to waste anybody's time. If he don't wanna come, then he don't got to."

"And he won't want to."

Ben stepped toward the front door. "Alright then, Reggie."

"I ain't—" He cleared his throat. "I ain't got no kinda problem with it. Just a waste of time is all. I'm tryin to help you."

"And I appreciate that."

"But to drag my boy along with you . . ." Reggie frowned and looked at Ben with disapproval.

"I ain't gonna drag nobody." Ben shrugged. "I'm just gonna ask."

"No . . . you—damnit. You ain't listenin."

"It ain't that long a drive. It'll be—"

"You ain't takin my boy out there!" Reggie cried. "You understand me? So quit makin like you are."

Ben stared at the man. He'd known Reggie for a long time, had never heard him yell, had never seen him this angry. But this wasn't quite anger. It felt like something else. "Reggie, how come you don't want me to take Frank out there?"

The man's lips snagged on his teeth. He tried to smile but couldn't seem to manage it.

"Tell me what was wrong with the school, Reggie." Ben's voice shook.

"I was just a janitor."

"Tell me about the school, or I'll ask Frank. I'll ask him and he'll say yes, Reggie."

"No," Reggie said casually, waving Ben's words away. Tears followed the contours of his struggling smile.

"He'll say yes. And me and him will drive up there and see for ourselves what it is. Tell me what was wrong with Blackwater."

"Nothin wrong with it."

"Damnit, Reggie! What was wrong with the school?"

"It wasn't a school." Reggie's eyes widened in surprise, as if he hadn't been the one who said it. It was a horrified look, one that Ben had only ever seen once before, on Deidra's face. Reggie froze like a child hiding from a monster that could hear you only if you breathed.

There was a burning in Ben's chest. He could taste bile in his throat as he watched Reggie's eyes turn red with tears and private terror.

"What was it?"

"Oh, God. Oh, goddamnit!" Reggie moaned. "I didn't do nothin. I don't know who told you I did, but I didn't do nothin to nobody."

"I ain't . . . That ain't what I'm here about. No one told me nothin, Reggie."

"Then what in the holy hell are you here for? Just leave it alone! Stop talking about it. Stop making me fucking think about it!"

"What's the symbol mean?" Ben urged, opening the book and pointing. "The boy and the moon."

"I don't know."

"Yeah, you do," Ben snapped. "Why would somebody send this to me?"

"The book?"

"No. The symbol."

"I don't know."

"Reggie—"

"They didn't have no Bibles when I was there. Weren't no books at all. Oh, *Jesus.* Oh my God."

"What was it then? If it wasn't a school, then what *was* it?"

"I don't know!" Reggie lost control of himself and wept. His glasses were smudged with tears. His breathing shuddered as it leveled. "Oh, Christ. Frankie's . . . I'm gonna wake up Frankie."

"He ain't here, Reggie. He's out with friends, you said."

Reggie breathed heavily. With unsteady legs, he moved toward his chair until he found it.

"Tell me, Reggie." Ben held the book out, and Reggie took it with pain in his eyes.

"I think it was a school back when it first started. Oh, jeez . . . My uncle. My uncle got me the job. And I was lucky to get it. Weren't a lot of work for black folks up in that part of Alabama. I was fifteen or so. My brother had already moved up to Baltimore, so it was just me and Momma, since my daddy was in a bad way.

"I just cleaned. That's it. I cleaned the floors. I cleaned the toilets. I didn't know nobody and didn't nobody know me. When I saw— I asked my uncle, 'How come you sent me to work in a place like that?' And he didn't know what I meant. Thought it was what it used to be back when it was a church thing." Reggie tapped his fingers against the cover of Ben's book. "Started as one little ol' building, for kids whose folks had died or given 'em up."

"Like an orphanage?"

"Yeah, kinda. Mostly. But it was a school. It was that too. Church members would send their kids to it just during the daytime if they wanted. Donation-type thing. It went on for a while like that. It was really nice. That's what everybody said. That it was real nice.

"They was building the place up all the time, adding new rooms and buildings. Buncha kids and lots of teachers and nuns and what have you. But for this or that reason, the church or churches maybe started getting less and less donation-wise. Or maybe they spent too much money on makin the place bigger. I don't know.

"Whoever ran that place or the committee or whatever, they made some kinda deal with the state so that they could keep it open, I guess. It was important. They didn't want to just . . . to just shut it down. It was state money for state students. That was the deal.

"This was all before I got there. I don't know how it went from what it was to what I seen. I'm fifteen years old. What the hell was I supposed to do?"

Ben looked at Reggie uncertainly. The man took a deep breath.

"The students that the state sent, there was something wrong with 'em. Some of 'em was . . . 'special needs' is what they'd call 'em now, I think. Rowdy kids. Or just simple ones. But there was other kinds too."

"What's that mean? Other kinds how?"

"I don't know. The kind that needs doctors. They was mean. That's what I heard. They just kept bringin 'em in until there weren't no more room left. Some of them kids couldn't have been there to learn. You couldn't teach 'em. They was *gone.*

"But it weren't just kids. Like how they put them dim older kids in the younger classrooms at Bradley Park? It was like that. But some of the people the state sent was *grown.* They had to be. Sent 'em because they had 'minds of children' or some such horseshit.

"Kids and grown-ups screamin at me or each other or themselves or nothin or everything."

Reggie's mouth trembled. "And I know," he said, shuddering, "I know you wanna say, 'That's called a *hospital,* Reg.' But it weren't. Some of them kids was just *kids.* Just regular kids. Put in that place . . . Put into rooms that was too big, made for bunkin together.

"There was this boy. Oh, goddamnit. There was this little boy that was sent there. I seen him come in. When he first got there, 'Yes, sir. No, sir,' all the way. He was good. He was a good boy, and that place took him . . ." Reggie gnashed his teeth and mimed his hands as if he were crushing something resilient into a ball.

"It was a rowdy place. A sick place with sick people. We did this thing at night, when it was time to sleep. We'd walk down the hallways sayin, 'Night's out! Lights out!' while we flipped the switches off. 'Night's out! Lights out!' Over and over. Got blacker than black in that place. They couldn't see nothin. They'd start screamin. They'd all be screamin.

"I worked there for a year and a half. I don't know nobody from there. I ain't seen nobody from there."

Ben tapped the book in Reggie's lap. "Do you recognize that name there? Someone named Beverly?"

"Did she work there?"

"Do you recognize the *name*?"

Reggie seemed to think for a moment, then shook his head. "And I don't want to, okay? They weren't all bad. The ones that lived there and the ones that worked there. They weren't. But you can't tell whoever you got this book from about me. You can't do it. *Please.*"

"I found it."

"Then you should leave it. For the life of me, I can't imagine that anyone who had anything to do with that place would want to remember it. Don't tell them about me, Ben. Please. *Please.*"

"Okay, Reggie," Ben said, standing. "I didn't mean to . . . you didn't do nothin."

Reggie sat in his chair, nodding silently to himself. "I chanted. That's the only thing I did, and that's too much. 'Night's out! Lights out!' Jesus Christ."

Ben leaned carefully over Reggie, then gently pulled the book from the man's tight hands.

"You can't take Frankie out there. You can't do it."

"I won't, Reggie," Ben said. "I promise that I won't."

Reggie sobbed behind him as Ben opened the door.

Outside, the gray clouds made the day look older than it was. Ben climbed into the truck but didn't start it. He opened the Bible and looked at Beverly's name. Somewhere behind him, a man was laughing.

In the rearview, Ben watched Frank smile in the middle of the street, shouting back through the window of the car that appeared to have dropped him off. His clothes were different. A uniform. Frank tapped the top of the car and walked up his driveway with light steps.

He looked so happy. Ben wasn't in the mood or condition to talk to Frank, and he knew that probably worked both ways. But Ben thought of Reggie, thought of Frank opening the door to his home and seeing his father unraveled in his favorite chair.

The truck door squeaked open, and Ben lifted himself out of the seat. "Hey, Frank!" Ben shouted. His old coworker turned with a smile that became confused. Frank didn't reply. He only waved. Then he went inside.

And when the tuh-teeth chewed his legs off, the guh-good thing yelled for help. "Pleeease! Suh-someone!"

But there was nuh-no one around to hear.

And the bad man just sssmiled.

47

Ben could see the scar in the glass almost as soon as he entered the parking lot. It looked like a crystal spiderweb, thin lines radiating out like spokes from a central hub—a kind of fractal geometry that seduces the eye, simple shapes made elegant by their array. But really, it was just a great big crack in the store's front door. A hole, actually, about the size of a baseball.

It had been there for three days. From what Ben had been able to find out, it had appeared sometime between the time he dropped the papers off with his dad and when the store opened a few hours later. Palmer's solution was to sit in his car at the back of the parking lot every night and wait for the vandal to return. Just knowing that the man was out there, breathing heavily and spying on the store, was close to the most annoying thing Ben could imagine.

The store was in absolute shambles, like the aftermath of a *Supermarket Sweep* episode, only everyone in town had been a contestant. It was the kind of ruin that was going to take about a week of slow rebuilding between trucks to fix, just in time to be undone by whatever white hell awaited those aisles in the small remaining preamble to Christmas.

Palmer had made no mention of any corresponding disarray in his office, no mention of Beverly's file. Each time Ben had seen the man, he'd felt his body tense, ready for a confrontation that never came. Maybe Palmer was biding his time. Or maybe Ben had covered his tracks better than he thought.

"Security to the front, please. Security to the front." Chelsea's voice floated from the intercom.

Ben couldn't help but grin. Chelsea had started asking him to walk her to her car. No threat of moonlight weirdos or toothless midnight panhandlers had ever done what Palmer's still-dented BMW had.

Ben slid the doors apart and stepped through them. He held his wrist in front of his waist and stood, back erect, scanning the parking lot like a bodyguard. Chelsea reached through the doors and shoved Ben's shoulder.

"Please be careful, ma'am. I am a weapon."

"Well, be a weapon away from the doors."

Ben moved forward an almost imperceptible amount.

"Ben!" Chelsea laughed. Her breath on the back of his neck as she tried to push him out of the way was the best thing he'd ever felt. Still, he moved and pressed the doors back together.

Most nights, they talked for only a few minutes, knowing that Palmer was watching them. Or maybe for other reasons too. It was hard for Ben to know. But this time, before Chelsea got into her car, she hugged him. And even though she lingered for a moment, Ben almost didn't react in time, almost didn't get his arms around her. But he did. He worried in those slow seconds that Palmer would flash his lights or honk his horn, but that didn't happen. And Ben was glad for it. Glad until he thought of Palmer's tape collection, thought of the couple at the deli cooler. But even that couldn't spoil things. Not entirely.

She pulled away, said that he was a real shit bodyguard, since someone could have just crept up behind him. Then she got in her car. Ben didn't respond. He wasn't even sure he said good night. He just smiled like a doofus and waved as she drove away.

Inside, Ben's feet moved inaudibly across the tiled floor. Above, the fluorescent tubes over every other aisle had been clicked off—an effort to mitigate some of the financial pressure created by Palmer finally having to turn the goddamn heater on. Ben had to squint his eyes to see some of the tags in the darker aisles. His peripheral was a playground. Phantom blurs and flashes teased him so much that Ben sometimes chased them through the store, followed them all the way to nothingness.

But the empty feeling that Ben had felt for so long wasn't there. That gray fog that enveloped him, the one that he could practically feel in his lungs, was gone. Ben could see through it, because he knew where to look. Because Ben had a plan.

In a few days, Ben was going to borrow his father's truck and drive to Alabama. He didn't know where Blackwater School had been or maybe even still was, but he knew where the Blackwater River flowed. That might be good enough. Even if he needed to go farther north than the river itself, it was just a matter of talking to people.

And maybe it *was* farther north. Maybe far enough that James Duchaine really didn't know what the symbol was. But if there were records of any kind, or if he could find someone who knew more than Reggie, then maybe Ben could figure out what in the holy hell was going on. How Palmer was involved with the school that wasn't a school. What message Beverly was trying to deliver.

Reggie had been terrified, reduced to a shaking child by just the thought of that place. So why the fuck was its logo scribbled on Eric's flyer?

"There's something wrong with Beverly," Marty had said—had screamed, actually—angry that Ben couldn't see what he did. But if Beverly had anything to do with Eric or these games, then why would *she* draw the symbol? Marty didn't see everything, didn't see how Palmer looked at Ben. How much the man enjoyed firing Beverly.

Then again, Marty had seen things that no one else had. Had seen Eric staring out from the summer trees, he said.

Had seen the Blackwater Bible sitting on the table.

And the golden boy vanishing into the sprawling woods.

Ben tried to talk it out with himself, saying these things aloud as he worked as if he were telling himself a story. Each time the tale began to strain credulity, Ben would start over. He never seemed to finish.

For the first time since he'd started working at the store, Ben started taking his breaks in the break room, and he didn't like it. The room just felt sad to Ben. Hopeless. Where employees burned through their days in the store, even when they weren't being paid for their time. But Ben let himself stew in the room because it was better than sitting outside, where Palmer could see.

When the sun finally began creeping through the glass, Ben wrapped up his work, hauling a few half-pallets of old stock back into Receiving. He tossed some pieces of cardboard into the baler like he was flicking enormous playing cards into a monster's mouth.

He was alone, but it sure didn't feel that way. It felt like he was back at the police station, sitting alone in a grim room, waiting for James Duchaine to come ask him more questions, staring at himself in a mirror while others stared through it.

As Ben headed toward the front of the store, he realized that the anxiety he'd felt all night had abated. He didn't want to see Palmer, but it was time for the man to show up. The anticipation was gone.

Even the sight of Palmer oozing out of his smashed-up coupe didn't faze Ben.

But the sirens did.

Cold water fell irregularly from the sky, the sun's brilliance hoarded selfishly by dull clouds. A police cruiser whipped by, skidding audibly as it stopped at the intersection of the town and the nothing beyond it. The sirens shrieked and wailed, seemingly coming from all directions at once.

Red and blue flashed like finale fireworks; sirens screeched like banshees carried by the power of their own voices. Five, no six police cars, still crying into the murky sky as they disappeared down the embankment. Wiping small drops of rainwater from his face, Ben turned toward Palmer and met the man's gaze. Had this been what he'd been waiting all night for?

His father's truck bobbed violently as it made a harsh turn into the parking lot. The yellow headlights flashed as the truck careened toward Ben.

With his father's arm frantically pumping, the window lowered. Words flew like gnats from his cotton-white lips, his eyes still adhered to the horizon. "Get in! Get in the car!"

"What is it, Pa? What the hell's goin on?"

"It's Eric. They found Eric!"

48

The truck fishtailed as it turned too quickly from the lot and struggled to find traction in the damp earth. Ben's shoulder thudded against the window. Bald tires screamed momentarily at a patch of gray asphalt before leaving it behind.

Ben's palms were tingling. He looked to his father, whose gawking eyes flitted wildly on the stretch of road ahead. The truck shook as it thundered over the craterous pavement, attempting to close the distance on the twinkling lights ahead of them.

"They *found* him?"

"What?" his father shouted over the roaring engine.

"They found him?" Ben yelled.

"I dunno." He clenched his fists around the wheel. "Yeah. Well, someone saw him. Someone said so, anyways. Someone called the house." Clint burned past a slow-moving tractor. "This morning. Phone woke me up. Next thing," he grunted as he swerved to miss a pothole, "next thing I know the police are at the door." He smiled uneasily through his beard. His eyes were tired and searching.

"Does Deidra know?"

"She's the one who answered the phone."

Ben and his father rode white-knuckled down the dirt road. Both men scanned the terrain for an indication that they should stop. Finally, as they crested a hill, Ben saw several police cars parked on the right side of the road. Colorful lights strobed, but the air was quiet now, save for the shouts of the officers standing by the tree line. Among them stood Lieutenant James Duchaine, hands cupped around his mouth as he bellowed into the rustling trees. Ben clenched his jaw so hard that it hurt.

"The man of the hour," said Duchaine.

"Is this it?" Clint panted as he jogged over. "Is this where he was?"

"This is where dispatch sent us." Noise crackled through Duchaine's radio; he listened for a moment before lowering the volume.

"Anything?" Ben's father asked impatiently.

"Not yet. Powell! Green! I said the other side!" He gestured dramatically across the road to the adjacent woods. "Deidra still at home? In case he makes his way back there?" Duchaine patted Clint's shoulder as the man nodded.

"What can we do?" Ben asked.

"Call for him. He'll hear your voices before any of ours."

And so they did. For the next two hours, Ben, his father, and half a dozen uniformed police officers shouted Eric's name into every pocket of air that a human voice could touch. They called, but the only thing that answered them was the wind.

It took Ben's mind a long time to catch up, to fully confront what was happening. It felt almost like he was phasing through time, bouncing along his own life with each unsteady movement, each foot stepping into a different part. One step and he was fifteen, screaming into the endless trees. Another and he was older but still in the same goddamn place.

Was this real? Three days ago, Ben had talked to Reggie about Blackwater School. The day before that, he'd broken into Beverly's home. Before that, Palmer's office. Twice. Before that and before that and before that and it never ended.

Still, Ben screamed as loud as he could, so loud and ferociously that he worried his voice was no longer inviting.

Duchaine leaned against a pine tree, jolted forward and checked the bark for sap, then reclined again. He took a swig from a large bottle of water and held it out in the direction of Ben and his father, who both declined. The sun burned a hole through the dark clouds and cast the forest in shadows.

"Shouldn't we have found something by now? Anything?" Clint said.

Duchaine checked his watch, then looked off listlessly into the distance. "I dunno. What do you make of all this, Ben?"

Weak echoes from faraway calls drifted through the branches. Duchaine spoke into his radio, and a garbled voice responded. Duchaine swished water around his teeth and then spit it into the dirt.

"Alright then," Duchaine said vaguely to the group, as he took the lead.

Clint was breathing heavily. Duchaine offered him the water bottle again and smiled faintly when the man accepted.

"No dogs this time either?" Ben asked.

"No dogs." Duchaine sighed, looking at the sun through the leaves and clouds until it overpowered his eyes.

"I . . ." Ben started. "I got a drawing I been workin on. Of Eric a little older. If you think it'd help—"

"How long after the call did we get here? Do you reckon we should have stopped sooner and then swept this way?" Clint asked.

"Witness said they were traveling north, so we set up a bit north of that hoping to cut 'em off."

"They?" questioned Ben.

"That's what the witness said." Duchaine glanced at Ben's father and then at a notepad he slid out of his pocket. He read in a slightly mechanical cadence. " 'I seen the kid traveling north past the cotton, coming away from town on Bayou Boulevard. East side of the road. Him and a blond-headed boy.' "

"Blond boy?" Ben's stomach turned.

Leaves and sticks crunched and cracked. Officer Duchaine headed in the sound's direction. Ben and his father followed. Circumventing a tangle of draping vines, the three men emerged to see two more men walking in their direction. One was an officer unknown to Ben. Another was a man Ben hadn't expected to see.

"Jacob!" Ben called as he quickened his pace, lifting his legs high to avoid toppled tree limbs ensnared by coils of thorns. "Did you see him? Are you sure it was him?" Ben reached to shake his hand.

"Sure as I can be. You find anything yet?" Jacob asked as he shook Ben's father's hand.

"No. Nothing," Ben replied. "You saw them around here?"

"Well, they was headed this way, anyhow."

"How long between when you saw them and when you called?" Duchaine asked.

"What about the blond kid?" Ben interjected.

"Couldn't have been more than twenty-five, thirty minutes."

"Why'd you wait so long?"

"I ain't got a phone in my *truck,* Lieutenant. I figured it'd take less time to drive to where I was goin and use the phone there than to drive all the way back home."

"And where were you going?"

"I don't see what that has to do—"

"What about the blond kid?" Ben repeated.

"I didn't get a good look at him."

"But you got a good look at the other boy? At Eric?" Clint pressed.

"Yessir."

"If you were heading in the same direction as them boys, then how'd you see their faces?" Duchaine asked. Even to Ben the attempt at nonchalance had failed.

"Only reason I paid them any mind at all was because they ran off when my truck come up behind them. I slowed down and looked, to make sure everything was okay. And the dark-haired boy waved at me from the bush before the other one pulled his hand down."

"How'd you come to call Clint first?"

Jacob reached into his back pocket and then unfolded the piece of paper he retrieved. "This was the boy I saw, the one who waved at me." He tapped his bruised nail against Eric's picture.

"Can I see that?" Duchaine asked, sliding the paper from between Jacob's fingers.

"Then they slipped farther in."

"You didn't go after them?" Clint asked.

"Nosir. All due respect, men like us"—he gestured at both their bellies—"have stronger suits than running through tight spaces. I was sure I'd never catch 'em, and I figured by the time I got back to my truck and headed down the way, they'd have even more of a head start."

"Where did you get this?" Duchaine rattled the paper gently. Jacob nodded to Ben.

The four men trampled through the woods. Only Clint was shouting Eric's name with any regularity, but if he noticed that fact, he didn't bring it up. Jacob didn't say anything at all and moved with the gait of a man who had walked into something he hadn't intended and didn't truly understand. James Duchaine's steps were as level as his stare, gliding from man to man, only dipping now and again to study the flyer he held pinched in his fingers like a failing boy's report card.

Ben just walked. His mind should have been aflame, but even when he tried to stoke it, nothing stirred. So he stopped trying. Maybe he knew. It sure felt like he did. Every time he looked at Duchaine, he thought he could feel that something was coming, and he thought he could feel that he wasn't ready for it at all. But he walked on, keeping pace with Duchaine even as Clint and Jacob outpaced them and took to new trajectories.

"Ya know, Jacob and your good friend Marty have lived across from each other for a long, *long* time. Don't you think it's interesting? That Marty says he seen Eric, and now his buddy neighbor says the same thing?"

"Not really, I don't. I talk to Jacob near every time I'm on that street."

"We been out here for a while now," Duchaine said. He got close enough that Ben could smell his sweat and asked with an almost playful tone, "What have you been up to?"

"What's that supposed to mean?"

Duchaine didn't respond, not right away. It was a few minutes before he spoke again. "Had a case with this guy. This was years and years ago, before you was born. Wife turned up dead one day. In the home. Door kicked in. Stabbed. Blood all over the place. He's covered. I mean, it's all over him. He'd moved the body around, tryin CPR, before he'd called for help.

"You see that kinda thing a lot. People forgetting themselves when something like that happens. Normal. All normal stuff in a situation like that.

"He was super cooperative. I mean coming down to the station anytime we needed. Answered all our questions. Seemed genuinely distraught. Just sad, you follow? And it was real. You could tell. It was real, and I mean *everyone* felt for this guy. Nice guy. Just helpful and friendly as could be given the tidal wave of shit that had washed over him.

"Only the thing was he did it. It's a long story, but he did it. The neighbors had a camera fixed on their driveway, but it caught this guy's too."

Ahead, Clint swam and clawed through brush, hollering for his little boy. Other voices penetrated the branches weakly, like they had fallen from the clouds and lost all their power on the descent.

"I watched the tape with him, with our guy. I watched him watch *him-*

self storm up to his own front door and kick it to pieces. Played it for him three times, and all he kept saying was 'That ain't me. That ain't me.'

"And he was tellin the truth, at least as far as his mind could handle. He really did believe what he was sayin, what he'd been sayin all along. Only it weren't the truth."

"Okay?" Ben said impatiently when Duchaine didn't continue.

"You got any thoughts at all on that story?"

"Jesus Christ," Ben spat. He quickened his pace, trying to catch up with his wandering father.

"Lead the way, Ben."

Ben turned back and hollered, "If I knew where he was, then we wouldn't be out here lookin for him, would we?"

"See, I think right here's exactly where we'd be."

"Hey! Lieutenant!" Ben stopped. "We're out here because Jacob called. Because he seen him!"

"Right. He seen whatever it was he thought he seen. Then he called your house."

"Fuck this," Ben said.

"Five years," Duchaine said, holding up splayed fingers. "Count 'em. Five years of takin your calls. Takin other people's calls about you. Drivin to houses that you thought was 'strange.' Because that's my *job.* Because I want to find your brother. Not for you. For *him.*

"And from the very start, from the very first goddamn day, you been yelling in my ear about all the different places I should look."

"Because you ain't done nothin! I been tryin to help and you ain't done a goddamn thing! You laughed right in my face when I told you what Marty said."

"Ben, you stir up a god-awful lot in me, but not once has it ever been laughter. I have never—*never*—laughed at you. I think all this is about as far away from funny as it gets." Duchaine paused to collect himself. "You killed Bob Prewitt. You killed Bob Prewitt, and then not even a year later you tell me about some trailer home that has too many locks on it. And then there's a school bus with a route you think is weird. And I let it go and let it go, because I knew that eventually it would unspool and we'd find our way to the end. But then Marty fucked with you a little, and you almost killed him too."

"That ain't what happened!"

"You don't see it that way, but you ain't the only one who's lookin at it. I'm lookin too, Ben. And what I see is someone who knows what all this is. Take away all the bullshit with the flyers and the logo. Take away all the games you play with yourself, and you know exactly where that boy is at. Because he's in the same goddamn place where you left him five years ago, and so help me God, you're gonna tell me where that is."

A wave rippled through Ben's body. "You think I *killed* him?" He muttered it so softly, it was almost for himself. Ben pivoted and looked into the trees, searching for his father, wanting his help while also hoping that he was nowhere near enough to hear that Ben needed it. "You think it was me?" Ben asked with a trembling voice.

"You don't think that he sees it?" Duchaine asked quietly, nodding toward Clint as he approached. "Doesn't see *you*? Because he does. Sees you draggin your brother through that store, yanking on his arm. Every time he looks at you I'd bet."

There was a sinking in Ben's stomach. No, that wasn't right. It was an absolute bottoming out.

"You mad at *me*? Cuz they seen what *you* done? They asked for a copy of the surveillance tape. Ain't no one persecutin you, Ben. Ain't no one responsible for what's goin on here but you."

"Hey!" Clint shouted at the two men. "What the hell are you just standin there for? Where you goin?" Clint asked as his son stepped heavily past him.

Ben turned and pointed behind his father. "Somewhere else. He ain't here to help. He ain't here to do nothin at all, except to fuck with me."

Clint grabbed Ben's arm as Ben moved to leave. "Hey. Ben. You need to calm it down, okay?"

"He thinks I know where Eric's at. I ain't gonna listen to his bullshit."

"Now hold on just a minute—" Clint tried.

"I ain't the one tellin tales here, Ben," Duchaine said, rattling the flyer. "I ain't fixin to apologize to you for that."

"Me? No." Duchaine chuckled. "You oughta apologize to your daddy. We got someone to answer that number twenty-four-seven, three-sixty-five—"

"And what a big help that was."

"Figure if your folks wasn't there when Jacob called. What then?"

"But they was," Ben said sharply. "They *was* there, and now we're out here lookin. All of us, 'cept for you, because you're too busy makin shit up and fuckin with me."

"We all gotta stay busy with somethin, though." Duchaine squeezed the flyer and shook it. "Ain't that right?" Duchaine held Ben's gaze; it felt like he was unpacking Ben's mind, rifling through his thoughts with unwelcome fingers.

"I know what you're doin. I ain't gonna admit to somethin I didn't do. I wish I knew half as much as you think. Hell"—Ben faced Duchaine squarely—"I wish it *was* me, so you could finally close a goddamn case.

"I told you everything, even when I knew you didn't care, and it don't fuckin matter! Marty told you right where Eric was and you missed him! Just like you miss everything. That's why there's fifteen fuckin posters on that board!"

"Ben?" Clint cut in. He wasn't staring into the forest anymore, wasn't pouring his baby boy's name into the trees. His father was just staring at him, stealing occasional glances at James Duchaine. "What're you talking about, Ben?"

Ben could feel the color leave his face and a kind of warm numbness take its place. Duchaine looked at Ben silently for a while, as if giving him the opportunity to answer the question, but Ben could only watch like a spectator of his own life.

"Few months ago," Duchaine began, "Ben here calls the station and says that one of his friends—Marty—said he seen Eric several months before that. I'm surprised he didn't tell you, Clint."

"What the hell's he talkin about, Ben?" Clint's fingers squeezed Ben's arm like a vise. *"Ben!"*

"He said he saw him. Marty said he seen him in the woods near our house."

"When?"

"A few months ago. I called him"—Ben pointed at Duchaine without looking—"and he said it never happened, said he never got any call from nobody about nothin. So I made the flyers. So I could look." Ben's voice was brittle.

"Jesus fucking Christ. We could've been looking. It could have been *me* that seen him if I was out looking for him."

"But you weren't!" Ben yelled. "You weren't looking for him. *I* was. Before and after Marty. I couldn't say nothin to you. To *her.* You act like you woulda been right there with me, but that ain't how it is, and you know it! I didn't know what to do. Marty said he seen him! Duchaine said he was a liar!"

"I talked to him," Duchaine said to Ben. "Talked to his tweaker mom too. Took his whole story down. Shoot, I asked everyone in the precinct, and not a one of 'em said that they ever got a call about your brother."

"You don't keep that kinda shit from me, Ben!"

"You seen what happened when I gave Deidra back the toy! What she was like!"

"What toy is that?" Duchaine asked.

"Please." Ben's lip was shaking as much as his voice. "Please, can we talk about all the things I done wrong later?"

The look on his father's face made Ben want to bury himself deep in the earth.

"You can keep pretendin that this is all because of me. Walk beside me the whole time if you want to. Just so long as we're walkin. Please, can we just look for him?"

"What else?" Clint snapped. "What else is there? He's got every pair of eyes on the payroll lookin for Eric. What *else*?"

Ben's uneasy gaze moved from Duchaine to Clint. Deep wrinkles crawled from the corners of his father's narrowed eyes. Horrified anticipation boiled in his expression, growing more palpable with every second that his son lingered in silence. Ben's fists bulged in his pants pockets. Deep in the trees, his brother's name bounced against the sky.

"Go home," Clint ordered.

"He needs to stay," Duchaine said curtly. "Clint—"

"You gonna arrest him, Jimmy? Go home."

"I wanna help, Pa."

"I don't want you out here."

"Pa, I—"

"Now, Ben!"

49

Neither man spoke as the truck sped down the road. Once or twice Clint smacked his palm against the steering wheel. Ben rested the side of his forehead against the cool glass. The store was a blur to Ben's right, and then suddenly everything was still when Clint stopped the car in the grass in front of his home.

"I can help," Ben said.

His father didn't reply. Ben slammed the side of his fist against the plastic trim of the truck's door, then flung it open and stepped outside. Clint reversed out of the yard right after Ben shut the door.

Ben climbed the steps to his porch, his eyes fixed on the door, expecting Deidra to come running out, but she didn't. And when Ben entered the house, he could see why.

It looked like there had been a burglary. Magazines and picture frames were scattered on the floor. In the kitchen, every drawer and cabinet was open, some with their contents spilled onto the tile beneath. A trash bag lay shredded near the refrigerator, coffee grounds and old food smeared into the grout. Somewhere in the house, Ben could hear a rummaging, like a raccoon scrambling through a dumpster.

In spite of the chaos, it didn't look like anything had been taken. The TV was still there. The VCR.

"Deidra?" Ben called, and the ruckus stopped.

His stepmother appeared in the hallway, her face a puzzle of concern and tentative joy. "Did you find him?" Her voice trembled. "No one's called or come by. Was he out there? Did you find him?"

"They're still looking . . ." Ben hesitated. "What happened?"

"I can't find him," she whimpered. "I don't know where he is."

"Can't find who?" Ben took a step forward.

"Stampie. He's *gone.* I put him in his room. I put him in there, but he isn't there now. I went . . ." She flailed her hands as if she had burned them. "I went to get him so that . . ." Her mouth trembled. "He's not there anymore. I searched all over."

Ben glanced past his stepmother, into his own open doorway.

"Where's Clint? Why aren't you out there looking? Why are you back?"

"They're still out there lookin," Ben said as he tried to squeeze past her.

It looked like God had picked up the box that was Ben's room and shaken it like a snow globe. Almost nothing was where it was supposed to be. His books. His clothes.

"I thought you took it," Deidra said.

"It's alright," Ben muttered.

It felt cold in the house now, though it might have just been something in Ben's blood. His small suitcase lay lopsided, leaning against one of the supports of his bed, his childhood piled carelessly on the carpet.

Through the walls, Ben could hear Deidra clawing and rummaging through everything they owned. How could she have lost that toy? Sitting on his bed, Ben tapped on his head as if it might shake an idea loose. He tried to think, but he didn't have the resources. Every time he heard a thud or a rumble, he flinched with irritation. He could hear her crying now, then cursing herself.

Ben was squeezing his head now, squeezing hard, just trying to get his breathing and thoughts to calm. Ben should be out there, not just sitting on his bed while his stepmom gutted the house. Instead, it was Duchaine walking side by side with Clint through those engulfing woods. What might he be saying? What stories might James Duchaine be telling?

Ben wrapped his arms around his pillow, tossed it aside, and then struck his fist against the side of his head once. Twice. He wanted to scream. How could she have lost that fucking toy?

She wouldn't have.

The thought swept into Ben's mind like a poison gas, suffocating every "but" and "what if" that tried to gain any ground at all. Because it was true. She wouldn't have lost it. Not her favorite thing. *Eric's* favorite thing. For the longest time, she wouldn't even set it down, wouldn't even let it out of her sight. *She didn't lose it.*

Deidra screamed and something crashed to the floor. Then she cursed and the ruckus continued.

Ben kicked at his childhood. A dirty note. Rocks. A midnight movie ticket. Photographs and the remnants of photographs. A lifetime of mementos saved during happy times, knowing that happiness couldn't last. He should have just put Stampie in here. No one would know that he'd found it. Then this wouldn't be happening. Ben scattered the menagerie with heavy hands. Safe and sound and secret, where no one knew—

"No . . ." Ben muttered. "No. Okay. Okay." His hands spasmed as they combed through his life.

A Micro Machine. A small plastic baseball hat. There was a ringing in his ears. His breath caught in his throat as he frantically shifted his valuables around like a child shuffling cards. "Please. *Please,*" Ben chanted.

The note tore, a toy cracked, but Ben didn't notice as he lowered himself to the ground and peered under his bed. "No. No." An origami bird. A late confession. A silver quarter. A note in a locker, a moonchild Bible, a padlocked door, a golden boy. It was all there. Everything was there—every single thing—but not Marty's lighter.

There was a soreness in the back of his neck, one that crawled into his skull. Ben opened his mouth as if the pain were an insect that was trying to escape. His head was a crowded theater before the lights dimmed. Chattering. Snickering. With a wobble, he climbed to his feet. He felt dizzy.

Marty knew about Stampie. Marty knew about *everything.*

And now Marty's most favorite thing in the whole world was gone.

Cold hands gripped rough corners as Ben made his way to the front door.

50

Curving trenches of rich dirt scarred the grass from Clint's hasty departure. There was a hollowness in Ben; he felt he might fall over at the polite insistence of the gentle winter wind. Each step felt unnatural in his legs, as unnatural as the thoughts in his mind.

The covered windows. Ben's breath shuddered. *The padlock.* Didn't he see it? Cool air stung his throat. His lungs quivered, wheezed. He saw it. He saw it and he didn't do a goddamn thing. Pebbles skipped into the grass as his aching legs carried him across the road. Frustrated at his own body, Ben cursed and bent, squeezing his knees in his palms. A screaming child who missed his toy rhino.

White pockmarks danced in his vision, lingering even when he closed his eyes.

Ben knew that he needed some sort of plan. What he would say. What he would do. But each time he tried, he couldn't see it through. He'd imagine himself walking up the steps, and then he'd be in Marty's home. He'd be at the front door, and then he'd be tearing a padlock off another one. There'd be no noise at all as he moved through an empty house. He needed more time to think.

The Cotter girls chased each other in their yard, stopping to look at Ben as he studied Marty's house. Chilled wind scuttled around his body. Ben saw the two little girls whispering to each other before he turned to face the silver windows. The glass felt like ice against his hands. His palms squeaked on the stubborn and slippery window. It wouldn't budge.

With hurried steps, Ben moved back to the porch. Grunting faintly, he squatted and scraped his fingers against damp soil and old stone until they dislodged one of the buried bricks at the foundation of the steps. Clutching the brick in one hand, he returned to the window and pressed his ear against it. Inside, he could hear the subdued murmurings of a small voice.

Ben turned to the sisters and waved them away. Jessica pulled little Ellen across the yard; they both disappeared around the side of their home. For a moment, Ben bobbed the brick in his palm, feeling the weight of his decision. He thought of the shattering glass and how it would spray on his baby brother.

He dropped the brick. Returning to the porch, Ben's hand hovered near the battered wooden door before falling back to his side. The porch bent under his shifting feet like a diving board. They wouldn't let him into the house. He knew that. Could he just force his way in? Ben's fingers grazed the brass doorknob. It shifted loosely in its socket as he enveloped it in his hand. His heart jackhammered in his chest when the knob turned freely.

The door opened with a groan into an empty room. There was music pumping from somewhere in the house, but nothing else. Everything was almost as quiet as Ben had imagined in his grasping visions of a plan. For a moment, the draft on his back called to him. He could walk out. He could leave. No one had seen him except for the Cotter girls. Was he alone? The old house creaked under his weight as he entered. He gently closed the door and stood in breathless silence. One step. Then another. The smell of mold burned in his nose, and a floating shape in his peripheral showed him that he wasn't alone at all.

"What 'n the hell're you doing in here?" Darlene snapped, standing in the doorway to the kitchen, a cigarette burning between her fingers.

Ben's words were choked in his throat. *Say it to her. Tell her just what in the hell you're doin in here.*

"You hear me?" She took a step toward Ben. "What're you doin in my house? You can't just come in here." Her nose scrunched in confusion at Ben's silence, and she spoke in a soft voice, like she was talking to a duckling who'd wandered into her path. "Go on. Get the fuck out then."

For a little while, Ben and Darlene stood in silence. Ben's tongue sat like concrete in his mouth. The Cotter girls squeed outside, and it seemed to Ben like that might go on being the only sound there was for the rest of time.

Tim appeared next to Darlene and looked at her uneasily. "What's going on, hon?"

"He just walked right in." Darlene laughed with frustration. "I told him to get out, and there he stands."

"You're a friend of Marty's, ain't ya?" Darlene's boyfriend said. "He's sleepin right now. Go on home, and we'll tell him that you come by."

Ben could feel his heart beating. His lungs made his chest heavy.

"Bit slow?" Tim whispered to Darlene.

Ben heard the house creaking behind him. When Ben turned and saw Aaron's confused stare reaching out through his sun-colored hair, he felt a wave of heat break across his back.

"Where'd you take him?" Ben heard himself say. Aaron disappeared down the hall, and Ben felt his legs twitch. "Hey!" Ben shouted. He might have followed, but Darlene yanked on his arm until he turned to face her.

"You need to get out of my house, boy. Right now," she snarled.

Ben turned back toward the hall, and she turned with him, blocking his path. When he took a step forward, Darlene struck him in the chest with her palm.

Footsteps thudded in the hallway. "Ben, what're you doing here?" Marty said. His tired eyes whipped across and then beyond Ben. When Aaron reappeared, Marty tucked the boy behind himself, and everyone was quiet for a long while.

Ben knew that this was it. More than anything else—more than coming into the home uninvited; more than what little he had said, incomprehensible as it was—this was his last chance to just walk away. And he could do that. He could just walk right out, same as he had walked right in. That's what it seemed like everyone wanted. Marty stared unblinkingly, his eyes no longer tired but wide and fearfully eager, like a child who'd lost count of how long ago an M-80 had swallowed its burning fuse.

Aaron peered out from behind Marty's arm. Ben could *see* Aaron, *see* him leading Eric by the hand down the dead road, glancing at the lost boy through his fair hair and telling him that his other life had been nothing but a dream.

"I want you to open that door," Ben finally said, pointing through the wall.

Marty glanced down the hall. "What? Ben, I don't know what you're—"

"Yeah you do." Ben's voice was resigned, almost defeated by his own words. "They seen him with Aaron."

"What? What the hell are you talking about?" Marty glanced at his brother. "Seen Aaron with who?"

"They seen him walking down the goddamn road," Ben bellowed, "with a kid with yellow hair." Ben grabbed at Aaron, and Marty shoved against his friend's large body. "It was Jacob that seen you," Ben said to the boy. "Where were you takin him?" He grabbed at Aaron's arm.

"You get away from my boys!" Darlene shrieked.

"Ben, what the fuck is wrong with you?" Marty grunted through scarred vocal cords, pushing against Ben's chest.

A scree erupted from down the hallway, and Ben felt his stomach roll. Marty shoved harder into Ben's chest, and Ben brought the palm of his hand hard against the side of his friend's face.

"What are—what do you think I did? I didn't do nothin!" Marty howled as Ben hit him again.

Frail fists collided with Ben's midsection. "Don't you touch them!" Ben turned and pushed Darlene away like a small dog.

"Tim!" she cried. "Do something!"

"I'm comin, goddamnit!" Cabinets slammed and dishes crashed in the kitchen.

At the back of the hallway, Ben could see the padlock resting against the door's molding. "He's been here the *whole time*? You said you'd help me look for him." There was a buzzing in Ben's skull. "You wrote in Beverly's file! What'd you even take me out to Beverly's for? For a joke?" Ben's voice quivered. "Because I'm so stupid? You never called nobody." A river of salt water merged with the snot under Ben's nose. "You took his toy from my house."

"He's killing him! Tim!"

The world seemed to be moving so quickly to Ben, who was only now becoming aware of a squirming movement in his aching hand. The black scab on Marty's neck felt rough against Ben's thumb as he squeezed. He could pop it, squeeze just a little harder and it would cave in like the inside seal of an asprin bottle. Ben watched with casual detachment as Aaron yanked and pulled on his arm, dragging his eyes to Marty's face as if he were changing a television channel. Marty struck Ben in the arms and chest. His face was a summer sunset just before dusk.

"I'm sorry," Marty rasped. Ben opened his hand and Marty collapsed onto the stained carpet, coughing and gasping. Ben looked at Marty uneasily. Pity flashed in his heart. He felt an impulse to help his friend, as if he had been harmed by strange hands. Sweeping Aaron aside, Ben pounded down the hallway. "Nothin' for Nothin'" by Cinderella played from Marty's stereo.

His hands fumbled with the padlock. Darlene yelled from the living room, but Ben could hear only sounds, not words. Bracing his shoulder against the door, Ben pushed and felt a bit of give. Ben smacked his palm against the wood and called his brother's name. His blood ran faster at the wailing cries that answered him. Again and again, his weight slammed against the door. A crack. Splitting wood. The latch burst from the strike plate and the door lunged forward, held shut by only the padlock now. Soft light seeped through the narrow opening. The rich smell of pine wafted into Ben's nose as he pressed his face against the molding, his eyes darting across the slivered glimpse of the room beyond.

Something cold and hard pressed against Ben's neck. "Don't you move an inch—"

But Ben was already turning. The gun's muzzle scraped across his cheek, and Ben's hands were on it before he could even contemplate what he was doing. Tim grunted and cussed. Darlene screamed. Marty rushed Aaron into the kitchen. Ben's hand wrapped around the barrel, the fingers of his other hand slipping against Tim's. Panic was setting into Ben's extremities now. Groping and squeezing, he wanted to let go. He wanted to let go and run and leave, but he couldn't.

"Don't," Ben snarled. Tim heaved his body into Ben's, and the two collided against the door. Another crack. More splitting wood.

"Kill him!" Darlene shrieked from the hallway. "Kill him!"

Ben's arms felt weak as they wrestled with Tim's. Something moved in Ben's hands. Ben flinched at the explosion, and suddenly the tension was gone. Tim took a step back, the pistol still trained on Ben, though his eyes were vacant. Ben's ears rang. He felt nauseated. He patted his hands against the spot on his body that held Tim's gaze but could feel nothing, could see nothing. From what Ben could tell, Tim seemed to be unharmed. At least clean of blood.

"Tim!" Darlene yelled.

Ben shuffled slightly to the side, but Tim's floating eyes sat in his skull unmoved. *He's not looking at me.* Ben turned. *What's—*

In the wall, just a few inches from the door, soft light poured from a jagged circular hole. The lock and its metal strap hung limp and useless on the molding, uprooted during the scuffle.

"What happened?" Darlene cried.

The door swung open with a gentle push from Ben. A desk lamp's yellow glow washed into the hall. Ben wrapped his arms around himself and buckled, bracing himself against the doorframe.

"No," he whimpered.

51

It felt to Ben like it was taking a long time for the police to arrive. Still scattered in the vast woodlands beyond the edge of town, they'd be searching for Eric for a while longer. Ben supposed he could leave. He could just walk right out. But he didn't. There would be no point to it, really. So he sat slumped with his back to the wall opposite the battered door. His jaw ached, and he rubbed it absently with the tips of his fingers. Marty had hit him several times. Now Marty, Tim, and Darlene were arguing in the living room. Darlene smacked Marty more than once. Aaron stared from the kitchen.

In front of Ben, fidgeting in a tall chair with a wicker back, sat a boy. He couldn't have been more than eight, maybe nine. In truth, it was very difficult to tell. His jaw strained and rocked from one side of his skull to the other, aligning with his upper teeth only when he would swallow forcefully. The old chair creaked and crackled as the boy rolled his head in vast, swooping motions. Sometimes, at the gesture's apex, he would moan or bleat. Bending and curling his fingers, he tried passively to move his arms about, but instead they flapped like chicken wings, pivoting near his wrists, which were bound to the armrests. His smile was wide and constant, but devoid of joy. Beside him, on the floor, was the cake plate that Ben had brought to Marty's house on Eric's birthday.

Ben could see daylight shining through the far wall of the boy's room where the bullet had passed through. An ineffective rustling in his legs urged Ben to move. But he just sat there. At that moment, Ben thought that would be okay, to just sit there forever, until time blew him away with the rest of the weathered building.

The voices quieted. Footsteps swept against the stiff carpet. Ben stared at the spot between his feet.

"I seen this tape in Palmer's office. Right after what happened with the baler. He had these videos and one of 'em was from the day that Eric went missing. And it was . . . it was *me* on that tape. I was . . . pullin on him, yankin on Eric's arm. I don't remember doin that. I don't remember it at all." Ben looked at Marty. "I . . . misunderstand things sometimes. I got this wrong. They seen Eric today with a boy with yellow hair. Jacob did. I'm really sorry, man. I got it wrong, and I'm sorry."

"That's a great story," Marty said flatly. "Tell me if you heard this one. You said that you couldn't do this alone no more, and so I tried to make it so you wouldn't have to. I tried to help you, Ben. I wanted to. But you're a piece of shit. A worthless fat fuck.

"I ain't gonna say that I hope you never find your brother. But I feel bad for him if you do. I feel bad for anyone that has to know you. That's it, though. We ain't got no more to say to each other. You can leave."

"I'd just as soon get picked up here. Spare my folks—" Ben scraped his tongue against the roof of his mouth to clear it of his bitter words.

"We ain't calling the cops."

Ben looked to Marty. The words seemed compassionate, but there was nothing but disdain in his eyes. "What's wrong with him?"

"He's autistic."

"Is he okay like that?" Ben asked, wringing his own wrist in his hand while staring at the boy.

"He hits himself. The doctors said it's something to do with stimulation."

Ben looked to the limp lock dangling from the doorframe. "The Cotter girl?"

"Walter didn't mean it. But they took him away anyhow, to that place where he got touch—" Marty's face tensed. He rubbed the wetness out of his eyes.

Ben looked at Walter, who chomped his teeth like a nutcracker and writhed in his restraints seemingly without being aware that they were there at all. He yelped painlessly, smiled, and rolled his head.

"Go on then," Marty said.

From the moment Ben stood to the moment he sat back on his bed, his legs trembled. His stepmother had closed the door to Eric's room. Ben could still hear her through the wall, her muted song punctuated by sobs. Relics of a past life lay scattered at his feet. He clenched his teeth and felt a sting in his jaw.

Gripping the edge of his trash can, Ben walked to his dresser and rifled through the contents of the bottom drawer, where he retrieved the doctored flyers he had produced. He rolled the stack in half and plunged it into the trash can. Ben pulled the card sleeve out of his back pocket. Old creases made a jigsaw of his brother's face. After a moment of consideration, Ben tossed the picture into his treasure box.

Handful by handful, Ben separated his books from his clothes from his CDs, stacking and folding and filing, returning everything to where it had been. His treasure box. Beverly's Bible. He wanted to stop; there was really no point in making his room look nice. But he couldn't find his sketchbook.

It had been hours since Jacob had put the day in motion. They were still out there, still wandering through the endless woods, calling out for a boy who would never be found, while Ben had been burning a friendship to the ground. Clint would be home eventually. Ben wondered what the man might tell Deidra. Then he found himself wondering how many times she might have watched that last tape of Ben and Eric.

The feeling of malaise wouldn't leave him, even when he found what he'd been looking for—a kind of goal that feels empty once you reach it. Ben set the sketchbook on his bedside table, then changed his mind.

All these addresses, these records. Ben squeezed his hand on the well-worn paper, tearing it from the spine, crushing it into a soft ball. Page after page wadded in the palm of Ben's large hand. Doodles. Drawings. That fucking symbol. Even as he tore and crushed the sheets, he knew that he shouldn't, that he'd regret it later. Maybe even as soon as he was finished. But he didn't stop. Gritting his teeth, Ben ripped and tore and squeezed until he reached Eric's portrait. And then his hand finally stopped.

"Fuck," he said, trembling.

The lump in Ben's throat made it hard to breathe. His hands shook as he cradled the book. "Eric, Age 8."

"Fuck," he whimpered again.

Eric's eyes were gone, voided and cratered with dark, heavy lines, like balls of pressed black straw. The mouth was a scribbled frown with no contours or care, a jagged ink gash that spoke into bubbles like a comic-book child, saying one thing and one thing only.

Ben knocked the sketchbook off his lap, but the page didn't turn. The book didn't close. Eric's drawing just kept staring at Ben through its scratchy eyes, kept speaking to him through its centipede frown.

HI BEN

"Don't k-kill me!" sssaid the good thing.

"Kill you?" asked the buh-bad man.

"No. I juh-just don't want yuh-you to run.

"You're mine forever now."

And he was.

52

Ben held the phone in his hand, his fingers hovering over the keypad in Customer Service. It had been six days since Ben had spoken to Marty for what he knew would be the last time. Duchaine and his men hadn't found anything in the woods—nothing but starlight, and when they found that, they suspended the search until daybreak. Clint walked the woods for far longer. Just how long, Ben didn't know, because his father hadn't come back home until Ben had already left for work. His father and the police had searched those woods for days, but they found exactly as much as they found that first day, exactly as much as they'd found years before.

Ben had gone by himself once. Not shouting for his brother, not even really looking for him. He'd walked silently and looked for Beverly's home. He hadn't found it, hadn't even found the gravel that seemed to lead in its direction. For the whole quiet journey, Ben thought about what Marty had said about God's sentry over all things. About that cosmic blink, shielding a divine eye from its creation. And about the possibility that maybe Jacob hadn't seen Eric, not because he'd simply seen a similar boy, but because there had been no boy at all. Just a moving sculpture of leaves and air that shouldn't exist but did.

Ben never made the drive to look for Blackwater. He hadn't been back to talk to Reggie. And even though the ticket was still in his pocket, he still hadn't gone to pick up the photos he'd had developed. He'd already seen the pictures in his dreams, though—seen him and Eric together, when Eric was still so little, as if the camera had been made with those images already in it. And other pictures too. Arms and legs with unnatural joints. The lipless smile of his brother's face in the grainy dark.

Ben didn't trust himself anymore. His mind. His beliefs. He'd been wrong: wrong about Bobby Prewitt, about Eric's tape, about Marty. Wrong about everything. Ben hadn't hurt Eric, not in the way Duchaine had said. The man was out of his goddamn mind. But Ben couldn't stop thinking about it, imagining worlds where Duchaine wasn't lying, worlds where he'd led Eric into the bathroom and pushed his face into the toilet until he stopped moving.

Even when Bobby Prewitt died, Ben hadn't felt so trapped, so entombed in his own skull. He could feel his thoughts scratching around in his brain, and he wanted them gone. He couldn't give his ideas to Duchaine. The man wouldn't take them even if they were complete, and they were far from fully formed. Whatever message Beverly was trying to relate about Palmer, about Blackwater, Ben couldn't figure it out. And he knew he wasn't going to. All he wanted was some kind of guarantee—a real promise that what he said would be considered—and that everything he'd found wouldn't just sit in some box somewhere. That it would all be used. To do what Duchaine hadn't ever tried to do. To do what Ben hadn't managed.

Ben stared at the flyer he'd taken off the board outside the store. Clenching his jaw, Ben dialed the number at the bottom. The line connected almost immediately.

"North Florida Missing Persons. This is Joyce."

"Hi," Ben said, "I'm calling about . . ." Ben searched Eric's flyer. "Case 152294."

"Okay," Joyce said. The sound of shuffling papers was audible even through the muffled connection. "Is there something you'd like to report?"

"Yeah." Ben tapped the phone against his skull lightly.

"Sir?"

"I can barely hear you. Is there somethin wrong with the line?" Ben waited for the woman to respond. When she didn't, he continued. "Should I call back?"

"I can hear you fine."

"Okay. I called once before. A while back . . . I think maybe it was you I spoke to?"

"I'm sorry, sir. But we can't—"

"Give out information of any kind. I know. Okay. Listen . . ." Ben paused. "I know that someone called you this past summer about seein this boy, alright? I know you can't say yes or no, but you look back sometime in May or June, and it'll be there. Then someone over there forwarded that information to Lieutenant James Duchaine.

"Now, I have some things I wanna tell you. But when you pass this along . . . I need your word that you'll pass it to someone other than that man. Anybody else."

"Sir—"

"Eric is my brother, okay? I'm his brother, and I got some things. And they matter. James Duchaine don't care. He doesn't give a damn about this kid. He didn't do nothin at all with that information you gave him. You understand? No cops ever came. I want to give you stuff to help. Don't tell me to take it to the police. I won't do it. But I'll bring it to you if you just tell me where.

"*Hello?*" Ben said after a few seconds.

"Two ninety-five Dunn Street."

"And you'll pass this along to someone who will do something?"

Joyce sighed, then paused. "Yes, sir."

"Okay," Ben said. He calmed his breathing, then continued. "Thank you. It's just that I been tryin. I been tryin real hard . . . I need help. That's all." Ben blew a trembling breath through his lips. "I wanna tell . . . I wanna tell you about a woman named Beverly."

53

The ringback tone played eight times before Ben gave up. He slammed the phone back on the hook and walked out of his house.

Ben's street shone brightly in the dark air; hundreds of colored bulbs poured out small puddles of light that coalesced into something much larger against the pregnant clouds. The town felt like it had a low ceiling, making the lights feel that much brighter. Radio stations played songs that were at once familiar and yet distinctly alien to their listeners—words of snow in a place that had never seen it. But the sky would show them something soon. Ben could feel it in the wind as he walked to work.

There was no 295 Dunn Street.

It had taken Ben three days to get ahold of his father's truck, but he'd finally driven it all the way down Dunn. And then all the way back up. He wanted to talk to someone in person. Ben hadn't brought the Bible or the graffitied flyer. He hadn't even picked up the pictures yet. The woman he'd spoken to hadn't seemed all that intrigued by the things Ben had said. She did a poor job of hiding it, and it took Ben a while to accept that that was his fault. He knew that they got calls from crackpots all the time, intentional pranksters and delusional assholes who claimed to know or have or even be the victim. And he knew that's what he was to Joyce—another weirdo. Ben needed to let them see and consider him before he unloaded armfuls of sloppy evidence onto some desk. That was fine.

But after 240 Dunn, the road's name changed to Maple Street. And while there *was* a 295 Maple Street, it was a Laundromat.

Maybe he'd misheard. Maybe the woman had misspoken. Either way, when Ben called the number and no one answered, it took everything in Ben's power to resist smashing the phone into pieces. He couldn't call from home, not if he was going to yell.

Outside the store, Ben checked the phone number on the slip of paper in his hand against the one on Eric's bulletin board flyer. He checked it three times before he was satisfied that he hadn't misdialed. Then he flung the clear screen aside and snatched the flyer down, so he could just dial right from the source and stop worrying about it.

If he could show them, they'd understand. It just had to be organized. Intelligible. And complete. There was still one more thing Ben needed to do, one more thing he needed to get out of Palmer's office.

In the break room, Ben sat and chewed his food while he waited for the store to close. He ate most of his meals there now. It was quieter than his home, but it felt less lonely somehow. Sometimes Ben thought about Beverly as he sat at that empty table.

Chelsea's soft voice spoke through the intercom, addressing Ben by name. They hadn't spoken in a while, not since that lingering hug, in fact. It was only just occurring to Ben that she might like him.

Ben spent a lot of his time at the store. More than he ever had. Maybe more than anyone ever had. Sometimes he forgot to clock in or out, or forgot that he had remembered. And sometimes he slept there, just for a few hours, savoring sleep that was dreamless and dead.

Ben's watch woke him. The side of his face ached warmly from the pressure of his arm during his nap. He stretched his jaw slowly and blinked hard twice. He stood cautiously and unloaded his weight onto his sleep-stiff bad leg.

Moving toward the iron stairs, even Ben's heavy steps were soundless under the churning heater. The farther he moved down the corridor, the farther he moved from light, entering another part of the store that was plunged into darkness when midnight struck. Ben's hands swept along the wall for guidance. Mechanical shudders behind him felt like footsteps against the ground. Ahead, a pool of light fell from Palmer's office, dancing against the wall, quivering.

Everything was still and quiet, save the spindles driving the videotape. Ben flicked on the lights, then sat in Palmer's chair. He reached into his back pocket and slid out Eric's flyer, tapping its folded corner lightly on a stack of forms. He unfolded the paper and traced the crease out of Eric's face.

Every now and then, Ben's mania at Marty's house would flash through his mind. Just glimpses. Still frames from an event that Ben could hardly accept had actually happened. It made Ben want to cry, even though he didn't. Marty had been trying to help Ben since before they'd even met, since before Marty knew that the boy from the flyer even *had* a brother. Nothing at all had come from when Marty called, and try as he might, Ben couldn't delude himself into thinking that this call would be any different. But he'd give them everything, and then when he hung up the phone, he'd break Palmer's filing cabinet and take Beverly's folder. When Ben took the file, Palmer would likely notice, and Ben would be fired if he hadn't already quit. And then he could pretend that at long last he'd finally done all he could.

Ben hadn't decided if he'd look through it yet. Although he'd assigned the task to himself, it very much felt like he was running an errand for someone else. The people at Missing Persons hadn't asked for anything, but they needed it. Once they saw it, they'd know that. They'd know, and they'd be happy to have it.

But before he could give it to them, he needed a fucking address.

Ben punched in the number. It would be helpful if he could get some sense of anything else they might want. The ringback tone played once. Then it played again. Ben chewed the inside of his cheek. Was this their fucking day off? Duchaine had said that someone was always at the other end of this line, so why the hell wasn't someone picking up? He hoped Joyce would answer, so they could pick up where they'd left off, instead of Ben having to start from scratch. But that wasn't likely to happen, because Joyce didn't exist.

Ben slowly drew the receiver away from his ear. The beginnings of tears stung his eyes.

Somewhere—beyond a wall, through studs and nails, copper pipes and wires—somewhere behind him, Ben could hear a phone ringing.

54

Without thinking, Ben slammed the headset back onto the base, and the muffled ringing stopped. Immediately, his hands fumbled for the receiver and groped at the number pad, his blurry vision flicking from the flyer to the keys. He pressed the buttons carefully. He had to start over twice.

When the noise returned, Ben set the phone down on the desk and stood. He stayed there for a while, listening to the chime, while an acidic taste crept into the back of his throat. He tried to breathe slowly. His legs moved. The ringing was louder in the hallway, loudest to his right. He groped and clawed his way down the dark corridor, pressing his ear against each door. The hallway curved, and Ben followed it blindly. There, in the darkness straight ahead, he could make out a doorframe. Red light blazed through the slim gap at the bottom of the door and then disappeared. Louder. The ringing was louder now. Louder here. Ben moved forward. The red light returned, burning under the door like fire.

Ben felt for the doorknob and found that it turned freely. He pushed the door into the room, and when it pivoted back to him, he sent it crashing violently against whatever fragile thing lay behind it. The phone's ring was piercing, and for a few seconds, it was the only thing filling the room. Then the engulfing dark was beaten back by a surge of blistering red. As Ben stepped inside, the door shut forcefully behind him.

Another ring. More light coming from the same direction somewhere to Ben's right. What else? Ben glanced hurriedly. The light didn't touch everything, but it touched enough. Clothes in piles. Shorts. A dress. Darkness fell. What was that odor? More ringing that the room was too small to contain. Ben spun in the red glow, looking for a light switch. Books on shelves. Stacks of paper.

A wooden pallet. *Two* pallets. Thin bedsheets balled on the floor beside them. What was that *smell*? Ben stumbled in the dark, waiting for the light to return; his feet struck something that looked like a jack-in-the-box. His hands fumbled against volumes on an unsteady shelf, thumbing the pages of each spine he grabbed before casting it to the floor. A Bible. A children's book. A photo album. Smooth, cold laminated sheets brushed against his frantic fingers. The plastic smacked against itself like a dry mouth as Ben rifled the pages.

Children. Adults. All old pictures. Gray. Brown.

A little girl, harelipped. A solemn man.

Loose pictures spilled out of the book, and Ben caught them. A field. A woman with wild hair. Ben shuffled toward the brilliant light, stopped in the darkness, then held the book near the bulb for a better look. A sheet of paper slipped from its pages and hit somewhere near his feet in the darkness. The smell was worse here. White paper stood erect in a bucket. Bending to retrieve it, the smell overtook him. Effluvium dripped from the page as he pinched it out of the container. Excrement and urine fell away like melting ice.

HAVE YOU SEEN ME?

Ben's breath hung in the darkness. His heart pounded in his ears. The bulb burned again, shining through the paper and turning his brother's face into a crimson lamp. And that was it. At long last, Ben had found something that he didn't even know to look for, even though he'd been gaining on it all the time. He didn't really understand it—he couldn't possibly—but he still knew. He knew he'd found the heart of this place. And he knew it beat for him.

The bulb erupted again, splashing red light on everything in Ben's new world. And before him, on the wall, creeping from beneath frantic swaths of indecipherable colors, was a blood moon, smiling, fawning over its exuberant child. Scraped and carved and drawn and scratched and painted, they were everywhere—on the walls, on the ceiling—screaming out with each trill to their new guest, first asking, then demanding, that Ben smile too. That he join them in their forever dance.

Ben's head was pounding, the ringing telephone a chisel on his skull.

He grabbed the phone by its base, wanting to stop the clanging but afraid that it would take the light with it out of spite. Turning, Ben used the bulb on the phone as a spotlight, pulling on the cord and washing the light over the room's hidden corners.

The shadows were living things that scurried away from the light. And once it retreated, Ben could feel them crawling over his skin, holding him, embracing him. Each scream of the phone was a surprise, despite the rhythm. It was hard to breathe. Ben could see Eric, mangled and chittering across the floor. And then the light would reset the room and he'd be gone.

The phone cord brushed against his hand, a paper label sticking to the filth on his fingers. It said FAX. Following the line with his eyes, he watched as it hid in the blinking red darkness before finally disappearing altogether into the ceiling.

Ben couldn't move now. The clattering phone stunted the growth of any thought. He might never leave. That's what the room wanted, right? That's why it had brought him here, to stay and live forever until he crushed his skull between his own hands. Suddenly, it didn't feel like Ben had had anything at all to do with making this phone ring. There was someone else on the other end waiting for Ben to answer.

The phone smacked against the floor when Ben dropped it, but the ringing didn't stop. It became muted behind the closing door as Ben left the room. His eyes rang with the red light's memory. He tried to hold the room in his mind, to understand it. Rounding the corner, the soft glow from Palmer's office illuminated his way. His thoughts and legs both fought for balance.

Ben hung up the phone, and the distant ringing ceased. For what felt like a very long while, Ben just stood there next to Palmer's desk and his papers. With the filing cabinet behind him, Ben stared through the wide windows at the sprawling aisles of a lazy farm.

There was a fluttering in Ben's stomach, a kind of weightlessness in his guts. Ben still couldn't think, couldn't understand what he had just seen, or what any of it meant, or what he should do. He needed to think, needed time. Vacantly, Ben stared at the pictures in his hand. He hadn't realized he'd taken them out of that room. Wrinkled and creased, he'd squeezed them so tightly that his hand stung.

Ben didn't recognize the field. But—

Ben was running. He was halfway down the corridor, hurtling toward the bellowing heater, before he realized where he was. Clumsy feet tangled with each other as he plunged down the iron steps. His hands lashed out at the railing and caught it. *Marty never talked to anyone at Missing Persons.*

That was the first coherent thought that formed in Ben's mind as he stampeded through the store. He could feel the urgency of that fact in his panicked chest as he ran and pictured the woman with the wild hair. *Marty never talked to anyone at Missing Persons and neither did I.*

Not three days ago. Not months before. Someone had changed the phone number, and those calls had gone to that room.

Those calls had gone to Beverly.

The front doors rumbled as Ben pried them apart. Wind hurled icy rain into Ben's face. Light from the store's windows fought its way into the dark but succumbed quickly. Ben squinted and ran in alternating directions in front of the store calling for his brother, despite knowing in some meaningless, cognitive way that they'd be long gone by now.

Because Ben had given them a head start. How long? Two days. It couldn't be more than that. *What did you say?* He jogged into the emptiness of the parking lot. What had Ben said when he'd called? What had he told "Joyce"? *Think.* Had he mentioned Beverly's house? What had he *said*? Ben gripped the sides of his head and again screamed Eric's name into the air.

She had a head start. A big one. How fast could Beverly move with a struggling boy? And for how long? He didn't know the answers to those questions. But he knew *where.* He knew that much.

He stepped into the grass that bordered the parking lot and again screamed his brother's name. More steps now. Just a few more. He needed to call the police. How much time would that waste? How long would he spend trying to convince Duchaine or some deputy? He didn't even know Beverly's address.

The sky howled and spat in Ben's face.

But he'd find the house. By God, he would find it. Ben felt a current surge through his body, as if lightning had reached out to touch him. His legs fired like old pistons that ached from years of neglect. His body heaved with each step, steps that carried him deeper into the curtaining rain.

I can fix this, Ben thought. *I can fix everything.*

Somewhere in the distance, lightning lit the sky on fire, and it screamed in pain.

55

Ben ran next to the tree line, his feet pounding into the spongy earth. How far had they walked, him and Marty? Each opening in the bush called to Ben. Lightning flashed too quickly to be of any use. His feet slid in the shallow mud. Several times Ben ducked into the trees, only to be pushed back by them. When he finally came upon a void large enough to be a passage, he took it. Congested with branches and vines, the artery squeezed and tore, snagged and stabbed. This wasn't the same path. Ben pushed his body through and called for his brother. The sky seemed to answer with a roar, and then all at once it opened up.

The sound of the rainfall in the trees was deafening. Ben wiped water away from his face and pulled his shirt free of branches and thorns. A lingering throb coursed through Ben's hands, accented by the sting of new thorns as Ben continued to beat back the forest. His eyes peered half lidded through the tangled snares, slamming shut and pinching tightly when poked or scraped by the defending trees. At last, the tunnel opened up, and Ben searched for a landmark that might indicate that he was on the right path. But there was nothing.

The sky cracked and burst with light and sound. The tip of Ben's shoe caught on something hard. Tree bark dug and pulled against Ben's grasping hand. Ben hit the mud with a whimper and then pulled himself back up.

"Eric!" he yelled. "Eric, where are you?" His words fell apart. He shouldn't yell. Whatever Beverly's plan had been—changing the number, writing notes in her own file, the moonchild—she couldn't have known that Ben would find that room. She didn't know he was coming.

But neither did Eric. And he needed to.

Again the sky bellowed. Ben cradled his side, which stabbed with a cramp. The sound of rain played on, like a radio tuned to the wrong frequency. His chest heaved, lungs quivered. Doubled over, Ben dug his palms into his knees and wheezed.

"Eric!" Ben screamed.

The wind was so loud that Ben nearly missed what whispered on it.

"Olly olly oxen freeeee!"

Ben tried to yell again as he ran toward the sound, but his throat was choked. He'd heard it. That had been real. That had been *Eric.*

Even as the rain slackened, Ben's path was not any clearer. His shouts were ignored or unheard. The thunder rolled faintly in the distance, carried off by some traveling clouds. Water spattered against Ben's head and shoulders, falling not from the sky, but from the crooked trees above. More clouds loomed overhead, as dark and enveloping as the sky beyond them. Not spent but resting.

Ben felt dizzy, and his throat stung as he gasped in air. He winced at the stabbing pain in his chest, and his legs shook uncertainly underneath him as he walked a path that he found indistinguishable from all the others.

"Where—" he rasped, and hacked. "Where are you?"

Rich odors of mud and bark wafted into his nostrils as he breathed as quietly as he could, waiting for a reply that didn't come. Bracing himself on each trunk he passed, Ben trudged through the muck and grasped vines. *Please,* he thought, as he shambled along a path. *Please be real. Please be real.*

Each step was a concerted effort to keep walking. Ben wasn't even trying to run now. His movements were slow and plodding. Blinding currents of pain cracked from knee to hip. He leaned his shoulder against a large pine, then slid down with his back against the bark. Shivering, Ben plied his leg with his thumbs and the heels of his hand, but the usual relief refused to come. There was only agony.

Sobbing quietly, Ben picked at a couple spears of pine straw, splitting them from their sheaths and letting them fall to the damp earth between his knees. Only now did Ben have time to feel the full gravity of his mistake. He hadn't called anyone. But there was still time. He could still fix this. If he could make it back to town, he could call for help. Pressing his back against the tree, Ben struggled to his feet.

Water sheeted off the face of his watch as Ben wiped his index finger across it. He pressed a button, and the Indiglo light told him that dawn was still a few hours away. He made a halfhearted attempt to orient himself, then began walking.

He locked his knee and walked as he had when he first started moving under his own power after his accident. Each trunk became a waist to stumble into, each limb an outstretched arm. Ben hardly noticed when the rain started again. It came without fury, whipping only in occasional gusts of wind. Slowly and painfully, his foot swept the leaves at the end of his useless leg. *Just focus on the squeaking hinge, the whining brace. Just imagine the sound and concentrate on that.*

Ben wasn't sure how far he'd traveled, but he knew that he'd been moving for about two hours. Every few minutes, sometimes every few steps, he'd have to brace himself against a tree to take some of the weight off his leg. He tried making a crutch from a long stick, but the insides were soft with rot and it crumbled beneath his weight. Leaning against the rough bark of an evergreen, he searched the ground for a sturdier branch.

As he knelt, something moved in his peripheral, and he turned his head to meet it. The boy peered into the distance through his golden hair as he crept from around the tree. Frozen, Ben watched the boy take a step forward with delicate, careful feet.

Ben cleared his throat to speak. The boy jerked, turning on his heels and losing his balance in the mud. He looked at Ben with wide, fiery eyes as Ben grabbed him by the arm.

Ben studied the boy's face: his pointed nose, his high, sharp cheekbones. His blond hair.

"Oh, Jesus," Ben said. "You . . . You're the kid . . . the kid from Halloween. Beverly's grandson."

Rain pattered against leaves and dirt. The boy's mouth moved as if to speak but shut in silence.

"It was you," Ben said, slackening his grip in shock. "You were with my brother. My brother, Eric."

The boy's amber eyes glowed vibrantly for a moment. Ben felt the boy's arm slipping from his grip. He tightened his fist.

"Is he alive?" Ben demanded. The boy nodded, and Ben felt so weak he almost let the child go. "Do you know where he is? Where Beverly's house is at?" Again, the boy nodded. "Show me, okay?" Ben tried to calm his voice. "Show me, please."

The boy walked and Ben followed.

"Did she take you? Did she take you too?" The boy said nothing, but Ben's questions were so frantic that he hardly left time for an answer. "Is it far?" Ben waited longer this time, and the boy nodded.

They walked in silence for a while. The boy didn't speak or even look at Ben. He didn't look at much at all, for that matter—never seeming to consult his surroundings, walking as if he could see right through the trees and the night itself. Each time Ben asked if they were headed in the right direction, the boy simply nodded. Ben stopped asking when they passed the mangled car.

Faintly, the moonlight glistened on the thick mud of the woodland floor. Driving deep pockets into the earth, Ben pulled himself through the sticky ground. The boy walked more easily, his steps lighter and almost effortless; it was as if he walked on an invisible platform just above the unsteady, waterlogged earth. He hardly left any trail at all, but it was there. And although it was hard to see, Ben recognized the zagging pattern from a lifetime ago, when he had shattered a rancid jar of mayonnaise.

"Did you . . . did you put that flyer in my locker?" Ben asked.

Again, the boy nodded. But this time he turned and smiled.

Beverly must have made the boy tear down Eric's flyers, and the boy had reached out to Ben for help. And now here he was. Now they could help *each other*.

"When we get there," Ben said, lifting the boy over a fallen branch and then stepping clumsily over it himself, "you're going to run and get help, okay? Do you know how to get back to town?" Again, the boy dipped his chin. "You're gonna tell them where to go and who I am. My name's Ben. Ben. Can you remember that?" The boy nodded.

"What's *your* name?"

The boy turned his blazing eyes back toward Ben and shrugged his shoulders.

"Don't you got a name?"

Ben tightened his grip on the back of the boy's shirt. As he pulled the fabric, he could see the tangled knot of the twine necklace resting against his spine.

"Did you live with Eric? In that room in the store?" The boy bobbed his head slowly. "Did she treat him okay?" Ben's words caught in his throat. The boy did not answer. "Did she hurt him?" The boy shook his head. "Can't you talk?" Ben said with subdued frustration.

"Yes."

Then fucking talk, Ben thought. Damp leaves and clumps of fallen pine straw scattered in the wake of Ben's shifting feet. "It's gonna be okay," Ben said through chattering teeth. "I don't want you to worry about what's gonna happen. You're gonna be fine. She's not even gonna see you, okay?" The boy nodded.

Periodically, Ben tugged on the boy's shirt, reining him in like a horse who moved too fast. Too gradual to notice as it happened, the path had started widening and the ground grew to be made more of grass than dead leaves and branches. The trees thinned until Ben and the boy were nearly free from them altogether. Ben struggled against his leg and the slope of the land, pushing against damp bark whenever he had the chance.

The boy's shirt slipped from Ben's fist. Lunging, Ben called out for him to stop, but was cut short by the buckling of his leg. He panted, kneeling in the soft dirt. After a few steps the boy stopped and looked back, waiting. Ben stifled a yelp as the pain in his leg spiked, and he closed the distance to his guide. The boy's eyes blazed as he extended an arm behind himself, pointing.

In the distance, beyond the scattered trees and their beards of Spanish moss, was a home. It was almost impossible to see, tucked safely in the consuming night, save for the flat shine of a window. It was Beverly's home.

"Okay." Ben's voice was strained as he knelt in front of the boy. "Which way is town? Alright, you go that way, and you don't stop. You don't stop for nothin. There's a restaurant." Ben checked his watch. "The Finer

Diner. Do you know what I'm talking about? Okay, you go there and you use their phone. If they're not open, you break a window. The cops won't care. Don't stop for nothin, and don't come back here even if the cops try to make you. You got it?" Ben exhaled heavily and struggled to his feet. His eyes fell back on the boy's. "Does she know I'm coming?"

Chewing on the inside of his cheek, the boy nodded.

Ben turned back toward the house. Leaves rustled quietly under the boy's gentle steps. "Thank you," Ben called in a loud whisper, just as the boy was about to slip into the darkness.

"You're wuh-welcome," the boy replied.

56

Ben wobbled slightly on his numb legs as he made his way down the hill, his body sure of its footing only when the vibration of each step carried up to his torso. The sound of the wind chime drifted through the air as Ben limped down the hill, his stomach in knots. He had a bad taste in his mouth.

The steps had moaned when he climbed them with Marty, but they seemed to be too bloated with water to make any noise this time. Wind howled through the trees and around the house. The metal edges of the window screen that Marty had removed jostled lightly against the wet wood. Ben's whole body quaked with nerves and cold.

Gently, he turned the doorknob. It was unlocked.

The smell of old dust and mildew filled Ben's nose as he entered the void of the house. Ben crept with delicate steps into a home so dark it was as if only his peripheral had any vision left at all. Shadows danced in the corners of the room and then fled from his pupils. Ben knew he was standing in the living room, but only by memory. The coffee table, the chairs, the armoire—everything was buried under black. Ben groped at the air with damp hands and pulled himself through the darkness deeper into the house.

He stood in each doorway, squinting into the black boxes that made up the house, searching for movement, but finding only its illusion—the swirling dark that writhed only in his eyes.

In the kitchen, Ben cupped his hands against the window but could see only gyres of windblown rain. The lantern that was hanging next to the door squeaked as he lifted it from its hook and eyed the carbonized wick. He fumbled through the drawers. Can openers and wooden skewers. Rags and papers. Finally, his fingers brushed against something rough. The box rattled as he shook it. Two matches tumbled out of the package; one rolled against the side of his hand and then was lost.

The remaining match lit on the third strike, and Ben hurried it to the thirsty wick. His eyes gorged themselves too quickly as the flame burst to life and squinted in reflex. Dust floated like snowflakes in the stale air, rolling and swarming in the wake of the swinging lantern. Ben nearly screamed when he caught his own reflection in the window.

The house cracked against the wind. "Eric?" Ben whispered, turning and raising the light above his head as he moved back into the hallway. Ben's hand trembled as the lantern light filled the bedroom. The sheets were made. A chill swept across Ben's neck and he backed into the hallway. As he turned toward the opposite bedroom, the light washed over the living room.

He nearly dropped the lantern when he saw Beverly. She sat motionless in a tattered chair, the same chair Marty had thought he'd seen her in. She hadn't been here. Not then. But as Ben stared at the woman, her eyes fixed toward the dirty window in front of her, he thought that none of that meant that Marty hadn't seen her. No, Ben felt sure that the emptiness of the house had been the illusion.

A deep, ratcheting breath rumbled from her throat. "You shouldn't have come here," she said flatly. "Ain't nothing for you here."

She looked like a doll a child had arranged. Her head bobbed erratically. Her hands shook. The harsh light was unkind to her ancient face; shadows drew deep trenches in the wrinkles of her saurian skin. Her eyes seemed to seek the darkness of her skull, retreating from the lantern into dark pockets, flashing only at the occasional swing of the lamp. Each breath rolled loudly in her chest. She stifled a cough and hacked into a lace handkerchief.

"Eric!" Ben shouted.

"He can't hear you."

Ben ignored her. "Eric! Tell me where you are!"

The windows rattled as he stormed back into the hallway. He checked the other rooms again. Every drawer. Every creaking cabinet. He screamed his brother's name so many times it began to lose its meaning. When he paced back into the room Beverly occupied, she was looking at her watch.

"You look so stupid." Beverly leaned back in her chair, folding her handkerchief. Her head trembled around her motionless eyes.

Ben could feel the blood rushing to his face. The house shook as he stormed toward the old woman. Her lips curled back as she recoiled in the chair. Ben caught her by the wrist. It was thin and cold, her skin draped loosely over her bones. "Take me to him."

"No," Beverly said.

Ben squeezed, staring into her jaundiced eyes. He squeezed just a little, just enough that he could feel her bones start to bend toward one another like the thin walls of a tube of toothpaste.

Beverly gritted her teeth. "Alright!" she sneered at Ben. "Alright."

Ben's hand loosened and slid away before being snatched up again by Beverly's.

"Help me up, then."

The woman groaned; her crooked spine contorted her torso, while the swinging light shined on her weathered face. The two walked in single file down the narrow hallway. Ben had to take half-steps behind the old woman. One of her shoulders hung lower than the other, and she would occasionally brace it with her hand. A deep purple was bleeding into her papery skin where Ben had grabbed her.

The wind moaned against the roof while the windows flexed, returning reflections like fun-house mirrors. With her good arm, Beverly reached for the kerosene lantern. When Ben refused, the woman rolled her eyes, then grabbed for an old umbrella leaning against the wall near the back door. Again, Ben said no.

"I'm sick, you moron. I ain't goin out there without this."

They walked out of the house and into the rain.

Beverly shuffled slowly in the grass, angling the umbrella against the wind. Ben scrunched his face unconsciously at the cold spray. He looked at the back of Beverly's head and the blue veins traveling down her neck like the tentacles of a jellyfish.

"I know what you're thinking of doing," she yelled into the wind, her coarse white hair blowing wildly, exposing her hearing aids. "Don't do it."

Gusts surged, tugging against the umbrella.

"It would have all been okay," she said, or at least Ben thought he heard her say. Beverly raised her quivering arm and pointed toward the shed.

The ground squished beneath Ben's shoes, and the wind swirled into the umbrella, shaking it more forcefully this time.

"Is he in there?"

"No."

"What's in there?"

Beverly stopped and turned toward Ben. "You already seen what's in there and you know it." There was venom in her voice, and it made Ben feel almost as small as she was. He depressed the button on his watch and checked the time, trying to figure out how long it would take the boy to make it back to town.

She slid a key into the padlock and pulled on it. When she couldn't get it to open, she stepped aside and motioned to Ben, who yanked on the lock and then lifted it out of the metal loop. The flimsy door opened with a whine.

"Eric?" Ben shouted into the dark contours of the shed. "I can't see nothin in there," Ben snapped as he held the lantern into the void.

"There's nothing in there to see," she said, running her finger gently between her nose and lip. "That's for you. Get on in, and I'll bring Eric right to you."

"Quit playing games!" Ben's fist struck the side of the shed. The two stared at each other for a while. Their breath steamed in the chilled air. "I need to take him home."

"He's got one."

"A closet?"

The old woman nodded to herself with what looked like comprehension, tracing the gorges that ran from her averted eyes with her skeletal fingers. "A home don't care where it is. You got a place you live, Benjamin. It feel like a home to you?" The look on Beverly's face invited Ben to answer, but he didn't. "Everything was fine. Because we had each other. I lost the house. Fine. We made a new one and we was happy and things was good. And then *you.* You came to tear everything up. From right when I seen your application on that pig-faced prick's desk I knew it. And you wouldn't *leave.* You damn near kick in our door. Almost killed Martin. And you just kept on and kept on.

"Fine. Then *we* would leave. That's all we wanted. And you know how long we waited because of you? Waiting for someplace else to go? Then just waiting for them doors to be unlocked with clear passage? The one night when we was finally left alone, when we could finally get out, who do I see peeking through the glass?

"And then"—Beverly's mouth trembled—"I sent them away. By themselves. So they could move faster. And a man sees 'em? Then there's more men screamin Eric's name so loud and making him so scared that he has to come *back*?

"You and Martin and Frank and the cashier and then Bill and your fucking flyers and on and on. You trapped us in there! I couldn't even walk around in my own home. You cursed that place with glass that wouldn't break, with no way out. And here you are, in our way *again,* where nobody wants you and where you got no right to be."

"He's my brother!"

"And you hit him!" Beverly roared. Her mouth was snarled and tense, her lips almost invisible. "I *seen* you. You ain't got no claim to him that's worth anything at all, so go on. Just get already!" Beverly coughed violently into her handkerchief. It sounded like something was breaking in her chest. "I *love* him. You understand? You walk around askin after him"—Beverly mimed holding a sheet of paper—"but you beat on that boy. He was little and you beat on him.

"I'll let him die out here before I take you anywhere near him. By the time you get to that boy, he'll be nothin but bones, and he'll be happier for it."

"You gotta take me to him, Beverly. You're gonna take me to him or make him come to where we're at." Ben reached for Beverly's arm. She withdrew, bending her arm behind her back, but that was an easy chase for Ben. With her forearm in his grip, Beverly stopped trying to move. "I seen the other one, you know? I seen him out there in the woods, tryin to get away from you. And he did. You wanna know what *he's* doin for you? He's telling the cops where we're at, and when they get here, they're gonna make you take them to Eric. You don't have nobody, Ms. Beverly. Now call for him."

"No."

"Please." Ben's voice quaked as he squeezed Beverly's fragile wrist. "I just need him back."

The woman didn't respond, even as Ben squeezed harder; she pressed her lips together and refused to call out. But that's not to say that she was silent.

"Please," Ben pleaded as Beverly whimpered.

"He couldn't come even if he wanted to."

Ben didn't want to hurt her. He wasn't going to. He was going to stop. But he kept turning his wrist, more and more, until there was a pop in Beverly's arm. Beverly screamed, but not for Eric.

Ben let go almost immediately. Beverly's hand hung limply. The umbrella fell against the grass. Tears pooled in her eyes and she made a kind of moaning sound as she tucked her arm up next to her chest.

There were no voices on the wind. No one answered Beverly's cry. But Ben could still hear the echo of Beverly's voice in his ear, still feel the quick and brutal movements of her bones in his hand. He felt woozy. He'd broken her arm. It would never heal. It would always hurt. She wasn't going to take him to Eric, and it sure didn't seem like Eric was coming to them.

Beverly clutched her broken arm in the bend of her opposite elbow. Her head tremored as she stared up at Ben through glassy eyes.

"What now?"

57

Frail but unmoving, Beverly stood in the rain outside the crumbling shed. She was a paper doll that tore so easily that Ben was afraid to touch her again. If she died—hell, if she lost consciousness—then Ben would have no guide at all. Ben picked up the umbrella.

"That boy you're countin on," Beverly said, "he ain't gonna help you, son. I don't blame you for gettin it wrong. Truly, I don't. I love him more than I know how to say, but there ain't a person alive that understands the way that one thinks. I don't reckon the world's ever seen a boy like him before."

"He led me here," Ben said.

Beverly shrugged. "That don't mean nothin."

"Why would he do it then?"

Again, Beverly shrugged. "I don't pretend that I can see what he sees. But I know one thing: after Halloween, he thinks you're a tattletale, and he *hates* tattletales. Whatever you think is goin on here, you're wrong. I can promise you that."

The trees had dissolved into a sea of muddy black like a lazy painting. Ben peered into it but saw nothing, no flashing lights, no movement at all other than the swaying branches. Beverly's pallid face trembled from either cold or sickness, maybe both.

"Why don't you lock me in there?" Beverly asked, turning toward the shed. "Then you can have a look around."

"No," Ben said. "I ain't letting you out of my sight." He reached for her as she tried to back into the murky shed, and Beverly recoiled.

"Well, then hold the umbrella right at least." Her silver hair hung like wet yarn against her face.

Ben checked his watch. Beverly had brought them out here in hopes that Ben would step under that dark roof. And now she was trying to take his place. Where the fuck were the police? Ben rubbed the back of his neck. It itched like he had ants in his skin. Ben had just wanted a little time. Time enough for the cops to come. And she was giving it to him. She wasn't worried at all. *You're not the only one stalling here, you dumb fuck.*

The night seemed to writhe and contort like diluted ink. The quiet kid was getting Eric. While Ben wasted his time here, the golden boy was taking Eric somewhere. He was going to have to take Beverly back to town. She would know where Eric was or would be. The police could get her to talk. Could he carry her? For short distances at a time, he reckoned. He could drag her for longer, though. And he would. He would drag her for a hundred miles if that's what it took.

"We're going back to town," Ben said.

"Lead the way," Beverly said.

Ben balled his fists. He wanted to hurt her, but he couldn't, not even with words. She wasn't embarrassed about living in the store, about the red room, about the life she'd made for herself and stolen from others. Again, Ben looked to the dark, and it looked right back. *There's nothing for you here,* it seemed to say. Ben's jaw hurt from clenching his teeth, and suddenly words he hadn't intended to say spilled past them.

"I know about Blackwater School."

Beverly flinched. "And what do you *know*?"

Ben's words stalled. What could he possibly say about the place that would unbalance her? Reggie had talked for a few minutes. Beverly might have lived there for years. *Goddamnit.* "That when this is over, I hope they put you in a place just like it again."

"If you really knew anything about that place," Beverly said, "then you'd know that they'd do anything they could to keep me out of it."

When Ben had come here with Marty, they'd been at the top of a modest hill, with the property down and a little to the right. If he walked back in that direction, then maybe he could find the road. It was hard to visualize, hard to even imagine. Because the way it felt, there in that pocket of enveloping dark, was that they weren't *anywhere.* That there was no way back, because this place was all there was: a rotting house, a skeletal shed, and a sea of trees that stretched on to the edge of forever. That Marty and the golden boy had known some course that Ben did not, an invisible path through a labyrinth that Ben would never find his way out of.

As Ben reached out for the old woman, he heard something. It seemed far away, somewhere mingled with the endless shadow. Then, beneath the pattering of rain on dead leaves, there was another sound. A shuffling. Too soft for Beverly to hear, perhaps. She leaned against the shed and nursed her arm with her opposite palm, looking only at the tattered house across the yard.

Squinting, Ben held his breath in his lungs until they began to starve. His eyes tried desperately to parse the blackness from itself, slipping and fumbling at every frozen contour. But there was something. Ben could just make it out, like fingers dancing before sunbathed eyelids: the impression of a thing he could only imagine. And what he imagined moved his feet backward. Something that shifted and shuddered through the rotten undergrowth. He could hear it on the wind, couldn't he? Chittering through its broken jaw, pleading with a sneering mouth: *Itsmeitsmeitsme.*

Ben shook the sound from his ears and from his mind. He'd dreamed for long enough, imagined for too long. But he could see now. He could see that Beverly had been wrong, and it made him want to cry. His knees felt like they might buckle, and that would be fine, because it was over.

"Over here!" Ben shouted. "Officer!"

Beverly turned and raised her arm to shield her face from the stinging rain. Her expression made Ben uncomfortable. Maybe it was her relaxed silence, a countenance so stoic that Ben couldn't help but doubt his own eager eyes. But his eyes hadn't deceived him; they'd shown him exactly what was stirring in those woods. It was his mind that had failed him. And now it was screaming.

Wind swirled through the grass and whipped at the boy's blond hair.

"What're you doing here?" Ben yelled. "Why did you come back? You weren't supposed to come back!"

Beverly huffed, then threw her voice into the wind. "Did you bring him here? Hmm? Didja?" Beverly snapped as the boy moved in next to her. "That ain't what I told you to do."

"Did you tell someone?" Ben demanded, peering out past the quiet boy and into the sheet of blackness draped behind him. "Did you call for help?"

"What're you doin back here? Speak up now. *Speak up!*"

"Huh-he wuh-wouldn't—"

"Spit it out!"

"Hhhhhee wuh-wuh-wouldn't let me guh-g-go." The boy's face tensed each time his breath hung on a sound. His lips quivered in what was almost a snarl, as if he were angry at his own uncooperative mouth. There was a stiffness in both Beverly and the boy, as if invisible hands fastened their wrists by their sides.

"Are you okay?" Beverly finally asked, and the boy nodded, his amber eyes flashing in the darkness. "You know what has to happen now," she continued wearily.

When the boy smirked, Ben lunged for him, catching his arm and squeezing it like a vise.

"D-don't-t-t. Don't tuh-tou—" The meat of Ben's forearm slid across the boy's throat.

"Don't you hurt him!" Beverly screamed, lurching at Ben. He stepped back and dragged the boy.

"I just want him back. I don't want to do this," he pleaded, desperately trying to sound more resolved than sick.

"Do what?" Beverly asked.

Ben felt the boy's back press harder against his stomach. His arm grew warm in the tight curve of the boy's neck. "What do you reckon Eric will think if you let me do this?"

"What'll he think of *you* if you do it?"

Ben squeezed and felt the bulb of the golden boy's throat compress against his forearm. The boy struggled, but not as much as Ben had expected. He thought to press harder, but he didn't know what would happen if he did. But when Beverly didn't say anything, Ben squeezed anyway. He squeezed until the boy's feet were off the ground, and he watched the smug confidence wilt off Beverly's face.

"Let him go!" Beverly's whole body contorted as she screamed. "That's enough! Don't you hurt him!"

But Ben didn't move; the boy was so light that Ben thought he could hold him there for hours. But he didn't reckon he'd have to do anything close to that, not when he saw the pain in the old woman's face.

"I want my brother!" The boy's heel struck Ben's shin, but not hard enough to hurt. "You want to lose everything?" Ben's voice stung in his throat. He didn't know if he meant what he was saying. He didn't think he did.

"Alright!" Beverly shouted.

"No more games!"

"Let him go," Beverly moaned. Her eyes were wide and frightened. "I'll bring him to you. Just don't hurt my boy."

"You'll take me to him!" Ben snapped.

Beverly backed into the shed and was swallowed up by the unmoving shadow. Ben still held the boy as he rushed in after her, as if she might disappear within the small cube. Even when the woman tore through the black, he held the boy. Her face was twisted with feral madness. There was something in her hands. Her arm bowed where Ben had made a new joint. But still, she swung. Ben couldn't let go of the boy. And he couldn't get out of the way.

The teeth of the rake landed squarely in the meat of Ben's left leg, and he crumpled like a pile of old clothes. His mind collapsed in the pain. He wasn't even sure he was screaming.

A strange and vicious noise poured out of Beverly's mouth. Ben was only dimly aware of her movements, even as she twisted at the waist, bending more than Ben thought an old lady could. She grunted and pivoted. Ben moved his hand in front of his face in reflex, his other arm still pressed against the boy's chest. The rake handle struck Ben's wrist, sounding like gloved knuckles striking a winter door.

Ben yowled. Beverly pulled on the pole, and the wood slid against Ben's still-ringing forearm. The rusted prongs of the tool scraped against his shoulder. Turning his wrist, Ben felt for the handle, and when his palm found it, Ben closed his hand. Through the neural fire in his brain, Ben could make out only a single salient thought. *Don't let go.*

The metal teeth scratched against Ben's face. Beverly grunted, pulling on the wooden handle, pulling hard against Ben's grip. Finally, she threw the pole down. Then she crouched.

Ben felt her hands on his face, rough and cold. He thrashed his head but couldn't move it enough. *Don't let* go. Her thin fingers crept up toward his eyes, and nature shut them just before he could feel the pressure of her thumbs. The woman snarled as she strained to force her way into Ben's sockets. One hand was weaker.

He hadn't searched for the words. In truth, Ben wasn't even aware that he remembered them, much less that he was speaking. But he could hear Reggie's voice in the depths of his mind, could hear him chanting. And now Ben was chanting too.

"Night's out. Lights out," he said. "Night's out. Lights out." Again.

The pressure on his eyes disappeared. Through sore slits, Ben saw the paralyzed face of a woman being devoured by her own mind, hollow and vacant and inert. Something in her throat clicked. Her hands shook like a bad mime. And then all at once she was screaming, low and guttural, like a record played at the wrong speed. Her fist smashed into Ben's face. She swung her arms without any apparent concern or awareness of the fact that one of them was broken. Beverly didn't speak. There was nothing about the woman now that would lead one to believe that she even could. She swung her hands at Ben like that's all they'd been made for. The boy was laughing wildly in Ben's embrace.

Still, Ben chanted. Yelled. Bellowed the rhyme, and in a few short seconds it was done. The mask was gone. The woman stomped on Ben's leg with all her weight. Once. And then again.

Her fingers scraped at Ben's arm. Ben squeezed tighter while the boy kicked. Deep breaths through clenched teeth. The pain was otherworldly. Ben could feel his mind trying to escape, but he had to stay awake. He couldn't black out. Beverly's fingers wormed between Ben's forearm and the boy, until they reappeared with a piece of twine. She slipped the cord from around his neck. The red disk swung in the air like a pendulum until she tucked it into her pocket.

The quiet one reached for his mother as she disappeared.

58

Ben hadn't passed out. At least, he didn't think he had. He was aware that time was passing, though he couldn't do anything to stop it. He felt dull. Confused. Every bit of movement he tried to summon in his leg caused a riot in his nerves. He could only lie there, prostrate, buried alive in his own body.

Ben tried to roll onto his side and shrieked in pain. *The boy!* Ben must have loosened his grip; he couldn't feel him anymore. "Fuck!" Ben shouted. Again, he tried to move, and again his body wouldn't allow it.

The dark was nearly absolute. Beverly had taken the lantern, and what light escaped the clouds struggled through the warped wood, while wind rolled against the bones of the shed until they creaked. Ben craned his head against the dirt floor and looked behind him. The door was closed.

Tremulously, Ben guided his hand down to his left thigh, moving slowly as if he were trying to sneak up on it. His fingers slipped into the holes in his newly tattered jeans. Pain spiked in his leg, and Ben inhaled sharply. His fingers slipped against one another, and when he held them in front of his face, chasing what little light there was, he could see blood.

Ben groaned. He wasn't trapped exactly. If he could stand, he'd have no problem breaking the door open, but at the moment that "if" loomed large.

There was a clattering somewhere near him, somewhere in the shed. Lifting his head, Ben strained his eyes into the black. It was the boy, sitting or kneeling, Ben couldn't tell. But he was there, moving and making just enough noise that Ben was sure he wasn't hallucinating.

"Are you okay?" Ben asked. He received no reply.

Ben exhaled a trembling breath. He hadn't felt a thing. Eric had been so close, but he hadn't felt a goddamn thing at all, not while he worked below, not even while he kicked against the door with all his might as Marty lay dying on the concrete. Ben had hit that door so hard—hard enough that it had given just a little. One more kick might have done it. Just one.

Ben could hear the clinking of glass and the faint grinding of metal and grit, a hushed scraping somewhere in the dark. Nothing urgent. Nothing frantic.

What was the kid doing here? Why would Beverly abandon him? And why wasn't he trying to escape? He wasn't clawing at the broken ribs of the walls or at the warped door. Wasn't doing much of anything, from what Ben could tell.

"Do you know where he is?" Ben asked as he rolled painfully onto his back. The boy did not reply.

With great effort, Ben bent at the waist and sat up. His clothes were glued to his skin, pushing the chill all the way into his blood. He hovered his hands around the wound in his left thigh. It looked like black ink was spilling from the center of his leg. Reaching in his back pocket, Ben yanked his handkerchief free and folded it diagonally. Uncertain of exactly what he was doing, or if it was even necessary, Ben wrapped the cloth around his thigh, tying a tight knot.

Tucked into the shadows of the small building, Ben could finally make out the blond head of the quiet boy. Round pieces of glass glinted brilliantly each time they caught some of the minimal light that still survived in this place. The boy was stacking old jars.

"Do you know where Eric is?" Ben asked again.

The boy turned toward Ben, amber eyes blinking with the glass as the crawling moonlight waxed and waned through the space. He nodded his head.

"Will you take me to him?"

Again, the boy nodded.

Ben rolled onto his right elbow and tried to prop himself up. The boy didn't help, didn't even look at Ben as he struggled to his knees. He just kept stacking the jars, gently twisting and shimmying them to their balance point.

Ben tried and failed to stand. He struck the dirt floor with his knuckles, then paused for a moment to catch his breath.

"Is your neck okay?"

The boy nodded, turning toward the workbench.

"I wouldn't have really done it," Ben said. "Hurt you bad. I wouldn't have done that."

The boy shrugged in the dim glow, plucking a box of mason jars from the dust. "Why not?"

For the first time, Ben tried to think of this boy as something more than a path, to think of him as just a child. Ben watched as the boy chewed his cheek and stacked the jars, slowly and with care, like it was the most important thing he'd ever done. He'd lived in that place too, maybe for even longer than Eric had. What must this be like for him? He could be only as certain about his future now as Ben had been in the store the day he'd lost his brother. The same day, maybe, that this boy had found one. Ben watched as the frail child finished his tower of jars that stood taller than he did. The boy pressed the tip of his index finger against one jar and then another. The pillar rocked; he let them settle before he pushed again. He brushed his golden hair away from his fiery eyes and studied the rakes and shovels that hung from the wall. Lithe and beautiful, he traced his fingers across the rusted metal and then examined his skin, indifferent to his cell, his cellmate, and their warden.

Outside, the clouds flashed like a lightbulb was dying in their embrace, while wind moaned through the grasping trees.

"I . . . I don't wanna hurt nobody. Not even your momma. I just want my brother. And I know . . . I know that Eric's a brother to you too . . . And I ain't trying to take him away from you. I just have to bring him home."

The quiet one nodded, then pressed his fingers against the glass tower, sending it clattering to the dirt.

"But I promise," Ben said, almost pleading with the boy, "I won't let nothin happen to you. You helped me, okay? I'll keep you safe. We'll find your family and you'll be safe. You won't never have to see Beverly again."

The boy looked disbelievingly at Ben, as if Ben were a stupid child. A fat little boy being left behind on his school's track.

Then he smiled and shrugged.

59

Fiery pain whipped through Ben's leg as he stood. He didn't put any weight on it, but even hopping hurt almost too much to bear. Leaning down, Ben scooped up the rake that he'd snatched from Beverly. It wouldn't work very well as a crutch, but it was something.

As Ben approached the door, he could tell that if he put enough force into it, it would come off its hinges. Hell, the whole rotten wall might just give. He pressed his palm against the door and pushed, wanting to get some sense for its resistance. But it had none. The door swung freely.

Ben stood at the threshold looking stupidly over the wet grass. The boy had *chosen* to stay. Quick as he could, Ben turned, expecting some kind of attack. But the quiet one stood patiently waiting for Ben to step back out into the world.

Standing just outside the shed, Ben looked for the light Beverly was carrying, but he saw only wind blowing wild patterns in the stiff grass. Ben put his hand on the boy's shoulder and didn't have to say a word before the boy started walking.

The soft, damp earth sank under Ben's careful steps. He had to use the tooth end of the rake against the ground, because the pole would puncture the soil too easily. It felt, and probably very much looked, like Ben was rowing through the yawning forest.

Frogs and crickets bellowed and screeched so loudly that Ben could barely hear his own footfalls. Ben held the quiet boy's shirt like it was a greased rope, but the boy never pulled away. He walked slowly, and the time or two that Ben stumbled over some dead log or snarling bush, the boy waited silently for Ben to collect himself.

If Ben had lost consciousness in the shed, the boy could have hurt him then. Or he could have left, just as he could leave now. But he hadn't, and he wasn't. He'd helped Ben get here. But Ben didn't feel like he was being helped. *Why would she leave the door unlocked?*

Their course seemed less than straight to Ben. Rarely did he follow his own guiding light, but the kid, who earlier had not paused a single time as they walked to the old house, appeared to be taking more stock of his surroundings. Whether he was afraid to lose his way or he had yet to find it, Ben could not know. So he wrinkled the boy's shirt and followed step for step.

Thunder rumbled somewhere far away. The sky overhead was still blotted with clouds, but they had begun to grow thin and tired. Ben squinted into the black; the forest twinkled like a nebula. Suddenly, the child's shirt grew taut in Ben's fist, jerking his shoulder forward. Without any difficulty at all, the quiet one's small frame disappeared into the tangled mouth of a bush.

"Hey," Ben hissed, as the thorns bit into his forearm, but the boy kept pulling. Ben was strong enough to start to reel his guide back, but when he did, he both heard and felt the boy's shirt begin to tear. "Hey, damnit!" But the kid sank deeper and Ben had no choice but to follow. The brambles plucked at his skin and clothes. He stopped trying to negotiate his way through and lowered his head so the cellulose fangs would stab at his scalp rather than his eyes.

When they emerged, Ben released the shirt. The boy stood just in front of Ben, gazing into the trees. When Ben tried to speak, he was promptly shushed. Turning his head slightly, the child tapped his ear with his index finger. Ben pinched a final thorn from his cheek and listened. At first he heard nothing at all, only the wind and the smattering of water that it shook from the trees. But there was something else, wasn't there? Something either small or far away. A voice.

Ben strained to make out the words, but he could not. It was a sound more than a voice, and then it was nothing. Gone. Trampled under the sound of the boy's quick feet.

Moving quickly enough to keep him in sight, Ben lumbered behind the boy. He yanked the metal teeth of his inadequate crutch through the snarling undergrowth. He could hardly feel his leg at all now. Ben didn't bother calling out or demanding that the kid stop; he didn't want to waste the breath. If he lost the boy now, he knew that he would lose him forever. He would lose everything forever.

Suddenly, the quiet kid stopped moving. He wasn't looking around, wasn't searching. He stared straight ahead into the trees. And Ben stared with him. In the distance, beyond the columns of pine, a kerosene flame ambled and swayed. Fallen trees, slick with rainwater and moss, littered the ground in a decaying maze. Ben followed as silently as possible, stepping over the logs when he could and circumventing them when he couldn't. They moved slowly, but they were gaining on the swinging light of Beverly's lantern, gaining on it more and more until Ben could see her silhouette, her jagged shadow diffusing into the dark woods like the black ghost of a giant. When she would stop or slow, so would they.

She halted, swaying slowly with an unnatural rhythm. Ben aped the boy and folded himself behind a tree to watch the old woman. Wind crashed through the trees and mingled dead rain with what still tumbled from the inky sky. Beverly's lantern shook, and the warm glow sloshed against the trees like a cupful of light.

"Okay," she yelled into the roiling air.

Ben felt drunk, dizzy, like the word had shattered his inner ear and all the fluid had ridden away on a river of winter rain. All three of them—Ben, the boy, Beverly—faced the same direction, peering into the dark trees. Ben's hands were tingling.

"Come on out now!"

A single whimper slipped out of Ben's lips. His eyes darted across the rows of trees, stalling on every dancing shadow, waiting for Eric to emerge, for his brother to come home. But the trees stayed empty, and the only movement was right beside him.

The quiet boy stood and stepped into the light.

60

By the time Ben thought to grab him, the boy was already well out of reach. It wouldn't have mattered, though; Beverly was already turning, splashing her light onto his golden hair and into the trees around and behind Ben, who still hadn't stood, who felt quite unable to stand at all.

"Oh," the old woman said, not with surprise but detestation. "Where is he?"

Ben felt himself hunch away from the light, pressing himself tighter against the muddy trunk, exposing only the top of his head so that he could see. He knew that he should rise, that he was being called out and that he should answer. But he didn't. The quiet boy said nothing. For a while, neither of them did. They only looked at each other across the thin clearing. Finally, the boy raised his arm and held out his hand, palm upturned.

The old woman laughed. "Really?" Cold wind tossed her silver hair. Her smile grew and she laughed again, longer this time. "Didn't you say that those things didn't matter none? Isn't that what you said to your brother, when you took his toy from him? And now here you are. Followed me all the way out here because little baby wants his nuknuk."

Still the blond boy said nothing.

"You can have it," Beverly said. "Just tell me where he is. *Where is he?*"

The boy lowered his hand and turned his bright eyes toward Ben. As if he could somehow avoid the gaze, Ben looked away and pressed his forehead against the trunk, exhaling heavily. But he could still feel it: that amber stare cutting through the trees.

As Ben moved, Beverly swung the lantern and peered out at him. The kid turned back toward the old woman before she started speaking. "You chose the wrong boy to keep track of, son," she said.

"Eric!" Ben shouted. "Eric!" But only the wind replied. "Tell me where he is!"

"Eric!" The old woman's body contorted as she screamed. "Eric, come out!" Her voice scattered across the sky and died there. "I don't *know* where he is," she moaned. "He does." Beverly's face pinched as a tremor rolled through her body. "Where'd you take him?" she snapped. "Where is he?"

Again, the quiet boy only extended his hand.

"Give him what he wants, Beverly," Ben pleaded.

"Give him what *he* wants," the old woman muttered. She rubbed her drooping forearm and then moved the lantern from her bad arm to her good one. "I tried—" Her voice broke. "I tried for *so long* . . . and Eric was my reward. A gift. I knew it as soon as I seen him. I could feel it. That we was supposed to be a family. That something got mixed up somewhere and he'd wound up in the wrong spot. With you. The world got it wrong, and I fixed it. And when *he* let Eric out, and Martin called me, that was the world sayin that I got it *right.*

"No one ever loved him like I did. *No one.* Not you. You're just someone that slept in the same house as him. I know you don't believe it, don't see the sense of what's happened. Because you're on the bad end. It's darker there. I know, because I lived my whole life there. But *I* can see it.

"And what do *you* care?" Beverly yelled to the boy. "Just tell me where he's at. I see you! I see you shaking your hand. I'll give it back when you tell me where he is. You don't even have to say nothin. Just point!"

But the boy neither spoke nor pointed. The old lantern squeaked as it swung lightly in the breeze.

"He don't get what he wants. Not this time." A tremor rippled through her body and she sneered angrily. "He's a schemer, a pretender. I see what you are. I seen it since you was three years old. You ain't no boy.

"How do you think this ends, Ben? I don't know what this one did to make it so you found our home. Did you turn the ringer back on?" she asked the quiet one. "Did you leave the damn door open? What was it?"

The boy didn't respond. Beverly shook her head.

"He ain't helpin you. And if you think that this ends . . . that when the sun rises it'll be shinin on you and Eric's smiling faces, then you got it wrong. I just wanted you out of the store. Out of our *home.* All this"—with the arm that still worked, Beverly gestured to the world that surrounded them—"everything else came from this one's mind. I don't know what he's been playin at, what he did to bring all of this to pass. But I know he's been in your house. I know that much. That he put that drawing on Eric's paper.

"I promise you, Ben. I *promise* you that you don't want no part of whatever game this is."

"So just let him go!" Ben shouted. "Let them both go!"

"I did!" Beverly shrieked, pointing to the golden boy. "I let him go! I let him stay out here, when we lost the house, and he found us! Me and Eric! He followed us right to the store. Ruined our new home with his goddamn drawings all over the walls. Again! He could come and go as he pleased, and he wouldn't ever just *go*. And when he went out, it was for what?" she screamed at the boy, and gestured at Ben. "To play games with *him*?"

The boy didn't object, didn't say anything at all. He hadn't looked back at Ben. He just stood there with his arm outstretched and his palm turned toward the sky.

"He was tryin to lead me to you, to tell me about Blackwater."

"Then why didn't he just tell you?" Beverly said. "Hmm? He don't know anything about Blackwater. Nothin! 'Cept for that I hate it. I never said nothin. Never showed that symbol to *him.* But six years old and he finds it in my book and he just *knows.* Draws it on the walls. He scratched it into my oven so I'd have to look at it every day. Cuz he thinks it's funny, thinks they look the same. Well, this ain't that!" the woman hollered as she pulled the boy's necklace out of her pocket. Beverly sighed. "God almighty."

Ben didn't speak. He didn't know what he could say. Beverly seemed exhausted. The longer this went on, the greater the chance that she might just implode. The quiet one had some kind of effect on her that Ben could only hope might bring an end to all this.

"I been giving you what you wanted your whole life. A home. A family. Gave you more than I ever had. I tried *so hard* with you," she said to the boy. "You can stare at me with those eyes all you want, but you can't say I didn't do everything for you, didn't try to love you. And I did. I *did* love you. Even after I knew you was rotten, even after I knew I'd made a mistake, I still loved you. But you ain't chewin your way through me, boy."

The boy took one step forward and then another, his upturned palm held out. The old woman gritted her teeth, her eyes inflamed, her countenance reviling.

"This what you want?" she snapped, whipping the necklace as she shook her arm. "This what's important to *you*?"

The red ring dangled at the end of the twine like a hypnotist's medallion. When the boy reached for it, Ben worried that the old woman might snatch it away, that she might throw it into the dark woods. But she didn't. She held it as steady as her shaking arm would allow, even when the boy pulled at it.

"They wouldn't have bought this for you if they knew what you was. If they knew you like I do."

Just take it, Ben thought. *Just take it from her.* But the boy didn't take it. He didn't even try. And then Ben thought he understood. The boy didn't want to take it; he wanted her to *give* it to him. Beverly leaned down into the lantern light and spoke so softly to the boy that Ben couldn't hear. But her eyes said enough. They were the same eyes that Ben saw every time his stepmother looked at him.

The boy placed his hand on the lantern, right on the side of the glass that chambered the fire, snuffing out all the light to the left of the world. It stayed there long enough for Ben to think about how much it would hurt, long enough for Ben's legs to start moving. Beverly was looking right at the boy's palm when he finally moved his hand.

The globe burst like a glass grenade.

Kerosene surged in a flaming wave onto Beverly's head and torso. She tried to scream. Once. Then she folded in on herself, crumpling in a spasming heap. Shards of glass stuck out of her face like clear teeth.

Ben tried to take a step back but stumbled and fell. He covered his mouth but could still smell the burning skin and hair. Beverly's lower jaw slunk out of its socket and chattered rapidly, exposing her cracked and twisted teeth under her bisected upper lip. She gurgled once and rolled her eyes over to Ben. And then she was gone.

Shaking, Ben's arms finally failed him, and he fell backward onto his elbows. Tall trees swayed above, their branches reaching out for one another with dozens of thin, crooked fingers. Beverly's body burned in the dead rain. Blackened flakes of her hair were carried away by a cold, silent hearse that only birds could feel.

61

The quiet boy knelt over Beverly. Leaves crinkled against his small hands as he brushed and scattered them with care, but there was nothing reverent about his movements. His fingers plucked at the folds of the old woman's dress. Finally, the boy smiled faintly, withdrawing his necklace from where it had fallen. As he tied it around his neck, Ben couldn't help but stare. Flat and red, the disk looked like a piece of plastic jewelry made for a bull's nose. It was the grip ring from a pacifier.

It bounced against the quiet one's small chest. A crescent blood moon whose ends had been fused together, bobbing at the end of a string. Ben covered his nose with his forearm and stared—stared at the boy and his happy walk, stared at the crimson prize dangling from his neck.

"Okay" was all the boy said before he walked past Ben and back into the thick dark.

Ben groped for the rake, stabbing it into the dirt and pulling himself to his feet. His leg shook, then buckled, and he braced himself against a tree. His eyes lingered on Beverly for a moment, her face splayed and puckered like a rodent's. Bones, blood, and flesh. That was all. Something had moved those things through the world and ruined a small corner of it forever. A pillar of salt spilled over the soil of other people's lives. And now all was still.

Ahead, Ben could hear the *slink-clink* of a Zippo. Ben wiped his palms against his shirt. The residue of human smoke had leached into his clothes. The smell followed him as he caught up with the boy and the metal whispers of Marty's lighter.

"This ain't that," Beverly had said. But Ben could see it. The moonchild in the red ring of the boy's necklace. The crescent curves. The twine body. It was almost irresistible to Ben's eye, stronger in sensation the longer he looked.

The boy found it funny. But it wasn't. Separated by time and place and everything that mattered, the Blackwater beacon and this boy's treasure had found each other anyway. They'd overcome their own histories, because their beginnings were conjoined to their end, an invisible coupling buried somewhere in the machinery of the world. There was nothing funny in that.

This child had been in Ben's home, had probably been the one who'd written in Beverly's file. And his sketchbook. Those swirling and scribbled eyes. "HI BEN."

"Why didn't you get the police? Hmm? Hey! Why did you come *back*?"

"Juh-just to see," the boy replied.

"See what?"

They didn't talk any more after that. And Ben no longer held the boy's shirt as they walked, though he knew he should. He told himself that he didn't think the kid would run, but the truth was that Ben simply didn't want to touch him. The quiet one walked less timidly now, trampling through the undergrowth with the high and bouncy steps of a real boy, leading Ben through the trees, showing him the way . . . and leading Ben back past Beverly's home, showing him that they hadn't needed to follow the woman at all. It had been a special trip.

Ben would need to go to the doctor. He thought he could feel the muscle of his thigh moving freely under his torn skin, like it had somehow become disconnected from the bone. He needed to rest. Maybe he finally could when this was all over. It was hard to walk at a steady pace, but when Ben stopped, so did the boy.

Each time the stuttering boy led them into a clearing, Ben's eyes darted into its murky edges, ready to use his crutch as a weapon if he had to. The fact was that Ben didn't know where he was being led or what he was being led to. All he could do was follow and hope.

"Is this a trap?" Ben asked.

The boy didn't turn, and when he spoke it sounded sincere. "I dunno."

When his guide finally stopped, Ben was thankful, for no other reason than he could rest for longer than a breath. He leaned against a tree. It didn't even occur to him that they might be done walking. It didn't occur to him until he saw the boy gesture ahead of himself, shooing Ben deeper into the undergrowth as he stared with his burning, expectant eyes.

Ben obeyed. He didn't even think about it. Limbs and thorns tore at his clothes and skin as he pushed his way into the overgrowth; he didn't think about that either. He looked back only once, just before the boy was lost from view entirely. He was nothing more than a shadow now, sunken in the crowding woods.

"Cuh-come out, come out, whu-wherever you aaaaaare!" the boy yelled.

The sound echoed through the trees, and a chill rolled up Ben's spine, right to the base of his skull. Then, behind Ben, the woods answered. "Olly olly oxen free!"

"Oh, God," Ben blubbered. He pushed through the trees in the direction of the sound. It was far away, but it didn't feel like it. It felt so close. "Eric! Eric, I'm coming!"

Gritting his teeth, Ben pushed through the tangle. Every second step, his left leg would falter, but Ben didn't slow. He didn't need that leg. He could drag it. So he did, pulling it along and parting the brittle pine straw, driving gouges into the soft dirt. Barreling so hard into the branches that they snapped. Shouting his brother's name with every scraping step, waiting for the voice to answer, and trying again when it refused. He moved his eyes over and around the glistening trunk of every tree, turned at every noise.

"Come out, come out, wherever you are!" Ben waited with his breath stuck in his throat, but there was no reply. Nothing at all. "Come out!" Ben pleaded.

How far away had the voice sounded? Shouldn't he have reached it by now? Ben hadn't gone off course. He'd been so careful. But there was nothing—nothing but more goddamn trees. "Eric! Please!"

Ben pulled in another breath and cupped his hands around his mouth, but the yell collapsed in his chest. His foot had struck something so hard and unyielding that it made his whole leg hum. It lay tucked into the bed of the forest, half covered in soggy leaves and pine needles, something alien and strange in this place of unending wood, something metal. Its rungs glistening with moisture. Delicately, Ben swung his lame leg and kicked the forest away from the ladder.

At first Ben didn't understand. In fact, he nearly stepped away from it altogether—he wasn't looking for a *ladder.* But then he stopped. And after a moment, he looked up, up into the trees, following them until they disappeared in the mouth of the hungry sky. "Eric?" Ben called tentatively, expecting only silence in return. But there was a voice.

It had been tiny and fleeting, but Ben had heard it. Somewhere in the towering trees above, the voice had finally answered. He called to it again, frantically searching the branches. The voice didn't reply, but it didn't matter. Ben plunged his hands into the slippery leaves, wrestling the aluminum ladder from the clutches of the undergrowth.

The trees all looked the same, giant pillars reaching deep into the purple black. Day would be coming soon, but not soon enough to wait for. Nothing could come that quickly.

Ben's arms shook as he heaved the ladder; the cold metal clattered against the thick pine, rumbling all the way down into the ground near his feet. He felt weak and dreamy as he took his first step, weaker still the more he took. His eyes saw nothing but clouds and stars above, crooked wood in front. "Eric!" he shouted. And under the hushed rustling of the wind, Eric replied—not with a word, but a sound, and a sound was all Ben needed.

Ben had chosen the wrong tree. "I'm coming, Eric! I'm coming for you." Ben whimpered as he adjusted his hands around the damp, cold sides of the ladder. Twice he slipped as he descended; his leg hardly worked at all now. Grunting, Ben jerked the ladder off the ground and away from the tree, straining and yanking against every branch that tried to snag it.

Here! This one! Dirt and dead leaves scattered onto his face as Ben pulled himself up. His feet slipped off the rungs with almost every step. His leg was screaming, but his mind screamed right back. Higher and higher he climbed. Each step brought more limbs and needles, more jagged plates of waterlogged bark. Ben's hands clawed viciously at the rungs now. His knuckles were raw from scraping against the tree in his mania.

And then, as if the darkness itself had grown weary, it simply gave up.

"Oh my God," Ben sobbed. Mucus bubbled in his nose. "Oh, *God*!"

Eric clutched the thick trunk of the mighty pine with both arms, his weight unnoticed by the large branch on which he sat.

It was like looking in his sketchbook.

The contours of Eric's face were different, more severe somehow. Gaunt and hollow, his cheeks were shallow caves. The chestnut hair that had rolled and curled so much like his mother's was tightly cropped. But everything else was right, just as Ben had drawn. He wished he could show his brother. For some reason, that wish burned the brightest in his heart, that he could show he hadn't needed to see Eric's face to know it.

Ben's whole body shook as he pulled himself higher. Shivering from the cold wind, Eric was whimpering as he curled against the wet trunk just above the end of the ladder.

"Eric, I'm here. I'm here. It's okay now," Ben called softly as he wrapped his fingers around the last rung. The boy's eyes shifted, never landing squarely on Ben for more than a moment. He squirmed as much as his confinement would allow. "Don't be scared. I'm gonna take you home."

Blinking tears away, Ben gripped the ladder with one hand and reached his arm out, first to wrap it around his brother, then just to touch him a little when the boy recoiled. "It's alright. Everything's alright now . . ." A chuckle freed itself from somewhere deep in Ben's chest, and then he was crying. "I've missed you so much. Momma and Daddy are waiting. They've got a whole mess of presents for you. You can open 'em just as soon as we get back home."

When Ben reached for him again, Eric seemed to whimper more loudly, pressing his cheek into the jagged bark and stretching his arms around the trunk as far as he could. And as he did, Ben could see the black dome eyes and dull gray horns of a stuffed rhinoceros.

"Is that Stampie, bud?" Ben asked with a struggling smile. "Hey, that's great. You got him . . . You got him back."

Eric finally looked at Ben: a searching gaze that groped for something Ben didn't think he understood.

"What is it, bud? Tell me what I can do." If he could just know what Eric wanted, then he could give it to him.

The wind slowed. Everything seemed to slow. And out of that calm, Eric's noises grew in intensity. Ben wiped his running nose on his shoulder and stared into his brother's eyes. Tentatively, Ben reached his hand out again, letting it hover in the chilled air for a moment before slowly drawing it back toward his chest. Eric wasn't whimpering. He was humming.

Ben carried the tune with his brother. It sounded lighter now, much lighter than when Beverly sang it. And a bit more in key too. It sounded almost as good as when Deidra would sing it—Ben's breath hitched when he realized that. She never sang this song anymore. Ben couldn't seem to swallow the lump in his throat. So he hummed around it. Even when his voice fluttered, he kept humming with his brother. This wasn't Beverly's song. This was magic given to Eric by his mother. A song that beat monsters back into the dark.

"Are you really real?" Eric whispered.

"I am," Ben sobbed. "It's me."

Slowly, Eric plucked a green pine needle free from its stubby quiver. His hand trembled as he floated it toward Ben. The boy's face was calm, but his eyes flicked from Ben's to the needle and back again. The point made a dent in Ben's forearm that deepened until the thin green rod buckled and snapped. Ben smiled and looked back to his brother's face. Then he stopped smiling.

Light seemed to dance in the boy's eyes, a sparkle that made Ben's heart pound. Because he hadn't gotten them right. He wasn't even close. "It's me," Ben said again, reaching for the boy one more time.

"I thought you was pretend," Eric whimpered as he dropped the pine needle like it was aflame. The boy folded inward, squeezing his stuffed toy in the crook of his elbow. The child's tiny chest began to heave as his eyes grew so wide they seemed to lose their lids entirely. Then he screamed.

He screamed louder than Ben thought a boy could. A scream of fear and anger. A scream of hate. It was so sharp and gouging that Ben was already recoiling as Eric's feet and hands began striking him violently in the face and shoulder.

"Quit it, Eric! It's me! It's Ben!" He tried to protect his face with the hand that wasn't gripping the ladder. "Stop it, Eric!"

Eric shrieked, driving his feet and fingernails into Ben. His stoic, placid face was gone—Ben couldn't even picture it anymore. It had been consumed by something more savage, more primal. The boy's skin clung to his cheeks like cellophane as he screamed and lashed. One of his shoes smashed against Ben's fingers. "Eric, stop! It's me!" Ben reached for his brother. "It's okay," he said as softly as he could to the frightened boy. "It's gonna be okay now."

The sole of Eric's shoe collided with the bridge of Ben's nose. His balance wavered, and he tried to stiffen himself to compensate, but his bad leg had finally had enough. The pain was immense. Ben didn't even feel the smooth metal of the ladder's rung slip from his grasp.

62

Butterflies danced in Ben's stomach as he fell. His teeth pressed so tightly together that one of them fractured at the root, but he didn't feel it. His arms and legs swam in the cold air, trying to regain balance that came only through the inevitable and unmoving earth.

Everything was cold, even colder than it should have been, Ben thought. Someone was crying. How long had he been here? he wondered. Was he still in the tree? Ben didn't think he was still in the tree. That was above him. If he could just move, he could see where he was. If he could just move at all. Just move.

It hurt to breathe. Ben had to try for it, like reaching for air that doesn't want to be caught, like inhaling through a coffee straw. That's what it felt like.

If he could just move he could breathe better. Get this weight off his chest. It was crushing him. Even if he couldn't see it, it was crushing him. Just move a little. Move a little and breathe. Someone was crying.

He could hear his heartbeat—distant footsteps that seemed to send ripples through the whole world. Not every time, but enough to notice. His head hurt. It hurt so badly.

Someone was crying. Eric was crying. Ben tried to sit up, to move toward his brother's wailing moans, but he couldn't. His legs spasmed when he heard Eric call for help. Again and again the boy cried out, and again and again Ben's body said no. He felt like he might sleep.

Don't leave. Don't leave him there. Not like this.

There were voices now. Maybe just one. Ben wanted to stand; he needed to. But his legs didn't belong to him anymore, not in any sense that mattered. The ladder rattled. Through dim eyes, Ben watched Eric climb down to the dirt. Small footsteps, crunching leaves.

"Hey, buddy," Ben said. Or maybe he didn't say it. He thought he had. Someone else was talking now, talking to Eric. For just a moment Ben thought it was Marty. He'd like to talk to Marty. Ben tried to turn his head, but he couldn't. It didn't matter. The sun was coming up, casting purple spears of light through the trees, but everything looked so dark to Ben; every second it grew harder for him to keep his eyes open. Sleep would be nice. He thought it might be dreamless. He could hear the person well enough now. The voice didn't belong to his friend.

"You huh-hurt?"

"No."

"Then wuh-why you cruh-cryin?"

"He tried to get me," Eric sobbed. "Where *were* you?"

"You wuh-want him to guh-get mmme too?"

"It was uh accident. I didn't mean to hurt him. He falled. What if he didn't?"

"Then I guh-guess he'd have you," the boy said casually, nudging Ben with the tip of his shoe.

"Where's Momma at?" Eric asked after a while.

"Nowhere."

"I heard screamin."

"Yup."

Eric held his own elbows. His face scrunched, squeezing water from his eyes. The quiet boy smacked the back of Eric's head with his palm. Ben tried to talk, to say something to his brother, but his jaw would only chatter silently.

"Yuh-you oughta cry. This is all be-cuh-cause of yooou. You nuh-know who he is?"

"The bad man," Eric whispered like a boy telling a secret.

The golden boy smiled and shrugged. "So what're you suh-sad for? You want to guh-get him medicine?"

Eric looked at Ben's face for a long time, studied it, and then slowly shook his head. "No."

Ben used his fingers to walk his hand through the dirt and toward his body. He wanted to show Eric the photograph, though he didn't know why. It wasn't to help him remember. It wasn't for any useful reason at all, really. Ben stopped moving his hand before he remembered that he didn't have the photo.

"What're we gonna do?" Eric asked, still sniffling through hitching and shuddering breaths. "Without Momma?"

"We? Thu-there ain't no we."

"I can't go with you?"

Don't say it. Don't say it to him.

The boy sighed as he squatted next to Ben, running his eyes from Ben's feet to just above his scalp. The red pacifier ring slid and bounced under the boy's thin shirt. His fingers rested against Ben's chest, then they pushed down. Ben wheezed and grimaced in pain while the boy watched in fascination. "Wow," he whispered to himself.

Behind the boy, Eric bawled hysterically, trying to talk but making only noises while he hugged Stampie tight to his chest.

"I guess it wuh-*was* a trap," the boy whispered to Ben. "I been tuh-tellin him stories. Nuh-never said it was you, though. He decided that all on huh-his own." His breath was warm against Ben's ear, fighting the chill that seemed to be coming from his own bones. The boy poked Ben's arm and asked, "Can't *yuh-you* talk?" He smiled and sat, resting his forearms on his bent knees. He glanced at Eric. "Wuh-we can go to the outssside all the time now. Yuh-you and me."

"Can't we go home?" Eric whined.

"That ain't huh-home. We ain't going buh-back there," he shouted over his shoulder.

"What about our stuff? Momma's pictures."

The boy chewed his cheek and seemed to consider the question. "I'll tuh-take caaare of it. Your stuff. Ah-I'll get it, if you quit yer whinin. Ah-I'll do a cleanup day all by muh-myself."

"I can do it," Eric said.

"No. Buh-but you can help muh-me with him. Now suh-sing somethin."

At first the melody seemed strangled by his unhappy throat, but gradually the notes escaped, weaving themselves over and around the courting of songbirds in the morning sky.

"Hey," the boy said excitedly, leaning toward Ben again, "you ever guh-get that present I left for yuh-you? With all them other sssshiny ones? The nuh-newspaper one in the clean room?"

The boy's eyes flashed gold in the creeping sun. He tapped his knuckles against Ben's chest.

Knock. Knock. Knock.

Leaves shuffled. Eric's small fingers wrapped around Ben's wrist, and Ben curled his own like a plant moving to welcome the sunlight. But even that small exertion was too much for him. His fingers uncoiled as Eric hummed above him. Ben's heart broke with its last beat.

He felt Eric tugging on his arm. Then he felt nothing at all.

Epilogue: A Flyer on the Wall

"C'mon, man," Marty said, sighing. Walter squealed and writhed in his chair, his mouth open but deftly dodging the spoon. "Fine. If you don't want it, then I'm gonna eat every last bit." He slipped the spoon into his own mouth and regretted it immediately.

It wasn't the taste—something about the texture of chicken and gravy puree didn't work. Marty gagged and Walter groaned a laugh until the spoon found its way into his mouth. He chewed, smacked, and swallowed. "There we go," Marty said softly, cleaning the edges of his brother's mouth with the spoon.

"Marty!" his mother called from somewhere in the house. He shut the door behind him and walked into the living room. Scratching the dry and cracked scar on his neck, Marty looked impatiently at his mother. She pointed at the front door, then walked back into the kitchen.

Sunlight poured through the door as Marty opened it, and he squinted. He'd been in Walter's room for a while, longer than he'd realized, it seemed. It took a beat or two before Marty recognized the man on his porch, but the man introduced himself all the same.

"Marty? I'm Ben's dad. Clint." The man put his hand out, and Marty snaked his arm through the door and shook it. "Jacob told me where you lived. I hope I ain't intrudin."

Marty looked across the dirt road. Jacob waved lazily from his porch and Marty waved back as he stepped outside. The sun felt good against his bare chest. He fished his cigarettes out of his jeans, then felt for his lighter until he remembered that he was still groping for the wrong shape. Marty dug the BIC lighter out of his pocket. "You ain't," Marty said with a puff of smoke.

Clint pulled at his beard lightly. "I don't know if you heard, but Ben's gone missing."

A squeal tore through the house. Marty brushed ash off his chest with the side of his hand. "What do you mean exactly?"

"He ain't been home a week now. Ain't nobody at work seen him. I know you two is real close, so I was wonderin if you heard from him or know where he went to." Clint put his palm up. "Now if he just took off and wants to be by himself, that's fine. I'll leave him be. I just want to know that he's alright."

"I ain't heard nothin." Marty ran his tongue over his sore tooth. "I didn't even know he was gone."

"Not many people really . . . *took* to Ben. He never brought anyone around. Never much talked about anybody with me, 'cept for you. You were the only friend he had."

"I know," Marty said after a while. Beyond the walls, Walter's cries seemed to move unimpeded through the home. Marty wished that his mom would just go in there and feed him for once. He hoped that Clint wouldn't care enough to ask.

"He talked about you all the time," Clint said. "Working at that store was hard for him. I'm not sure how much he told you about his baby brother, but I think you made working at that place easier for him." Marty lowered his eyes. "Him having a friend was . . . You meant a lot to him, and I could really use your help, son." The man's voice wavered a little. Marty looked at his swollen eyes.

"Did he ever say anything about leaving?" Clint asked. "Do you think he might have just taken off?"

Marty looked at the father of someone who used to be his friend, someone who he'd tried to help, only to be accused of something horrible. He knew that he could end this right here, that all he had to say was yes. That Ben had talked about leaving. That he'd burned down his own life and might have decided to just take off and leave it behind. All he had to do was say yes.

Marty pulled on his cigarette, then flicked the ashes over the railing of the porch. "No. Lemme get my shoes."

—

"That's quite a hole there," James Duchaine said, gesturing through the large window to the circular breach in the store's glass door. Even up here, he could see the back wheel of his cruiser parked just out front. He knew Bill Palmer could too and that he wouldn't like it. Duchaine's radio chirped in his ear. He leaned away, then turned a knob near his waist. "Oughta get that fixed."

Bill Palmer stood from his chair and scowled at the sight. "Someone threw a rock. Probably those same little shits that smashed up my car. 'Ain't no way a rock did that.' That's what the sales rep said. Said that somebody must have pounded on it. I said, 'What the hell difference does that make? It fuckin broke!' He tells me that I gotta resubmit the claim if I want the warranty to honor the replacement."

"It's always somethin," Duchaine muttered. "Alright then, Bill. You know what I come by for. You mind if I close this door?"

"You can try." Palmer sighed as he eased himself back into his chair. He lowered his head as if he might avoid the sound of the broken door scraping the tile. "I'll tell you the same as I told his daddy. I don't know where Ben is or how come he left."

"No idea at all?"

"None. All I know is that I get here and the front door's wide open. Now I got bag boys and little ol' cashiers that are having to throw my trucks."

"So you figure what, exactly? That he just decided to call it quits like that?" Duchaine ran his fingers over the rippled burn on his arm. It couldn't itch, but sometimes it felt like it did.

Palmer shrugged. "Happens more often than you think."

Duchaine laced his fingers together in his lap and studied the man, whom he'd never found to be all that interesting. He was the living counterpart to the desk that sat between them: sloppy and disorganized, unkempt and unraveled.

"Between you and me," Duchaine said, "if Ben's gone . . ." The man shrugged. "That boy had a lot of problems."

"You ain't gotta tell me," Palmer replied. "You know he broke into my office. At least once that I know of. Real pain in the ass."

Duchaine smiled and nodded. "So why'd you let him keep workin here?"

"How do you mean?"

"Well, I mean, I know how Ben could be. Strong as all hell, so he could do the job. But a little hysterical sometimes. He thought you had a big-time hard-on for him, and I reckon that's something he wouldn't've hid too well. And I know you know who he was—what happened with his brother, I mean—so I'm just wonderin why you kept him working here."

"Well, I felt bad about what had happened with his brother. Thought maybe I owed it to him." Palmer squared some of his papers, despite the fact that his desk was covered with them, forcing order and neatness now where he could.

The officer nodded, then furrowed his brow. "But—and set me straight if I'm wrong—I was told that you fired Ben after you found out who he was."

Duchaine's eyes lingered, waiting to see what else the man might say. Then he let them wander over the endless forms, piled and scattered. Duchaine wasn't looking for anything in particular, but he wanted Palmer to see him looking all the same. This desk was like a man caught nude in the middle of a room: no hope to conceal anything.

His radio crackled again, and Duchaine's eyes snagged for just a moment on some deep scratches that peeked out from beneath the paper blanket. Just a few lines carved into the wood.

"See, the thing is," Duchaine started, "Ben had an awful lot to say about you, Bill. I ain't gonna repeat what he said or what it is he thought you did, but I've known Ben for a long, long time. Hell, I know him better than some people I've known for longer. Some people in my own damn family.

"I seen all sortsa people mess with that boy. He gets confused about a lot of stuff, but he's not a capricious type. And however wrong he mighta been about God knows what, there ain't nothin about Ben that would let him walk away—not from this town, not from this store. And not from you."

Bill Palmer pushed himself back in his chair and crossed his arms. "I don't give a good goddamn why Ben left or where he might have gone. You said the same thing yourself."

"No, Bill. I might not be all that upset *that* he's gone, but I'm real interested in the why. I confronted him, you understand? Two weeks ago, I brought the world down on him, and then for a week straight he kept comin on back here. Every night. Stockin shelves in your little store. And then all of a sudden . . ." Duchaine snapped his fingers.

"You listen to me, Jimmy. I don't mind tellin you what I know, but I'll be goddamned if I'm gonna let you sit here and accuse me of anything."

"I ain't accusing you of nothin, Bill. We're just talkin."

—

Their drive was a long and quiet one. Three grocery stores and a handful of shopping centers. Clint had made about a hundred or so flyers, and Marty helped the man hang them and read the map for places they might want to visit. They didn't really talk. Marty didn't have anything he wanted to say.

For the whole ride, Marty tried to build something in his head that made sense. They'd talked about wanting to leave town, or at least Marty had. Had Ben? Marty tried to remember. When he'd told Ben that they had no more to say to each other, he'd meant it. And if he never heard from his former friend again, that would be just fine. But this didn't feel fine.

Clint seemed less certain. He said only that things were tough at home for Ben, tough all around. Then he just shook his head and stared at the road. Marty didn't want to tell the man anything—not about Beverly, not about the Blackwater symbol. He truly didn't know what any of it amounted to anyway. Whatever path Ben had been on had flown so far off course that he wasn't sure he wanted to travel it with Clint.

By the time they stopped the truck in the parking lot of the store, they had fewer sheets of paper but still far too many.

"I know this don't really look like him," Clint finally said, looking at the stack of flyers in his lap. "We ain't taken any pictures in a long time, I guess . . . I found this picture in his room. Had a hole cut out of it, and it took me a whole day to realize that that hole . . . that hole was from when we made Eric's flyer. Same goddamn picture." Clint slammed his hand against the steering wheel. "I told Ben to quit this job. I found him another one, and I shoulda pushed him harder . . . I thought maybe he needed this." Clint slapped his hand against the wheel three more times, then pushed his way out of the truck.

Marty got out and lit a cigarette. He looked at Ben's flyer as he took a drag. It really didn't look much like Ben at all. The face was way too round, the eyes too happy.

"Shit!" Marty said, slapping his hand against the hood. "I got a picture of Ben. Well, I don't *got it* got it, but it's at the photo place up the street."

"Alright then," Clint said. "We can go and get it when we're done here."

Marty realized then that he didn't have the ticket, but he didn't say anything. He'd talk about that problem when it introduced itself.

Blowing hot air into his cold hands, Marty walked toward the store, passing a Crown Victoria with sleeping strobes. A cop car parked right in front of where he, Frank, and Ben used to sit every night. Marty hesitated, then slid the acrylic glass of the bulletin board to the side and thumbed off a sheet of paper from his stack. He took the time to square the edges, leveling the paper under the arched bubbly letters of the HAVE YOU SEEN ME? banner.

Pressing his fingers against the tack, Marty read the flyer text one more time. And again tried to understand why he had to read it at all.

"My name is BEN."

It was only when Marty thought that he should move Ben's flyer so that it would be next to his brother's that he realized Eric's was gone. Marty sighed and considered what he ought to do. He could see Clint leaning against the idling truck, his listless, voided stare washing over the store. Marty tried to imagine what the man might be thinking, but he knew that he could not. He didn't have the referent.

Turning toward the sound of the whining doors, Marty looked without interest at the passing customers, then at a boy with a bloated backpack and a stack of binders in his arms. Marty smiled and nodded out of politeness, but as he did he thought he experienced a moment of recognition. Was it one of Aaron's friends? No. The young boy looked through Marty and into the parking lot, paying him no regard at all. And suddenly Marty knew him again.

"Hey," Marty said, approaching the boy. "Hey, you're that kid."

He made sure not to touch him but instead raised his palm to him, as if a gesture might hold him in place. And it did.

"That's where I know you from." The boy shrugged. "I wanna say I'm sorry about that day. I shouldn'ta grabbed you like that. There was a missin kid, and I seen you leavin . . ."

Whether the boy understood or cared was a mystery to Marty.

"Anyways," Marty continued, thumbing off a small stack of papers, "if you see this guy, that's the number you call right there. Give some to your friends or your teachers even."

Marty wedged the flyers between two of the binders.

"Hey," Marty said, gently touching the kid's arm, "you understand? What I'm telling you, I mean. It'd be a big-time help to me and that man there."

The kid stared at Marty's hand until Marty withdrew it. He searched for understanding in the boy's golden eyes but found what felt like annoyance or even contempt.

"Fuh-fine," he finally said. The boy chewed the inside of his cheek and turned, walking slowly into the parking lot.

"Sorry again!" Marty hollered, but the boy made no response. He shifted his cargo in his arms, then passed close enough by Clint's truck that he had to dodge the side mirror. But he didn't pay the vehicle any mind. As Marty made his own way to the truck, he couldn't help but notice that the boy didn't seem to pay any mind to anything.

Marty leaned against the driver's side of the truck, next to Clint, then bent sideways to grab the map off the console. He didn't look at it. His eyes kept returning to the boy, who walked until there were no more vehicles left to pass, right to the edge of the lot. His hair drank in the sun like a sponge: soft gold blowing in the wind.

"That's James Duchaine's car," Clint said, nodding toward the store.

Marty turned toward the cruiser. "He here askin after Ben?"

Clint grunted. "I would be very surprised to learn that was the case. He thinks that Ben had something to do with what happened to Eric. He never said it, but he thinks it. And here he is. Another one of my boys missin, and . . ." Clint slammed the side of his fist against the truck.

Marty pulled on his cigarette and squinted at the horizon opposite the store, searching for the boy with the yellow hair. Finally, he found him moving slowly along the tree line, encumbered by his cargo. It was strange. Curious, that was all. This wandering boy who'd walked right out of the parking lot and onto the sprawling dirt, away from the store and toward nothing at all. Marty wondered where he might be heading. And when the boy fed himself to the trees and disappeared from sight, Marty turned back toward Clint, words perched on his tongue.

Marty thought to speak, but Clint was in another world, staring with red-rimmed eyes back at Earth, studying the great mural of smiling children just outside the store's entrance. In and out, customers and workers filed, lost in conversations, lost in thought. Like a little boy, Clint appeared to be trying to will the world to his preferences, to will these people to stop and turn for just a second. To just look at the goddamn board.

But they didn't look.

No one ever does.

Author's Note

About twelve years ago, I graduated from college and couldn't find work. While I subjected myself to bad interviews for bad jobs, most of my friends were skipping town, bound for better days in bigger cities. Eventually, I got tired of looking, so I jammed my degrees into my filing cabinet and took an overnight job at a grocery store while I tried to figure my life out.

The job itself was bullshit. I mean it was tedious beyond belief. Reading barcodes. Stacking cans and boxes. That's it. Forever. The end. Even better: you're out of sync with everyone in town, tucking yourself into bed while they're ordering lunch, shotgunning cans of Steel Reserve in the parking lot while they're sipping coffee. It was a one-two punch of terrible hours and unfulfilling tasks.

Of course, I didn't know any of this going in. All I knew was that I needed cash and that the guy who was supposed to show me the ropes was some dude named Brian.

There wasn't really that much for Brian to show me ("Where's this box go?" "Here." "Oh, okay."), so we spent most of that first night talking. He was a couple years younger than me. Still in college, he was studying to be an accountant, despite hating it, while working at the grocery store, despite hating that too. Brian was loud, prone to mock incredulity, and crass. He dressed like a runner, which I thought was dumb, until he told me that he ran cross-country for the university in all his abundant free time—when he wasn't studying, or in class, or working ten-hour night shifts. What an asshole. He smiled with his whole face and laughed with his whole body. I liked him right away.

For over a year and a half we worked together almost every night. By all rights, that should have gotten pretty old pretty quick. But it never did. Just one of those things, I guess. I liked Brian all the time. Our breaks were so long they bordered on paid vacations. We talked and laughed, shared books and movies, argued. We made each other smarter, better. We helped each other, covered for each other, and competed with each other. He bet me I couldn't smoke a loaf of French bread like a cigar. I won (if you can call it that). And I bet him that he couldn't eat that whole seven-layer bean dip with an expiration date that, while hard to read, had certainly long since passed. He won (if you can call it that).

Amid the ebb and flow of new coworkers, Brian was one of the few bright spots in a sea of dim weirdos. There were others too, of course. And if they're reading this, they know who they are. It wasn't often, but sometimes it was perfect. Sometimes just shooting the shit outside in the sticky air turned a place where I had to be into one where I wanted to be. Turned what I thought was a slump into one of the best times of my life.

Brian helped me edit the paper that I submitted with my grad school applications, telling me that commas weren't a garnish and to just get to the point. I'm not sure I'll ever master either of those things, but that paper got me a scholarship offer. When I put in my notice at the store, Brian said that it was "about fuckin time."

We stayed in touch after I moved away—not as much as we could have, but then it never is. That's the wrong way to think about it anyway.

We finally caught up a few years ago, a proper hangout face-to-face. It turned out Brian didn't hate grocery; he hated the managers. So he just got himself promoted above them all until he was running his own store, one of the youngest in the company's history. He looked good. Happy. We didn't talk much about the old days. We didn't need them anymore, I guess.

The night ended with Brian singing "Bohemian Rhapsody" at a karaoke bar. That was the last time I saw him, sometime around Christmas of 2015.

In April of 2017, Brian was killed in a traffic accident.

The book you're holding draws heavily from that time in my life twelve years ago, and the personality of the character Marty shares a lot of qualities with my friend Brian. He helped me edit my first book, *Penpal,* so I had hoped that he would read this one and see flashes of himself and get a kick out of it. I never got to tell him that he was in this story, so I'm telling all of you. He was one of my favorite people. A great friend. And a great man.

I miss you, Brian. I liked you all the time. Easiest thing I've ever done. This book is for you.

years ago, and the personality of the character Marty shares a lot of qualities with my friend Brian. He helped me edit my first book, *Pemberley*, so I had hoped that he would read this one and see flashes of himself and get a kick out of it. I never got to tell him that he was in this story, so I'm telling all of you. He was one of my favorite people. A great friend. And a great man.

I miss you, Brian. I liked you all the time. Easiest thing I've ever done. This book is for you.